EVERYMAN,
I WILL GO WITH THEE,
AND BE THY GUIDE,
IN THY MOST NEED
TO GO BY THY SIDE

KATHERINE MANSFIELD

The Garden Party
and Other Stories

EVERYMAN'S LIBRARY

Alfred A. Knopf New York

48

Printed and bound in Germany

CONTENTS

INTRODUCTION

Katherine Mansfield lived from 1888 to 1923; thus she was the contemporary of D. H. Lawrence and Virginia Woolf – who were her friends – and of James Joyce, whom she met once and whose work she admired; and also of P. G. Wodehouse, J. B. Priestley and Ethel M. Dell, to set her against some other successful writers of her generation. But she was an original, both in her technique as a writer and in the way she chose to live her life; a modernist, an innovator, an experimenter. During her lifetime she was successful in one sense; most of her stories were published in magazines, and three collections appeared, *In a German Pension* in 1911, *Bliss* in 1920 and *The Garden Party* in 1922. The first was briefly hailed for its 'impishness', the two later ones generally but not universally applauded. This degree of success did not bring her wealth; nor did it save her from ill health. For the last five years of her life she was dying of tuberculosis but – like Keats, like Chekhov, with both of whom she felt a bitter sense of kinship – she wrote against time and her own dissolution. It is not surprising that the total body of her work is small, and that it is uneven in quality.

There was a Katherine Mansfield who was in love with little things – tiny children, small animals, pet names, frail old ladies, dolls' houses – and who sought a saintly purity in her life and art, at any rate as her husband John Middleton Murry presented her to the world. This exquisite person is at odds with the writer of many of her stories, and has taken a salutary knock from recent biographies (Jeffrey Meyers 1978, Antony Alpers 1980); both show her as a complicated and far from virtuous young woman who fought life hard, giving blows as well as receiving them. Murry, who in life loved her, failed her and felt guilty about her, was her literary adviser from 1912 until her death ten years later, and thereafter responsible for the publication of posthumous stories and fragments; in this way he inevitably presented and controlled her literary as well as her personal image. The merest glance at Murry's own published novels suggests that he had no feeling at all for fiction; but, in his grief, he wanted the world to see everything she had written. The result is that the *Collected Stories* are loaded with sentimental scraps which have done her a disservice.

Murry's subsequent publication of fat volumes of her diaries and letters established the vision of the tragic, sensitive person while deflecting attention from her actual work – the work she had wanted to be judged by. A cult arose, both in her native New Zealand where she is properly a source of pride, and in France, where many of her stories are set and where she lived a good deal, died and was buried. The cults, unfortunately, helped to emphasize those whimsical and self-pitying aspects of her work that are least attractive. It looks as though, to appreciate what is best in her writing, you have to accept what was bad – or at any rate complicated – in her character.

The most perceptive critical approaches have come from her fellow writers. Mansfield has appealed to those who see themselves as subverters of the established social order, and respond to that aspect of her work; Christopher Isherwood and Angus Wilson are both admirers. Brigid Brophy has written boldly and convincingly of the cruel, witchlike qualities of many of the stories. Elizabeth Bowen singled out the isolation of her characters, the sense that they do not know how to reach one another: 'the indelible mark' of her own loneliness, suggested Miss Bowen, after she had uprooted herself from New Zealand. The most telling critical commentary comes from V. S. Pritchett, himself an incomparable writer of stories. In 1946 he described her as 'one of those key writers who in their generation make a new point of departure' by destroying many of the existing formal conventions: 'liquefying' is the word he uses. He particularly admires her gift for listening well, and his summary of her virtues seems absolutely just:

her economy, the boldness of her comic gift, her speed, her dramatic changes of the point of interest, her power to dissolve and reassemble a character and situation by a few lines...

It is this technical virtuosity that Pritchett most appreciates. (The self-revelation of the journals does not interest him at all.)

Katherine Mansfield herself wrote, a few weeks before her death: 'I am tired of my little stories like birds bred in cages.' It is true that her scope and scale are restricted; but the harshness of her verdict on herself was unjust to her truly original gift. Some, but by no means all her stories are 'bred in cages'.

This volume sets out to present the work most likely to challenge the attention of readers a century after her birth. The Mansfield who writes here is a tough, adventurous, humorous, observant colonial girl, hard on others and hard on herself. Her best stories are miracles of construction, spare, sharp and cool. There are no tricks in them, only an attentiveness to detail, a watchfulness so acute that it sometimes verges on the sinister; a watchfulness that is evident from the start, and never leaves her. Nothing mattered to her more than her work, and she was never satisfied with it; that is why so much of it is so good.

She was born into the well-to-do family of Harold Beauchamp, an import-export agent of English descent, in Wellington, New Zealand. She was the third daughter and, she felt, the misfit of the family; two more girls, one of whom died, and a boy followed. Katherine was originally Kathleen, but she began early to experiment with different names; she was always fascinated by the idea of being someone else, something other than what she was. Many names were tried out before she settled for 'Katherine' and her own middle name of 'Mansfield', taken from her maternal grandmother.

Her parents were frequent visitors to England – still in those days known as Home – and in 1903 they took their three eldest daughters to London in order to install them in Queen's College, Harley Street. Queen's College, an excellent girls' school, had been founded fifty years earlier by F. D. Maurice to help improve the education and status of women and, although it was a thoroughly ladylike institution, it was not over-conventional in its approach. The girls were granted considerable social and intellectual freedom; New Women emerged from it, and Katherine was among their number. She was taught German by a would-be Aesthete, a young man called Walter Rippmann who enjoyed inspiring impressionable girls and introducing them to the works of Ibsen, Shaw, Oscar Wilde and other turn-of-the-century writers. Wilde's particular blend of sentimentality, laughter and social concern made its mark on her imagination; but, although a few fragments of purple prose and some fairy stories survive from her schooldays, it was above all the idea of the superiority of the Artist to the common person that impressed itself upon her, rather unhappily perhaps. (She also learnt enough about Wilde's personal history to examine her own adolescent sexual uncertainties with a mixture of triumphant fascination and penitent terror.)

The years at Queen's were crucial. It is unfair to say they redeemed the philistinism of Katherine's background, since it was after all her parents' decision to send her in pursuit of the higher things she acquired at Queen's; but the Beauchamp household was not book-lined and she had not enjoyed there the hours in a library that Virginia Woolf took for granted, much to Katherine's later envy. Queen's also allowed her the experience of dominating an appreciative audience for the first time; she made friends who found her bewitching and extraordinary. One of these, Ida Baker, remained loyally devoted to her until her death, and to her memory for half a century afterwards; in her nineties she sought to convey to me the irresistible spell that Katherine laid upon her, by the power of her personality, her physical presence and beautiful voice – in which of course no colonial twang was allowed.

Her declared ambition during the school years was to become a professional musician. She played the cello, and began to fall in love with a family of musicians, the Trowells, also from New Zealand, who had come to England to train their gifted twin sons, Arnold and Garnet; soon they were to play an important part in her life.

When Harold and Annie Beauchamp came to collect their daughters, Katherine went back to New Zealand willingly enough; but she was determined to return to England and become an Artist. The Trowells also travelled back to New

Zealand and there the father taught Katherine the cello (in her journal he was hailed as 'my father') and the boys became her romantic idols. They were part of the sacred world of Art; Mr Beauchamp was merely an increasingly successful businessman whose ambitions for his daughters, despite his adventurousness in sending them to school, lay in the direction of social accomplishments and good marriages. The Trowells were poor; the boys wore velvet jackets, smoked and had unsteady friends. The rift between the prosperous, solid, dull world of the bourgeois father and insistently ladylike mother on the one hand, and the precarious dedicated *vie de Bohème* on the other, seemed unbridgable.

The Trowells returned to Europe. Two things happened now. Katherine went in for some sexual experiments which sound normal enough for a high-spirited young woman, but were dramatized by Katherine herself to the point where they upset her family. '*We* were virgins,' her younger sister explained many years later, to justify the family's attitude and fear of a scandal which might even jeopardize the marriage chances of the others. Katherine transgressed against the rules of her tribe; but she also succeeded in publishing some vignettes in a Melbourne paper; and this persuaded her father that she might have a talent for something other than causing scandal. She was sent off, or allowed to go, a sort of remittance woman with the promise of £100 a year from her father, in the summer of 1908. Her own description of what she was giving up comes from an unpublished and fragmentary early story:

On the other hand lay the Suitable Appropriate Existence, the days full of perpetual Society functions, the hours full of clothes discussions, the waste of life. 'The stifling atmosphere would kill me' she thought. The days, weeks, months, years of it all. Her father, with his successful characteristic respectable face, crying 'Now is the time. What have I got for my money? Come along, deck yourself out, show the world that you are expensive.'

On her arrival in London she had a room in a Westbourne Park hostel for young ladies; her allowance, which had to be collected from a banker of her father's designation; a few friends from her schooldays, notably the devoted Ida; and the

Trowells, living cosily in St John's Wood. Garnet Trowell, the more passive of the twins, became the object of Katherine's passionate attention; her love letters address him as 'husband'. They became lovers; Katherine appears to have been the instigator of the whole affair. But the Trowell family, when they realized what was happening, disapproved; Garnet departed for a spell with a touring opera company; and Katherine suddenly married another man, also a musician, a singer called George Bowden. She did not inform her parents and she left him almost at once; he formed the impression she was sexually involved with Ida. When her mother arrived in England to see what was going on she found Katherine pregnant – by Garnet – unwilling to live with her legal husband and once again (for there had been an incident in New Zealand) suspected of sexual inversion.

Her reaction was to take Katherine to Bad Wörishofen, a spa in Germany, for her 'health', and leave her there. She herself sailed straight back to Wellington and cut Katherine out of her will on arrival. Such bizarre and primitive assumptions about family love, sexual behaviour and money were not unusual for their time. Later, Katherine wrote wistfully and lovingly of her mother in her diaries and letters, and it is hard to guess what her real feelings were. But it is worth noting that the character of Linda Burnell in 'Prelude' and 'At the Bay', is that of a woman who knows herself incapable of love towards her children.

The experience of Wörishofen in 1909 was all the same of great importance to Katherine. Here she miscarried of her child, but began to write with serious, professional intentions and found material that she could crystallize into effective stories. Here also she first read Chekhov, probably in a German translation. Unfortunately the reading of Chekhov was not a straightforward blessing, a handing down of the lesson of a master to an eager pupil: Mansfield plagiarized one of his stories ('Sleepyhead' in his version, 'The Child-who-was-Tired' in hers) and offered it for publication in England later without mentioning its derivation. Her extreme reluctance to allow *In a German Pension* (in which it also appeared) to be reprinted after she became well known may be due to this. And this was not the only time-bomb set ticking in Germany. The man who probably showed her the Chekhov was a literary Pole, Floryan Sobieniowski; in all the gallery of her ill-chosen lovers he is one of the worst, for he afterwards blackmailed her with the love letters she wrote him. The letters may of course have contained references to the Chekhov plagiary as well as their love affair; at all events, Katherine convinced Murry it was worth paying for them in 1920; and in 1946 Murry supported Sobieniowski's application to the Royal Literary Fund for financial assistance. Considering that Murry knew him to be a blackmailer, it leads one to wonder what revelations he feared from him even then (Murry published new editions of Katherine's Journals and Letters in the early fifties).

Sobieniowski may have been responsible for another disaster; in 1910 Katherine had an operation which she described as 'for peritonitis' but which in fact involved the removal of an ovary. It appears that she was suffering from a venereal disease; the effect of this operation must have been to diminish the possibility of bearing a child very considerably; but this she never admitted. So she became trapped in two areas of deception: one about the plagiarized story, which must have frightened and tormented her over the years; the other about her health and ability to become a mother as she longed to.

Whatever her adventures in Europe in the autumn of 1909, she returned to England at the end of the year to be welcomed by the faithful Ida and, at the suggestion of her husband, with whom she resumed a temporary friendship of sorts, submitted a story to the political and literary magazine, the *New Age*. This was something like a precursor of the *New Statesman*; and the editor, A. R. Orage, a brilliant, attractive, self-educated, unstable man, accepted the Chekhov-inspired story first and continued to print her work enthusiastically. The *New Age* circle was lively, free-thinking, left-wing and for a while at any rate feminist; Edward Carpenter wrote for it, Sickert drew for it, Shaw helped to finance it and the young D. H. Lawrence read it. Katherine began to be a figure in the small circle of literary London – the tea and buns, not the champagne sector. She was always poor, and settled where she could: in a small flat on the Gray's Inn Road from 1910 to 1912.

She was living here when her first collection, made up largely of stories first published in the *New Age*, appeared. The publisher, Stephen Swift, was yet another of the rogues who appear so regularly in Katherine's life; although hailed by friends as 'the English Tolstoy', he was in fact a bigamist and a crook. But this was not apparent in December 1911 when *In a German Pension* appeared and enjoyed a modest success; in the same month Katherine met John Middleton Murry, a good-looking Oxford undergraduate who was already co-editing an avant-garde magazine, *Rhythm*, and wished to be a writer himself. Murry had been well educated at Christ's Hospital; he was unhappy at Oxford, snobbish and socially uncertain, uncomfortable about his humble origins. He was also an acute and clever critic. Katherine helped to persuade him to leave Oxford, offered him a room in her flat, fell in love with him and seduced him.

They were not able to marry for some years, and their relationship was always unsatisfactory, with many separations and infidelities on both sides. It became nevertheless the emotional centre of her life and, however, disappointed and impatient she grew with Murry, she clung increasingly to the idea of its sanctity as the years went by. Murry's own copious confessional writing reveals him as emotionally childlike throughout the years of his association with Katherine, and it is hard to think that he was helpful to her in any way except as a playmate ('Tig' and 'Wig', 'the two Tigers', 'Bogey', 'Broomy', 'Boy' were some of the names they gave one another). He was certainly quite incapable of looking after her when she was ill, which was often, or of keeping her housed and fed at any time. Their life was nomadic and uncomfortable to a degree, and the only person who attempted to care for Katherine in any practical way was Ida, who as a consequence bore the brunt of Katherine's considerable rages. This was partly because she was not Murry (whose presence Katherine would have preferred) and also because she was

neither very practical despite her good intentions, nor beautiful, quick and charming as Katherine liked her companions to
be. But if anyone was the wife needed by Katherine Mansfield
it was Ida, who worshipped her with true, fixed love and total
sexual innocence.

For a while Katherine and Murry lived the life of weekend
cottages, trips to Paris, little magazines and literary quarrels,
ebbing and flowing friendships with other couples. Murry and
Orage disliked one another. There was a famous quarrel with
the sculptor Gaudier-Brezska; and presently another unmarried couple, D. H. Lawrence and Frieda, were drawn to them.
When the war came, both Lawrence and Murry had exemp-
tion from military service; but it was a difficult time. In 1915
Katherine's only brother, Leslie, arrived to join up, to be
killed within a few months in an accident. She had been
vacillating between Murry and a French writer, Francis
Carco, and spending a good deal of time in Paris; but after the
shock of Leslie's death she set off for the south of France with
Ida, because her health was so poor.

The Mediterranean did her good; she began to write what
would become 'Prelude', and Murry came to join her. But
from this relatively happy period they allowed themselves to
be summoned back to England by the Lawrences, who had
found two cottages in Cornwall and wished to have companions in their simple life. As might have been predicted, the
couples quarrelled disastrously; Katherine was aghast at the
violence of Frieda and Lawrence, and Lawrence, hoping that
Murry would become his loving disciple, soon began to feel
that he was treacherous. Frieda complained of Katherine's
'terrible gift of nearness, she can come so close'. They
separated.

For a while Katherine and Murry's life whirled around an
increasingly smart set. They met, and Murry flirted with,
Lady Ottoline Morrell, and spent weekends at Garsington.
Katherine flirted too, with Bertrand Russell. They were
introduced to the Woolfs; Katherine and Virginia, although
suspicious of one another at first, became friends, despite
professional jealousy. Katherine gave her longest finished

work yet, 'Prelude', to the Woolfs to print on their Hogarth Press.

In December 1917 Katherine, suffering from a chill, sent for a doctor who told her she had a spot on her lung and must go abroad at once; she went alone and settled down in Bandol in the south of France to write. Soon after Ida arrived, uninvited, Katherine suffered her first haemorrhage. The two women then set off to return to England, and were trapped for three weeks in Paris, which was under bombardment at the time. It was scarcely the way to treat tuberculosis. Back in London, she and Murry were married at last; by October she was warned that she had only four years to live unless she went into a sanatorium. From now on her life was a series of restless movements between London, France and Switzerland, always in search of an alleviation that was not to be found for her lung condition. She continued to write. She was unable to settle anywhere for long and sought a miracle she did not believe in herself; she renewed links with old friends, wrote affectionately to her father (her mother was dead) and finally banished Ida and Murry from her life. She spent her last weeks in the curious establishment near Fontainebleau of a Russian guru, Gurdjieff, who, although he was undoubtedly a charlatan, cannot be blamed for taking her in at her own request and giving her some illusory sense of purpose. Murry, invited for a visit in January 1923, was there when she died of a haemorrhage. He and Ida, both present at the funeral, continued to quarrel about her for years afterwards, and wrote conflicting accounts of her; Ida's book, *Katherine Mansfield, The Memories of L.M.* (Ida's pen name was Lesley Moore), published in 1971, though scrappy and not always reliable, is well worth reading.

She was mourned for a long time by Virginia Woolf, who recorded dreams of her in her diary and confessed to jealousy of her abilities as a writer. Leonard Woolf, who had liked and admired Katherine, wrote that he considered Murry had spoiled a creature 'by nature ... gay, cynical, amoral, ribald, witty'.

The pattern of Katherine Mansfield's life is both pathetic and almost ludicrously retributive: for every rash, false or wild thing she did she suffered a heavy punishment of the kind a Victorian novelist might have inflicted on an erring heroine. But the moral climate of her stories has nothing to do with sinful subplots and retribution, although it has to do with danger and vulnerability and the deadening of the spirit. The stories, published first in the *New Age*, were very consciously of a new age. Up-to-dateness was their distinctive mark, in their themes, their tone and their technique. Mansfield worked out for herself the modernist creed that a story can be coherent without a plot that moves from A to B to C, her point of departure being simply the idea of inhabiting other selves than her own. 'Would you not like to try all sorts of lives – one is so very small – but that is the satisfaction of writing – one can impersonate so many people' she wrote in a letter to a cousin when she was only seventeen. She practised a little as a *diseuse* in her Westbourne Park hostel days and had ambitions towards the stage; some of her early pieces are written in the form of dramatic sketches. To inhabit a character you must watch and listen with preternatural acuteness, snatching up scraps of speech and behaviour that come your way and using them to suggest a whole world. And this is what she learnt to do, using whatever scraps of her past and present that she could.

The earlier stories in this collection are the work of an angry young woman, acutely alive to the problems and plights of women in a world in which power of all kinds lay with men, and mocking of the pomposity of the established male and the complicity of many women with it: this theme appears in 'Frau Brechenmacher', in 'A Birthday', in 'Bains Turcs', in 'The Swing of the Pendulum', in 'The Little Governess', and crops up later too, notably in 'The Daughters of the Late Colonel' and 'Honeymoon'. Indeed, the twin themes of women crushed by male power and women subverting that power are rarely absent from her stories, although they are often present by implication rather than directly. Her first story, 'The Tiredness of Rosabel', was written at the height of the suffragette movement's activities; but stories are not necessarily mirrors of political movements, and Katherine was never a suffragette; in fact she ran laughing from the intensities of the only meeting she attended in London, not because she was out of sympathy with its general aims, but because she could not confine her vision of life to those terms. Rosabel looks at first glance like a simple rendering of the consciousness of a girl working in a hat shop; but there is more to it than that.

The story follows Rosabel home to her lodgings after her day's work and shows her daydreams of luxury, inspired by the young woman who has bought a hat from her, and the young woman's escort, who has murmured a word of flattery to Rosabel during the transaction. Rosabel is a girl who buys violets rather than a proper evening meal, who despises the advertisements in the bus and the cheap romance being read by another girl, and who laughs at the memory of her stupid customers; but the banality of her own imagination is not glossed over. She sustains herself in a bleak life – picking her way through the mud of the London streets endlessly, not having enough to eat, living in an uncomfortable and lonely room – with dreams. And here the story bites, for the dreams that sustain Rosabel also make her vulnerable since, it is implied, the only escape from the humiliating realities of her life lies through the admiration of the sort of men who accompany young ladies into the shop where she works, and spare her an appraising glance. No harm is done in the story but to Rosabel's imagination, which has in any case been given nothing else to turn to but thin fantasy; it is not terrifying, like the end of 'The Little Governess', where the heroine is brought to the brink of the pit, but neither is it a simple, tender-hearted tale.

The relationship between dreams and danger appears again in 'Frau Brechenmacher Attends a Wedding'. The name of the heroine and some of the physical details are taken from Bad Wörishofen, but the story is about something much more general: about the bullying of a young woman, and about the echo it draws from the mind of the older woman called on to observe it. The bitterness of Frau Brechenmacher lies in the contrast between the emotions that are supposed to be aroused by a wedding and the actual occasion under observation, which is one of gross maltreatment. A simple young unmarried mother is being married off to a man she does not like; the woman who observes it, a good solid wife and mother of five, finds herself remembering more than she really cares to about her own wedding. (When one reflects that Katherine herself had, at the time of writing, been recently rejected by her own solid, bourgeois mother of five, 'Frau Brechenmacher' speaks volumes for her power to abstract herself from personal experience.)

The thread of Mansfield's own experience runs through most of her stories, and yet very few of them are autobiographical in a strict sense, and her 'German' stories are not necessarily about Germany at all. 'Frau Brechenmacher' is a cry against the stupidity and brutality of men and the women who support their arrangements, through sentimentality or weakness; it is written with feminist rage, and is clearly protective towards its matronly heroine, showing how her complicity in the degrading wedding celebrations has come about through the way in which she too had been made a victim. But Mansfield is equally protective and affectionate towards Andreas Binzer of 'A Birthday', which is quite recognizably set in Wellington, New Zealand. It is a calmer and a funnier story than 'Frau Brechenmacher'. Here already is the childishly pompous, self-important man who will appear later in 'Prelude'; the delicate wife (unseen, in pain, giving birth with difficulty upstairs); the excitable, exasperating, good-natured servant girl and the gentle, tired grandmother summoned up in two perfect lines:

Andreas, watching her, saw her face suddenly change; a fine network of wrinkles seemed to pull over it from under the skin surface.

Binzer's character is delicately and slyly drawn after Katherine's father; quick temper, easily aroused sense of grievance, tendency to blustering self-dramatization. In the course of the story he himself almost endures the pains of childbirth; and in a scene that is remarkable for a writer of twenty-two, he is shown examining a photograph of his wife and troubled by its secretive smile. The more he looks at the picture, taken when she was a bride, the more dissatisfied he grows because she does not look as his wife, as the mother of the son he is confidently awaiting, should look. He decides to get rid of the picture; it is as though the real woman is to be abolished in the service of the woman who is Binzer's wife, the mother of his son, the mother of a son who is going to be a partner in the firm. The story is not insistent, and remains purely comic; but it is comedy to make patriarchs tremble.

'The Swing of the Pendulum', while it takes up the themes of vulnerable women and brutal men, is really remarkable for something else again. It is a study in self-knowledge; the observer of the satirical early stories (such as 'Bains Turcs', a cheerful, savage blast against prurience) turns her sardonic eye on herself to devastating effect. The scene is, as in Rosabel, a single room high up in a house where the heroine has taken lodgings. She is penniless, alone, waiting for her lover to arrive (clearly Katherine is drawing on the year 1909 when she wandered in Europe). The landlady is mistrustful and abusive, as a landlady of that period would be towards a young woman with no visible means of support. The girl's self-dramatization is one theme: her rapidly and comically changing spectrum of feelings about the landlady, about the absent lover Casimir, about the other man who arrives, about the room, the weather, her plight. The other theme is the way in which she deals with her situation in practice. She has a series of encounters. The first is a spirited one with the landlady, the second a straightforward one with an unexpected and unknown caller. Then, in an interlude, she recreates this man and his possibilities in her imagination; she will get something out of him, he is a glamorous and worldly creature who will help her, and so on. Summoning him back, she finds of course that he does not treat her at all as she hoped, but as a prostitute. For a moment she is in real danger; there is a sexual struggle from which she saves herself only by biting through his glove to his hand so that she hurts and frightens him in turn. He leaves. And then instantly her thoughts fly to Casimir who – the reader knows – is going to be little more support than the visitor. For all her resourcefulness and courage, she cannot resist the idea that some man will smooth her path. It is a vital and intelligent piece of writing, physically vivid and unsettling in its clear-sighted account of its high-spirited and appallingly vulnerable heroine.

Violence, suppressed and overt, appears often enough in Mansfield stories. 'Millie' and 'The Woman at the Store', both squarely set in the New Zealand outback, both contain offstage murders. But they are not sensational: they are laconically told and have the ring of truth about the bleakness, emptiness and isolation of colonial life at that time. Nothing is picturesque: flies, the smell of cabbages in the garden, drunkenness to combat loneliness, a society without graces, its women reduced to hysteria by the circumstances in which they are forced to live. The tone is cold; remarkably for Mansfield, there is a thoroughly repellent small child in 'The Woman at the Store'; and the atmosphere of the sparsely inhabited wilderness is grimly conjured up:

There is no twilight in our savage New Zealand days, but a curious half-hour when everything appears grotesque – it frightens – as though the savage spirit of the country walked abroad and sneered at what it saw.

There is something of Dickens' surreal genius in such a phrase; although it was not until some years later that Mansfield talked of learning from Dickens: 'I am not reading Dickens *idly*,' she wrote to Murry in 1918.

'Millie' is an accomplished study in hysteria; 'The Woman at the Store' suggests that alongside the student of deviant human behaviour was a first-rate reporter at work too. Here is the inside of the store:

It was a large room, the walls plastered with old pages of English periodicals. Queen Victoria's Jubilee appeared to be the most recent number. A table with an ironing board and wash-tub on it, some wooden forms, a black horsehair sofa and some broken cane chairs pushed against the walls. The mantelpiece above the stove was draped in pink paper, further ornamented with dried grasses and ferns and a coloured print of Richard Seddon ... Flies buzzed in circles round the ceiling, and treacle papers and bundles of dried clover were pinned to the window curtains.

(Richard Seddon, whose picture adorns the room, was a prime minister of New Zealand – and also a close friend of Harold Beauchamp.)

It is this same cool reporter's eye that makes 'An Indiscreet Journey' so interesting, because in this case she is observing nothing less than the 1914–18 war in action, not in its heroics or horror even, but in the casualness, the muddle and confusion of the French army just behind the lines in 1915, the brief look at the weedy soldier with the bandage newly removed from his eyes who cannot control their watering as he sits in a café. Madame behind the till comments on his disgustingness:

> '*Mais vous savez, c'est un peu dégoûtant, ça,*' she said severely. '*Ah, oui, Madame,*' answered the soldiers, watching her bent head and pretty hands, as she arranged for the hundredth time a frill of lace on her lifted bosom.

This story is directly drawn from her own experience, when she made a visit to her lover Francis Carco while he was serving at Gray, near Dijon, on the Saône. The foolhardy journey into the war zone was carried out in a spirit of reckless adventurousness; Katherine had wanted an erotic adventure and fancied herself in love. By the time she came to write, her feelings for Carco had been brushed aside; he became the 'little corporal' with curly lashes, the least significant feature of the story. Almost banishing the personal and romantic, Mansfield has drawn instead a picture of the interaction of civilian and military life in which irreverence for the great theme of war and insistence on detail captures a vanished moment of history. There are not many war stories by women; this is a little classic.

'Bliss' is one of Mansfield's best-known stories. It was disliked by Virginia Woolf and has worried many critics since: the satire on the conversation of London intellectuals is crudely done, and the point is obscure. Yet it is one of her few stories in which she seems to be straining after a point rather than in confident control of the shape of her story.

What 'Bliss' establishes is a mood: a mood of elation, almost mania. The subject is a young English wife and mother,

Bertha, who is shown in this state of heightened emotion as she prepares for a dinner party in her own house. Bertha is an idle person, with nothing to do but shopping and fruit and flower arrangement and the enjoyment of a sort of affectionate contempt for her husband Harry: 'what a boy he was in some ways'. She has no sexual feeling, and regards this as a happy condition of modern marriage; but she is capable of an excited response to other women – a type of response Mansfield described clearly without feeling obliged to make approving or disapproving noises. The story swings rather uneasily between precise description of this kind and rather broad satire on the literati who gather at Bertha's table. There is some very sharp observation of the jockeying between Bertha and her baby's nurse for possession of the baby. The language in which Bertha speaks to herself about her happiness has a brilliant sheen upon it; and she and Harry are sharply drawn, if slightly brittle, variants on the classic Mansfield couple, he a self-indulgent breadwinner, 'a little ridiculous perhaps', she cold and supersensitive. But instead of allowing them to play their parts she forces a plot on them; and as soon as we are told about Bertha desiring her husband for the first time, the story loses power and almost collapses. It becomes absurd, and is kept afloat only by Mansfield's power to sustain a mood and by her acute visual touches. If it is not the disaster that 'Marriage à la Mode' is (a companion story about smart Londoners), it does have a sense of strain which is absent from her best work.

Whereas 'Prelude' and its continuation 'At the Bay' are virtually flawless in their rendering of a family, the Burnells, with another boyish, self-indulgent breadwinner and cold, delicate wife. The comedy here has an absolutely sure note, and the point of these stories, the longest she wrote, does not lie in any twist of plot. They are about memory and understanding, about things not being what they seem; about order and escape and the hatred which inhabits Alice, Beryl and Linda. Katherine Mansfield is not remembering her childhood, the explanation often given for the brilliance of this writing; almost nothing she tells us in them could have been known to her as a child. It is obvious that the little world evoked in

'Prelude' bears a considerable resemblance to the Beauchamp family's existence; and yet the story she wrote in 1915 and 1916 rests on something quite different from what the child of the 1890s saw and felt. In her journals and letters there is no hint of what she is doing in the stories; her memories are all tender, as are her letters home. But the stories are a different matter: gently, tenderly even, she strips the family, exposing alongside its cheerful absurdities the pretensions and cruelties of the household. The grandmother makes order and allays fears for a while; the children are innocent, though they are learning the duplicities of adult behaviour; but the young women rage in their several ways against the lies in which they are trapped. The effect is peculiar: a world that is lost, and mourned because it is lost, is simultaneously savaged; a pastoral is peopled by witches.

'A Married Man's Story' experiments in a different sort of eeriness. It departs boldly and effectively form Mansfield's usual imaginative territories, with its mystery and its curious, muted male narrator. It is a fragment that feels very like the beginning of a full-length novel; and it is thoroughly absorbing with its confession of a hypocrite and wife-hater who gradually wins the sympathies of the reader with his reminiscences of his own starved childhood. There is a flavour of Dickens again; and of all her unfinished stories it is the one that most cries out for completion. Two other stories, 'This Flower' and 'The Man Without a Temperament', use the theme of a woman vulnerable through ill-health and the agonies of mutual deception arising from such a situation. One shows a man failing at a crucial moment through crass stupidity and insensitivity (the story is deliberately ambiguous as to whether the doctor has diagnosed disease or pregnancy: either way, the diagnosis isolates the woman from the man). In the other story the man supports his invalid wife with infinite, agonized patience that puts them both upon the rack. These are stories written on a knife-edge, from which self-pity is miraculously just absent. From the same period 'Carnation' is a slight but perfect evocation – it almost gives off a steamy smell – of a hot afternoon in a classroom of dreamy, giggly, ripe girls with their minds on anything but what the French master is reading to them. It was Mansfield's compliment to her old school, which she celebrates more for its distractions than for its teaching: impudent, and truthful, one suspects.

'The Daughters of the Late Colonel' has been generally acknowledged as one of Mansfield's finest stories, with stress on its comic virtues. It is comedy of course, but a comedy that offers an almost flawless description of two sisters who have been rendered unfit for life: not entirely a laughing matter. They are unable to decide anything; to control anyone; to find any enjoyment or to value themselves at all. The death of their tyrannical father leaves them like beached whales gasping to be refloated in the element of someone else's will; but of course they won't be. It is not written satirically, at the expense of the sisters, but affectionately; and so quietly, without pity or emphasis, that it is quite possible to enjoy its jokes about early twentieth-century genteel womanhood and miss the devastating nature of what it is saying.

The remaining stories cluster round one theme, which is the fragility of the young as they prepare to enjoy life and find that there are spectres at the feast. In their different ways Fenella on the Picton boat, Laura at her mother's garden party, Leila at her first ball and Fanny on her honeymoon are all faced with the same *memento mori* – Fenella's mother's death and father's grief, only half realized as yet, cloud the excitement of the voyage with her grandmother; Laura's visit to the house of the dead workman in her silly, pretty clothes; Leila's encounter with the odious little fat middle-aged man who predicts her future and Fanny's solitary self-questioning after she has heard the tattered old Spaniard sing at the café. All these stories are written with the lightest of touch, and all insist on the beauty and pleasure of the world, the luxuries of the garden party, cream cakes and new hats, silk dresses and flowers, the lights and scents of the ball, the gorgeous Mediterranean 'lapping the land as though it loved it'.

Other late stories such as 'The Fly' and 'The Canary' have attracted much critical attention, perhaps because they cry their symbolism so loudly – too loudly, I think, to work well as stories, whatever they do for critics. Yet 'Honeymoon' has had almost no attention and was dismissed as a 'soufflé' and a 'farewell to her sparkling Riviera manner' by Antony Alpers; it is a more interesting story than this suggests. 'Honeymoon' is indeed set beside the Mediterranean and describes a silly little pair, George and Fanny, enjoying their happiness in the sunshine, eating chocolate éclairs and talking to each other in the tones of P. G. Wodehouse. George, putting Fanny's hand into his pocket, is reminded pleasantly of how he kept a white mouse in his pocket at school. She, not very bright perhaps, but infinitely more thoughtful, raises a question:

'Do you feel', she said softly, 'that you really know me now? But really, really know *me*?'
He gave a broad, childish grin. 'I should jolly well think I do,' he said emphatically. 'Why, what's up?'

George's pleasant idiocy is pushed further and further; there is nothing wrong with him except that he is an intolerable ass, and we know that Fanny, mouselike and insignificant as she is, is going to discover this soon enough, and to her cost.

When the band on the terrace where they are having tea is joined by an old man in a battered suit who sings an incomprehensible, mad, grieving song in Spanish, Fanny's response is:

Is life like this too? thought Fanny. There are people like this. There is suffering. And she looked at that gorgeous sea, lapping the land as though it loved it, and the sky, bright with the brightness before evening. Had she and George the right to be so happy? Wasn't it cruel? There must be something else in life which made all these things possible. What was it? She turned to George.

Fanny is a simple soul, but she at least sees what is before her eyes and responds with feelings that are appropriate. But George has been thinking quite different thoughts, and is only concerned to hurry Fanny away 'before the old codger begins squawking again'. The insouciant surface is hardly ruffled; but the attentive reader has seen both the future of George and Fanny, and the abyss.

'Honeymoon' is strong enough to stand on its own; but it is difficult not to recall that it was written when Mansfield knew herself to be dying, when she was herself the spectre at any feast, a *memento mori* for all who saw her. The light touch is the sign of artistry; it is also the sign of courage.

It is sixty years since Katherine Mansfield died and the world of her stories has gone; the language spoken by her characters, their way of life, their preoccupations are all foreign now. Written to announce a new age, they have become, like all good writing, a key to the foreign land of the past. Not the least of the pleasures of reading her stories is that they show us the world as it was; or as it appeared to a young woman determined to live several lives in her three decades, and endowed with a rare spirit. Each of the stories in this collection is a fresh and memorable response to a world she found challenging, exasperating and ridiculous, and yet enjoyed with a passionate, unflagging zest.

Claire Tomalin

SELECT BIBLIOGRAPHY

WORKS

In a German Pension, Stephen Swift, 1911.
Prelude, Hogarth Press, 1918.
Je Ne Parle Pas Français, Heron Press, 1920.
Bliss and other stories, Constable, 1920.
The Garden Party and other stories, Constable, 1922.
The Dove's Nest and other stories, Constable, 1923.
Something Childish and other stories, Constable, 1924.
The Aloe, Constable, 1930, and Carcanet, 1983.
Stories (omnibus edition), Constable, 1945.
Undiscovered Country, Longman, 1974 (all the New Zealand stories arranged by Ian A. Gordon).

The Journal of Katherine Mansfield, ed. J. M. Murry, Constable, 1927; new expanded edition, 1954.
Letters, ed. J. M. Murry (2 vols.), Constable, 1928.
Letters to J. M. Murry, ed. J. M. Murry, Constable, 1951.
Novels and Novelists (Katherine Mansfield's reviews), ed. J. M. Murry, Constable, 1930.
The Urewera Notebook, ed. Ian A. Gordon, Oxford University Press, 1980. (Text of journal kept by Katherine Mansfield on trip to the outback in 1907. Adolescent moodiness, but also raw material for some of the later New Zealand stories.)
Unpublished MSS., ed. Margaret Scott, *Turnbull Library Record*, Wellington, NZ, March 1970, November 1970, May 1971, October 1973, May 1974. Story 'Brave Love', ed. M. Scott, *Landfall*, Christchurch, NZ, quarterly, March 1972.
Two issues of *Adam International Review*, ed. Miron Grindea, contain Katherine Mansfield letters: No. 300 dated 1963–5 and Nos. 370–75 (one issue, entitled *Katherine Mansfield – fifty years after*, has letters to Virginia Woolf, Bertrand Russell, and Richard Murry, and juvenilia).
Katherine Mansfield: Letters & Journals, ed. C. K. Stead, Allen Lane & Penguin, 1977 (heavily abridged, with linking passages but no index).
The Collected Letters of Katherine Mansfield, ed. Vincent O'Sullivan and Margaret Scott, Oxford University Press, 1984 and 1987 (Vol. I, 1903–17, Vol. II, 1918–19; three more volumes to come. These are

impeccably edited and produced, and are indispensable to anyone interested in K.M.).

BIOGRAPHICAL

SIR HAROLD BEAUCHAMP, *Reminiscences and Recollections*, New Plymouth, NZ, 1937. Hard-to-get-hold-of, very self-revealing autobiography of Katherine Mansfield's father.

ANTONY ALPERS, *Katherine Mansfield, A Biography*, Cape, 1953. The pioneering work, still very interesting.

CLAIRE TOMALIN, *Katherine Mansfield: A Secret Life*, Viking, 1987, Penguin paperback, 1988.

IDA BAKER, *Katherine Mansfield, The Memories of LM*, Michael Joseph, 1971. Indispensable account by Katherine Mansfield's closest friend of her point of view.

VINCENT O'SULLIVAN, *Katherine Mansfield's New Zealand*, Golden Press, Auckland, NZ, 1974. Very well-produced picture book with interesting caption notes.

JEFFREY MEYERS, *Katherine Mansfield, A Biography*, Hamish Hamilton, 1978. Unsympathetic but detailed.

JOHN CARSWELL, *Lives and Letters*, Faber, 1978. Good if generally hostile account of Mansfield and Murry; especially useful on the *New Age* circle, and on Koteliansky.

ANTONY ALPERS, *The Life of Katherine Mansfield*, Cape, 1980. Alpers' second, massively enlarged biography: the standard work, now available in paperback, Oxford University Press.

CRITICAL

DESMOND McCARTHY article in *New Statesman*, January 1921.

REBECCA WEST article in *New Statesman*, March 1922.

DAVID DAICHES, *New Literary Values*, Oliver & Boyd, 1936.

V. S. PRITCHETT article in *New Statesman*, February 1946.

SYLVIA BERKMAN, *Katherine Mansfield, A Critical Study*, New Haven, Conn., 1951.

ELIZABETH BOWEN, introduction to *Selected Stories*, Collins, 1957.

BRIGID BROPHY article in *London Magazine*, December 1962.

CHRISTOPHER ISHERWOOD in *Exhumations*, Eyre Methuen, 1966.

VINCENT O'SULLIVAN article in *Landfall*, Christchurch, NZ, quarterly, June 1975.

C. K. STEAD article in *New Review*, 1977.

WALTER ALLEN, *The Short Story in English*, Oxford University Press, 1981.

CHRONOLOGY

DATE	AUTHOR'S LIFE	LITERARY CONTEXT
1888	Born in New Zealand, 14 October.	
1897	First story published.	
1901		
1903	Attends Queens College, London. Meets 'L.M.'	
1905		E. M. Forster: *Where Angels Fear to Tread*.
1906	Returns to New Zealand.	
1908	Returns to London.	Stein: *Three Lives*. E. M. Forster: *A Room With a View*.
1907		E. M. Forster: *The Longest Journey*.
1909	Marries and separates from George Bowden. Becomes pregnant and miscarries. Stays in Bavaria.	
1910	Returns to England. Meets Orage and writes for *New Age*.	E. M. Forster: *Howards End*.
1911	Second pregnancy aborted. Meets John Middleton Murry. *In A German Pension*.	Lawrence: *The White Peacock*. Colette: *The Vagabond*.
1912	Meets Henri and Sophie Gaudier-Brzeska.	
1913	Meets D. H. Lawrence.	Lawrence: *Sons and Lovers*. Proust: *Swann's Way*. Fournier: *Le Grand Meaulnes*. Mann: *Death in Venice*.
1914		Joyce: *Dubliners*. Lawrence: *The Prussian Officer*. Gide: *Caves of the Vatican*.
1915	Brother killed in World War I.	Lawrence: *The Rainbow*. Woolf: *The Voyage Out*.
1915–38		Richardson: *Pilgrimage* (in thirteen volumes).
1916		Joyce: *Portrait of the Artist*.
1917		

DATE	AUTHOR'S LIFE	LITERARY CONTEXT
1918	Marries Middleton Murry. TB positively diagnosed. Lives in south of France. Mother dies.	Joyce: *Exiles.* Wyndham Lewis: *Tarr.* Proust: *Within a Budding Grove.*
1919	Murry becomes editor of *Athenaeum.* Katherine Mansfield Visits Italy.	Woolf: *Night and Day.* Kafka: *In the Penal Colony.* Gide: *Pastoral Symphony.*
1920	*Bliss and other stories.*	Lawrence: *The Lost Girl* and *Women in Love.* Proust: *The Guermantes Way.* Colette: *Chéri.*
1921	Stays in Swiss Alps.	Huxley: *Crome Yellow.* Woolf: *Monday or Tuesday.* Proust: *Cities of the Plain.*
1922	Goes to stay at Prieure, near Paris, for treatment. *The Garden Party.*	Joyce: *Ulysses.* Lawrence: *Aaron's Rod.* Woolf: *Jacob's Room.*
1923	Dies, 9 January. *The Dove's Nest. Poems.*	Huxley: *Antic Hay.* Lawrence: *Kangaroo.* Proust: *The Captive.* Mann: *Felix Krull.* Svevo: *The Conscience of Zeno.*
1924	*Something Childish.*	E. M. Forster: *A Passage to India.* Hemingway: *In Our Time.* Lawrence: *England, My England.* Mann: *The Magic Mountain.*
1925		Dos Passos: *Manhattan Transfer.* Fitzgerald: *The Great Gatsby.* Woolf: *Mrs Dalloway.* Proust: *The Sweet Cheat Gone.* Kafka: *The Trial.*
1926		Faulkner: *Soldier's Pay.* Hemingway: *The Sun Also Rises.* Lawrence: *The Plumed Serpent.* Kafka: *The Castle.* Gide: *The Counterfeiters* and *If It Die . . . .* Colette: *The Last of Chéri.*
1927	*Journal.*	Woolf: *To the Lighthouse.* Hemingway: *Men Without Women.* Kafka: *Amerika.*

CHRONOLOGY

DATE	AUTHOR'S LIFE	LITERARY CONTEXT
1928	*Letters.*	Huxley: *Point Counter Point.* Joyce: *Anna Livia Plurabelle.* Lawrence: *Lady Chatterley's Lover.* Woolf: *Orlando.*
1929		Compton Burnett: *Brothers and Sisters.* Faulkner: *The Sound and the Fury.* Hemingway: *A Farewell to Arms.* Woolf: *A Room of One's Own.* Colette: *Sido.*
1930	*The Aloe.*	Faulkner: *As I Lay Dying.* Hesse: *Narziss and Goldmund.* Lawrence: *The Virgin and The Gypsy.* Lewis: The Apes of God. Musil: *The Man Without Qualities* vol. 1.

CHRONOLOGY

The Tiredness of Rosabel

At the corner of Oxford Circus Rosabel bought a bunch of violets, and that was practically the reason why she had so little tea—for a scone and a boiled egg and a cup of cocoa at Lyons are not ample sufficiency after a hard day's work in a millinery establishment. As she swung on to the step of the Atlas bus, grabbed her skirt with one hand and clung to the railing with the other, Rosabel thought she would have sacrificed her soul for a good dinner—roast duck and green peas, chestnut stuffing, pudding with brandy sauce—something hot and strong and filling. She sat down next to a girl very much her own age who was reading *Anna Lombard* in a cheap, paper-covered edition, and the rain had tear-spattered the pages. Rosabel looked out of the windows; the street was blurred and misty, but light striking on the panes turned their dullness to opal and silver, and the jewellers' shops seen through this, were fairy palaces. Her feet were horribly wet, and she knew the bottom of her skirt and petticoat would be coated with black, greasy mud. There was a sickening smell of warm humanity—it seemed to be oozing out of everybody in the bus—and everybody had the same expression, sitting so still, staring in front of them. How many times had she read these advertisements—'Sapolio Saves Time, Saves Labour'—'Heinz's Tomato Sauce'—and the inane, annoying dialogue between doctor and judge concerning the superlative merits of 'Lamplough's Pyretic Saline'. She glanced at the book which the girl read so earnestly, mouthing the words in a way that Rosabel detested, licking her first finger and thumb each time that she turned the page. She could not see very clearly; it was something about a hot, voluptuous night, a band playing, and a girl with lovely, white shoulders. Oh, heavens! Rosabel stirred suddenly and unfastened the two top buttons of her coat . . . she felt almost stifled. Through her half-closed eyes the whole row of people on the opposite seat seemed to resolve into one fatuous, staring face . . . .

And this was her corner. She stumbled a little on her way out and lurched against the girl next to her. 'I beg your pardon,' said

Rosabel, but the girl did not even look up. Rosabel saw that she was smiling as she read.

Westbourne Grove looked as she had always imagined Venice to look at night, mysterious, dark, even the hansoms were like gondolas dodging up and down, and the lights trailing luridly—tongues of flame licking the wet street—magic fish swimming in the Grand Canal. She was more than glad to reach Richmond Road, but from the corner of the street until she came to No. 26 she thought of those four flights of stairs. Oh, why four flights! It was really criminal to expect people to live so high up. Every house ought to have a lift, something simple and inexpensive, or else an electric staircase like the one at Earl's Court—but four flights! When she stood in the hall and saw the first flight ahead of her and the stuffed albatross head on the landing, glimmering ghost-like in the light of the little gas jet, she almost cried. Well, they had to be faced; it was very like bicycling up a steep hill, but there was not the satisfaction of flying down the other side . . . .

Her own room at last! She closed the door, lit the gas, took off her hat and coat, skirt, blouse, unhooked her old flannel dressing-gown from behind the door, pulled it on, then unlaced her boots—on consideration her stockings were not wet enough to change. She went over to the wash-stand. The jug had not been filled again today. There was just enough water to soak the sponge, and the enamel was coming off the basin—that was the second time she had scratched her chin.

It was just seven o'clock. If she pulled the blind up and put out the gas it was much more restful—Rosabel did not want to read. So she knelt down on the floor, pillowing her arms on the window-sill . . . just one little sheet of glass between her and the great wet world outside!

She began to think of all that had happened during the day. Would she ever forget that awful woman in the grey mackintosh who had wanted a trimmed motor-cap—'something purple with something rosy each side'—or the girl who had tried on every hat in the shop and then said she would 'call in tomorrow and decide definitely'. Rosabel could not help smiling; the excuse was worn so thin . . . .

But there had been one other—a girl with beautiful red hair and white skin and eyes the colour of that green ribbon shot with gold they had got from Paris last week. Rosabel had seen her electric brougham at the door; a man had come in with her, quite a young man, and so well dressed.

'What is it exactly that I want, Harry?' she had said, as Rosabel took the pins out of her hat, untied her veil, and gave her a hand-mirror.

'You must have a black hat,' he had answered, 'a black hat with a feather that goes right round it and then round your neck and ties in a bow under your chin, and the ends tuck into your belt—a decent-sized feather.'

The girl glanced at Rosabel laughingly. 'Have you any hats like that?'

They had been very hard to please; Harry would demand the impossible, and Rosabel was almost in despair. Then she remembered the big, untouched box upstairs.

'Oh, one moment, Madam,' she had said. 'I think perhaps I can show you something that will please you better.' She had run up, breathlessly, cut the cords, scattered the tissue paper, and yes, there was the very hat—rather large, soft, with a great, curled feather, and a black velvet rose, nothing else. They had been charmed. The girl had put it on and then handed it to Rosabel.

'Let me see how it looks on you,' she said, frowning a little, very serious indeed.

Rosabel turned to the mirror and placed it on her brown hair, then faced them.

'Oh, Harry, isn't it adorable,' the girl cried, 'I must have that!' She smiled again at Rosabel. 'It suits you beautifully.'

A sudden, ridiculous feeling of anger had seized Rosabel. She longed to throw the lovely, perishable thing in the girl's face, and bent over the hat, flushing.

'It's exquisitely finished off inside, Madam,' she said. The girl swept out to her brougham, and left Harry to pay and bring the box with him.

'I shall go straight home and put it on before I come out to lunch with you,' Rosabel heard her say.

The man leant over her as she made out the bill, then, as he counted the money into her hand—'Ever been painted?' he said.

'No,' said Rosabel shortly, realising the swift change in his voice, the slight tinge of insolence, of familiarity.

'Oh, well you ought to be,' said Harry. 'You've got such a damned pretty little figure.'

Rosabel did not pay the slightest attention. How handsome he had been! She had thought of no one else all day; his face fascinated her; she could see clearly his fine, straight eyebrows, and his hair grew back from his forehead with just the slightest suspicion of crisp curl, his laughing, disdainful mouth. She saw again his slim hands counting the money into hers .... Rosabel suddenly pushed the hair back from her face, her forehead was hot ... if those slim hands could rest one moment ... the luck of that girl!

Suppose they changed places. Rosabel would drive home with him, of course they were in love with each other, but not engaged, very nearly, and she would say—'I won't be one moment.' He would wait in the brougham while her maid took the hat-box upstairs, following Rosabel. Then the great, white and pink bedroom with roses everywhere in dull silver vases. She would sit down before the mirror and the little French maid would fasten her hat and find her a thin, fine veil and another pair of white suède gloves—a button had come off the gloves she had worn that morning. She had scented her furs and gloves and handkerchief, taken a big muff and run downstairs. The butler opened the door, Harry was waiting, they drove away together .... *That* was life, thought Rosabel! On the way to the Carlton they stopped at Gerard's, Harry bought her great sprays of Parma violets, filled her hands with them.

'Oh, they are sweet!' she said, holding them against her face.

'It is as you always should be,' said Harry, 'with your hands full of violets.'

(Rosabel realised that her knees were getting stiff; she sat down on the floor and leant her head against the wall.) Oh, that lunch! The table covered with flowers, a band hidden behind a grove of palms playing music that fired her blood like wine—the soup, and oysters, and pigeons, and creamed potatoes, and champagne, of course, and afterwards coffee and cigarettes. She would lean over the table fingering her glass with one hand, talking with that charming gaiety which Harry so appreciated. Afterwards a matinée, something that gripped them both, and then tea at the 'Cottage'.

'Sugar? Milk? Cream?' The little homely questions seemed to suggest a joyous intimacy. And then home again in the dusk, and the scent of the Parma violets seemed to drench the air with their sweetness.

'I'll call for you at nine,' he said as he left her.

The fire had been lighted in her boudoir, the curtains drawn, there were a great pile of letters waiting her—invitations for the Opera, dinners, balls, a weekend on the river, a motor tour—she glanced through them listlessly as she went upstairs to dress. A fire in her bedroom, too, and her beautiful, shining dress spread on the bed—white tulle over silver, silver shoes, silver scarf, a little silver fan. Rosabel knew that she was the most famous woman at the ball that night; men paid her homage, a foreign Prince desired to be presented to this English wonder. Yes, it was a voluptuous night, a band playing, and *her* lovely white shoulders . . . .

But she became very tired. Harry took her home, and came in with her for just one moment. The fire was out in the drawing-room, but the sleepy maid waited for her in her boudoir. She took off her cloak, dismissed the servant, and went over to the fire-place, and stood peeling off her gloves; the firelight shone on her hair, Harry came across the room and caught her in his arms—'Rosabel, Rosabel, Rosabel . . . .' Oh, the haven of those arms, and she was very tired.

(The real Rosabel, the girl crouched on the floor in the dark, laughed aloud, and put her hand up to her hot mouth.)

Of course they rode in the park next morning, the engagement had been announced in the *Court Circular*, all the world knew, all the world was shaking hands with her . . . .

They were married shortly afterwards at St. George's, Hanover Square, and motored down to Harry's old ancestral home for the honeymoon; the peasants in the village curtseyed to them as they passed; under the folds of the rug he pressed her convulsively. And that night she wore again her white and silver frock. She was tired after the journey and went upstairs to bed . . . quite early . . . .

The real Rosabel got up from the floor and undressed slowly, folding her clothes over the back of a chair. She slipped over her head her coarse, calico nightdress, and took the pins out of her hair—the soft, brown flood of it fell round her, warmly. Then she blew out the candle and groped her way into bed, pulling the blankets and grimy 'honeycomb' quilt closely round her neck, cuddling down in the darkness . . . .

So she slept and dreamed, and smiled in her sleep, and once threw out her arm to feel for something which was not there, dreaming still.

And the night passed. Presently the cold fingers of dawn closed over her uncovered hand; grey light flooded the full room. Rosabel shivered, drew a little gasping breath, sat up. And because her heritage was that tragic optimism, which is all too often the only inheritance of youth, still half asleep, she smiled, with a little nervous tremor round her mouth.

Frau Brechenmacher Attends a Wedding

Getting ready was a terrible business. After supper Frau Brechenmacher packed four of the five babies to bed, allowing R. a to stay with her and help to polish the buttons of Herr Brechenmacher's uniform. Then she ran over his best shirt with a hot iron, polished his boots, and put a stitch or two into his black satin necktie.

'Rosa,' she said, 'fetch my dress and hang it in front of the stove to get the creases out. Now, mind, you must look after the children and not sit up later than half-past eight, and not touch the lamp—you know what will happen if you do.'

'Yes, mamma,' said Rosa, who was nine and felt old enough to manage a thousand lamps. 'But let me stay up—the "Bub" may wake and want some milk.'

'Half-past eight!' said the Frau. 'I'll make the father tell you too.'

Rosa drew down the corners of her mouth.

'But ... but ...'

'Here comes the father. You go into the bedroom and fetch my blue silk handkerchief. You can wear my black shawl while I'm out—there now!'

Rosa dragged it off her mother's shoulders and wound it carefully round her own, tying the two ends in a knot at the back. After all, she reflected, if she had to go to bed at half-past eight she would keep the shawl on. Which resolution comforted her absolutely.

'Now then, where are my clothes?' cried Herr Brechenmacher, hanging his empty letter-bag behind the door and stamping the snow out of his boots. 'Nothing ready, of course, and everybody at the wedding by this time. I heard the music as I passed. What are you doing? You're not dressed. You can't go like that.'

'Here they are—all ready for you on the table, and some warm water in the tin basin. Dip your head in. Rosa, give your father the towel. Everything ready except the trousers. I haven't had time to shorten them. You must tuck the ends into your boots until we get there.'

'Nu,' said the Herr, 'there isn't room to turn. I want the light. You go and dress in the passage.'

Dressing in the dark was nothing to Frau Brechenmacher. She hooked her skirt and bodice, fastened her handkerchief round her neck with a beautiful brooch that had four medals to the Virgin dangling from it, and then drew on her cloak and hood.

'Here, come and fasten this buckle,' called Herr Brechenmacher. He stood in the kitchen puffing himself out, the buttons on his blue uniform shining with an enthusiasm which nothing but official buttons could possibly possess. 'How do I look?'

'Wonderful,' replied the little Frau, straining at the waist buckle and giving him a little pull here, a little tug there. 'Rosa, come and look at your father.'

Herr Brechenmacher strode up and down the kitchen, was helped on with his coat, then waited while the Frau lighted the lantern.

'Now, then—finished at last! Come along.'

'The lamp, Rosa,' warned the Frau, slamming the front door behind them.

Snow had not fallen all day; the frozen ground was slippery as an icepond. She had not been out of the house for weeks past, and the day had so flurried her that she felt muddled and stupid—felt that Rosa had pushed her out of the house and her man was running away from her.

'Wait, wait!' she cried.

'No. I'll get my feet damp—you hurry.'

It was easier when they came into the village. There were fences to cling to, and leading from the railway station to the Gasthaus a little path of cinders had been strewn for the benefit of the wedding guests.

The Gasthaus was very festive. Lights shone out from every window, wreaths of fir twigs hung from the ledges. Branches decorated the front doors, which swung open, and in the hall the landlord voiced his superiority by bullying the waitresses, who ran about continually with glasses of beer, trays of cups and saucers, and bottles of wine.

'Up the stairs—up the stairs!' boomed the landlord. 'Leave your coats on the landing.'

Herr Brechenmacher, completely overawed by this grand manner, so far forgot his rights as a husband as to beg his wife's pardon for jostling her against the banisters in his efforts to get ahead of everybody else.

Herr Brechenmacher's colleagues greeted him with acclamation as he entered the door of the Festsaal, and the Frau straightened her brooch and folded her hands, assuming the air of dignity becoming to the wife of a postman and the mother of five children. Beautiful indeed was the Festsaal. Three long tables were grouped at one end, the remainder of the floor space cleared for dancing. Oil lamps, hanging from the ceiling, shed a warm, bright light on the walls decorated with paper flowers and garlands; shed a warmer, brighter light on the red faces of the guests in their best clothes.

At the head of the centre table sat the bride and bridegroom, she in a white dress trimmed with stripes and bows of coloured ribbon, giving her the appearance of an iced cake all ready to be cut and served in neat little pieces to the bridegroom beside her, who wore a suit of white clothes much too large for him and a white silk tie that rose half-way up his collar. Grouped about them, with a fine regard for dignity and precedence, sat their parents and relations; and perched on a stool at the bride's right hand a little girl in a crumpled muslin dress with a wreath of forget-me-nots hanging over one ear. Everybody was laughing and talking, shaking hands, clinking glasses, stamping on the floor—a stench of beer and perspiration filled the air.

Frau Brechenmacher, following her man down the room after greeting the bridal party, knew that she was going to enjoy herself. She seemed to fill out and become rosy and warm as she sniffed that familiar festive smell. Somebody pulled at her skirt, and, looking down, she saw Frau Rupp, the butcher's wife, who pulled out an empty chair and begged her to sit beside her.

'Fritz will get you some beer,' she said. 'My dear, your skirt is open at the back. We could not help laughing as you walked up the room with the white tape of your petticoat showing!'

'But how frightful!' said Frau Brechenmacher, collapsing into her chair and biting her lip.

'Na, it's over now,' said Frau Rupp, stretching her fat hands over the table and regarding her three mourning rings with intense enjoyment; 'but one must be careful, especially at a wedding.'

'And such a wedding as this,' cried Frau Ledermann, who sat on the other side of Frau Brechenmacher. 'Fancy Theresa bringing that child with her. It's her own child, you know, my dear, and it's going to live with them. That's what I call a sin against the Church for a free-born child to attend its own mother's wedding.'

The three women sat and stared at the bride, who remained very still, with a little vacant smile on her lips, only her eyes shifting uneasily from side to side.

'Beer they've given it, too,' whispered Frau Rupp, 'and white wine and an ice. It never did have a stomach; she ought to have left it at home.'

Frau Brechenmacher turned round and looked towards the bride's mother. She never took her eyes off her daughter, but wrinkled her brown forehead like an old monkey, and nodded now and again very solemnly. Her hands shook as she raised her beer mug, and when she had drunk she spat on the floor and savagely wiped her mouth with her sleeve. Then the music started and she followed Theresa with her eyes, looking suspiciously at each man who danced with her.

'Cheer up, old woman,' shouted her husband, digging her in the ribs; 'this isn't Theresa's funeral.' He winked at the guests, who broke into loud laughter.

'I *am* cheerful,' mumbled the old woman, and beat upon the table with her fist, keeping time to the music, proving she was not out of the festivities.

'She can't forget how wild Theresa has been,' said Frau Ledermann. 'Who could—with the child there? I heard that last Sunday evening Theresa had hysterics and said that she would not marry this man. They had to get the priest to her.'

'Where is the other one?' asked Frau Brechenmacher. 'Why didn't he marry her?'

The woman shrugged her shoulders.

'Gone—disappeared. He was a traveller, and only stayed at their house two nights. He was selling shirt buttons—I bought some myself, and they were beautiful shirt buttons—but what a pig of a fellow! I can't think what he saw in such a plain girl—but you never know. Her mother says she's been like fire ever since she was sixteen!'

Frau Brechenmacher looked down at her beer and blew a little hole in the froth.

'That's not how a wedding should be,' she said; 'it's not religion to love two men.'

'Nice time she'll have with this one,' Frau Rupp exclaimed. 'He was lodging with me last summer and I had to get rid of him. He never changed his clothes once in two months, and when I spoke to him of the smell in his room he told me he was sure it floated up from the shop. Ah, every wife has her cross. Isn't that true, my dear?'

Frau Brechenmacher saw her husband among his colleagues at the next table. He was drinking far too much, she knew— gesticulating wildly, the saliva spluttering out of his mouth as he talked.

'Yes,' she assented, 'that's true. Girls have a lot to learn.'

Wedged in between these two fat old women, the Frau had no hope of being asked to dance. She watched the couples going round and round; she forgot her five babies and her man and felt almost like a girl again. The music sounded sad and sweet. Her roughened hands clasped and unclasped themselves in the folds of her skirt. While the music went on she was afraid to look anybody in the face, and she smiled with a little nervous tremor round the mouth.

'But, my God,' Frau Rupp cried, 'they've given that child of Theresa's a piece of sausage. It's to keep her quiet. There's going to be a presentation now—your man has to speak.'

Frau Brechenmacher sat up stiffly. The music ceased, and the dancers took their places again at the tables.

Herr Brechenmacher alone remained standing—he held in his hands a big silver coffee-pot. Everybody laughed at his speech, except the Frau; everybody roared at his grimaces, and at the way he carried the coffee-pot to the bridal pair, as if it were a baby he was holding.

She lifted the lid, peeped in, then shut it down with a little scream and sat biting her lips. The bridegroom wrenched the pot away from her and drew forth a baby's bottle and two little

cradles holding china dolls. As he dandled these treasures before
Theresa the hot room seemed to heave and sway with laughter.

Frau Brechenmacher did not think it funny. She stared round at
the laughing faces, and suddenly they all seemed strange to her.
She wanted to go home and never come out again. She imagined
that all these people were laughing at her, more people than there
were in the room even—all laughing at her because they were so
much stronger than she was.

They walked home in silence. Herr Brechenmacher strode
ahead, she stumbled after him. White and forsaken lay the road
from the railway station to their house—a cold rush of wind blew
her hood from her face, and suddenly she remembered how they
had come home together the first night. Now they had five babies
and twice as much money; *but*—

'Na, what is it all for?' she muttered, and not until she had
reached home and prepared a little supper of meat and bread for
her man did she stop asking herself that silly question.

Herr Brechenmacher broke the bread into his plate, smeared it
round with his fork and chewed greedily.

'Good?' she asked, leaning her arms on the table and pillowing
her breast against them.

'But fine!'

He took a piece of the crumb, wiped it round his plate edge, and
held it up to her mouth. She shook her head.

'Not hungry,' she said.

'But it is one of the best pieces, and full of the fat.'

He cleared the plate; then pulled off his boots and flung them
into a corner.

'Not much of a wedding,' he said, stretching out his feet and
wriggling his toes in the worsted socks.

'N—no,' she replied, taking up the discarded boots and placing
them on the oven to dry.

Herr Brechenmacher yawned and stretched himself, and then
looked up at her, grinning.

'Remember the night that we came home? You were an
innocent one, you were.'

'Get along! Such a time ago I forget.' Well she remembered.

'Such a clout on the ear as you gave me . . . . But I soon taught you.'

'Oh, don't start talking. You've too much beer. Come to bed.'

He tilted back in his chair, chuckling with laughter.

'That's not what you said to me that night. God, the trouble you gave me!'

But the little Frau seized the candle and went into the next room. The children were all soundly sleeping. She stripped the mattress off the baby's bed to see if he was still dry, then began unfastening her blouse and skirt.

'Always the same,' she said—'all over the world the same; but, God in heaven—but *stupid*.'

Then even the memory of the wedding faded quite. She lay down on the bed and put her arm across her face like a child who expected to be hurt as Herr Brechenmacher lurched in.

The Swing of the Pendulum

The landlady knocked at the door.

'Come in,' said Viola.

'There is a letter for you,' said the landlady, 'a special letter'—she held the green envelope in a corner of her dingy apron.

'Thanks.' Viola, kneeling on the floor, poking at the little dusty stove, stretched out her hand. 'Any answer?'

'No; the messenger has gone.'

'Oh, all right!' She did not look the landlady in the face; she was ashamed of not having paid her rent, and wondered grimly, without any hope, if the woman would begin to bluster again.

'About this money owing to me—' said the landlady.

'Oh, the Lord—off she goes!' thought Viola, turning her back on the woman and making a grimace at the stove.

'It's settle— or it's go!' The landlady raised her voice; she began to bawl. 'I'm a lady, I am, and a respectable woman, I'll have you know. I'll have no lice in my house, sneaking their way into the furniture and eating up everything. It's cash—or out you go before twelve o'clock tomorrow.'

Viola felt rather than saw the woman's gesture. She shot out her arm in a stupid helpless way, as though a dirty pigeon had suddenly flown at her face. 'Filthy old beast! Ugh! And the smell of her—like stale cheese and damp washing.'

'Very well!' she answered shortly; 'it's cash down or I leave tomorrow. All right: don't shout.'

It was extraordinary—always before this woman came near her she trembled in her shoes—even the sound of those flat feet stumping up the stairs made her feel sick, but once they were face to face she felt immensely calm and indifferent, and could not understand why she even worried about money, nor why she sneaked out of the house on tiptoe, not even daring to shut the door after her in case the landlady should hear and shout something terrible, nor why she spent nights pacing up and down her room—drawing up sharply before the mirror and saying to a tragic reflection: 'Money, money, money!' When she was alone her poverty was like a huge dream-mountain on which her feet were fast rooted—aching with the ache of the size of the thing—but if it came to definite action, with no time for imaginings, her dream-mountain dwindled into a. beastly 'hold-your-nose' affair, to be passed by as quickly as possible, with anger and a strong sense of superiority.

The landlady bounced out of the room, banging the door, so that it shook and rattled as though it had listened to the conversation and fully sympathised with the old hag.

Squatting on her heels, Viola opened the letter. It was from Casimir:

'I shall be with you at three o'clock this afternoon—and must be off again this evening. All news when we meet. I hope you are happier than I.—Casimir.'

'Huh! how kind!' she sneered; 'how condescending. Too good of you, really!' She sprang to her feet, crumbling the letter in her hands. 'And how are you to know that I shall stick here awaiting your pleasure until three o'clock this afternoon?' But she knew she would; her rage was only half sincere. She longed to see Casimir, for she was confident that this time she would make him understand the situation.... 'For, as it is, it's intolerable—intolerable!' she muttered.

It was ten o'clock in the morning of a grey day curiously lighted by pale flashes of sunshine. Searched by these flashes her room looked tumbled and grimed. She pulled down the window-blinds—but they gave a persistent, whitish glare which was just as bad. The only thing of life in the room was a jar of hyacinths given her by the landlady's daughter: it stood on the table exuding a sickly perfume from its plump petals; there were even rich buds unfolding, and the leaves shone like oil.

Viola went over to the wash-stand, poured some water into the enamel basin, and sponged her face and neck. She dipped her face into the water, opened her eyes, and shook her head from side to side—it was exhilarating. She did it three times. 'I suppose I could drown myself if I stayed under long enough,' she thought. 'I wonder how long it takes to become unconscious?... Often read of women drowning in a bucket. I wonder if any air enters by the ears—if the basin would have to be as deep as a bucket?' She experimented—gripped the wash-stand with both hands and slowly sank her head into the water, when again there was a knock on the door. Not the landlady this time—it must be Casimir. With her face and hair dripping, with her petticoat bodice unbuttoned, she ran and opened it.

A strange man stood against the lintel—seeing her, he opened his eyes very wide and smiled delightfully. 'Excuse me—does Fräulein Schäfer live here?'

'No; never heard of her.' His smile was so infectious, she wanted to smile too—and the water had made her feel so fresh and rosy.

The strange man appeared overwhelmed with astonishment. 'She doesn't?' he cried. 'She is out, you mean!'

'No, she's not living here,' answered Viola.

'But—pardon—one moment.' He moved from the door lintel, standing squarely in front of her. He unbuttoned his greatcoat and drew a slip of paper from the breast pocket, smoothing it in his gloved fingers before handing it to her.

'Yes, that's the address, right enough, but there must be a mistake in the number. So many lodging-houses in this street, you know, and so big.'

Drops of water fell from her hair on to the paper. She burst out laughing. 'Oh, *how* dreadful I must look—one moment!' She ran back to the wash-stand and caught up a towel. The door was still open. After all, there was nothing more to be said. Why on earth had she asked him to wait a moment? She folded the towel round her shoulders, and returned to the door, suddenly grave. 'I'm sorry; I know no such name?' in a sharp voice.

Said the strange man: 'Sorry, too. Have you been living here long?'

'Er—yes—a long time.' She began to close the door slowly.

'Well—good morning, thanks so much. Hope I haven't been a bother.'

'Good morning.'

She heard him walk down the passage and then pause—lighting a cigarette. Yes—a faint scent of delicious cigarette smoke penetrated her room. She sniffed at it, smiling again. Well, that had been a fascinating interlude! He looked so amazingly happy:

his heavy clothes and big buttoned gloves; his beautifully brushed hair... and that smile... 'Jolly' was the word—just a well-fed boy with the world for his playground. People like that did one good—one felt 'made over' at the sight of them. *Sane* they were—so sane and solid. You could depend on them never having one mad impulse from the day they were born until the day they died. And Life was in league with them—jumped them on her knee—quite rightly too. At that moment she noticed Casimir's letter, crumpled up on the floor—the smile faded. Staring at the letter she began braiding her hair—a dull feeling of rage crept through her—she seemed to be braiding it into her brain, and binding it, tightly, above her head... Of course that had been the mistake all along. What had? Oh, Casimir's frightful seriousness. If she had been happy when they first met she never would have looked at him—but they had been like two patients in the same hospital ward—each finding comfort in the sickness of the other—sweet foundation for a love episode! Misfortune had knocked their heads together: they had looked at each other, stunned with the conflict and sympathized... 'I wish I could step outside the whole affair and just judge it—then I'd find a way out. I certainly was in love with Casimir... Oh, be sincere for once.' She flopped down on the bed and hid her face in the pillow. 'I was not in love. I wanted somebody to look after me—and keep me until my work began to sell—and he kept bothers with other men away. And what would have happened if he hadn't come along? I would have spent my wretched little pittance, and then— Yes, that was what decided me, thinking about that "then". He was the only solution. And I believed in him then. I thought his work had only to be recognised once, and he'd roll in wealth. I thought perhaps we might be poor for a month—but he said, if only he could have me, the stimulus... Funny, if it wasn't so damned tragic! Exactly the contrary has happened—he hasn't had a thing published for months—neither have I—but then I didn't expect to. Yes, the truth is, I'm hard and bitter, and I have neither faith nor love for unsuccessful men. I always end by despising them as I despise Casimir. I suppose it's the savage pride of the female who likes to think the man to whom she has given herself must be a very great chief indeed. But to stew in this disgusting house while

Casimir scours the land in the hope of finding one editorial open door—it's humiliating. It's changed my whole nature. I wasn't born for poverty—I only flower among really jolly people, and people who never are worried.'

The figure of the strange man rose before her—would not be dismissed. 'That was the man for me, after all is said and done—a man without a care—who'd give me everything I want and with whom I'd always feel that sense of life and of being in touch with the world. I never wanted to fight—it was thrust on me. Really, there's a fount of happiness in me, that is drying up, little by little, in this hateful existence. I'll be dead if this goes on—and'—she stirred in the bed and flung out her arms—'I want passion, and love, and adventure—I yearn for them. Why should I stay here and rot?—I am rotting!' she cried, comforting herself with the sound of her breaking voice. 'But if I tell Casimir all this when he comes this afternoon, and he says, "Go"—as he certainly will—that's another thing I loathe about him,—he's under my thumb—what should I do then—where should I go to?' There was nowhere. 'I don't want to work—or carve out my own path. I want ease and any amount of nursing in the lap of luxury. There is only one thing I'm fitted for, and that is to be a great courtesan.' But she did not know how to go about it. She was frightened to go into the streets—she heard of such awful things happening to those women—men with diseases—or men who didn't pay— besides, the idea of a strange man every night—no, that was out of the question. 'If I'd the clothes I would go to a really good hotel and find some wealthy man... like the strange man this morning. He would be ideal. Oh, if I only had his address—I am sure I would fascinate him. I'd keep him laughing all day—I'd make him give me unlimited money.' At the thought she grew warm and soft. She began to dream of a wonderful house, and of presses full of clothes and of perfumes. She saw herself stepping into carriages—looking at the strange man with a mysterious, voluptuous glance—she practised the glance, lying on the bed—and never another worry, just drugged with happiness. That was the life for her. Well, the thing to do was to let Casimir go on his wild-goose chase that evening, and while he was away—What! Also—please to remember—there was the rent to be paid before twelve next morning, and she hadn't the money for a square meal. At the thought of food she felt a sharp twinge in her stomach, a sensation as though there were a hand in her stomach, squeezing it dry. She was terribly hungry—all Casimir's fault—and that man had lived on the fat of the land ever since he was born. He looked as though he could order a magnificent dinner. Oh, why hadn't she played her cards better?—he'd been sent by Providence—and she'd snubbed him. 'If I had that time over again, I'd be safe by now.' And instead of the ordinary man who had spoken with her at the door her mind created a brilliant, laughing image, who would treat her like a queen... 'There's only one thing I could not stand—that he should be coarse or vulgar. Well, he wasn't—he was obviously a man of the world, and the way he apologised... I have enough faith in my own power and beauty to know I could make a man treat me just as I wanted to be treated.'... It floated into her dreams—that sweet scent of cigarette smoke. And then she remembered that she had heard nobody go down the stone stairs. Was it possible that the strange man was still there?... The thought was too absurd—Life didn't play tricks like that—and yet—she was quite conscious of his nearness. Very quietly she got up, unhooked from the back of the door a long white gown, buttoned it on—smiling slyly. She did not know what was going to happen. She only thought: 'Oh, what fun!' and that they were playing a delicious game—this strange man and she. Very gently she turned the door-handle, screwing up her face and biting her lip as the lock snapped back. Of course, there he was—leaning against the banister rail. He wheeled round as she slipped into the passage.

'Da,' she muttered, folding her gown tightly around her, 'I must go downstairs and fetch some wood. Brr! the cold!'

'There isn't any wood,' volunteered the strange man. She gave a little cry of astonishment, and then tossed her head.

'You, again,' she said scornfully, conscious the while of his merry eye, and the fresh, strong smell of his healthy body.

'The landlady shouted out there was no wood left. I just saw her go out to buy some.'

'Story—story!' she longed to cry. He came quite close to her, stood over her and whispered:

'Aren't you going to ask me to finish my cigarette in your room?'

She nodded. 'You may if you want to!'

In that moment together in the passage a miracle had happened. Her room was quite changed—it was full of sweet light and the scent of hyacinth flowers. Even the furniture appeared different—exciting. Quick as a flash she remembered childish parties when they had played charades, and one side had left the room and come in again to act a word—just what she was doing now. The strange man went over to the stove and sat down in her armchair. She did not want him to talk or come near her—it was enough to see him in the room, so secure and happy. How hungry she had been for the nearness of someone like that—who knew nothing at all about her—and made no demands—but just lived. Viola ran over to the table and put her arms round the jar of hyacinths.

'Beautiful! Beautiful!' she cried—burying her head in the flowers—and sniffing greedily at the scent. Over the leaves she looked at the man and laughed.

'You are a funny little thing,' said he lazily.

'Why? Because I love flowers?'

'I'd far rather you loved other things,' said the strange man slowly. She broke off a little pink petal and smiled at it.

'Let me send you some flowers,' said the strange man. 'I'll send you a roomful if you'd like them.'

His voice frightened her slightly. 'Oh no, thanks—this one is quite enough for me.'

'No, it isn't'—in a teasing voice.

'What a stupid remark!' thought Viola, and looking at him again he did not seem quite so jolly. She noticed that his eyes were set too closely together—and they were too small. Horrible thought, that he should prove stupid.

'What do you do all day?' she asked hastily.

'Nothing.'

'Nothing at all?'

'Why should I do anything?'

'Oh, don't imagine for one moment that I condemn such widsom—only it sounds too good to be true!'

'What's that?'—he craned forward. 'What sounds too good to be true?' Yes—there was no denying it—he looked silly.

'I suppose the searching after Fraulein Schäfer doesn't occupy all your days.'

'Oh no'—he smiled broadly—'that's very good! By Jove! no. I drive a good bit—are you keen on horses?'

She nodded. 'Love them'.

'You must come driving with me—I've got a fine pair of greys. Will you?'

'Pretty I'd look perched behind greys in my one and only hat,' thought she. Aloud: 'I'd love to.' Her easy acceptance pleased him.

'How about tomorrow?' he suggested. 'Suppose you have lunch with me tomorrow and I take you driving.'

After all—this was just a game. 'Yes, I'm not busy tomorrow,' she said.

A little pause—then the strange man patted his leg. 'Why don't you come and sit down?' he said.

She pretended not to see and swung on to the table. 'Oh, I'm all right here.'

'No, you're not'—again the teasing voice. 'Come and sit on my knee.'

'Oh no,' said Viola very heartily, suddenly busy with her hair.

'Why not?'

'I don't want to.'

'Oh, come along'—impatiently.

She shook her head from side to side. 'I wouldn't dream of such a thing.'

At that he got up and came over to her. 'Funny little pussy cat!' He put up one hand to touch her hair.

'Don't' she said—and slipped off the table. 'I—I think it's time you went now.' She was quite frightened now—thinking only: 'This man must be got rid of as quickly as possible.'

'Oh, but you don't want me to go?'

'Yes, I do—I'm very busy.'

'Busy. What does the pussy cat do all day?'

'Lots and lots of things!' She wanted to push him out of the room and slam the door on him—idiot—fool—cruel disappointment.

'What's she frowning for?' he asked. 'Is she worried about anything?' Suddenly serious: 'I say—you know, are you in any financial difficulty. Do you want money? I'll give it to you if you like!'

'Money! Steady on the brake—don't lose your head!'—so she spoke to herself.

'I'll give you two hundred marks if you'll kiss me.'

'Oh, boo! What a condition! And I don't want to kiss you—I don't like kissing. Please go!'

'Yes—you do!—yes, you do.' He caught hold of her arms above the elbows. She struggled, and was quite amazed to realize how angry she felt.

'Let me go—immediately!' she cried—and he slipped one arm round her body, and drew her towards him—like a bar of iron across her back—that arm.

'Leave me alone, I tell you! Don't be mean! I didn't want this to happen when you came into my room. How dare you.'

'Well, kiss me and I'll go!'

It was too idiotic—dodging that stupid, smiling face.

'I won't kiss you!—you brute!—I won't!' Somehow she slipped out of his arms and ran to the wall—stood back against it—breathing quickly.

'Get out!' she stammered. 'Go on now, clear out!'

At that moment, when he was not touching her, she quite enjoyed herself. She thrilled at her own angry voice. 'To think I should talk to a man like that!' An angry flush spread over his face—his lips curled back, showing his teeth—just like a dog, thought Viola. He made a rush at her, and held her against the wall—pressed upon her with all the weight of his body. This time she could not get free.

'I won't kiss you. I won't. Stop doing that! Ugh! you're like a dog—you ought to find lovers round lamp-posts—you beast—you fiend!'

He did not answer. With an expression of the most absurd determination he pressed ever more heavily upon her. He did not even look at her—but rapped out in a sharp voice: 'Keep quiet—keep quiet.'

'Gar-r! Why are men so strong?' She began to cry. 'Go away—I don't want you, you dirty creature. I want to murder you. Oh, my God! if I had a knife.'

'Don't be silly—come and be good!' He dragged her towards the bed.

'Do you suppose I'm a light woman?' she snarled, and swooping over she fastened her teeth in his glove.

'Ach! don't do that—you are hurting me!'

She did not let go, but her heart said, 'Thank the Lord I thought of this.'

'Stop this minute—you vixen—you bitch.' He threw her away from him. She saw with joy that his eyes were full of tears. 'You've really hurt me,' he said in a choking voice.

'Of course I have. I meant to. That's nothing to what I'll do if you touch me again.'

The strange man picked up his hat. 'No, thanks,' he said grimly. 'But I'll not forget this—I'll go to your landlady.'

'Pooh!' She shrugged her shoulders and laughed. 'I'll tell her you forced your way in here and tried to assault me. Who will she believe?—with your bitten hand. You go and find your Schäfers.'

A sensation of glorious, intoxicating happiness flooded Viola. She rolled her eyes at him. 'If you don't go away this moment I'll bite you again,' she said, and the absurd words started her laughing. Even when the door was closed, hearing him descending the stairs, she laughed, and danced about the room.

What a morning! Oh, chalk it up. That was her first fight, and she'd won—she'd conquered that beast—all by herself. Her hands were still trembling. She pulled up the sleeve of her gown—great red marks on her arms. 'My ribs will be blue. I'll be blue all over,' she reflected. 'If only that beloved Casimir could have seen us.' And the feeling of rage and disgust against Casimir had totally disappeared. How could the poor darling help not having any money? It was her fault as much as his, and he, just like her, was apart from the world, fighting it, just as she had done. If only three o'clock would come. She saw herself running towards him and putting her arms round his neck. 'My blessed one! Of course we are bound to win. Do you love me still? Oh, I have been horrible lately.'

A Birthday

Andreas Binzer woke slowly. He turned over on the narrow bed and stretched himself—yawned—opening his mouth as widely as possible and bringing his teeth together afterwards with a sharp 'click'. The sound of that click fascinated him; he repeated it quickly several times, with a snapping movement of the jaws. What teeth! he thought. Sound as a bell, every man jack of them. Never had one out, never had one stopped. That comes of no tomfoolery in eating, and a good regular brushing night and morning. He raised himself on his left elbow and waved his right arm over the side of the bed to feel for the chair where he put his watch and chain overnight. No chair was there—of course, he'd forgotten, there wasn't a chair in this wretched spare room. Had to put the confounded thing under his pillow. 'Half-past eight, Sunday, breakfast at nine—time for the bath'—his brain ticked to the watch. He sprang out of bed and went over to the window. The venetian blind was broken, hung fan-shaped over the upper pane. 'That blind must be mended. I'll get the office boy to drop in and fix it on his way home tomorrow—he's a good hand at blinds. Give him twopence and he'll do it as well a a carpenter. Anna could do it herself if she was all right. So would I, for the matter of that, but I don't like to trust myself on rickety step-ladders.' He looked up at the sky: it shone, strangely white, unflecked with cloud; he looked down at the row of garden strips and back yards. The fence of these gardens was built along the edge of a gully, spanned by an iron suspension bridge, and the people had a wretched habit of throwing their empty tins over the fence into the gully. Just like them, of course! Andreas started counting the tins, and decided, viciously, to write a letter to the papers about it and sign it—sign it in full.

The servant girl came out of their back door into the yard, carrying his boots. She threw one down on the ground, thrust her hand into the other, and stared at it, sucking in her cheeks. Suddenly, she bent forward, spat on the toecap, and started polishing with a brush rooted out of her apron pocket. 'Slut of a girl! Heaven knows what infectious disease may be breeding now in that boot. Anna must get rid of the girl—even if she has to do without one for a bit—as soon as she's up and about again. The way she chucked one boot down and then spat upon the other! She didn't care whose boots she'd got hold of. *She* had no false notions of the respect due to the master of the house.' He turned away from the window and switched his bath towel from the wash-stand rail, sick at heart. 'I'm too sensitive for a man—that's what's the matter with me. Have been from the beginning, and will be to the end.'

There was a gentle knock at the door and his mother came in. She closed the door after her and leant against it. Andreas noticed that her cap was crooked, and a long tail of hair hung over her shoulder. He went forward and kissed her.

'Good morning, mother; how's Anna?'

The old woman spoke quickly, clasping and unclasping her hands.

'Andreas, please go to Doctor Erb as soon as you are dressed.'

'Why,' he said, 'is she bad?'

Frau Binzer nodded, and Andreas, watching her, saw her face suddenly change; a fine network of wrinkles seemed to pull over it from under the skin surface.

'Sit down on the bed a moment,' he said. 'Been up all night?'

'Yes. No, I won't sit down, I must go back to her. Anna has been in pain all night. She wouldn't have you disturbed before because she said you looked so run down yesterday. You told her you had caught a cold and been very worried.'

Straightaway Andreas felt that he was being accused.

'Well, she made me tell her, worried it out of me; you know the way she does.'

Again Frau Binzer nodded.

'Oh yes, I know. She says, is your cold better, and there's a warm undervest for you in the left-hand corner of the big drawer.'

Quite automatically Andreas cleared his throat twice.

'Yes,' he answered. 'Tell her my throat certainly feels looser. I suppose I'd better not disturb her?'

'No, and besides, *time*, Andreas.'

'I'll be ready in five minutes.'

They went into the passage. As Frau Binzer opened the door of the front bedroom, a long wail came from the room.

That shocked and terrified Andreas. He dashed into the bathroom, turned on both taps as far as they would go, cleaned his teeth and pared his nails while the water was running.

'Frightful business, frightful business,' he heard himself whispering. 'And I can't understand it. It isn't as though it were her first—it's her third. Old Schäfer told me, yesterday, his wife simply "dropped" her fourth. Anna ought to have had a qualified nurse. Mother gives way to her. Mother spoils her. I wonder what she meant by saying I'd worried Anna yesterday. Nice remark to make to a husband at a time like this. Unstrung, I suppose—and my sensitiveness again.'

When he went into the kitchen for his boots, the servant girl was bent over the stove, cooking breakfast. 'Breathing into that, now, I suppose,' thought Andreas, and was very short with the servant girl. She did not notice. She was full of terrified joy and importance in the goings-on upstairs. She felt she was learning the secrets of life with every breath she drew. Had laid the table that morning saying, 'Boy,' as she put down the first dish, 'Girl,' as she placed the second—it had worked out with the saltspoon to 'Boy'. 'For two pins I'd tell the master that, to comfort him, like,' she decided. But the master gave her no opening.

'Put an extra cup and saucer on the table,' he said; 'the doctor may want some coffee.'

'The doctor, sir?' The servant girl whipped a spoon out of a pan, and spilt two drops of grease on the stove. 'Shall I fry something extra?' But the master had gone, slamming the door after him. He walked down the street—there was nobody about at all—dead and alive this place on Sunday morning. As he crossed the suspension bridge a strong stench of fennel and decayed refuse streamed from the gulley, and again Andreas began concocting a letter. He turned into the main road. The shutters were still up before the shops. Scraps of newspaper, hay and fruit skins strewed the pavement; the gutters were choked with the leavings of Saturday night. Two dogs sprawled in the middle of the road, scuffling and biting. Only the public-house at the corner was open; a young barman slopped water over the doorstep.

Fastidiously, his lip curling, Andreas picked his way through the water. 'Extraordinary how I am noticing things this morning. It's partly the effect of Sunday. I loathe a Sunday when Anna's tied by the leg and the children are away. On Sunday a man has the right to expect his family. Everything here's filthy, the whole place might be down with the plague, and will be, too, if this street's not swept away. I'd like to have a hand on the government ropes.' He braced his shoulders. 'Doctor Erb is at breakfast,' the maid informed him. She showed him into the waiting-room, a dark and musty place, with some ferns under a glass-case by the window. 'He says he won't be a minute, please, sir, and there is a paper on the table.'

'Unhealthy hole,' thought Binzer, walking over to the window and drumming his fingers on the glass fern-shade. 'At breakfast, is he? That's the mistake I made: turning out early on an empty stomach.'

A milk cart rattled down the street, the driver standing at the back, cracking a whip; he wore an immense geranium flower stuck in the lapel of his coat. Firm as a rock he stood, bending back a little in the swaying cart. Andreas craned his neck to watch him all the way down the road, even after he had gone, listening for the sharp sound of those rattling cans.

'H'm, not much wrong with him,' he reflected. 'Wouldn't mind a taste of that life myself. Up early, work all over by eleven o'clock, nothing to do but loaf about all day until milking time.' Which he knew was an exaggeration, but he wanted to pity himself.

The maid opened the door, and stood aside for Doctor Erb. Andreas wheeled round; the two men shook hands.

'Well, Binzer,' said the doctor jovially, brushing some crumbs from a pearl-coloured waistcoat, 'son and heir becoming importunate?'

Up went Binzer's spirits with a bound. Son and heir, by Jove! He was glad to have to deal with a man again. And a sane fellow this, who came across this sort of thing every day of the week.

'That's about the measure of it, Doctor,' he answered, smiling and picking up his hat. 'Mother dragged me out of bed this morning with imperative orders to bring you along.'

'Gig will be round in a minute. Drive back with me, won't you? Extraordinary, sultry day; you're as red as a beetroot already.'

Andreas affected to laugh. The doctor had one annoying habit—imagined he had the right to poke fun at everybody simply because he was a doctor. 'The man's riddled with conceit, like all these professionals,' Andreas decided.

'What sort of night did Frau Binzer have?' asked the doctor. 'Ah, here's the gig. Tell me on the way up. Sit as near the middle as you can, will you, Binzer? Your weight tilts it over a bit one side—that's the worst of you successful business men.'

'Two stone heavier than I, if he's a pound,' thought Andreas. 'The man may be all right in his profession—but heaven preserve me.'

'Off you go, my beauty.' Doctor Erb flicked the little brown mare. 'Did your wife get any sleep last night?'

'No; I don't think she did,' answered Andreas shortly. 'To tell you the truth, I'm not satisfied that she hasn't a nurse.'

'Oh, your mother's worth a dozen nurses,' cried the doctor, with immense gusto. 'To tell you the truth, I'm not keen on nurses—too raw—raw as rump-steak. They wrestle for a baby as though they were wrestling with Death for the body of Patroclus.... Ever seen that picture by an English artist. Leighton? Wonderful thing—full of sinew!'

'There he goes again,' thought Andreas, 'airing off his knowledge to make a fool of me.'

'Now your mother—she's firm—she's capable. Does what she's told with a fund of sympathy. Look at these shops we're passing — they're festering sores. How on earth this government can tolerate—'

'They're not so bad—sound enough—only want a coat of paint.'

The doctor whistled a little tune and flicked the mare again.

'Well, I hope the young shaver won't give his mother too much trouble,' he said. 'Here we are.'

A skinny little boy, who had been sliding up and down the back seat of the gig, sprang out and held the horse's head. Andreas went straight into the dining-room and left the servant girl to take the doctor upstairs. He sat down, poured out some coffee, and bit through half a roll before helping himself to fish. Then he noticed there was no hot plate for the fish—the whole house was at sixes and sevens. He rang the bell, but the servant girl came in with a tray holding a bowl of soup and a hot plate.

'I've been keeping them on the stove,' she simpered.

'Ah, thanks, that's very kind of you.' As he swallowed the soup his heart warmed to this fool of a girl.

'Oh, it's a good thing Doctor Erb has come,' volunteered the servant girl, who was bursting from want of sympathy.

'H'm, h'm,' said Andreas.

She waited a moment, expectantly, rolling her eyes, then in full loathing of mankind went back to the kitchen and vowed herself to sterility.

Andreas cleared the soup bowl, and cleared the fish. As he ate, the room slowly darkened. A faint wind sprang up and beat the tree branches against the window. The dining-room looked over the breakwater of the harbour, and the sea swung heavily in rolling waves. Wind crept round the house, moaning drearily.

'We're in for a storm. That means I'm boxed up here all day. Well, there's one blessing; it'll clear the air.' He heard the servant girl rushing importantly round the house, slamming windows. Then he caught a glimpse of her in the garden unpegging tea towels from the line across the lawn. She was a worker, there was no doubt about that. He took up a book, and wheeled his armchair over to the window. But it was useless. Too dark to read; he didn't believe in straining his eyes, and gas at ten o'clock in the morning seemed absurd. So he slipped down in the chair, leaned his elbows on the padded arms and gave himself up, for once, to idle dreaming. 'A boy? Yes, it was bound to be a boy this time. ' 'What's your family, Binzer?' 'Oh, I've two girls and a boy!' A very nice little number. Of course he was the last man to have a favourite child, but a man needed a son. 'I'm working up the business for my son! Binzer & Son! It would mean living very tight for the next ten years, cutting expenses as fine as possible; and then—'

A tremendous gust of wind sprang upon the house, seized it, shook it, dropped, only to grip the more tightly. The waves swelled up along the breakwater and were whipped with broken foam. Over the white sky flew tattered streamers of grey cloud.

Andreas felt quite relieved to hear Doctor Erb coming down the stairs; he got up and lit the gas.

'Mind if I smoke in here?' asked Doctor Erb, lighting a cigarette before Andreas had time to answer. 'You don't smoke, do you? No time to indulge in pernicious little habits!'

'How is she now?' asked Andreas, loathing the man.

'Oh, well as can be expected, poor little soul. She begged me to come down and have a look at you. Said she knew you were worrying.' With laughing eyes the doctor looked at the breakfast-table. 'Managed to peck a bit, I see, eh?'

'Hoo-wih!' shouted the wind, shaking the window-sashes.

'Pity—this weather,' said Doctor Erb.

'Yes, it gets on Anna's nerves, and it's just nerve she wants.'

'Eh, what's that?' retorted the doctor. 'Nerve! Man alive! She's got twice the nerve of you and me rolled into one. Nerve! she's nothing but nerve. A woman who works as she does about the house and has three children in four years thrown in with the dusting, so to speak!'

He pitched his half-smoked cigarette into the fire-place and frowned at the window.

'Now *he's* accusing me,' thought Andreas. 'That's the second time this morning—first mother and now this man taking advantage of my sensitiveness.' He could not trust himself to speak, and rang the bell for the servant girl.

'Clear away the breakfast things,' he ordered. 'I can't have them messing about on the table till dinner!'

'Don't be hard on the girl,' coaxed Doctor Erb. 'She's got twice the work to do today.'

At that Binzer's anger blazed out.

'I'll trouble you, Doctor, not to interfere between me and my servants!' And he felt a fool at the same moment for not saying 'servant'.

Doctor Erb was not perturbed. He shook his head, thrust his hands into his pockets, and began balancing himself on toe and heel.

'You're jagged by the weather,' he said wryly, 'nothing else. A great pity—this storm. You know climate has an immense effect upon birth. A fine day perks a woman—gives her heart for her business. Good weather is as necessary to a confinement as it is to a washing day. Not bad—that last remark of mine—for a professional fossil, eh?'

Andreas made no reply.

'Well, I'll be getting back to my patient. Why don't you take a walk, and clear your head? That's the idea for you.'

'No,' he answered, 'I won't do that; it's too rough.'

He went back to his chair by the window. While the servant girl cleared away he pretended to read. . . then his dreams! It seemed years since he had had the time to himself to dream like that—he never had a breathing space. Saddled with work all day, and couldn't shake it off in the evening like other men. Besides, Anna was interested—they talked of practically nothing else together. Excellent mother she'd make for a boy; she had a grip of things.

Church bells started ringing through the windy air, now sounding as though from very far away, then again as though all the churches in the town had been suddenly transplanted into their street. They stirred something in him, those bells, something vague and tender. Just about that time Anna would call him from the hall. 'Andreas, come and have your coat brushed. I'm ready.' Then off they would go, she hanging on his arm, and looking up at him. She certainly was a little thing. He remembered once saying when they were engaged, 'Just as high as my heart,' and she had jumped on to a stool and pulled his head down, laughing. A kid in those days, younger than her children in nature, brighter, more 'go' and 'spirit' in her. The way she'd run down the road to meet him after business! And the way she laughed when they were looking for a house. By Jove! that laugh of hers! At the memory he grinned, then grew suddenly grave. Marriage certainly changed a woman far more than it did a man. Talk about sobering down. She had lost all her go in two months! Well, once this boy business was over she'd get stronger. He began to plan a little trip for them. He'd take her away and they'd loaf about together somewhere. After all, dash it, they were young still. She'd got into a groove; he'd have to force her out of it, that's all.

He got up and went into the drawing-room, carefully shut the door and took Anna's photograph from the top of the piano. She wore a white dress with a big bow of some soft stuff under the chin, and stood, a little stiffly, holding a sheaf of artifical poppies and corn in her hands. Delicate she looked even then; her masses of hair gave her that look. She seemed to droop under the heavy braids of it, and yet she was smiling. Andreas caught his breath sharply. She was his wife—that girl. Posh! it had only been taken four years ago. He held it close to him, bent forward and kissed it. Then rubbed the glass with the back of his hand. At that moment, fainter than he had heard in the passage, more terrifying, Andreas heard again that wailing cry. The wind caught it up in mocking echo, blew it over the house-tops, down the street, far away from him. He flung out his arms, 'I'm so damnably helpless,' he said, and then, to the picture, 'Perhaps it's not as bad as it sounds; perhaps it is just my sensitiveness.' In the half-light of the drawing-room the smile seemed to deepen in Anna's portrait, and to become secret, even cruel. 'No,' he reflected, 'that smile is not at all her happiest expression—it was a mistake to let her have it taken smiling like that. She doesn't look like my wife—like the mother of my son.' Yes, that was it, she did not look like the mother of a son who was going to be a partner in the firm. The picture got on his nerves; he held it in different lights, looked at it from a distance, sideways, spent, it seemed to Andreas afterwards, a whole lifetime trying to fit it in. The more he played with it the deeper grew his dislike of it. Thrice he carried it over to the fire-place and decided to chuck it behind the Japanese umbrella in the grate; then he thought it absurd to waste an expensive frame. There was no good in beating about the bush. Anna looked like a stranger—abnormal, a freak—it might be a picture taken just before or after death.

Suddenly he realised that the wind had dropped, that the whole house was still, terribly still. Cold and pale, with a disgusting feeling that spiders were creeping up his spine and across his face, he stood in the centre of the drawing-room, hearing Doctor Erb's footsteps descending the stairs.

He saw Doctor Erb come into the room; the room seemed to change into a great glass bowl that spun round, and Doctor Erb seemed to swim through this glass bowl towards him, like a goldfish in a pearl-coloured waistcoat.

'My beloved wife has passed away!' He wanted to shout it out before the doctor spoke...

'Well, she's hooked a boy this time!' said Doctor Erb. Andreas staggered forward.

'Look out. Keep on your pins,' said Doctor Erb, catching Binzer's arm, and murmuring, as he felt it, 'Flabby as butter.'

A glow spread all over Andreas. He was exultant.

'Well, by God! Nobody can accuse *me* of not knowing what suffering is,' he said.

Millie

Millie stood leaning against the veranda until the men were out of sight. When they were far down the road Willie Cox turned round on his horse and waved. But she didn't wave back. She nodded her head a little and made a grimace. Not a bad young fellow, Willie Cox, but a bit too free and easy for her taste. Oh, my word! it was hot. Enough to fry your hair!

Millie put her handkerchief over her head and shaded her eyes with her hand. In the distance along the dusty road she could see the horses, like brown spots dancing up and down, and when she looked away from them and over the burnt paddocks she could see them still—just before her eyes, jumping like mosquitoes. It was half-past two in the afternoon. The sun hung in the faded blue sky like a burning mirror, and away beyond the paddocks the blue mountains quivered and leapt like the sea.

Sid wouldn't be back until half-past ten. He had ridden over to the township with four of the boys to help hunt down the young fellow who'd murdered Mr Williamson. Such a dreadful thing! And Mrs Williamson left all alone with all those kids. Funny! she couldn't think of Mr Williamson being dead! He was such a one for a joke. Always having a lark. Willie Cox said they found him in the barn, shot bang through the head, and the young English 'Johnny' who'd been on the station learning farming—disappeared. Funny! she couldn't think of anyone shooting Mr Williamson, and him so popular and all. My word! when they caught that young man! Well, you couldn't be sorry for a young fellow like that. As Sid said, if he wasn't strung up where would they all be? A man like that doesn't stop at one go. There was blood all over the barn. And Willie Cox said he was that knocked out he picked a cigarette up out of the blood and smoked it. My word! he must have been half dotty.

Millie went back into the kitchen. She put some ashes on the stove and sprinkled them with water. Languidly, the sweat pouring down her face, and dropping off her nose and chin, she cleared away the dinner, and going into the bedroom, stared at herself in the fly-specked mirror, and wiped her face and neck with a towel. She didn't know what was the matter with herself that afternoon. She could have a good cry—just for nothing—and then change her blouse and have a good cup of tea. Yes, she felt like that!

She flopped down on the side of the bed and stared at the coloured print on the wall opposite, *Garden Party at Windsor Castle*. In the foreground emerald lawns planted with immense oak trees, and in their grateful shade a muddle of ladies and gentlemen and parasols and little tables. The background was filled with the towers of Windsor Castle, flying three Union Jacks, and in the middle of the picture the old Queen, like a tea-cosy with a head on top of it. 'I wonder if it really looked like that.' Millie stared at the flowery ladies, who simpered back at her. 'I wouldn't care for that sort of thing. Too much side. What with the Queen an' one thing an' another.'

Over the packing-case dressing-table there was a large photograph of her and Sid, taken on their wedding day. Nice picture that—if you *do* like. She was sitting down in a basket chair, in her cream cashmere and satin ribbons, and Sid, standing with one hand on her shoulder, looking at her bouquet. And behind them there were some fern trees and a waterfall, and Mount Cook in the distance, covered with snow. She had almost forgotten her wedding day; time did pass so, and if you hadn't anyone to talk things over with, they soon dropped out of your mind. 'I wunner why we never had no kids . . . . ' She shrugged her shoulders—gave it up. 'Well, *I've* never missed them. I wouldn't be surprised if Sid had, though. He's softer than me.'

And then she sat quiet, thinking of nothing at all, her red swollen hands rolled in her apron, her feet stuck out in front of her, her little head with the thick screw of dark hair drooped on her chest. *Tick-tick* went the kitchen clock, the ashes clinked in the grate, and the venetian blind knocked against the kitchen window. Quite suddenly Millie felt frightened. A queer trembling started inside her—in her stomach—and then spread all over to her knees and hands. 'There's somebody about.' She tiptoed to the door and peered into the kitchen. Nobody there; the veranda doors were closed, the blinds were down, and in the dusky light the white face of the clock shone, and the furniture seemed to bulge and breathe . . . and listen, too. The clock—the ashes—and the venetian—and then again—something else, like steps in the back yard. 'Go an' see what it is, Millie Evans.'

She darted to the back door, opened it, and at the same moment someone ducked behind the wood pile. 'Who's that?' she cried, in a loud, bold voice. 'Come out o' that! I seen yer. I know where y'are. I got my gun. Come out from behind of that wood stack!' She was not frightened any more. She was furiously angry. Her heart banged like a drum. 'I'll teach you to play tricks with a woman,' she yelled, and she took a gun from the kitchen corner, and dashed down the veranda steps, across the glaring yard to the other side of the wood stack. A young man lay there, on his stomach, one arm across his face. 'Get up! You're shamming!' Still holding the gun she kicked him in the shoulders. He gave no sign. 'Oh, my God, I believe he's dead.' She knelt down, seized hold of him, and turned him over on his back. He rolled like a sack. She crouched back on her haunches, staring; her lips and nostrils fluttered with horror.

He was not much more than a boy, with fair hair and a growth of fair down on his lips and chin. His eyes were open, rolled up, showing the whites, and his face was patched with dust caked with sweat. He wore a cotton shirt and trousers, with sandshoes on his feet. One of the trousers was stuck to his leg with a patch of dark blood. 'I *can't*,' said Millie, and then, 'You've got to.' She bent over and felt his heart. 'Wait a minute,' she stammered, 'wait a minute,' and she ran into the house for brandy and a pail of water. 'What are you going to do, Millie Evans? Oh, I don't know. I never seen anyone in a dead faint before.' She knelt down, put her arm under the boy's head and poured some brandy between his lips. It spilled down both sides of his mouth. She dipped a corner of her apron in the water and wiped his face and his hair and his throat, with fingers that trembled. Under the dust and sweat his face gleamed, white as her apron, and thin, and puckered in little lines. A strange dreadful feeling gripped Millie Evans' bosom—some seed that had never flourished there, unfolded and struck deep roots and burst into painful leaf. 'Are yer coming round? Feeling all right again?' The boy breathed

sharply, half choked, his eyelids quivered, and he moved his head
from side to side. 'You're better,' said Millie, smoothing his hair.
'Feeling fine now again, ain't yer?' The pain in her bosom half
suffocated her. 'It's no good you crying, Millie Evans. You got to
keep your head.' Quite suddenly he sat up and leaned against the
wood pile, away from her, staring on the ground. 'There now!'
cried Millie Evans, in a strange, shaking voice.

The boy turned and looked at her, still not speaking, but his
eyes were so full of pain and terror that she had to shut her teeth
and clench her hands to stop from crying. After a long pause he
said, in the little voice of a child talking in his sleep, 'I'm hungry.'
His lips quivered. She scrambled to her feet and stood over him.
'You come right into the house and have a sit-down meal,' she
said. 'Can you walk?' 'Yes,' he whispered, and swaying he
followed her across the glaring yard to the veranda. At the bottom
step he paused, looking at her again. 'I'm not coming in,' he said.
He sat on the veranda step in the little pool of shade that lay round
the house. Millie watched him. 'When did yer last 'ave anything to
eat?' He shook his head. She cut a chunk off the greasy corned beef
and a round of bread plastered with butter; but when she brought
it he was standing up, glancing round him, and paid no attention
to the plate of food. 'When are they coming back?' he stammered.

At that moment she knew. She stood, holding the plate, staring.
He was Harrison. He was the English johnny who'd killed Mr
Williamson. 'I know who you are,' she said, very slowly, 'yer can't
fox me. That's who you are. I must have been blind in me two eyes
not to 'ave known from the first.' He made a movement with his
hands as though that was all nothing. 'When are they coming
back?' And she meant to say, 'Any minute. They're on their way
now.' Instead she said to the dreadful, frightened face, 'Not till
'arf-past ten.' He sat down, leaning against one of the veranda
poles. His face broke up into little quivers. He shut his eyes, and
tears streamed down his cheeks. 'Nothing but a kid. An' all them
fellows after 'im. 'E don't stand any more of a chance than a kid
would.' 'Try a bit of beef,' said Millie. 'It's the food you want.
Something to steady your stomach.' She moved across the
veranda and sat down beside him, the plate on her knees.
''Ere—try a bit.' She broke the bread and butter into little pieces,

and she thought, 'They won't ketch him. Not if I can 'elp it. Men is all beasts. I don't care wot 'e's done, or wot 'e 'asn't done. See 'im through, Millie Evans. 'E's nothink but a sick kid.'

Millie lay on her back, her eyes wide open, listening. Sid turned over, hunched the quilt round his shoulders, muttered 'Good night, ole girl.' She heard Willie Cox and the other chap drop their clothes on to the kitchen floor, and then their voices, and Willie Cox saying, 'Lie down, Gumboil. Lie down, yer little devil,' to his dog. The house dropped quiet. She lay and listened. Little pulses tapped in her body, listening, too. It was hot. She was frightened to move because of Sid. ''E must get off. 'E must. I don't care anythink about justice an' all the rot they've bin spoutin' tonight,' she thought savagely. ''Ow are yer to know what anythink's like till yer *do* know. It's all rot.' She strained to the silence. He ought to be moving.... Before there was a sound from outside, Willie Cox's Gumboil got up and padded sharply across the kitchen floor and sniffed at the back door. Terror started up in Millie. 'What's that dog doing? Uh! What a fool that young fellow is with a dog 'anging about. Why don't 'e lie down an' sleep.' The dog stopped, but she knew it was listening.

Suddenly, with a sound that made her cry out in horror the dog started barking and rushing to and fro. 'What's that? What's up?' Sid flung out of bed. 'It ain't nothink. It's only Gumboil. Sid, Sid!' She clutched his arm, but he shook her off. 'My Christ, there's somethink up. My God!' Sid flung into his trousers. Willie Cox opened the back door. Gumboil in a fury darted out into the yard, round the corner of the house. 'Sid, there's someone in the paddock,' roared the other chap. 'What is it—what's that?' Sid dashed out on to the front veranda. ''Ere, Millie, take the lantin. Willie, some skunk's got 'old of one of the 'orses.' The three men bolted out of the house, and at the same moment Millie saw Harrison dash across the paddock on Sid's horse and down the road. 'Millie, bring that blasted lantin.' She ran in her bare feet, her nightdress flicking her legs. They were after him in a flash. And at the sight of Harrison in the distance, and the three men hot after, a strange mad joy smothered everything else. She rushed into the road—she laughed and shrieked and danced in the dust, jigging the lantern. 'A—ah! Arter 'im, Sid! A—a—a—h! Ketch him, Willie. Go it! Go it! A—ah, Sid! Shoot 'im down. Shoot 'im!'

The Woman at the Store

All that day the heat was terrible. The wind blew close to the ground; it rooted among the tussock grass, slithered along the road, so that the white pumice dust swirled in our faces, settled and sifted over us and was like a dry-skin itching for growth on our bodies. The horses stumbled along, coughing and chuffing. The pack-horse was sick—with a big open sore rubbed under the belly. Now and again she stopped short, threw back her head, looked at us as though she were going to cry, and whinnied. Hundreds of larks shrilled; the sky was slate colour, and the sound of the larks reminded me of slate pencils scraping over its surface. There was nothing to be seen but wave after wave of tussock grass, patched with purple orchids and manuka bushes covered with thick spider webs.

Jo rode ahead. He wore a blue galatea shirt, corduroy trousers and riding boots. A white handkerchief, spotted with red—it looked as though his nose had been bleeding on it—was knotted round his throat. Wisps of white hair straggled from under his wideawake—his moustache and eyebrows were called white—he slouched in the saddle, grunting. Not once that day had he sung

'I don't care, for don't you see,
My wife's mother was in front of me!'

It was the first day we had been without it for a month, and now there seemed something uncanny in his silence. Jim rode beside me, white as a clown; his black eyes glittered and he kept shooting out his tongue and moistening his lips. He was dressed in a Jaeger vest and a pair of blue duck trousers, fastened round the waist with a plaited leather belt. We had hardly spoken since dawn. At noon we had lunched off fly biscuits and apricots by the side of a swampy creek.

'My stomach feels like the crop of a hen,' said Jo. 'Now then, Jim, you're the bright boy of the party—where's this 'ere store you kep' on talking about. "Oh yes," you says, "I know a fine store, with a paddock for the horses and a creek runnin' through, owned by a friend of mine who'll give yer a bottle of whisky before 'e shakes hands with yer." I'd like ter see that place—merely as a matter of curiosity—not that I'd ever doubt yer word—as yer know very well—*but* ... '

Jim laughed. 'Don't forget there's a woman too, Jo, with blue eyes and yellow hair, who'll promise you something else before she shakes hands with you. Put that in your pipe and smoke it.'

'The heat's making you balmy,' said Jo. But he dug his knees into the horse. We shambled on. I half fell asleep and had a sort of uneasy dream that the horses were not moving forward at all—then that I was on a rocking-horse, and my old mother was scolding me for raising such a fearful dust from the drawing-room carpet. 'You've entirely worn off the pattern of the carpet,' I heard her saying, and she gave the reins a tug. I snivelled and woke to find Jim leaning over me, maliciously smiling.

'That was a case of all but,' said he. 'I just caught you. What's up? Been bye-bye?'

'No!' I raised my head. 'Thank the Lord we're arriving somewhere.'

We were on the brow of the hill, and below us there was a whare roofed with corrugated iron. It stood in a garden, rather far back from the road—a big paddock opposite, and a creek and a clump of young willow trees. A thin line of blue smoke stood up straight from the chimney of the whare; and as I looked a woman came out, followed by a child and a sheep dog—the woman carrying what appeared to me a black stick. She made gestures at us. The horses put on a final spurt, Jo took off his wideawake, shouted, threw out his chest, and began singing 'I don't care, for don't you see ... ' The sun pushed through the pale clouds and shed a vivid light over the scene. It gleamed on the woman's yellow hair, over her flapping pinafore and the rifle she was carrying. The child hid behind her, and the yellow dog, a mangy beast, scuttled back into the whare, his tail between his legs. We drew rein and dismounted.

'Hallo,' screamed the woman. 'I thought you was three 'awks. My kid comes runnin' in ter me. "Mumma," says she, "there's three brown things comin' over the 'ill," says she. An' I comes out smart, I can tell yer. "They'll be 'awks," I says to her. Oh, the 'awks about 'ere, yer wouldn't believe.'

The 'kid' gave us the benefit of one eye from behind the woman's pinafore—then retired again.

'Where's your old man?' asked Jim.

The woman blinked rapidly, screwing up her face.

'Away shearin'. Bin away a month. I suppose ye're not goin' to stop, are yer? There's a storm comin' up.'

'You bet we are,' said Jo. 'So you're on your lonely, missus?'

She stood, pleating the frills of her pinafore, and glancing from one to the other of us, like a hungry bird. I smiled at the thought of how Jim had pulled Jo's leg about her. Certainly her eyes were blue, and what hair she had was yellow, but ugly. She was a figure of fun. Looking at her, you felt there was nothing but sticks and wires under that pinafore—her front teeth were knocked out, she had red, pulpy hands and she wore on her feet a pair of dirty Bluchers.

'I'll go and turn out the horses,' said Jim. 'Got any embrocation? Poi's rubbed herself to hell!'

''Arf a mo!' The woman stood silent a moment, her nostrils expanding as she breathed. Then she shouted violently, 'I'd rather you didn't stop... You *can't*, and there's the end of it. I don't let out that paddock any more. You'll have to go on; I ain't got nothing!'

'Well, I'm blest!' said Jo heavily. He pulled me aside. 'Gone a bit off 'er dot,' he whispered. 'Too much alone, *you know*,' very significantly. 'Turn the sympathetic tap on 'er, she'll come round all right.'

But there was no need—she had come round by herself.
'Stop if yer like!' she muttered, shrugging her shoulders. To me—'I'll give yer the embrocation if yer come along.'

'Right-o, I'll take it down to them.' We walked together up the garden path. It was planted on both sides with cabbages. They smelled like stale dish-water. Of flowers there were double poppies and sweet-williams. One little patch was divided off by pawa shells—presumably it belonged to the child—for she ran from her mother and began to grub in it with a broken clothes-peg. The yellow dog lay across the doorstep, biting fleas; the woman kicked him away.

'Gar-r, get away, you beast ... the place ain't tidy. I 'aven't 'ad time ter fix things today—been ironing. Come right in.'

It was a large room, the walls plastered with old pages of English periodicals. Queen Victoria's Jubilee appeared to be the most recent number. A table with an ironing board and wash-tub on it, some wooden forms, a black horsehair sofa and some broken cane chairs pushed against the walls. The mantelpiece above the stove was draped in pink paper, further ornamented with dried grasses and ferns and a coloured print of Richard Seddon. There were four doors—one, judging from the smell, led into the 'Store', one on to the 'backyard', through a third I saw the bedroom. Flies buzzed in circles round the ceiling, and treacle papers and bundles of dried clover were pinned to the window curtains.

I was alone in the room; she had gone into the store for the embrocation. I heard her stamping about and muttering to herself: 'I got some, now where did I put that bottle? . . . It's behind the pickles . . . no, it ain't.' I cleared a place on the table and sat there, swinging my legs. Down in the paddock I could hear Jo singing and the sound of hammer strokes as Jim drove in the tent pegs. It was sunset. There is no twilight in our New Zealand days, but a curious half-hour when everything appears grotesque—it frightens—as though the savage spirit of the country walked abroad and sneered at what it saw. Sitting alone in the hideous room I grew afraid. The woman next door was a long time finding that stuff. What was she doing in there? Once I thought I heard her bang her hands down on the counter, and once she half moaned, turning it into a cough and clearing her throat. I wanted to shout 'Buck up!' but I kept silent.

'Good Lord, what a life!' I thought. 'Imagine being here day in, day out, with that rat of a child and a mangy dog. Imagine bothering about ironing. *Mad,* of course she's mad! Wonder how long she's been here—wonder if I could get her to talk.'

At that moment she poked her head round the door.

'Wot was it yer wanted?' she asked.

'Embrocation.'

'Oh, I forgot. I got it, it was in front of the pickle jars.' She handed me the bottle.

'My, you do look tired, you do! Shall I knock yer up a few scones for supper! There's some tongue in the store, too, and I'll cook yer a cabbage if you fancy it.'

'Right-o.' I smiled at her. 'Come down to the paddock and bring the kid for tea.'

She shook her head, pursing up her mouth.

'Oh no. I don't fancy it. I'll send the kid down with the things and a billy of milk. Shall I knock up a few extry scones to take with yer termorrow?'

'Thanks.'

She came and stood by the door.

'How old is the kid?'

'Six—come next Christmas. I 'ad a bit of trouble with 'er one way an' another. I 'adn't any milk till a month after she was born and she sickened like a cow.'

'She's not like you—takes after her father?' Just as the woman had shouted her refusal at us before, she shouted at me then.

'No, she don't! She's the dead spit of me. Any fool could see that. Come on in now, Else, you stop messing in the dirt.'

I met Jo climbing over the paddock fence.

'What's the old bitch got in the store?' he asked.

'Don't know—didn't look.'

'Well, of all the fools. Jim's slanging you. What have you been doing all the time?'

'She couldn't find this stuff. Oh, my shakes, you are smart!'

Jo had washed, combed his wet hair in a line across his forehead, and buttoned a coat over his shirt. He grinned.

Jim snatched the embrocation from me. I went to the end of the paddock where the willows grew and bathed in the creek. The water was clear and soft as oil. Along the edges held by the grass and rushes white foam tumbled and bubbled. I lay in the water and looked up at the trees that were still a moment, then quivered lightly and again were still. The air smelt of rain. I forgot about the woman and the kid until I came back to the tent. Jim lay by the fire watching the billy boil.

I asked where Jo was, and if the kid had brought our supper.

'Pooh,' said Jim, rolling over and looking up at the sky. 'Didn't you see how Jo had been titivating? He said to me before he went up to the whare,"Dang it! she'll look better by night light—at any rate, my buck, she's female flesh!"'

'You had Jo about her looks—you had me too.'

'No—look here. I can't make it out. It's four years since I came
past this way and I stopped here two days. The husband was a pal
of mine once, down the West Coast—a fine, big chap, with a voice
on him like a trombone. She's been barmaid down the Coast—as
pretty as a wax doll. The coach used to come this way then once a
fortnight, that was before they opened the railway up Napier way,
and she had no end of a time! Told me once in a confidential
moment that she knew one hundred and twenty-five different
ways of kissing!'

'Oh, go on, Jim! She isn't the same woman!'

''Course she is. I can't make it out. What I think is the old man's
cleared out and left her: that's all my eye about shearing. Sweet
life! The only people who come through now are Maoris and
sundowners!'

Through the dark we saw the gleam of the kid's pinafore. She
trailed over to us with a basket in her hand, the milk billy in the
other. I unpacked the basket, the child standing by.

'Come over here,' said Jim, snapping his fingers at her.

She went, the lamp from the inside of the tent cast a bright light
over her. A mean, undersized brat, with whitish hair and weak
eyes. She stood, legs wide apart and her stomach protruding.

'What do you do all day?' asked Jim.

She scraped out one ear with her little finger, looked at the result
and said, 'Draw.'

'Huh! What do you draw? Leave your ears alone!'

'Pictures.'

'What on?'

'Bits of butter paper an' a pencil of my Mumma's.'

'Boh! What a lot of words at one time!' Jim rolled his eyes at
her. 'Baa-lambs and moo-cows?'

'No, everything. I'll draw all of you when you're gone, and your
horses and the tent, and that one'—she pointed to me—'with no
clothes on in the creek. I looked at her where she couldn't see me
from.'

'Thanks very much. How ripping of you,' said Jim. 'Where's
Dad?'

The kid pouted. 'I won't tell you because I don't like yer face!'
She started operations on the other ear.

'Here,' I said. 'Take the basket, get along home and tell the other man supper's ready.'

'I don't want to.'

'I'll give you a box on the ear if you don't,' said Jim savagely.

'Hie! I'll tell Mumma. I'll tell Mumma.' The kid fled.

We ate until we were full, and had arrived at the smoke stage before Jo came back, very flushed and jaunty, a whisky bottle in his hand.

'Ave a drink—you two!' he shouted, carrying off matters with a high hand. 'Ere, shove along the cups.'

'One hundred and twenty-five different ways,' I murmured to Jim.

'What's that? Oh! stow it!' said Jo. 'Why 'ave you always got your knife into me. You gas like a kid at a Sunday School beano. She wants us to go there tonight and have a comfortable chat. I'—he waved his hand airily—'I got 'er round.'

'Trust you for that,' laughed Jim. 'But did she tell you where the old man's got to?'

Jo looked up. 'Shearing! You 'eard 'er, you fool!'

The woman had fixed up the room, even to a light bouquet of sweet-williams on the table. She and I sat one side of the table, Jo and Jim the other. An oil lamp was set between us, the whisky bottle and glasses, and a jug of water. The kid knelt against one of the forms, drawing on butter paper; I wondered, grimly, if she was attempting the creek episode. But Jo had been right about night time. The woman's hair was tumbled—two red spots burned in her cheeks—her eyes shone—and we knew that they were kissing feet under the table. She had changed the blue pinafore for a white calico dressing-jacket and a black skirt—the kid was decorated to the extent of a blue sateen hair ribbon. In the stifling room, with the flies buzzing against the ceiling and dropping on to the table, we got slowly drunk.

'Now listen to me,' shouted the woman, banging her fist on the table. 'It's six years since I was married, and four miscarriages. I says to 'im, I says, what do you think I'm doin' up 'ere? If you was back at the Coast I'd 'ave you lynched for child murder. Over and over I tells 'im—you've broken my spirit and spoiled my looks, and wot for—that's wot I'm driving at.' She clutched her head with her hands and stared round at us. Speaking rapidly, 'Oh, some days—an' months of them—I'ear them two words knockin' inside me all the time—"Wot for!" but sometimes I'll be cooking the spuds an' I lifts the lid off to give 'em a prong and I 'ears, quite suddin again, "Wot for!" Oh! I don't mean only the spuds and the kid—I mean—I mean,' she hiccoughed—'you know what I mean, Mr Jo.'

'I know,' said Jo, scratching his head.

'Trouble with me is,' she leaned across the table, 'he left me too much alone. When the coach stopped coming, sometimes he'd go away days, sometimes he'd go away weeks, and leave me ter look after the store. Back 'e'd come—pleased as Punch. "Oh, 'allo,' 'e'd say. "'Ow are you gettin' on? Come and give us a kiss." Sometimes I'd turn a bit nasty, and then 'e'd go off again, and if I took it all right, 'e'd wait till 'e could twist me round 'is finger, then 'e'd say, "Well, so long, I'm off," and do you think I could keep 'im?—not me!'

'Mumma,' bleated the kid, 'I made a picture of them on the 'ill, an' you an' me an' the dog down below.'

'Shut your mouth!' said the woman.

A vivid flash of lightning played over the room—we heard the mutter of thunder.

'Good thing that's broke loose,' said Jo. 'I've 'ad it in me 'ead for three days.'

'Where's your old man now?' asked Jim slowly.

The woman blubbered and dropped her head on to the table. 'Jim, 'e's gone shearin' and left me alone again,' she wailed.

''Ere, look out for the glasses,' said Jo. 'Cheer-o, 'ave another drop. No good cryin' over spilt 'usbands! You, Jim, you blasted cuckoo!'

'Mr Jo,' said the woman, drying her eyes on her jacket frill, 'you're a gent, an' if I was a secret woman I'd place any confidence in your 'ands. I don't mind if I do 'ave a glass on that.'

Every moment the lightning grew more vivid and the thunder sounded nearer. Jim and I were silent—the kid never moved from her bench. She poked her tongue out and blew on her paper as she drew.

'It's the loneliness,' said the woman, addressing Jo—he made sheep's eyes at her—'and bein' shut up 'ere like a broody 'en.' He reached his hand across the table and held hers, and though the position looked most uncomfortable when they wanted to pass the water and whisky, their hands stuck together as though glued. I pushed back my chair and went over to the kid, who immediately sat flat down on her artistic achievements and made a face at me.

'You're not to look,' said she.

'Oh, come on, don't be nasty!' Jim came over to us, and we were just drunk enough to wheedle the kid into showing us. And those drawings of hers were extraordinary and repulsively vulgar. The creations of a lunatic's cleverness. There was no doubt about it, the kid's mind was diseased. While she showed them to us, she worked herself up into a mad excitement, laughing and trembling, and shooting out her arms.

'Mumma,' she yelled. 'Now I'm going to draw them what you told me I never was to—now I am.'

The woman rushed from the table and beat the child's head with the flat of her hand.

'I'll smack you with yer clothes turned up if yer dare say that again,' she bawled.

Jo was too drunk to notice, but Jim caught her by the arm. The kid did not utter a cry. She drifted over to the window and began picking flies from the treacle paper.

We returned to the table—Jim and I sitting one side, the woman and Jo, touching shoulders, the other. We listened to the thunder, saying stupidly, 'That was a near one,' 'There it goes again,' and Jo, at a heavy hit, 'Now we're off,' 'Steady on the brake,' until the rain began to fall, sharp as cannon shot on the iron roof.

'You'd better doss here for the night,' said the woman.

'That's right,' assented Jo, evidently in the know about this move.

'Bring up yer things from the tent. You two can doss in the store along with the kid—she's used to sleep in there and won't mind you.'

'Oh, Mumma, I never did,' interrupted the kid.

'Shut yer lies! An' Mr Jo can 'ave this room.'

It sounded a ridiculous arrangement, but it was useless to

attempt to cross them, they were too far gone. While the woman sketched the plan of action, Jo sat, abnormally solemn and red, his eyes bulging, and pulling at his moustache.

'Give us a lantern' said Jim, 'I'll go down to the paddock.' We two went together. Rain whipped our faces, the land was light as though a bush fire was raging. We behaved like two children let loose in the thick of an adventure, laughed and shouted to each other, and came back to the whare to find the kid already bedded in the counter of the store. The woman brought us a lamp. Jo took his bundle from Jim, the door was shut.

'Good night all,' shouted Jo.

Jim and I sat on two sacks of potatoes. For the life of us we could not stop laughing. Strings of onions and half-hams dangled from the ceiling—wherever we looked there were advertisements for 'Camp Coffee' and tinned meats. We pointed at them, tried to read them aloud—overcome with laughter and hiccoughs. The kid in the counter stared at us. She threw off her blanket and scrambled to the floor, where she stood in her grey flannel nightgown rubbing one leg against the other. We paid no attention to her.

'Wot are you laughing at?' she said uneasily.

'You!' shouted Jim. 'The red tribe of you, my child.'

She flew into a rage and beat herself with her hands. 'I won't be laughed at, you curs—you.' He swooped down upon the child and swung her on to the counter.

'Go to sleep, Miss Smarty—or make a drawing—here's a pencil—you can use Mumma's account book.'

Through the rain we heard Jo creak over the boarding of the next room—the sound of a door being opened—then shut to.

'It's the loneliness,' whispered Jim.

'One hundred and twenty-five different ways—alas! my poor brother!'

The kid tore out a page and flung it at me.

'There you are,' she said. 'Now I done it ter spite Mumma for shutting me up 'ere with you two. I done the one she told me I never ought to. I done the one she told me she'd shoot me if I did. Don't care! Don't care!'

The kid had drawn the picture of the woman shooting at a man with a rook rifle and then digging a hole to bury him in.

She jumped off the counter and squirmed about on the floor biting her nails.

Jim and I sat till dawn with the drawing beside us. The rain ceased, the little kid fell asleep, breathing loudly. We got up, stole out of the whare, down into the paddock. White clouds floated over a pink sky—a chill wind blew; the air smelled of wet grass. Just as we swung into the saddle Jo came out of the whare—he motioned to us to ride on.

'I'll pick you up later,' he shouted.

A bend in the road, and the whole place disappeared.

Bains Turcs

'Third storey—to the left, Madame,' said the cashier, handing me a pink ticket. 'One moment—I will ring for the elevator.' Her black satin skirt swished across the scarlet and gold hall, and she stood among the artificial palms, her white neck and powdered face topped with masses of gleaming orange hair—like an over-ripe fungus bursting from a thick, black stem. She rang and rang. 'A thousand pardons, Madame. It is disgraceful. A new attendant. He leaves this week.' With her fingers on the bell she peered into the cage as though she expected to see him, lying on the floor, like a dead bird. 'It is disgraceful.' There appeared from nowhere a tiny figure disguised in a peaked cap and dirty white cotton gloves. 'Here you are!' she scolded. 'Where have you been? What have you been doing?' For answer the figure hid its face behind one of the white cotton gloves and sneezed twice. 'Ugh! Disgusting! Take Madame to the third storey!' The midget stepped aside, bowed, entered after me and clashed the gates to. We ascended, very slowly, to an accompaniment of sneezes and prolonged, half-whistling sniffs. I asked the top of the patent-leather cap: 'Have you a cold?' 'It is the air, Madame,' replied the creature, speaking through its nose with a restrained air of great relish, 'one is never dry here. Third floor—*if* you please,' sneezing over my ten-centime tip.

I walked along a tiled corridor decorated with advertisements for lingerie and bust improvers—was allotted a tiny cabin and a blue print chemise and told to undress and find the Warm Room as soon as possible. Through the matchboard walls and from the corridor sounded cries and laughter and snatches of conversation.

'Are you ready?'

'Are you coming out now?'

'Wait till you see me!'

'Berthe—Berthe!'

'One moment! One moment! Immediately!'

I undressed quickly and carelessly, feeling like one of a troupe of little schoolgirls let loose in a swimming-bath.

The Warm Room was not large. It had terra-cotta painted walls with a fringe of peacocks, and a glass roof through which one could see the sky, pale and unreal as a photographer's background screen. Some round tables strewn with shabby fashion journals, a marble basin in the centre of the room, filled with yellow lilies, and on the long, towel-enveloped chairs a number of ladies, apparently languid as the flowers . . . . I lay back with a cloth over my head, and the air, smelling of jungles and circuses and damp washing, made me begin to dream . . . . Yes, it might have been very fascinating to have married an explorer . . . and lived in a jungle, as long as he didn't shoot anything or take anything captive. I detest performing beasts. Oh . . . those circuses at home . . . the tent in the paddock and the children swarming over the fence to stare at the wagons and at the clown making up, with his glass stuck on the wagon wheel—and the steam organ playing the 'Honeysuckle and the Bee' much too fast . . . over and over. I know what this air reminds me of—a game of follow-my-leader among the clothes hung out to dry . . . .

The door opened. Two tall blonde women in red and white check gowns came in and took the chairs opposite mine. One of them carried a box of mandarins wrapped in silver paper and the other a manicure set. They were very stout, with gay, bold faces, and quantities of exquisite whipped fair hair.

Before sitting down they glanced round the room, looked the other women up and down, turned to each other, grimaced, whispered something, and one of them said, offering the box, 'Have a mandarin?' At that they started laughing—they lay back and shook, and each time they caught sight of each other broke out afresh.

'Ah, that was too good,' cried one, wiping her eyes very carefully, just at the corners. 'You and I, coming in here, quite serious, you know, very correct—and looking round the room—and—and as a result of our *careful* inspection—I offer you a mandarin. No, it's too funny. I must remember that. It's good enough for a music-hall. Have a mandarin?'

'But I cannot imagine,' said the other, 'why women look so hideous in Turkish baths—like beef-steaks in chemises. Is it the women—or is it the air? Look at that one, for instance—the skinny one, reading a book and sweating at the moustache—and those two over in the corner, discussing whether or not they ought to tell their non-existent babies how babies come—and ... Heavens! Look at this one coming in. Take the box, dear. Have all the mandarins.'

The newcomer was a short, stout little woman with flat, white feet, and a black mackintosh cap over her hair. She walked up and down the room, swinging her arms, in affected unconcern, glancing contemptuously at the laughing women, and rang the bell for the attendant. It was answered immediately by Berthe, half naked and sprinkled with soapsuds. 'Well, what is it, Madame? I've no time ...'

'Please bring me a hand towel,' said the Mackintosh Cap in German.

'Pardon? I do not understand. Do you speak French?'

'*Non,*' said the Mackintosh Cap.

'Ber-the!' shrieked one of the blonde women, 'have a mandarin. Oh, *mon Dieu,* I shall die of laughing.'

The Mackintosh Cap went through a pantomime of finding herself wet and rubbing herself dry. '*Verstehen Sie?*'

'*Mais non, Madame,*' said Berthe, watching with round eyes that snapped with laughter, and she left the Mackintosh Cap, winked at the blonde women, came over, felt them as though they had been a pair of prize poultry, said 'You are doing very well,' and disappeared again.

The Mackintosh Cap sat down on the edge of a chair, snatched a fashion journal, smacked over the crackling pages and pretended to read, while the blonde women leaned back eating the mandarins and throwing the peelings into the lily basin. A scent of fruit, fresh and penetrating, hung on the air. I looked round at the other women. Yes, they were hideous, lying back, red and moist, with dull eyes and lank hair, the only little energy they had vented in shocked prudery at the behaviour of the two blondes. Suddenly I discovered Mackintosh Cap staring at me over the top of her fashion journal, so intently that I took flight and went into the hot room. But in vain! Mackintosh Cap followed after and planted herself in front of me.

'I know,' she said, confident and confiding, 'that you can speak

German. I saw it in your face just now. Wasn't that a scandal about the attendant refusing me a towel? I shall speak to the management about that, and I shall get my husband to write them a letter this evening. Things always come better from a man, don't they? No,' she said, rubbing her yellowish arms, 'I've never been in such a scandalous place—and four francs fifty to pay! Naturally, I shall not give a tip. You wouldn't, would you? Not after that scandal about a hand-towel .... I've a great mind to complain about those women as well. Those two that keep on laughing and eating. Do you know who they are?' She shook her head. 'They're not respectable women—you can tell at a glance. At least I can, any married woman can. They're nothing but a couple of street women. I've never been so insulted in my life. Laughing at me, mind you! The great big fat pigs like that! And I haven't sweated at all properly, just because of them. I got so angry that the sweat turned in instead of out; it does in excitement, you know, sometimes, and now instead of losing my cold I wouldn't be surprised if I brought on a fever.'

I walked round the hot room in misery pursued by the Mackintosh Cap until the two blonde women came in, and seeing her, burst into another fit of laughter. To my rage and disgust Mackintosh Cap sidled up to me, smiled meaningly, and drew down her mouth. 'I don't care,' she said, in her hideous German voice. 'I shouldn't lower myself by paying any attention to a couple of street women. If my husband knew he'd never get over it. Dreadfully particular he is. We've been married six years. We come from Pfalzburg. It's a nice town. Four children I have living, and it was really to get over the shock of the fifth that we came here. The fifth,' she whispered, padding after me, 'was born, a fine healthy child, and it never breathed! Well, after nine months, a woman can't help being disappointed, can she?'

I moved towards the vapour room. 'Are you going in there?' she said. 'I wouldn't if I were you. Those two have gone in. They may think you want to strike up an acquaintance with them. You never know women like that.' At that moment they came out, wrapping themselves in the rough gowns, and passing Mackintosh Cap like disdainful queens. 'Are you going to take your chemise off in the vapour room?' asked she. 'Don't mind me, you know. Woman is woman, and besides, if you'd rather, I won't look at you. I know—I used to be like that. I wouldn't mind betting,' she went on savagely, 'those filthy women had a good look at each other. Pooh! women like that. You can't shock them. And don't they look dreadful? Bold, and all that false hair. That manicure box one of them had was fitted up with gold. Well, I don't suppose it was real, but I think it was disgusting to bring it. One might at least cut one's nails in private, don't you think? I *cannot* see,' she said, 'what men see in such women. No, a husband and children and a home to look after, that's what a woman needs. That's what my husband says. Fancy one of these hussies peeling potatoes or choosing the meat! Are you going already?'

I flew to find Berthe, and all the time I was soaped and smacked and sprayed and thrown in a cold-water tank I could not get out of my mind the ugly, wretched figure of the little German with a good husband and four children, railing against the two fresh beauties who had never peeled potatoes nor chosen the right meat. In the ante-room I saw them once again. They were dressed in blue. One was pinning on a bunch of violets, the other buttoning a pair of ivory suede gloves. In their charming feathered hats and furs they stood talking. 'Yes, there they are,' said a voice at my elbow.

And there was Mackintosh Cap, transformed, in a blue and white check blouse and crochet collar, with the little waist and large hips of the German woman and a terrible bird nest, which Pfalzburg doubtless called *Reisehut,* on her head. 'How do you suppose they can afford clothes like that? The horrible, low creatures. No, they're enough to make a young girl think twice.' And as the two walked out of the ante-room, Mackintosh Cap stared after them, her sallow face all mouth and eyes, like the face of a hungry child before a forbidden table.

An Indiscreet Journey

She is like St Anne. Yes, the concierge is the image of St Anne, with that black cloth over her head, the wisps of grey hair hanging, and the tiny smoking lamp in her hand. Really very beautiful, I thought, smiling at St Anne, who said severely: 'Six o'clock. You have only just got time. There is a bowl of milk on the writing-table.' I jumped out of my pyjamas and into a basin of cold water like any English lady in any French novel. The concierge, persuaded that I was on my way to prison cells and death by bayonets, opened the shutters and the cold clear light came through. A little steamer hooted on the river; a cart with two horses at a gallop flung past. The rapid swirling water; the tall black trees on the far side, grouped together like negroes conversing. Sinister, very, I thought, as I buttoned on my age-old Burberry. (That Burberry was very significant. It did not belong to me. I had borrowed it from a friend. My eye lighted upon it hanging in her little dark hall. The very thing! The perfect and adequate disguise—an old Burberry. Lions have been faced in a Burberry. Ladies have been rescued from open boats in mountainous seas wrapped in nothing else. An old Burberry seems to me the sign and the token of the undisputed venerable traveller, I decided, leaving my purple peg-top with the real seal collar and cuffs in exchange.)

'You will never get there,' said the concierge, watching me turn up the collar. 'Never! Never!' I ran down the echoing stairs—strange they sounded, like a piano flicked by a sleepy housemaid—and on to the Quai. 'Why so fast, *ma mignonne?*' said a lovely little boy in coloured socks, dancing in front of the electric lotus buds that curve over the entrance to the Métro. Alas! there was not even time to blow him a kiss. When I arrived at the big station I had only four minutes to spare, and the platform entrance was crowded and packed with soldiers, their yellow papers in one hand and big untidy bundles. The Commissaire of

Police stood on one side, a Nameless Official on the other. Will he let me pass? Will he? He was an old man with a fat swollen face covered with big warts. Horn-rimmed spectacles squatted on his nose. Trembling, I made an effort. I conjured up my sweetest early-morning smile and handed it with the papers. But the delicate thing fluttered against the horn spectacles and fell. Nevertheless, he let me pass, and I ran, ran in and out among the soldiers and up the high steps into the yellow-painted carriage.

'Does one go direct to X?' I asked the collector who dug at my ticket with a pair of forceps and handed it back again. 'No, Mademoiselle, you must change at X.Y.Z.'

'At—?'

'X.Y.Z.'

Again I had not heard. 'At what time do we arrive there, if you please?'

'One o'clock.' But that was no good to me. I hadn't a watch. Oh, well—later.

Ah! the train had begun to move. The train was on my side. It swung out of the station, and soon we were passing the vegetable gardens, passing the tall, blind houses to let, passing the servants beating carpets. Up already and walking in the fields, rosy from the rivers and the red-fringed pools, the sun lighted upon the swinging train and stroked my muff and told me to take that Burberry. I was not alone in the carriage. An old woman sat opposite, her skirt turned back over her knees, a bonnet of black lace on her head. In her fat hands, adorned with a wedding and two mourning rings, she held a letter. Slowly, slowly she sipped a sentence, and then looked up and out of the window, her lips trembling a little, and then another sentence, and again the old face turned to the light, tasting it .... Two soldiers leaned out of the window, their heads nearly touching—one of them was whistling, the other had his coat fastened with some rusty safety-pins. And now there were soldiers everywhere working on the railway line, leaning against trucks or standing hands on hips, eyes fixed on the train as though they expected at least one camera at every window. And now we were passing big wooden sheds like rigged-up dancing halls or seaside pavilions, each flying a flag. In and out of them walked the Red Cross men; the wounded sat against the walls sunning themselves. At all the bridges, the crossings, the stations, a *petit soldat,* all boots and bayonet. Forlorn and desolate he looked, like a little comic picture waiting for the joke to be written underneath. Is there really such a thing as war? Are all these laughing voices really going to the war? These dark woods lighted so mysteriously by the white stems of the birch and the ash—these watery fields with the big birds flying over—these rivers green and blue in the light—have battles been fought in places like these?

What beautiful cemeteries we are passing! They flash gay in the sun. They seem to be full of cornflowers and poppies and daisies. How can there be so many flowers at this time of the year? But they are not flowers at all. They are bunches of ribbons tied on to the soldiers' graves.

I glanced up and caught the old woman's eye. She smiled and folded the letter. 'It is from my son—the first we have had since October. I am taking it to my daughter-in-law.'

' ... ?'

'Yes, very good,' said the old woman, shaking down her skirt and putting her arm through the handle of her basket. 'He wants me to send him some handkerchiefs and a piece of stout string.'

What is the name of the station where I have to change? Perhaps I shall never know. I got up and leaned my arms across the window rail, my feet crossed. One cheek burned as in infancy on the way to the seaside. When the war is over I shall have a barge and drift along these rivers with a white cat and a pot of mignonette to bear me company.

Down the side of the hill filed the troops, winking red and blue in the light. Far away, but plainly to be seen, some more flew by on bicycles. But really, *ma France adorée,* this uniform is ridiculous. Your soldiers are stamped upon your bosom like bright irreverent transfers.

The train slowed down, stopped .... Everybody was getting out except me. A big boy, his sabots tied to his back with a piece of string, the inside of his tin wine cup stained a lovely impossible pink, looked very friendly. Does one change here perhaps for X? Another whose képi had come out of a wet paper cracker swung my suitcase to earth. What darlings soldiers are! '*Merci bien, Monsieur, vous êtes tout à fait aimable ....* ' 'Not this way,' said a bayonet. 'Nor this,' said another. So I followed the crowd. 'Your passport, Mademoiselle ....' '*We, Sir Edward Grey ...*' I ran through the muddy square and into the buffet.

A green room with a stove jutting out and tables on each side. On the counter, beautiful with coloured bottles, a woman leans, her breasts in her folded arms. Through an open door I can see a kitchen, and the cook in a white coat breaking eggs into a bowl and tossing the shells into a corner. The blue and red coats of the men who are eating hang upon the walls. Their short swords and belts are piled upon chairs. Heavens! what a noise. The sunny air seemed all broken up and trembling with it. A little boy, very pale, swung from table to table, taking the orders, and poured me out a glass of purple coffee. *Ssssh,* came from the eggs. They were in a pan. The woman rushed from behind the counter and began to help the boy. *Toute de suite, tout' suite!* she chirruped to the loud impatient voices. There came a clatter of plates and the pop-pop of corks being drawn.

Suddenly in the doorway I saw someone with a pail of fish—brown speckled fish, like the fish one sees in a glass case, swimming through forests of beautiful pressed sea-weed. He was an old man in a tattered jacket, standing humbly, waiting for someone to attend to him. A thin beard fell over his chest, his eyes under the tufted eyebrows were bent on the pail he carried. He looked as though he had escaped from some holy picture, and was entreating the soldiers' pardon for being there at all....

But what could I have done? I could not arrive at X. with two fishes hanging on a straw; and I am sure it is a penal offence in France to throw fish out of railway-carriage windows, I thought, miserably climbing into a smaller, shabbier train. Perhaps I might have taken them to—*ah, mon Dieu*—I had forgotten the name of my uncle and aunt again! Buffard, Buffon—what was it? Again I read the unfamiliar letter in the familiar handwriting.

'MY DEAR NIECE,

Now that the weather is more settled, your uncle and I would be charmed if you would pay us a little visit. Telegraph me when you are coming. I shall meet you outside the station if I am free. Otherwise our good friend, Madame Grinçon, who lives in the little

toll-house by the bridge, *juste en face de la gare,* will
conduct you to our home. *Je vous embrasse bien
tendrement.*   JULIE BOIFFARD.'

A visiting card was enclosed: *M. Paul Boiffard.*
     Boiffard—of course that was the name. *Ma tante Julie et mon
oncle Paul*—suddenly they were there with me, more real, more
solid than any relations I had ever known. I saw *tante Julie*
bridling, with the soup-tureen in her hands, and *oncle Paul* sitting
at the table with a red and white napkin tied round his neck.
Boiffard—Boiffard—I must remember the name. Supposing the
Commissaire Militaire should ask me who the relations were I
was going to and I muddled the name—Oh, how fatal!
Buffard—no, Boiffard. And then for the first time, folding Aunt
Julie's letter, I saw scrawled in a corner of the empty back page:
Venez vite, vite. Strange impulsive woman! My heart began to
beat . . . .
     'Ah, we are not far off now,' said the lady opposite. 'You are
going to X, Mademoiselle?'
     '*Oui, Madame.*'
     'I also . . . . You have been there before?'
     'No, Madame. This is the first time.'
     'Really, it is a strange time for a visit.'
     I smiled faintly, and tried to keep my eyes off her hat. She was
quite an ordinary little woman, but she wore a black velvet toque,
with an incredibly surprised looking sea-gull camped on the very
top of it. Its round eyes, fixed on me so inquiringly, were almost
too much to bear. I had a dreadful impulse to shoo it away, or to
lean forward and inform her of its presence . . . .
     '*Excusez-moi, Madame,* but perhaps you have not remarked
there is an *espèce de* sea-gull *couché sur votre chapeau.*'
     Could the bird be there on purpose? I must not laugh I must not
laugh. Had she ever looked at herself in a glass with that bird on
her head?
     'It is very difficult to get into X at present, to pass the station,'
she said, and she shook her head with the sea-gull at me. 'Ah, such
an affair. One must sign one's name and state one's business.'
     'Really, is it as bad as all that?'

'But naturally. You see the whole place is in the hands of the military, and'—she shrugged—'they have to be strict. Many people do not get beyond the station at all. They arrive. They are put in the waiting-room, and there they remain.'

Did I or did I not detect in her voice a strange, insulting relish?

'I suppose such strictness is absolutely necessary,' I said coldly stroking my muff.

'Necessary,' she cried. 'I should think so. Why, Mademoiselle, you cannot imagine what it would be like otherwise! You know what women are like about soldiers'—she raised a final hand—'mad, completely mad. But—' and she gave a little laugh of triumph—'they could not get into X. *Mon Dieu,* no! There is no question about that.'

'I don't suppose they even try,' said I.

'Don't you?' said the sea-gull.

Madame said nothing for a moment. 'Of course the authorities are very hard on the men. It means instant imprisonment, and then—off to the firing-line without a word.'

'What are *you* going to X for?' said the sea-gull. 'What on earth are *you* doing here?'

'Are you making a long stay in X, Mademoiselle?'

She had won, she had won. I was terrified. A lamp-post swam past the train with the fatal name upon it. I could hardly breathe—the train had stopped. I smiled gaily at Madame and danced down the steps to the platform

It was a hot little room, completely furnished, with two colonels seated at two tables. They were large grey-whiskered men with a touch of burnt red on their cheeks. Sumptuous and omnipotent they looked. One smoked what ladies love to call a heavy Egyptian cigarette, with a long creamy ash, the other toyed with a gilded pen. Their heads rolled on their tight collars, like big over-ripe fruits. I had a terrible feeling, as I handed my passport and ticket, that a soldier would step forward and tell me to kneel. I would have knelt without question.

'What's this?' said God I, querulously. He did not like my passport at all. The very sight of it seemed to annoy him. He waved a dissenting hand at it, with a *'Non, je ne peux pas manger ça,'* air.

'But it won't do. It won't do at all, you know. Look,—read for yourself,' and he glanced with extreme distaste at my photograph, and then with even greater distaste his pebble eyes looked at me.

'Of course the photograph is deplorable,' I said, scarcely breathing with terror, 'but it has been viséd and viséd.'

He raised his big bulk and went to over to God II.

'Courage!' I said to my muff and held it firmly, 'Courage!'

God II held up a finger to me, and I produced Aunt Julie's letter and her card. But he did not seem to feel the slightest interest in her. He stamped my passport idly, scribbled a word on my ticket, and I was on the platform again.

'That way—you pass out that way.'

Terribly pale, with a faint smile on his lips, his hand at salute, stood the little corporal. I gave no sign, I am sure I gave no sign. He stepped behind me.

'And then follow me as though you do not see me,' I heard him half whisper, half sing.

How fast he went, through the slippery mud towards a bridge. He had a postman's bag on his back, a paper parcel and the *Matin* in his hand. We seemed to dodge through a maze of policemen, and I could not keep up at all with the little corporal who began to whistle. From the toll-house 'our good friend, Madame Grinçon', her hands wrapped in a shawl, watched our coming, and against the toll-house there leaned a tiny faded cab. *Montez vite, vite!* said the little corporal, hurling my suitcase, the postman's bag, the paper parcel and the *Matin* on to the floor.

'A-ie! A-ie! Do not be so mad. Do not ride yourself. You will be seen,' wailed 'our good friend, Madame Grinçon.'

'*Ah, je m'en f . . .* ' said the little corporal.

The driver jerked into activity. He lashed the bony horse and away we flew, both doors, which were the complete sides of the cab, flapping and banging.

'*Bon jour, mon amie.*'

'*Bon jour, mon ami.*'

And then we swooped down and clutched at the banging doors. They would not keep shut. They were fools of doors.

'Lean back, let me do it!' I cried. 'Policemen are as thick as violets everywhere.'

At the barracks the horse reared up and stopped. A crowd of laughing faces blotted the window.

'*Prends ça, mon vieux,*' said the little corporal, handing the paper parcel.

'It's all right,' called someone.

We waved, we were off again. By a river, down a strange white street, with the little houses on either side, gay in the late sunlight.

'Jump out as soon as he stops again. The door will be open. Run straight inside. I will follow. The man is already paid. I know you will like the house. It is quite white. And the room is white too, and the people are—'

'White as snow.'

We looked at each other. We began to laugh. 'Now,' said the little corporal.

Out I flew and in at the door. There stood, presumably, my Aunt Julie. There in the background hovered, I supposed, my Uncle Paul.

'*Bon jour, Madame!*' '*Bon jour, Monsieur!*'

'It is all right, you are safe,' said my Aunt Julie. Heavens, how I loved her! And she opened the door of the white room and shut it upon us. Down went the suitcase, the postman's bag, the *Matin*. I threw my passport up into the air, and the little corporal caught it.

II

What an extraordinary thing. We had been there to lunch and to dinner each day; but now in the dusk and alone I could not find it. I clop-clopped in my borrowed *sabots* through the greasy mud, right to the end of the village, and there was not a sign of it. I could not even remember what it looked like, or if there was a name painted on the outside, or any bottles or tables showing at the window. Already the village houses were sealed for the night behind big wooden shutters. Strange and mysterious they looked in the ragged drifting light and thin rain, like a company of beggars perched on the hill-side, their bosoms full of rich unlawful gold. There was nobody about but the soldiers. A group of wounded stood under a lamp-post, petting a mangy, shivering dog. Up the street came four big boys singing:

'*Dodo, mon homme, fais vit' dodo ...*'

and swung off down the hill to their sheds behind the railway station. They seemed to take the last breath of the day with them. I began to walk slowly back.

'It must have been one of these houses. I remember it stood far back from the road—and there were no steps, not even a porch—one seemed to walk right through the window.' And then quite suddenly the waiting-boy came out of just such a place. He saw me and grinned cheerfully, and began to whistle through his teeth.

'*Bon soir, mon petit.*'

'*Bon soir, Madame.*' And he followed me up the café to our special table, right at the far end by the window, and marked by a bunch of violets that I had left in a glass there yesterday.

'You are two?' asked the waiting-boy, flicking the table with a red and white cloth. His long swinging steps echoed over the bare floor. He disappeared into the kitchen and came back to light the lamp that hung from the ceiling under a spreading shade, like a haymaker's hat. Warm light shone on the empty place that was really a barn, set out with dilapidated tables and chairs. Into the middle of the room a black stove jutted. At one side of it there was a table with a row of bottles on it, behind which Madame sat and took the money and made entries in a red book. Opposite her desk a door led into the kitchen. The walls were covered with creamy paper patterned all over with green and swollen trees—hundreds and hundreds of trees reared their mushroom heads to the ceiling. I began to wonder who had chosen the paper and why. Did Madame think it was beautiful, or that it was a gay and lovely thing to eat one's dinner at all seasons in the middle of a forest . . . . On either side of the clock there hung a picture: one, a young gentleman in black tights wooing a pear-shaped lady in yellow over the back of a garden seat, *Premier Rencontre;* two, the black and yellow in amorous confusion, *Triomphe d'Amour.*

The clock ticked to a soothing lilt, *C'est ça, c'est ça.* In the kitchen the waiting-boy was washing up. I heard the ghostly chatter of the dishes.

And years passed. Perhaps the war is long since over—there is no village outside at all—the streets are quiet under the grass. I have an idea this is the sort of thing one will do on the very last day of all—sit in an empty café and listen to a clock ticking until—

Madame came through the kitchen door, nodded to me and took her seat behind the table, her plump hands folded on the red book. *Ping* went the door. A handful of soldiers came in, took off their coats and began to play cards, chaffing and poking fun at the pretty waiting-boy, who threw up his little round head, rubbed his thick fringe out of his eyes and cheeked them back in his broken voice. Sometimes his voice boomed up from his throat, deep and harsh, and then in the middle of a sentence it broke and scattered in a funny squeaking. He seemed to enjoy it himself. You would not have been surprised if he had walked into the kitchen on his hands and brought back your dinner turning a catherine-wheel.

Ping went the door again. Two more men came in. They sat at the table nearest Madame, and she leaned to them with a birdlike movement, her head on one side. Oh, they had a grievance! The Lieutenant was a fool—nosing about—springing out at them— and they'd only been sewing on buttons. Yes, that was all—sewing on buttons, and up comes this young spark. 'Now then, what are you up to?' They mimicked the idiotic voice. Madame drew down her mouth, nodding sympathy. The waiting-boy served them with glasses. He took a bottle of some orange-stuff and put it on the table edge. A shout from the card-players made him turn sharply, and crash! over went the bottle, spilling on the table, the floor—smash! to tinkling atoms. An amazed silence. Through it the drip-drip of the wine from the table on to the floor. It looked very strange dropping so slowly, as though the table were crying. Then there came a roar from the card-players. 'You'll catch it, my lad! That's the style! Now you've done it! ... *Sept, huit, neuf.*' They started playing again. The waiting-boy never said a word. He stood, his head bent, his hands spread out, and then he knelt and gathered up the glass, piece by piece, and soaked the wine up with a cloth. Only when Madame cried cheerfully, 'You wait until *he* finds out,' did he raise his head.

'He can't say anything, if I pay for it,' he muttered, his face jerking, and he marched off into the kitchen with the soaking cloth.

'*Il pleure de colère,*' said Madame delightedly, patting her hair with her plump hands.

The café slowly filled. It grew very warm. Blue smoke mounted from the tables and hung about the haymaker's hat in misty wreaths. There was a suffocating smell of onion soup and boots and damp cloth. In the din the door sounded again. It opened to let in a weed of a fellow, who stood with his back against it, one hand shading his eyes.

'Hullo! you've got the bandage off?'

'How does it feel, *mon vieux?*'

'Let's have a look at them.'

But he made no reply. He shrugged and walked unsteadily to a table, sat down and leant against the wall. Slowly his hand fell. In his white face his eyes showed, pink as a rabbit's. They brimmed and spilled, brimmed and spilled. He dragged a white cloth out of his pocket and wiped them.

'It's the smoke,' said someone. 'It's the smoke tickles them up for you.'

His comrades watched him a bit, watched his eyes fill again, again brim over. The water ran down his face, off his chin on to the table. He rubbed the place with his coat-sleeve, and then, as though forgetful, went on rubbing, rubbing with his hand across the table, staring in front of him. And then he started shaking his head to the movement of his hand. He gave a loud strange groan and dragged out the cloth again.

'*Huit, neuf, dix,*' said the card-players.

'*P'tit,* some more bread.'

'Two coffees.'

'*Un Picon!*'

The waiting-boy, quite recovered, but with scarlet cheeks, ran to and fro. A tremendous quarrel flared up among the card-players, raged for two minutes, and died in flickering laughter. 'Ooof!' groaned the man with the eyes, rocking and mopping. But nobody paid any attention to him except Madame. She made a little grimace at her two soldiers.

'*Mais vous savez, c'est un peu dégoûtant, ça,*' she said severely.

'*Ah, oui, Madame,*' answered the soldiers, watching her bent head and pretty hands, as she arranged for the hundredth time a frill of lace on her lifted bosom.

'*V'là, Monsieur!*' cawed the waiting-boy over his shoulder to me. For some silly reason I pretended not to hear, and I leaned over the table smelling the violets, until the little corporal's hand closed over mine.

'Shall we have *un peu de charcuterie* to begin with?' he asked tenderly.

III

'In England,' said the blue-eyed soldier, 'you drink whisky with your meals. *N'est-ce pas, Mademoiselle?* A little glass of whisky neat before eating. Whisky and soda with your *bifteks,* and after, more whisky with hot water and lemon.'

'Is it true that?' asked his great friend who sat opposite, a big red-faced chap with a black beard and large moist eyes and hair that looked as though it had been cut with a sewing-maching.

'Well, not quite true,' said I.

'*Si, si,*' cried the blue-eyed soldier. 'I ought to know. I'm in business. English travellers come to my place, and it's always the same thing.'

'Bah, I can't stand whisky,' said the little corporal. 'It's too disgusting the morning after. Do you remember, *ma fille*, the whisky in that little bar at Montmartre?'

'*Souvenir tendre,*' sighed Blackbeard, putting two fingers in the breast of his coat and letting his head fall. He was very drunk.

'But I know something that you've never tasted,' said the blue-eyed soldier, pointing a finger at me; 'something really good.' *Cluck* he went with his tongue. '*E-patant!* And the curious thing is that you'd hardly know it from whisky except that it's'—he felt with his hand for the word—'finer, sweeter perhaps, not so sharp, and it leaves you feeling gay as a rabbit next morning.'

'What is it called?'

'Mirabelle!' He rolled the word round his mouth, under his tongue. 'Ah-ha, that's the stuff.'

'I could eat another mushroom,' said Blackbeard. 'I would like another mushroom very much. I am sure I could eat another mushroom if Mademoiselle gave it to me out of her hand.'

'You ought to try it,' said the blue-eyed soldier, leaning both hands on the table and speaking so seriously that I began to wonder how much more sober he was than Blackbeard. 'You ought to try it, and tonight. I would like you to tell me if you don't think it's like whisky.'

'Perhaps they've got it here,' said the little corporal, and he called the waiting-boy. '*P'tit!*'

'*Non, Monsieur,*' said the boy, who never stopped smiling. He served us with dessert plates painted with blue parrots and horned beetles.

'What is the name for this in English?' said Blackbeard, pointing. I told him 'Parrot.'

'Ah, *mon Dieu!* . . . Pair-rot . . . . ' He put his arms round his plate. 'I love you, *ma petite* pair-rot. You are sweet, you are blonde, you are English. You do not know the difference between whisky and mirabelle.'

The little corporal and I looked at each other, laughing. He squeezed up his eyes when he laughed, so that you saw nothing but the long curly lashes.

'Well, I know a place where they do keep it,' said the blue-eyed soldier. '*Café des Amis.* We'll go there—I'll pay—I'll pay for the whole lot of us.' His gesture embraced thousands of pounds.

But with a loud whirring noise the clock on the wall struck half-past eight; and no soldier is allowed in a café after eight o'clock at night.

'It is fast,' said the blue-eyed soldier. The little corporal's watch said the same. So did the immense turnip that Blackbeard produced and carefully deposited on the head of one of the horned beetles.

'Ah, well, we'll take the risk,' said the blue-eyed soldier, and he thrust his arms into the cardboard coat. 'It's worth it,' he said. 'It's worth it. Just you wait.'

Outside, stars shone between wispy clouds and the moon fluttered like a candle flame over a pointed spire. The shadows of the dark plume-like trees waved on the white houses. Not a soul to be seen. No sound to be heard but the *Hsh! Hsh!* of a far-away train, like a big beast shuffling in its sleep.

'You are cold,' whispered the little corporal. 'You are cold, *ma fille.*'

'No, really not.'

'But you are trembling.'

'Yes, but I'm not cold.'

'What are the women like in England?' asked Blackbeard. 'After the war is over I shall go to England. I shall find a little English woman and marry—and her pair-rot.' He gave a loud choking laugh.

'Fool!' said the blue-eyed soldier, shaking him; and he leant over to me. 'It is only after the second glass that you really taste it,' he whispered. 'The second little glass and then—ah!—then you know.'

Café des Amis gleamed in the moonlight. We glanced quickly up and down the road. We ran up the four wooden steps, and opened the ringing glass door into a low room lighted with a hanging lamp, where about ten people were dining. They were seated on two benches at a narrow table.

'Soldiers!' screamed a woman, leaping up from behind a white soup-tureen—a scrag of a woman in a black shawl. 'Soldiers! At this hour! Look at that clock, look at it.' And she pointed to the clock with the dripping ladle.

'It's fast,' said the blue-eyed soldier. 'It's fast, Madame. And don't make so much noise, I beg of you. We will drink and we will go.'

'Will you?' she cried, running round the table and planting herself in front of us. 'That's just what you won't do. Coming into an honest woman's house this hour of the night—making a scene—getting the police after you. Ah, no! Ah, no! It's a disgrace, that's what it is.'

'Sh!' said the little corporal, holding up his hand. Dead silence. In the silence we heard steps passing.

'The police,' whispered Blackbeard, winking at a pretty girl with rings in her ears, who smiled back at him, saucy. 'Sh!'

The faces lifted, listening. 'How beautiful they are!' I thought. 'They are like a family party having supper in the New Testament . . . .' The steps died away.

'Serve you very well right if you had been caught,' scolded the angry woman. 'I'm sorry on your account that the police didn't come. You deserve it—you deserve it.'

'A little glass of mirabelle and we will go,' persisted the blue-eyed soldier.

Still scolding and muttering she took four glasses from the

cupboard and a big bottle. 'But you're not going to drink in here. Don't you believe it.' The little corporal ran into the kitchen. 'Not there! Not there! Idiot!' she cried. 'Can't you see there's a window there, and a wall opposite where the police come every evening to ...'

'Sh!' Another scare.

'You are mad and you will end in prison,—all four of you,' said the woman. She flounced out of the room. We tiptoed after her into a dark smelling scullery, full of pans of greasy water, of salad leaves and meat-bones.

'There now,' she said, putting down the glasses. 'Drink and go!'

'Ah, at last!' The blue-eyed soldier's happy voice trickled through the dark. 'What do you think? Isn't it just as I said? Hasn't it got a taste of excellent—*ex-cellent* whisky?'

The Little Governess

Oh, dear, how she wished that it wasn't night-time. She'd have much rather travelled by day, much much rather. But the lady at the Governess Bureau said: 'You had better take an evening boat and then if you get into a compartment for "Ladies Only" in the train you will be far safer than sleeping in a foreign hotel. Don't go out of the carriage; don't walk about the corridors and *be sure* to lock the lavatory door if you go there. The train arrives at Munich at eight o'clock, and Frau Arnholdt says that the Hotel Grunewald is only one minute away. A porter can take you there. She will arrive at six the same evening, so you will have a nice quiet day to rest after the journey and rub up your German. And when you want anything to eat I would advise you to pop into the nearest baker's and get a bun and some coffee. You haven't been abroad before, have you?' 'No.' 'Well, I always tell my girls that it's better to mistrust people at first rather than trust them and it's safer to suspect people of evil intentions rather than good ones. . . . It sounds rather hard but we've got to be women of the world, haven't we?'

It had been nice in the Ladies' Cabin. The stewardess was so kind and changed her money for her and tucked up her feet. She lay on one of the hard pink-sprigged couches and watched the other passengers, friendly and natural, pinning their hats to the bolsters, taking off their boots and skirts, opening dressing-cases and arranging mysterious rustling little packages, tying their heads up in veils before lying down. *Thud, thud, thud,* went the steady screw of the steamer. The stewardess pulled a green shade over the light and sat down by the stove, her skirt turned back over her knees, a long piece of knitting on her lap. On a shelf above her head there was a water-bottle with a tight bunch of flowers stuck in it. 'I like travelling very much,' thought the little governess. She smiled and yielded to the warm rocking.

But when the boat stopped and she went up on deck, her dress-basket in one hand, her rug and umbrella in the other, a cold, strange wind flew under her hat. She looked up at the masts and spars of the ship, black against a green glittering sky, and down to the dark landing-stage where strange muffled figures lounged, waiting; she moved forward with the sleepy flock, all knowing where to go to and what to do except her, and she felt afraid. Just a little—just enough to wish—oh, to wish that it was daytime and that one of those women who had smiled at her in the glass, when they both did their hair in the Ladies' Cabin, was somewhere near now. 'Tickets, please. Show your tickets. Have your tickets ready.' She went down the gangway balancing herself carefully on her heels. Then a man in a black leather cap came forward and touched her on the arm. 'Where for, Miss?' He spoke English—he must be a guard or a stationmaster with a cap like that. She had scarcely answered when he pounced on her dress-basket. 'This way,' he shouted, in a rude, determined voice, and elbowing his way he strode past the people. 'But I don't want a porter.' What a horrible man! 'I don't want a porter. I want to carry it myself.' She had to run to keep up with him, and her anger, far stronger than she, ran before her and snatched the bag out of the wretch's hand. He paid no attention at all, but swung on down the long dark platform, and across a railway line. 'He is a robber.' She was sure he was a robber as she stepped between the silvery rails and felt the cinders crunch under her shoes. On the other side—oh, thank goodness!—there was a train with Munich written on it. The man stopped by the huge lighted carriages. 'Second class?' asked the insolent voice. 'Yes, a Ladies' compartment.' She was quite out of breath. She opened her little purse to find something small enough to give this horrible man while he tossed her dress-basket into the rack of an empty carriage that had a ticket, *Dames Seules,* gummed on the window. She got into the train and handed him twenty centimes. 'What's this?' shouted the man, glaring at the money and then at her, holding it up to his nose, sniffing at it as though he had never in his life seen, much less held, such a sum. 'It's a franc. You know that, don't you? It's a franc. That's my fare!' A franc! Did he imagine that she was going to give him a franc for playing a trick like that just because she was a girl and travelling alone at night? Never, never! She squeezed her purse in her hand and simply did not see him—she looked at a view of St. Malo on the wall opposite and simply did not hear him. 'Ah, no. Ah, no. Four sous. You make a mistake. Here, take it. It's a franc I want.' He leapt on to the step of the train and threw the money on to her lap. Trembling with terror she screwed herself tight, tight, and put out an icy hand and took the money—stowed it away in her hand. 'That's all you're going to get,' she said. For a minute or two she felt his sharp eyes pricking her all over, while he nodded slowly, pulling down his mouth: 'Ve-ry well. *Trrrès bien.*' He shrugged his shoulders and disappeared into the dark. Oh, the relief! How simply terrible that had been! As she stood up to feel if the dress-basket was firm she caught sight of herself in the mirror, quite white, with big round eyes. She untied her 'motor veil' and unbuttoned her green cape. 'But it's all over now,' she said to the mirror face, feeling in some way that it was more frightened than she.

People began to assemble on the platform. They stood together in little groups talking; a strange light from the station lamps painted their faces almost green. A little boy in red clattered up with a huge tea-wagon and leaned against it, whistling and flicking his boots with a serviette. A woman in a black alpaca apron pushed a barrow with pillows for hire. Dreamy and vacant she looked—like a woman wheeling a perambulator—up and down, up and down—with a sleeping baby inside it. Wreaths of white smoke floated up from somewhere and hung below the roof like misty vines. 'How strange it all is,' thought the little governess, 'and the middle of the night, too.' She looked out from her safe corner, frightened no longer but proud that she had not given that franc. 'I can look after myself—of course I can. The great thing is not to—' Suddenly from the corridor there came a stamping of feet and men's voices, high and broken with snatches of loud laughter. They were coming her way. The little governess shrank into her corner as four young men in bowler hats passed, staring through the door and window. One of them, bursting with the joke, pointed to the notice *Dames Seules* and the four bent down the better to see the one little girl in the corner. Oh dear, they were in the carriage next door. She heard them tramping about, and then a sudden hush followed by a tall thin fellow with a tiny black moustache who flung her door open. 'If Mademoiselle cares to come in with us,' he said, in French. She saw the others crowding behind him, peeping under his arm and over his shoulder, and she sat very straight and still. 'If Mademoiselle will do us the honour,' mocked the tall man. One of them could be quiet no longer; his laughter went off in a loud crack. 'Mademoiselle is serious,' persisted the young man, bowing and grimacing. He took off his hat with a flourish, and she was alone again.

'*En voiture. En voi-ture!*' Someone ran up and down beside the train. 'I wish it wasn't night-time. I wish there was another woman in the carriage. I'm frightened of the men next door.' The little governess looked out to see her porter coming back again—the same man making for her carriage with his arms full of luggage. But—but what *was* he doing? He put his thumb nail under the label *Dames Seules* and tore it right off, and then stood aside squinting at her while an old man wrapped in a plaid cape climbed up the high step. 'But this is a ladies' compartment.' 'Oh no, Mademoiselle, you make a mistake. No, no I assure you. Merci, Monsieur.' '*En voi-turre!*' A shrill whistle. The porter stepped off triumphant and the train started. For a moment or two big tears brimmed her eyes and through them she saw the old man unwinding a scarf from his neck and untying the flaps of his Jaeger cap. He looked very old. Ninety at least. He had a white moustache and big gold-rimmed spectacles with little blue eyes behind them and pink wrinkled cheeks. A nice face—and charming the way he bent forward and said in halting French: 'Do I disturb you, Mademoiselle? Would you rather I took all these things out of the rack and found another carriage?' What! that old man have to move all those heavy things just because she ... 'No, it's quite all right. You don't disturb me at all.' 'Ah, a thousand thanks.' He sat down opposite her and unbuttoned the cape of his enormous coat and flung it off his shoulders.

The train seemed glad to have left the station. With a long leap it sprang into the dark. She rubbed a place in the window with her glove but she could see nothing—just a tree outspread like a black fan or a scatter of lights, or the line of a hill, solemn and huge. In the carriage next door the young men started singing '*Un, deux, trois.*' They sang the same song over and over at the tops of their voices.

'I never could have dared to go to sleep if I had been alone,' she decided. 'I *couldn't* have put my feet up or even taken off my hat.' The singing gave her a queer little tremble in her stomach and, hugging herself to stop it, with her arms crossed under her cape, she felt really glad to have the old man in the carriage with her. Careful to see that he was not looking she peeped at him through her long lashes. He sat extremely upright, the chest thrown out, the chin well in, knees pressed together, reading a German paper. That was why he spoke French so funnily. He was a German. Something in the army, she supposed—a Colonel or a General—once, of course, not now; he was too old for that now. How spick and span he looked for an old man. He wore a pearl pin stuck in his black tie and a ring with a dark red stone on his little finger; the tip of a white silk handkerchief showed in the pocket of his double-breasted jacket. Somehow, altogether, he was really nice to look at. Most old men were so horrid. She couldn't bear them doddery—or they had a disgusting cough or something. But not having a beard—that made all the difference—and then his cheeks were so pink and his moustache so very white. Down went the German paper and the old man leaned forward with the same delightful courtesy: 'Do you speak German, Mademoiselle?' '*Ja, ein wenig, mehr als Französisch,*' said the little governess, blushing a deep pink colour that spread slowly over her cheeks and made her blue eyes look almost black. 'Ach, so!' The old man bowed graciously. 'Then perhaps you would care to look at some illustrated papers.' He slipped a rubber band from a little roll of them and handed them across. 'Thank you very much.' She was very fond of looking at pictures, but first she would take off her hat and gloves. So she stood up, unpinned the brown straw and put it neatly in the rack beside the dress-basket, stripped off her brown kid gloves, paired them in a tight roll and put them in the crown of the hat for safety, and then sat down again, more comfortably this time, her feet crossed, the papers on her lap. How kindly the old man in the corner watched her bare little hand turning over the big white pages, watched her lips moving as she pronounced the long words to herself, rested upon her hair that fairly blazed under the light. Alas! how tragic for a little governess to possess hair that made one think of tangerines and marigolds, of apricots and tortoiseshell cats and champagne! Perhaps that was what the old man was thinking as he gazed and gazed, and that not even the dark ugly clothes could disguise her soft beauty. Perhaps the flush that licked his cheeks and lips was a flush of rage that anyone so young and tender should have to travel alone and unprotected through the night. Who knows he was not murmuring in his sentimental German fashion: *'Ja, es ist eine Tragödie!* Would to God I were the child's grandpapa!'

'Thank you very much. They were very interesting.' She smiled prettily handing back the papers. 'But you speak German extremely well,' said the old man. 'You have been in Germany before, of course?' 'Oh no, this is the first time'—a little pause, then—'this is the first time that I have ever been abroad at all.' 'Really! I am surprised. You gave me the impression, if I may say so, that you were accustomed to travelling.' 'Oh, well—I have been about a good deal in England, and to Scotland, once.' 'So. I myself have been in England once, but I could not learn English.' He raised one hand and shook his head, laughing. 'No, it was too difficult for me....."Ow-do-you-do. Please vich is ze vay to Leicestaire Squaare."' She laughed too. 'Foreigners always say ... ' They had quite a little talk about it. 'But you will like Munich,' said the old man. 'Munich is a wonderful city. Museums, pictures, galleries, fine buildings and shops, concerts, theatres, restaurants—all are in Munich. I have travelled all over Europe many, many times in my life, but it is always to Munich that I return. You will enjoy yourself there.' 'I am not going to *stay* in Munich,' said the little governess, and she added shyly, 'I am going to a post as governess to a doctor's family in Augsburg.' 'Ah, that was it.' Augsburg he knew. Augsburg—well—was not beautiful. A solid manufacturing town. But if Germany was new to her he hoped she would find something interesting there too. 'I am sure I shall.' 'But what a pity not to see Munich before you go. You ought to take a little holiday on your way'—he smiled—'and store up some pleasant memories.' 'I am afraid I could not do *that*,' said the little governess, shaking her head, suddenly important and serious. 'And also, if one is alone ... ' He quite understood. He bowed, serious too. They were silent after that.

The train shattered on, baring its dark, flaming breast to the hills and to the valleys. It was warm in the carriage. She seemed to lean against the dark rushing and to be carried away and away. Little sounds made themselves heard; steps in the corridor, doors opening and shutting—a murmur of voices—whistling.... Then the window was pricked with long needles of rain.... But it did not matter ... it was outside ... and she had her umbrella ... she pouted, sighed, opened and shut her hands once and fell fast asleep.

'Pardon! Pardon!' The sliding back of the carriage door woke her with a start. What had happened? Someone had come in and gone out again. The old man sat in his corner, more upright than ever, his hands in the pockets of his coat, frowning heavily. 'Ha! ha! ha!' came from the carriage next door. Still half asleep, she put her hands to her hair to make sure it wasn't a dream. 'Disgraceful!' muttered the old man more to himself than to her. 'Common, vulgar fellows! I am afraid they disturbed you, gracious Fräulein, blundering in here like that.' No, not really. She was just going to wake up, and she took out her silver watch to look at the time. Half-past four. A cold blue light filled the window panes. Now when she rubbed a place she could see bright patches of fields, a clump of white houses like mushrooms, a road 'like a picture' with poplar trees on either side, a thread of river. How pretty it was! How pretty and how different! Even those pink clouds in the sky looked foreign. It was cold, but she pretended that it was far colder and rubbed her hands together and shivered, pulling at the collar of her coat because she was so happy.

The train began to slow down. The engine gave a long shrill whistle. They were coming to a town. Taller houses, pink and yellow, glided by, fast asleep behind their green eyelids, and guarded by the poplar trees that quivered in the blue air as if on tiptoes, listening. In one house a woman opened the shutters, flung a red and white mattress across the window frame and stood staring at the train. A pale woman with black hair and a white woollen shawl over her shoulders. More women appeared at the doors and at the windows of the sleeping houses. There came a flock of sheep. The shepherd wore a blue blouse and pointed wooden shoes. Look! look what flowers—and by the railway station too! Standard roses like bridesmaids' bouquets, white geraniums, waxy pink ones that you would *never* see out of a greenhouse at home. Slower and slower. A man with a watering-can was spraying the platform. 'A-a-a-ah!' Somebody came running and waving his arms. A huge fat woman waddled through the glass doors of the station with a tray of strawberries. Oh, she was thirsty! She was very thirsty! 'A-a-a-ah!' The same somebody ran back again. The train stopped.

The old man pulled his coat round him and got up, smiling at her. He murmured something she didn't quite catch, but she smiled back at him as he left the carriage. While he was away the little governess looked at herself again in the glass, shook and patted herself with the precise practical care of a girl who is old enough to travel by herself and has nobody else to assure her that she is 'quite all right behind'. Thirsty and thirsty! The air tasted of water. She let down the window and the fat woman with the strawberries passed as if on purpose, holding up the tray to her. '*Nein, danke,*' said the little governess, looking at the big berries on their gleaming leaves. '*Wei viel?*' she asked as the fat woman moved away. 'Two marks fifty, Fräulein.' 'Good gracious!' She came in from the window and sat down in the corner, very sobered for a minute. Half a crown! 'H-o-o-o-o-e-e-e!' shrieked the train, gathering itself together to be off again. She hoped the old man wouldn't be left behind. Oh, it was daylight—everything was lovely if only she hadn't been so thirsty. Where *was* the old man—oh, here he was—she dimpled at him as though he were an old accepted friend as he closed the door and, turning, took from under his cape a basket of the strawberries. 'If Fräulein would honour me by accepting these . . . ' 'What, for me?' But she drew back and raised her hands as though he were about to put a wild little kitten on her lap.

'Certainly, for you,' said the old man. 'For myself it is twenty years since I was brave enough to eat strawberries.' 'Oh, thank you so very much. *Danke bestens,*' she stammered, '*sie sind so sehr schön!*' 'Eat them and see,' said the old man, looking pleased and friendly. 'You won't have even one?' 'No, no, no.' Timidly and charmingly her hand hovered. They were so big and juicy she had to take two bites to them—the juice ran all down her fingers—and it was while she munched the berries that she first thought of the old man as her grandfather. What a perfect grandfather he would make! Just like one out of a book!

The sun came out, the pink clouds in the sky, the strawberry clouds were eaten by the blue. 'Are they good?' asked the old man. 'As good as they look?'

When she had eaten them she felt she had known him for years. She told him about Frau Arnholdt and how she had got the place. Did he know the Hotel Grunewald? Frau Arnholdt would not arrive until the evening. He listened, listened until he knew as much about the affair as she did, until he said—not looking at her—but smoothing the palms of his brown suède gloves together: 'I wonder if you would let me show you a little of Munich today. Nothing much—but just perhaps a picture gallery and the Englischer Garten. It seems such a pity that you should have to spend the day at the hotel, and also a little uncomfortable ... in a strange place. *Nicht wahr?* You would be back there by the early afternoon or whenever you wish, of course, and you would give an old man a great deal of pleasure.'

It was not until long after she had said 'Yes'—because the moment she had said it and he had thanked her he began telling her about his travels in Turkey and attar of roses—that she wondered whether she had done wrong. After all, she really did not know him. But he was so old and he had been so very kind—not to mention the strawberries. . . . And she couldn't have explained the reason why she said 'No,' and it was her *last* day in a way, her last day to really enjoy herself in. 'Was I wrong? Was I?' A drop of sunlight fell into her hands and lay there, warm and quivering. 'If I might accompany you as far as the hotel,' he suggested, 'and call for you again at about ten o'clock.' He took out his pocket-book and handed her a card. 'Herr Regierung srat. . . . ' He had a title! Well, it was *bound* to be all right! So after that the little governess gave herself up to the excitement of being really abroad, to looking out and reading the foreign advertise-ment signs, to being told about the places they came to—having her attention and enjoyment looked after by the charming old

grandfather—until they reached Munich and the Hauptbahnhof.
'Porter! Porter!' He found her a porter, disposed of his own
luggage in a few words, guided her through the bewildering
crowd out of the station down the clean white steps into the white
road to the hotel. He explained who she was to the manager as
though all this had been bound to happen, and then for one
moment her little hand lost itself in the big brown suède ones. 'I
will call for you at ten o'clock.' He was gone.

'This way, Fräulein,' said the waiter, who had been dodging
behind the manager's back, all eyes and ears for the strange
couple. She followed him up two flights of stairs into a dark
bedroom. He dashed down her dress-basket and pulled up a
clattering, dusty blind. Ugh! what an ugly, cold room—what
enormous furniture! Fancy spending the day in here! 'Is this the
room Frau Arnholdt ordered?' asked the little governess. The
waiter had a curious way of staring as if there was something
funny about her. He pursed up his lips about to whistle, and then
changed his mind. '*Gewiss,*' he said. Well, why didn't he go? Why
did he stare so? '*Gehen Sie,*' said the little governess, with frigid
English simplicity. His little eyes, like currants, nearly popped out
of his doughy cheeks. '*Gehen Sie sofort,*' she repeated icily. At the
door he turned. 'And the gentleman,' said he, 'shall I show the
gentleman upstairs when he comes?'

Over the white streets big white clouds fringed with silver—and
sunshine everywhere. Fat, fat coachmen driving fat cabs; funny
women with little round hats cleaning the tramway lines; people
laughing and pushing against one another; trees on both sides of
the streets and everywhere you looked almost, immense
fountains; a noise of laughing from the footpaths or the middle of
the streets or the open windows. And beside her, more beautifully
brushed than ever, with a rolled umbrella in one hand and yellow
gloves instead of brown ones, her grandfather who had asked her
to spend the day. She wanted to run, she wanted to hang on his
arm, she wanted to cry every minute, 'Oh, I am so frightfully
happy!' He guided her across the roads, stood still while she
'looked', and his kind eyes beamed on her and he said 'just
whatever you wish'. She ate two white sausages and two little rolls

of fresh bread at eleven o'clock in the morning and she drank some beer, which he told her wasn't intoxicating, wasn't at all like English beer, out of a glass like a flower vase. And then they took a cab and really she must have seen thousands and thousands of wonderful classical pictures in about a quarter of an hour! 'I shall have to think them over when I am alone. . . . ' But when they came out of the picture gallery it was raining. The grandfather unfurled his umbrella and held it over the little governess. They started to walk to the restaurant for lunch. She, very close beside him so that he should have some of the umbrella too. 'It goes easier,' he remarked in a detached way, 'if you take my arm, Fräulein. And besides it is the custom in Germany.' So she took his arm and walked beside him while he pointed out the famous statues, so interested that he quite forgot to put down the umbrella even when the rain was long over.

After lunch they went to a café to hear a gypsy band, but she did not like that at all. Ugh! such horrible men were there with heads like eggs and cuts on their faces, so she turned her chair and cupped her burning cheeks in her hands and watched her old friend instead. . . . Then they went to the Englischer Garten.

'I wonder what the time is,' asked the little governess. 'My watch has stopped. I forgot to wind it in the train last night. We've seen such a lot of things that I feel it must be quite late.' 'Late!' He stopped in front of her laughing and shaking his head in a way she had begun to know. 'Then you have not really enjoyed yourself. Late! Why, we have not had any ice-cream yet!' 'Oh, but I have enjoyed myself,' she cried, distressed, 'more than I can possibly say. It has been wonderful! Only Frau Arnholdt is to be at the hotel at six and I ought to be there by five.' 'So you shall. After the ice-cream I shall put you into a cab and you can go there comfortably.' She was happy again. The chocolate ice-cream melted—melted in little sips a long way down. The shadows of the trees danced on the tablecloths, and she sat with her back safely turned to the ornamental clock that pointed to twenty-five minutes to seven. 'Really and truly,' said the little governess earnestly, 'this has been the happiest day of my life. I've never even imagined such a day.' In spite of the ice-cream her grateful baby heart glowed with love for the fairy grandfather.

So they walked out of the garden down a long alley. The day was nearly over. 'You see those big buildings opposite,' said the old man. 'The third storey—that is where I live. I and the old housekeeper who looks after me.' She was very interested. 'Now just before I find a cab for you, will you come and see my little "home" and let me give you a bottle of the attar of roses I told you about in the train? For remembrance?' She would love to. 'I've never seen a bachelor's flat in my life,' laughed the little governess.

The passage was quite dark. 'Ah, I suppose my old woman has gone out to buy me a chicken. One moment.' He opened a door and stood aside for her to pass, a little shy but curious, into a strange room. She did not know quite what to say. It wasn't pretty. In a way it was very ugly—but neat, and, she supposed, comfortable for such an old man. 'Well, what do you think of it?' He knelt down and took from a cupboard a round tray with two pink glasses and a tall pink bottle. 'Two little bedrooms beyond,' he said gaily, 'and a kitchen. It's enough, eh?' 'Oh, quite enough.' 'And if ever you should be in Munich and care to spend a day or two—why, there is always a little nest—a wing of a chicken, and a salad, and an old man delighted to be your host once more and many many times, dear little Fräulein!' He took the stopper out of the bottle and poured some wine into the two pink glasses. His hand shook and the wine spilled over the tray. It was very quiet in the room. She said: 'I think I ought to go now.' 'But you will have a tiny glass of wine with me—just one before you go?' said the old man. 'No, really no. I never drink wine. I—I have promised never to touch wine or anything like that.' And though he pleaded and though she felt dreadfully rude, especially when he seemed to take it to heart so, she was quite determined. 'No, *really,* please.' 'Well, will you just sit down on the sofa for five minutes and let me drink your health?' The little governess sat down on the edge of the red velvet couch and he sat down beside her and drank her health at a gulp. 'Have you really been happy today?' asked the old man, turning round, so close beside her that she felt his knee twitching against hers. Before she could answer he held her hands. 'And are you going to give me one little kiss before you go?' he asked, drawing her closer still.

It was a dream! It wasn't true! It wasn't the same old man at all.

Ah, how horrible! The little governess stared at him in terror. 'No, no, no!' she stammered, struggling out of his hands. 'One little kiss. A kiss. What is it? Just a kiss, dear little Fräulein. A kiss.' He pushed his face forward, his lips smiling broadly; and how his little blue eyes gleamed behind the spectacles! 'Never—never. How can you!' She sprang up, but he was too quick and he held her against the wall, pressed against her his hard old body and his twitching knee, and though she shook her head from side to side, distracted, kissed her on the mouth. On the mouth! Where not a soul who wasn't a near relation had ever kissed her before. . . .

She ran, ran down the street until she found a broad road with tram lines and a policeman standing in the middle like a clockwork doll. 'I want to get a tram to the Hauptbahnhof,' sobbed the little governess. 'Fräulein?' She wrung her hands at him. 'The Hauptbahnhof. There—there's one now,' and while he watched very much surprised, the little girl with her hat on one side, crying without a handkerchief, sprang on to the tram—not seeing the conductor's eyebrows, nor hearing the *hochwohlgebildete Dame* talking her over with a scandalised friend. She rocked herself and cried out loud and said 'Ah, ah!' pressing her hands to her mouth. 'She has been to the dentist,' shrilled a fat old woman, too stupid to be uncharitable. '*Na, sagen Sie 'mal*, what toothache! The child hasn't one left in her mouth.' While the tram swung and jangled through a world full of old men with twitching knees.

When the little governess reached the hall of the Hotel Grunewald the same waiter who had come into her room in the morning was standing by a table, polishing a tray of glasses. The sight of the little governess seemed to fill him out with some inexplicable important content. He was ready for her question; his answer came pat and suave. 'Yes, Fräulein, the lady has been here. I told her that you had arrived and gone out again immediately with a gentleman. She asked me when you were coming back again—but of course I could not say. And then she went to the manager.' He took up a glass from the table, held it up to the light, looked at it with one eye closed, and started polishing it with a corner of his apron. ' . . . ?' 'Pardon, Fräulein? Ach, no,

Fräulein. The manager could tell her nothing—nothing.' He shook his head and smiled at the brilliant glass. 'Where is the lady now?' asked the little governess, shuddering so violently that she had to hold her handkerchief up to her mouth. 'How should I know?' cried the waiter, and as he swooped past her to pounce upon a new arrival his heart beat so hard against his ribs that he nearly chuckled aloud. 'That's it! that's it!' he thought. 'That will show her.' And as he swung the new arrival's box on to his shoulders—hoop!—as though he were a giant and the box a feather, he minced over again the little governess's words, '*Gehen Sie. Gehen Sie sofort.* Shall I! Shall I!' he shouted to himself.

Prelude

I

There was not an inch of room for Lottie and Kezia in the buggy. When Pat swung them on top of the luggage they wobbled; the grandmother's lap was full and Linda Burnell could not possibly have held a lump of a child on hers for any distance. Isabel, very superior, was perched beside the new handy-man on the driver's seat. Holdalls, bags and boxes were piled upon the floor. 'These are absolute necessities that I will not let out of my sight for one instant,' said Linda Burnell, her voice trembling with fatigue and excitement.

Lottie and Kezia stood on the patch of lawn just inside the gate all ready for the fray in their coats with brass anchor buttons and little round caps with battleship ribbons. Hand in hand, they stared with round solemn eyes, first at the absolute necessities and then at their mother.

'We shall simply have to leave them. That is all. We shall simply have to cast them off,' said Linda Burnell. A strange little laugh flew from her lips; she leaned back against the buttoned leather cushions and shut her eyes, her lips trembling with laughter. Happily at that moment Mrs Samuel Josephs, who had been watching the scene from behind her drawing-room blind, waddled down the garden path.

'Why nod leave the chudren with be for the afterdoon, Brs Burnell? They could go on the dray with the storeban when he comes in the eveding. Those thigs on the path have to go, dod't they?'

'Yes, everything outside the house is supposed to go,' said Linda Burnell, and she waved a white hand at the tables and chairs standing on their heads on the front lawn. How absurd they looked! Either they ought to be the other way up, or Lottie and Kezia ought to stand on their heads, too. And she longed to say: 'Stand on your heads, children, and wait for the storeman.' It seemed to her that would be so exquisitely funny that she could not attend to Mrs Samuel Josephs.

The fat creaking body leaned across the gate, and the big jelly of a face smiled. 'Dod't you worry, Brs Burnell. Loddie and Kezia can have tea with my chudren in the dursery, and I'll see theb on the dray afterwards.'

The grandmother considered. 'Yes, it really is quite the best plan. We are very obliged to you, Mrs Samuel Josephs. Children, say "thank you" to Mrs Samuel Josephs.'

Two subdued chirrups: 'Thank you, Mrs Samuel Josephs.'

'And be good little girls, and—come closer—' they advanced, 'don't forget to tell Mrs Samuel Josephs when you want to ...'

'No, granma.'

'Dod't worry, Brs Burnell.'

At the last moment Kezia let go Lottie's hand and darted towards the buggy.

'I want to kiss my granma goodbye again.'

But she was too late. The buggy rolled off up the road, Isabel bursting with pride, her nose turned up at all the world, Linda Burnell prostrated, and the grandmother rummaging among the very curious oddments she had had put in her black silk reticule at the last moment, for something to give her daughter. The buggy twinkled away in the sunlight and fine golden dust up the hill and over. Kezia bit her lip, but Lottie, carefully finding her handkerchief first, set up a wail.

'Mother! Granma!'

Mrs Samuel Josephs, like a huge warm black silk tea-cosy, enveloped her.

'It's all right, by dear. Be a brave child. You come and blay in the dursery!'

She put her arm round weeping Lottie and led her away. Kezia followed, making a face at Mrs Samuel Josephs' placket, which was undone as usual, with two long pink corset laces hanging out of it....

Lottie's weeping died down as she mounted the stairs, but the sight of her at the nursery door with swollen eyes and a blob of a nose gave great satisfaction to the S.J.'s who sat on two benches before a long table covered with American cloth and set out with immense plates of bread and dripping and two brown jugs that faintly steamed.

'Hullo! You've been crying!'

'Ooh! Your eyes have gone right in.'

'Doesn't her nose look funny.'

'You're all red-and-patchy.'

Lottie was quite a success. She felt it and swelled, smiling timidly.

'Go and sid by Zaidee, ducky,' said Mrs Samuel Josephs, 'and Kezia, you sid ad the end by Boses.'

Moses grinned and gave her a nip as she sat down; but she pretended not to notice. She did hate boys.

'Which will you have?' asked Stanley, leaning across the table very politely, and smiling at her. 'Which will you have to begin with—strawberries and cream or bread and dripping?'

'Strawberries and cream, please,' said she.

'Ah-h-h-h.' How they all laughed and beat the table with their teaspoons. Wasn't that a take-in! Wasn't it now! Didn't he fox her! Good old Stan!

'Ma! She thought it was real.'

Even Mrs Samuel Josephs, pouring out the milk and water, could not help smiling. 'You bustn't tease theb on their last day,' she wheezed.

But Kezia bit a big piece out of her bread and dripping, and then stood the piece up on her plate. With the bite out it made a dear little sort of gate. Pooh! She didn't care! A tear rolled down her cheek, but she wasn't crying. She couldn't have cried in front of those awful Samuel Josephs. She sat with her head bent, and as the tear dripped slowly down, she caught it with a neat little whisk of her tongue and ate it before any of them had seen.

II

After tea Kezia wandered back to their own house. Slowly she walked up the back steps, and through the scullery into the kitchen. Nothing was left in it but a lump of gritty yellow soap in one corner of the kitchen window-sill and a piece of flannel stained with blue bag in another. The fireplace was choked up with rubbish. She poked among it but found nothing except a hair-tidy with a heart painted on it that had belonged to the servant girl. Even that she left lying, and she trailed through the narrow passage into the drawing-room. The Venetian blind was pulled down but not drawn close. Long pencil rays of sunlight shone through and the wavy shadow of a bush outside danced on the gold lines. Now it was still, now it began to flutter again, and now it came almost as far as her feet. Zoom! Zoom! a bluebottle knocked against the ceiling; the carpet-tacks had little bits of red fluff sticking to them.

The dining-room window had a square of coloured glass at each corner. One was blue and one was yellow. Kezia bent down to have one more look at a blue lawn with blue arum lilies growing at the gate, and then at a yellow lawn with yellow lilies and a yellow fence. As she looked a little Chinese Lottie came out on to the lawn and began to dust the tables and chairs with a corner of her pinafore. Was that really Lottie? Kezia was not quite sure until she had looked through the ordinary window.

Upstairs in her father's and mother's room she found a pill box black and shiny outside and red in, holding a blob of cotton wool.

'I could keep a bird's egg in that,' she decided.

In the servant girl's room there was a stay-button stuck in a crack of the floor, and in another crack some beads and a long needle. She knew there was nothing in her grandmother's room; she had watched her pack. She went over to the window and leaned against it, pressing her hands to the pane.

Kezia liked to stand so before the window. She liked the feeling of the cold shining glass against her hot palms, and she liked to watch the funny white tops that came on her fingers when she pressed them hard against the pane. As she stood there, the day flickered out and dark came. With the dark crept the wind snuffling and howling. The windows of the empty house shook, a creaking came from the walls and floors, a piece of loose iron on the roof banged forlornly. Kezia was suddenly quite, quite still, with wide open eyes and knees pressed together. She was frightened. She wanted to call Lottie and to go on calling all the while she ran downstairs and out of the house. But IT was just behind her, waiting at the door, at the head of the stairs, at the bottom of the stairs, hiding in the passage, ready to dart out at the back door. But Lottie was at the back door, too.

'Kezia!' she called cheerfully. 'The storeman's here. Everything is on the dray and three horses, Kezia. Mrs Samuel Josephs has given us a big shawl to wear round us, and she says to button up your coat. She won't come out because of asthma.'

Lottie was very important.

'Now then you kids,' called the storeman. He hooked his big thumbs under their arms and up they swung. Lottie arranged the shawl 'most beautifully' and the storeman tucked up their feet in a piece of old blanket.

'Lift up. Easy does it.'

They might have been a couple of young ponies. The storeman felt over the cords holding his load, unhooked the brakechain from the wheel, and whistling, he swung up beside them.

'Keep close to me,' said Lottie, 'because otherwise you pull the shawl away from my side, Kezia.'

But Kezia edged up to the storeman. He towered beside her big as a giant and he smelled of nuts and new wooden boxes.

III

It was the first time that Lottie and Kezia had ever been out so late. Everything looked different—the painted wooden houses far smaller than they did by day, the gardens far bigger and wilder. Bright stars speckled the sky and the moon hung over the harbour dabbling the waves with gold. They could see the lighthouse shining on Quarantine Island, and the green lights on the old coal hulks.

'There comes the Picton boat,' said the storeman, pointing to a little steamer all hung with bright beads.

But when they reached the top of the hill and began to go down the other side the harbour disappeared, and although they were still in the town they were quite lost. Other carts rattled past. Everybody knew the storeman.

'Night, Fred.'

'Night O,' he shouted.

Kezia liked very much to hear him. Whenever a cart appeared in the distance she looked up and waited for his voice. He was an old friend; and she and her grandmother had often been to his place to buy grapes. The storeman lived alone in a cottage that had a glasshouse against one wall built by himself. All the glasshouse was spanned and arched over with one beautiful vine. He took her brown basket from her, lined it with three large leaves, and then he felt in his belt for a little horn knife, reached up and snapped off a big blue cluster and laid it on the leaves so tenderly that Kezia held her breath to watch. He was a very big man. He wore brown velvet trousers, and he had a long brown beard. But he never wore a collar, not even on Sunday. The back of his neck was burnt bright red.

'Where are we now?' Every few minutes one of the children asked him the question.

'Why, this is Hawk Street, or Charlotte Crescent.'

'Of course it is,' Lottie pricked up her ears at the last name; she always felt that Charlotte Crescent belonged specially to her. Very few people had streets with the same name as theirs.

'Look, Kezia, there is Charlotte Crescent. Doesn't it look different?' Now everything familiar was left behind. Now the big dray rattled into unknown country, along new roads with high clay banks on either side, up steep hills, down into bushy valleys, through wide shallow rivers. Further and further. Lottie's head wagged; she drooped, she slipped half into Kezia's lap and lay there. But Kezia could not open her eyes wide enough. The wind blew and she shivered; but her cheeks and ears burned.

'Do stars ever blow about?' she asked.

'Not to notice,' said the storeman.

'We've got a nuncle and a naunt living near our new house,' said Kezia. 'They have got two children, Pip, the eldest is called, and the youngest's name is Rags. He's got a ram. He has to feed it with a nenamuel teapot and a glove top over the spout. He's going to show us. What is the difference between a ram and a sheep?'

'Well, a ram has horns and runs for you.'

Kezia considered. 'I don't want to see it frightfully,' she said. 'I hate rushing animals like dogs and parrots. I often dream that animals rush at me—even camels—and while they are rushing, their heads swell e-enormous.'

The storeman said nothing. Kezia peered up at him, screwing up her eyes. Then she put her finger out and stroked his sleeve; it felt hairy. 'Are we near?' she asked.

'Not far off, now,' answered the storeman. 'Getting tired?'

'Well, I'm not an atom bit sleepy,' said Kezia. 'But my eyes keep curling up in such a funny sort of way.' She gave a long sigh, and to stop her eyes from curling she shut them.... When she opened them again they were clanking through a drive that cut through the garden like a whiplash, looping suddenly an island of green, and behind the island, but out of sight until you came upon it, was the house. It was long and low built, with a pillared veranda and balcony all the way round. The soft white bulk of it lay stretched upon the green garden like a sleeping beast. And now one and now another of the windows leaped into light. someone was walking through the empty rooms carrying a lamp. From the window downstairs the light of a fire flickered. A strange beautiful excitement seemed to stream from the house in quivering ripples.

'Where are we?' said Lottie, sitting up. Her reefer cap was all on one side and on her cheek there was the print of an anchor button she had pressed against while sleeping. Tenderly the storeman lifted her, set her cap straight, and pulled down her crumpled clothes. She stood blinking on the lowest veranda step watching Kezia, who seemed to come flying through the air to her feet.

'Ooh!' cried Kezia, flinging up her arms. The grandmother came out of the dark hall carrying a little lamp. She was smiling.

'You found your way in the dark?' said she.

'Perfectly well.'

But Lottie staggered on the lowest veranda step like a bird fallen out of the nest. If she stood still for a moment she fell asleep; if she leaned against anything her eyes closed. She could not walk another step.

'Kezia,' said the grandmother, 'can I trust you to carry the lamp?'

'Yes, my granma.'

The old woman bent down and gave the bright breathing thing into her hands and then she caught up drunken Lottie. 'This way.'

Through a square hall filled with bales and hundreds of parrots (but the parrots were only on the wallpaper) down a narrow passage where the parrots persisted in flying past Kezia with her lamp.

'Be very quiet,' warned the grandmother, putting down Lottie and opening the dining-room door. 'Poor little mother has got such a headache.'

Linda Burnell, in a long cane chair, with her feet on a hassock and a plaid over her knees, lay before a crackling fire. Burnell and Beryl sat at the table in the middle of the room eating a dish of fried chops and drinking tea out of a brown china teapot. Over the back of her mother's chair leaned Isabel. She had a comb in her fingers and in a gentle absorbed fashion she was combing the curls from her mother's forehead. Outside the pool of lamp and firelight the room stretched dark and bare to the hollow windows.

'Are those the children?' But Linda did not really care; she did not even open her eyes to see.

'Put down the lamp, Kezia,' said Aunt Beryl, 'or we shall have the house on fire before we are out of packing cases. More tea, Stanley?'

'Well, you might just give me five-eighths of a cup,' said Burnell, leaning across the table. 'Have another chop, Beryl. Tip-top meat, isn't it? Not too lean and not too fat.' He turned to his wife. 'You're sure you won't change your mind, Linda darling?'

'The very thought of it is enough.' She raised one eyebrow in the way she had. The grandmother brought the children bread and milk and they sat up to table, flushed and sleepy behind the wavy steam.

'I had meat for my supper,' said Isabel, still combing gently.

'I had a whole chop for my supper, the bone and all and Worcester sauce. Didn't I father?'

'Oh, don't boast, Isabel,' said Aunt Beryl.

Isabel looked astounded. 'I wasn't boasting, was I, Mummy? I never thought of boasting. I thought they would like to know. I meant to tell them.'

'Very well. That's enough,' said Burnell. He pushed back his plate, took a toothpick out of his pocket and began picking his strong white teeth.

'You might see that Fred has a bite of something in the kitchen before he goes, will you, mother?'

'Yes, Stanley.' The old woman turned to go.

'Oh, hold on half a jiffy. I suppose nobody knows where my

slippers were put? I suppose I shall not be able to get at them for a month or two—what?'

'Yes,' came from Linda. 'In the top of the canvas holdall marked "urgent necessities". '

'Well, you might get them for me, will you, mother?'

'Yes, Stanley.'

Burnell got up, stretched himself, and going over to the fire he turned his back to it and lifted up his coat tails.

'By Jove, this is a pretty pickle. Eh, Beryl?'

Beryl, sipping tea, her elbows on the table, smiled over the cup at him. She wore an unfamiliar pink pinafore; the sleeves of her blouse were rolled up to her shoulders showing her lovely freckled arms, and she had let her hair fall down her back in a long pigtail.

'How long do you think it will take to get straight—couple of weeks—eh?' he chaffed.

'Good heavens, no,' said Beryl airily. 'The worst is over already. The servant girl and I have simply slaved all day, and ever since mother came she has worked like a horse, too. We have never sat down for a moment. We have had a day.'

Stanley scented a rebuke.

'Well, I suppose you did not expect me to rush away from the office and nail carpets—did you?'

'Certainly not,' laughed Beryl. She put down her cup and ran out of the dining-room.

'What the hell does she expect us to do?' asked Stanley. 'Sit down and fan herself with a palm-leaf fan while I have a gang of professionals to do the job? By Jove, if she can't do a hand's turn occasionally without shouting about it in return for ... '

And he gloomed as the chops began to fight the tea in his sensitive stomach. But Linda put up a hand and dragged him down to the side of her long chair.

'This is a wretched time for you, old boy,' she said. Her cheeks were very white, but she smiled and curled her fingers into the big red hand she held. Burnell became quiet. Suddenly he began to whistle 'Pure as a lily, joyous and free'—a good sign.

'Think you're going to like it?' he asked.

'I don't want to tell you, but I think I ought to, mother,' said Isabel. 'Kezia is drinking tea out of Aunt Beryl's cup.'

IV

They were taken off to bed by the grandmother. She went first with a candle; the stairs rang to their climbing feet. Isabel and Lottie lay in a room to themselves, Kezia curled in her grandmother's soft bed.

'Aren't there going to be any sheets, my granma?'

'No, not tonight.'

'It's tickly,' said Kezia, 'but it's like Indians.' She dragged her grandmother down to her and kissed her under the chin.

'Come to bed soon and be my Indian brave.'

'What a silly you are,' said the old woman, tucking her in as she loved to be tucked.

'Aren't you going to leave me a candle?'

'No. Sh—h. Go to sleep.'

'Well, can I have the door left open?'

She rolled herself up into a round but she did not go to sleep. From all over the house came the sound of steps. The house itself creaked and popped. Loud whispering voices came from downstairs. Once she heard Aunt Beryl's rush of high laughter, and once she heard a loud trumpeting from Burnell blowing his nose. Outside the window hundreds of black cats with yellow eyes sat in the sky watching her—but she was not frightened. Lottie was saying to Isabel:

'I'm going to say my prayers in bed tonight.'

'No, you can't, Lottie.' Isabel was very firm. 'God only excuses you saying your prayers in bed if you've got a temperature.' So Lottie yielded:

> 'Gentle Jesus meek anmile,
> Look pon a little chile.
> Pity me, simple Lizzie,
> Suffer me to come to thee.'

And then they lay down back to back, their little behinds just touching, and fell asleep.

Standing in a pool of moonlight Beryl Fairfield undressed herself. She was tired, but she pretended to be more tired than she really was—letting her clothes fall, pushing back with a languid gesture her warm, heavy hair.

'Oh, how tired I am—very tired.'

She shut her eyes a moment, but her lips smiled. Her breath rose and fell in her breast like two fanning wings. The window was wide open; it was warm, and somewhere out there in the garden a young man, dark and slender, with mocking eyes, tiptoed among the bushes, and gathered the flowers into a big bouquet, and slipped under her window and held it up to her. She saw herself bending forward. He thrust his head among the bright waxy flowers, sly and laughing. 'No, no,' said Beryl. She turned from the window and dropped her nightgown over her head.

'How frightfully unreasonable Stanley is sometimes,' she thought, buttoning. And then as she lay down, there came the old thought, the cruel thought—ah, if only she had money of her own.

A young man, immensely rich, has just arrived from England. He meets her quite by chance.... The new governor is unmarried.... There is a ball at Government house.... Who is that exquisite creature in eau-de-nil satin? Beryl Fairfield....

'The thing that pleases me,' said Stanley, leaning against the side of the bed and giving himself a good scratch on his shoulders and back before turning in, 'is that I've got the place dirt cheap, Linda. I was talking about it to little Wally Bell today and he said he simply could not understand why they had accepted my figure. You see land about here is bound to become more and more valuable ... in about ten years' time ... of course we shall have to go very slow and cut down expenses as fine as possible. Not asleep—are you?'

'No, dear, I've heard every word,' said Linda.

He sprang into bed, leaned over her and blew out the candle.

'Good night, Mr Business Man,' said she, and she took hold of his head by the ears and gave him a quick kiss. Her faint far-away voice seemed to come from a deep well.

'Good night, darling.' He slipped his arm under her neck and drew her to him.

'Yes, clasp me,' said the faint voice from the deep well.

Pat the handy-man sprawled in his little room behind the kitchen. His sponge-bag, coat and trousers hung from the door-peg like a hanged man. From the edge of the blanket his twisted toes protruded, and on the floor beside him there was an empty cane bird-cage. He looked like a comic picture.

'Honk, honk,' came from the servant girl. She had adenoids.

Last to go to bed was the grandmother.

'What. Not asleep yet?'

'No, I'm waiting for you,' said Kezia. The old woman sighed and lay down beside her. Kezia thrust her head under her grandmother's arm and gave a little squeak. But the old woman only pressed her faintly, and sighed again, took out her teeth, and put them in a glass of water beside her on the floor.

In the garden some tiny owls, perched on the branches of a lace-bark tree, called: 'More pork; more pork.' And far away in the bush there sounded a harsh rapid chatter: 'Ha-ha-ha ... Ha-ha-ha.'

V

Dawn came sharp and chill with red clouds on a faint green sky and drops of water on every leaf and blade. A breeze blew over the garden, dropping dew and dropping petals, shivered over the drenched paddocks, and was lost in the sombre bush. In the sky some tiny stars floated for a moment and then they were gone—they were dissolved like bubbles. And plain to be heard in the early quiet was the sound of the creek in the paddock running over the brown stones, running in and out of the sandy hollows, hiding under clumps of dark berry bushes, spilling into a swamp of yellow water flowers and cresses.

And then at the first beam of sun the birds began. Big cheeky birds, starlings and mynahs, whistled on the lawns, the little birds, the goldfinches and linnets and fan-tails, flicked from bough to bough. A lovely kingfisher perched on the paddock fence preening his rich beauty, and a *tui* sang his three notes and laughed and sang them again.

'How loud the birds are,' said Linda in her dream. She was walking with her father through a green paddock sprinkled with daisies. Suddenly he bent down and parted the grasses and showed her a tiny ball of fluff just at her feet. 'Oh, papa, the darling.' She made a cup of her hands and caught the tiny bird and stroked its head with her finger. It was quite tame. But a funny thing happened. As she stroked it began to swell, it ruffled and pouched, it grew bigger and bigger and its round eyes seemed to smile knowingly at her. Now her arms were hardly wide enough to hold it and she dropped it into her apron. It had become a baby with a big naked head and a gaping bird-mouth, opening and shutting. Her father broke into a loud clattering laugh and she woke to see Burnell standing by the windows rattling the Venetian blind up to the very top.

'Hullo,' he said. 'Didn't wake you, did I? Nothing much wrong with the weather this morning.'

He was enormously pleased. Weather like this set a final seal on his bargain. He felt, somehow, that he had bought the lovely day, too—got it chucked in dirt cheap with the house and ground. He dashed off to his bath and Linda turned over and raised herself on one elbow to see the room by daylight. All the furniture had found a place—all the old paraphernalia, as she expressed it. Even the photographs were on the mantelpiece and the medicine bottles on the shelf above the washstand. Her clothes lay across a chair— her outdoor things, a purple cape and a round hat with a plume in it. Looking at them she wished that she was going away from this house, too. And she saw herself driving away from them all in a little buggy, driving away from everybody and not even waving.

Back came Stanley girt with a towel, glowing and slapping his thighs. He pitched the wet towel on top of her hat and cape, and standing firm in the exact centre of a square of sunlight he began to do his exercises. Deep breathing, bending and squatting like a frog and shooting out his legs. He was so delighted with his firm, obedient body that he hit himself on the chest and gave a loud 'Ah'. But this amazing vigour seemed to set him worlds away from Linda. She lay on the white tumbled bed and watched him as if from the clouds.

'Oh, damn! Oh, blast!' said Stanley, who had butted into a crisp white shirt only to find that some idiot had fastened the neck-band and he was caught. He stalked over to Linda waving his arms.

'You look like a big fat turkey,' said she.

'Fat. I like that,' said Stanley. 'I haven't a square inch of fat on me. Feel that.'

'It's rock—it's iron,' mocked she.

'You'd be surprised,' said Stanley, as though this were intensely interesting, 'at the number of chaps at the club who have got a corporation. Young chaps, you know—men of my age.' He began parting his bushy ginger hair, his blue eyes fixed and round in the glass, his knees bent, because the dressing-table was always—confound it—a bit too low for him. 'Little Wally Bell, for instance,' and he straightened, describing upon himself an enormous curve with the hairbrush. 'I must say I've a perfect horror ... '

'My dear, don't worry. You'll never be fat. You are far too energetic.'

'Yes, yes, I suppose that's true,' said he, comforted for the hundredth time, and taking a pearl penknife out of his pocket he began to pare his nails.

'Breakfast, Stanley.' Beryl was at the door. 'Oh, Linda, mother says you are not to get up yet.' She popped her head in at the door. She had a big piece of syringa stuck through her hair.

'Everything we left on the veranda last night is simply sopping this morning. You should see poor dear mother wringing out the tables and the chairs. However, there is no harm done—' this with the faintest glance at Stanley.

'Have you told Pat to have the buggy round in time? It's a good six and a half miles to the office.'

'I can imagine what this early start for the office will be like,' thought Linda. 'It will be very high pressure indeed.'

'Pat, Pat.' She heard the servant girl calling. But Pat was evidently hard to find; the silly voice went baa—baaing through the garden.

Linda did not rest again until the final slam of the front door told her that Stanley was really gone.

Later she heard her children playing in the garden. Lottie's stolid, compact little voice cried: 'Ke—zia. Isa—bel.' She was always getting lost or losing people only to find them again, to her great surprise, round the next tree or the next corner. 'Oh, there you are after all.' They had been turned out after breakfast and told not to come back to the house until they were called. Isabel wheeled a neat pramload of prim dolls and Lottie was allowed for a great treat to walk beside her holding the doll's parasol over the face of the wax one.

'Where are you going to, Kezia?' asked Isabel, who longed to find some light and menial duty that Kezia might perform and so be roped in under her government.

'Oh, just away,' said Kezia....

Then she did not hear them any more. What a glare there was in the room. She hated blinds pulled up to the top at any time, but in the morning it was intolerable. She turned over to the wall and idly, with one finger, she traced a poppy on the wall-paper with a leaf and a stem and a fat bursting bud. In the quiet, and under her tracing finger, the poppy seemed to come alive. She could feel the sticky, silky petals, the stem, hairy like a gooseberry skin, the rough leaf and the tight glazed bud. Things had a habit of coming alive like that. Not only large substantial things like furniture but curtains and the patterns of stuffs and the fringes of quilts and cushions. How often she had seen the tassel fringe of her quilt change into a funny procession of dancers with priests attending.... For there were some tassels that did not dance at all but walked stately, bent forward as if praying or chanting. How often the medicine bottles had turned into a row of little men with brown top-hats on; and the washstand jug had a way of sitting in the basin like a fat bird in a round nest.

'I dreamed about birds last night,' thought Linda. What was it? She had forgotten. But the strangest part of this coming alive of things was what they did. They listened, they seemed to swell out with some mysterious important content, and when they were full she felt that they smiled. But it was not for her, only, their sly secret smile; they were members of a secret society and they smiled among themselves. Sometimes, when she had fallen asleep in the daytime, she woke and could not lift a finger, could not even turn her eyes to left or right because THEY were there; sometimes when she went out of a room and left it empty, she knew as she clicked the door to that THEY were filling it. And there were times in the evenings when she was upstairs, perhaps, and everybody else was down, when she could hardly escape from them. Then she could not hurry, she could not hum a tune; if she tried to say ever so carelessly—'Bother that old thimble'—THEY were not deceived. THEY knew how frightened she was; THEY saw how she turned her head away as she passed the mirror. What Linda always felt was that THEY wanted something of her, and she knew that if she gave herself up and was quiet, more than quiet, silent, motionless, something would really happen.

'It's very quiet now,' she thought. She opened her eyes wide, and she heard the silence spinning its soft endless web. How lightly she breathed; she scarcely had to breathe at all.

Yes, everything had come alive down to the minutest, tiniest particle, and she did not feel her bed, she floated, held up in the air. Only she seemed to be listening with her wide open watchful eyes, waiting for someone to come who just did not come, watching for something to happen that just did not happen.

VI

In the kitchen at the long deal table under the two windows old Mrs Fairfield was washing the breakfast dishes. The kitchen window looked out on to a big grass patch that led down to the vegetable garden and the rhubarb beds. On one side the grass patch was bordered by the scullery and wash-house and over this whitewahsed lean-to there grew a knotted vine. She had noticed yesterday that a few tiny corkscrew tendrils had come right through some cracks in the scullery ceiling and all the windows of the lean-to had a thick frill of ruffled green.

'I am very fond of a grape vine,' declared Mrs Fairfield, 'but I do not think that the grapes will ripen here. It takes Australian sun.' And she remembered how Beryl when she was a baby had been picking some white grapes from the vine on the back veranda of the Tasmanian house and she had been stung on the leg by a huge red ant. She saw Beryl in a little plaid dress with red ribbon tie-ups on the shoulders screaming so dreadfully that half the street rushed in. And how the child's leg had swelled! 'T—t—t—t!' Mrs Fairfield caught her breath remembering. 'Poor child, how terrifying it was.' And she set her lips tight and went over to the stove for some more hot water. The water frothed up in the big soapy bowl with pink and blue bubbles on top of the foam. Old Mrs Fairfield's arms were bare to the elbow and stained a bright pink. She wore a grey foulard dress patterned with large purple pansies, a white linen apron and a high cap shaped like a jelly mould of white muslin. At her throat there was a silver crescent moon with five little owls seated on it, and round her neck she wore a watch-guard made of black beads.

It was hard to believe that she had not been in that kitchen for years; she was so much a part of it. She put the crocks away with a sure, precise touch, moving leisurely and ample from the stove to the dresser, looking into the pantry and the larder as though there were not an unfamiliar corner. When she had finished, everything in the kitchen had become part of a series of patterns. She stood in the middle of the room wiping her hands on a check cloth; a smile beamed on her lips; she thought it looked very nice, very satisfactory.

'Mother! Mother! Are you there?' called Beryl.

'Yes, dear. Do you want me?'

'No. I'm coming,' and Beryl rushed in, very flushed, dragging with her two big pictures.

'Mother, whatever can I do with these awful hideous Chinese paintings that Chung Wah gave Stanley when he went bankrupt? It's absurd to say that they are valuable, because they were hanging in Chung Wah's fruit shop for months before. I can't make out why Stanley wants them kept. I'm sure he thinks them just as hideous as we do, but it's because of the frames,' she said spitefully. 'I suppose he thinks the frames might fetch something some day or other.'

'Why don't you hang them in the passage?' suggested Mrs Fairfield; 'they would not be much seen there.'

'I can't. There is no room. I've hung all the photographs of his office there before and after building, and the signed photos of his business friends, and that awful enlargement of Isabel lying on the mat in her singlet.' Her angry glance swept the placid kitchen. 'I know what I'll do. I'll hang them here. I will tell Stanley they got a little damp in the moving so I have put them in here for the time being.'

She dragged a chair forward, jumped on it, took a hammer and a big nail out of her pinafore pocket and banged away.

'There! That is enough! Hand me the picture, mother.'

'One moment, child.' Her mother was wiping over the carved ebony frame.

'Oh, mother, really you need not dust them. It would take years to dust all those little holes.' And she frowned at the top of her mother's head and bit her lip with impatience. Mother's deliberate way of doing things was simply maddening. It was old age, she supposed, loftily.

At last the two pictures were hung side by side. She jumped off the chair, stowing away the little hammer.

'They don't look so bad there, do they?' said she. 'And at any rate nobody need gaze at them except Pat and the servant girl—have I got a spider's web on my face, mother? I've been poking into that cupboard under the stairs and now something keeps tickling my nose.'

But before Mrs Fairfield had time to look Beryl had turned away. Someone tapped on the window: Linda was there, nodding and smiling. They heard the latch of the scullery door lift and she came in. She had no hat on; her hair stood upon her head in curling rings and she was wrapped up in an old cashmere shawl.

'I'm so hungry,' said Linda: 'where can I get something to eat, mother? This is the first time I've been in the kitchen. It says "mother" all over; everything is in pairs.'

'I will make you some tea,' said Mrs Fairfield, spreading a clean napkin over a corner of the table, 'and Beryl can have a cup with you.'

'Beryl, do you want half my gingerbread?' Linda waved the knife at her. 'Beryl, do you like the house now that we are here?'

'Oh yes, I like the house immensely and the garden is beautiful, but it feels very far away from everything to me. I can't imagine people coming out from town to see us in that dreadful jolting bus, and I am sure there is not anyone here to come and call. Of course it does not matter to you because—'

'But there's the buggy,' said Linda. 'Pat can drive you into town whenever you like.'

That was a consolation, certainly, but there was something at the back of Beryl's mind, something she did not even put into words for herself.

'Oh, well, at any rate it won't kill us,' she said dryly, putting down her empty cup and standing up and stretching. 'I am going to hang curtains.' And she ran away singing:

'How many thousand birds I see
That sing aloud from every tree ... '

' ... birds I see That sing aloud from every tree ... ' But when she reached the dining-room she stopped singing, her face changed; it became gloomy and sullen.

'One may as well rot here as anywhere else,' she muttered savagely, digging the stiff brass safety-pins into the red serge curtains.

The two left in the kitchen were quiet for a little. Linda leaned her cheek on her fingers and watched her mother. She thought her mother looked wonderfully beautiful with her back to the leafy window. There was something comforting in the sight of her that Linda felt she could never do without. She needed the sweet smell of her flesh, and the soft feel of her cheeks and her arms and shoulders still softer. She loved the way her hair curled, silver at her forehead, lighter at her neck and bright brown still in the big coil under the muslin cap. Exquisite were her mother's hands, and the two rings she wore seemed to melt into her creamy skin. And she was always so fresh, so delicious. The old woman could bear nothing but linen next to her body and she bathed in cold water winter and summer.

'Isn't there anything for me to do?' asked Linda.

'No, darling. I wish you would go into the garden and give an eye to your children; but that I know you will not do.'

'Of course I will, but you know Isabel is much more grown up than any of us.'

'Yes, but Kezia is not,' said Mrs Fairfield.

'Oh, Kezia has been tossed by a bull hours ago,' said Linda, winding herself up in her shawl again.

But no, Kezia had seen a bull through a hole in a knot of wood in the paling that separated the tennis lawn from the paddock. But she had not liked the bull frightfully, so she had walked away back through the orchard, up the grassy slope, along the path by the lace-bark tree and so into the spread tangled garden. She did not believe that she would ever not get lost in this garden. Twice she had found her way back to the big iron gates they had driven through the night before, and then had turned to walk up the drive that led to the house, but there were so many little paths on either side. On one side they all led into a tangle of tall dark trees and strange bushes with flat velvet leaves and feathery cream flowers that buzzed with flies when you shook them—this was the frightening side, and no garden at all. The little paths here were wet and clayey with tree roots spanned across them like the marks of big fowls' feet.

But on the other side of the drive there was a high box border and the paths had box edges and all of them led into a deeper and deeper tangle of flowers. The camellias were in bloom, white and crimson and pink and white striped with flashing leaves. You could not see a leaf on the syringa bushes for the white clusters. The roses were in flower—gentlemen's button-hole roses, little white ones, but far too full of insects to hold under anyone's nose, pink monthly roses with a ring of fallen petals round the bushes, cabbage roses on thick stalks, moss roses, always in bud, pink smooth beauties opening curl on curl, red ones so dark they seemed to turn back as they fell, and a certain exquisite cream kind with a slender red stem and bright scarlet leaves.

There were clumps of fairy bells, and all kinds of geraniums, and there were little trees of verbena and bluish lavender bushes and a bed of pelargoniums with velvet eyes and leaves like moths' wings. There was a bed of nothing but mignonette and another of nothing but pansies—borders of double and single daisies and all kinds of little tufty plants she had never seen before.

The red-hot pokers were taller than she; the Japanese sunflowers grew in a tiny jungle. She sat down on one of the box borders. By pressing hard at first it made a nice seat. But how dusty it was inside! Kezia bent down to look and sneezed and rubbed her nose.

And then she found herself at the top of the rolling grassy slope that led down to the orchard. . . . She looked down at the slope a moment; then she lay down on her back, gave a squeak and rolled over and over into the thick flowery orchard grass. As she lay waiting for things to stop spinning, she decided to go up to the house and ask the servant girl for an empty matchbox. She wanted to make a surprise for the grandmother. . . . First she would put a leaf inside with a big violet lying on it, then she would put a very small white picotee, perhaps, on each side of the violet, and then she would sprinkle some lavender on the top, but not to cover their heads.

She often made these surprises for the grandmother, and they were always most successful.

'Do you want a match, my granny?'

'Why, yes, child, I believe a match is just what I'm looking for.'

The grandmother slowly opened the box and came upon the picture inside.

'Good gracious, child! How you astonished me!'

'I can make her one every day here,' she thought, scrambling up the grass on her slippery shoes.

But on her way back to the house she came to that island that lay in the middle of the drive, dividing the drive into two arms that met in front of the house. The island was made of grass banked up high. Nothing grew on the top except one huge plant with thick, grey-green, thorny leaves, and out of the middle there sprang up a tall stout stem. Some of the leaves of the plant were so old that they curled up in the air no longer; they turned back, they were split and broken; some of them lay flat and withered on the ground.

Whatever could it be? She had never seen anything like it before. She stood and stared. And then she saw her mother coming down the path.

'Mother, what is it?'

Linda looked up at the fat swelling plant with its cruel leaves and fleshy stem. High above them, as though becalmed in the air, and yet holding so fast to the earth it grew from, it might have had claws instead of roots. The curving leaves seemed to be hiding something; the blind stem cut into the air as if no wind could ever shake it.

'That is an aloe, Kezia,' said her mother.

'Does it ever have any flowers?'

'Yes, Kezia,' and Linda smiled down at her, and half shut her eyes. 'Once every hundred years.'

VII

On his way home from the office Stanley Burnell stopped the

buggy at the Bodega, got out and bought a large bottle of oysters. At the Chinaman's shop next door he bought a pineapple in the pink of condition, and noticing a basket of fresh black cherries he told John to put him in a pound of those as well. The oysters and the pine he stowed away in the box under the front seat, but the cherries he kept in his hand.

Pat, the handy-man, leapt off the box and tucked him up again in the brown rug.

'Lift yer feet, Mr Burnell, while I give yer a fold under,' said he.

'Right! Right! First rate!' said Stanley. 'You can make straight for home now.'

Pat gave the grey mare a touch and the buggy sprang forward.

'I believe this man is a first-rate chap,' thought Stanley. He liked the look of him sitting up there in his neat brown coat and brown bowler. He liked the way Pat had tucked him in, and he liked his eyes. There was nothing servile about him—and if there was one thing he hated more than another it was servility. And he looked as if he was pleased with his job—happy and contented already.

The grey mare went very well; Burnell was impatient to be out of the town. He wanted to be home. Ah, it was splendid to live in the country—to get right out of that hole of a town once the office was closed; and this drive in the fresh warm air, knowing all the while that his own house was at the other end, with its garden and paddocks, its three tip-top cows and enough fowls and ducks to keep them in poultry, was splendid too.

As they left the town finally and bowled away up the deserted road his heart beat hard for joy. He rooted in the bag and began to eat the cherries, three or four at a time, chucking the stones over the side of the buggy. They were delicious, so plump and cold, without a spot or bruise on them.

Look at those two, now—black one side and white the other—perfect! A perfect little pair of Siamese twins. And he stuck them in his button-hole. . . . By Jove, he wouldn't mind giving that chap up there a handful—but no, better not. Better wait until he had been with him a bit longer.

He began to plan what he would do with his Saturday afternoons and his Sundays. He wouldn't go to the club for lunch on Saturday. No, cut away from the office as soon as possible and get them to give him a couple of slices of cold meat and half a lettuce when he got home. And then he'd get a few chaps out from town to play tennis in the afternoon. Not too many—three at most. Beryl was a good player, too.... He stretched out his right arm and slowly bent it, feeling the muscle.... A bath, a good rub-down, a cigar on the veranda after dinner....

On Sunday morning they would go to church—children and all. Which reminded him that he must hire a pew, in the sun if possible and well forward so as to be out of the draught from the door. In fancy he heard himself intoning extremely well: 'When thou did overcome the *Sharp*ness of Death Though didst open the *King*dom of heaven to *all* Believers.' And he saw the neat brass-edged card on the corner of the pew—Mr Stanley Burnell and family.... The rest of the day he'd loaf about with Linda.... Now they were walking about the garden; she was on his arm, and he was explaining to her at length what he intended doing at the office the week following. He heard her saying: 'My dear, I think that is most wise....' Talking things over with Linda was a wonderful help even though they were apt to drift away from the point.

Hang it all! They weren't getting along very fast. Pat had put the brake on again. Ugh! What a brute of a thing it was. He could feel it in the pit of his stomach.

A sort of panic overtook Burnell whenever he approached near home. Before he was well inside the gate he would shout to anyone within sight: 'Is everything all right?' And then he did not believe it was until he heard Linda say: 'Hullo! Are you home again?' That was the worst of living in the country—it took the deuce of a long time to get back.... But now they weren't far off. They were on the top of the last hill; it was a gentle slope all the way now and not more than half a mile.

Pat trailed the whip over the mare's back and he coaxed her 'Goop now. Goop now.'

It wanted a few minutes to sunset. Everything stood motionless bathed in bright, metallic light and from the paddocks on either side there streamed the milky scent of ripe grass. The iron gates were open. They dashed through and up the drive and round the island, stopping at the exact middle of the veranda.

'Did she satisfy yer, sir?' said Pat, getting off the box and grinning at his master.

'Very well indeed, Pat,' said Stanley.

Linda came out of the glass door; her voice rang in the shadowy quiet. 'Hullo! Are you home again?'

At the sound of her his heart beat so hard that he could hardly stop himself dashing up the steps and catching her in his arms.

'Yes, I'm home again. Is everything all right?'

Pat began to lead the buggy round to the side gate that opened into the courtyard.

'Here, half a moment,' said Burnell. 'Hand me those two parcels.' And he said to Linda, 'I've brought you back a bottle of oysters and a pineapple,' as though he had brought her back all the harvest of the earth.

They all went into the hall; Linda carried the oysters in one hand and the pineapple in the other. Burnell shut the glass door, threw his hat down, put his arms round her and strained her to him, kissing the top of her head, her ears, her lips, her eyes.

'Oh, dear! Oh, dear!' said she. 'Wait a moment. Let me put down these silly things,' and she put the bottle of oysters and the pine on a little carved chair. 'What have you got in your button-hole—cherries?' She took them out and hung them over his ear.

'Don't do that, darling. They are for you.'

So she took them off his ear again. 'You don't mind if I save them. They'd spoil my appetite for dinner. Come and see your children. They are having tea.'

The lamp was lighted on the nursery table. Mrs Fairfield was cutting and spreading bread and butter. The three little girls sat up to table wearing large bibs embroidered with their names. They wiped their mouths as their father came in ready to be kissed. The windows were open; a jar of wild flowers stood on the mantelpiece, and the lamp made a big soft bubble of light on the ceiling.

'You seem pretty snug, mother,' said Burnell, blinking at the light. Isabel and Lottie sat one on either side of the table, Kezia at the bottom—the place at the top was empty.

'That's where my boy ought to sit,' thought Stanley. He

tightened his arm round Linda's shoulder. By God, he was a perfect fool to feel as happy as this!

'We are, Stanley. We are very snug,' said Mrs Fairfield, cutting Kezia's bread into fingers.

'Like it better than town—eh, children?' asked Burnell.

'Oh, yes,' said the three little girls, and Isabel added as an afterthought: 'Thank you very much indeed, father dear.'

'Come upstairs,' said Linda. 'I'll bring your slippers.'

But the stairs were too narrow for them to go up arm in arm. It was quite dark in the room. He heard her ring tapping on the marble mantelpiece as she felt for the matches.

'I've got some, darling. I'll light the candles.'

But instead he came up behind her and again he put his arms round her and pressed her head into his shoulder.

'I'm so confoundedly happy,' he said.

'Are you?' She turned and put her hands on his breast and looked up at him.

'I don't know what has come over me,' he protested.

It was quite dark outside now and heavy dew was falling. When Linda shut the window the cold dew touched her finger tips. Far away a dog barked. 'I believe there is going to be a moon,' she said.

At the words, and with the cold wet dew on her fingers, she felt as thought the moon had risen—that she was being strangely discovered in a flood of cold light. She shivered; she came away from the window and sat down upon the box ottoman beside Stanley.

In the dining-room, by the flicker of a wood fire, Beryl sat on a hassock playing the guitar. She had bathed and changed all her clothes. Now she wore a white muslin dress with black spots on it and in her hair she had pinned a black silk rose.

> Nature has gone to her rest, love,
> See, we are alone.
> Give me your hand to press, love,
> Lightly within my own.

She played and sang half to herself, for she was watching herself playing and singing. The firelight gleamed on her shoes, on the ruddy belly of the guitar, and on her white fingers....

'If I were outside the window and looked in and saw myself I really would be rather struck,' thought she. Still more softly she played the accompaniment—not singing now but listening.

'... The first time that I ever saw you, little girl—oh, you had no idea that you were not alone—you were sitting with your little feet upon a hassock, playing the guitar. God, I can never forget....' Beryl flung up her head and began to sing again:

'Even the moon is aweary ...'

But there came a loud bang at the door. The servant girl's crimson face popped through.

'Please, Miss Beryl, I've got to come and lay.'

'Certainly, Alice,' said Beryl, in a voice of ice. She put the guitar in a corner. Alice lunged in with a heavy black iron tray.

'Well, I have had a job with that oving,' said she. 'I can't get nothing to brown.'

'Really!' said Beryl.

But no, she could not stand that fool of a girl. She ran into the dark drawing-room and began walking up and down.... Oh, she was restless, restless. There was a mirror over the mantel. She leaned her arms along and looked at her pale shadow in it. How beautiful she looked, but there was nobody to see, nobody.

'Why must you suffer so?' said the face in the mirror. 'You were not made for suffering.... Smile!'

Beryl smiled, and really her smile was so adorable that she smiled again—but this time because she could not help it.

VIII

'Good morning, Mrs Jones.'

'Oh, good morning, Mrs Smith. I'm so glad to see you. Have you brought your children?'

'Yes, I've brought both my twins. I have had another baby since I saw you last, but she came so suddenly that I haven't had time to make her any clothes yet. So I left her.... How is your husband?'

'Oh, he is very well, thank you. At least he had an awful cold but Queen Victoria—she's my godmother, you know—sent him a case of pineapples and that cured it im—mediately. Is that your new servant?'

'Yes, her name's Gwen. I've only had her two days. Oh, Gwen, this is my friend, Mrs Smith.'

'Good morning, Mrs Smith. Dinner won't be ready for about ten minutes.'

'I don't think you ought to introduce me to the servant. I think I ought to just begin talking to her.'

'Well, she's more of a lady-help than a servant and you do introduce lady-helps, I know, because Mrs Samuel Josephs had one.'

'Oh, well, it doesn't matter,' said the servant carelessly, beating up a chocolate custard with half a broken clothes peg. The dinner was baking beautifully on a concrete step. She began to lay the cloth on a pink garden seat. In front of each person she put two geranium leaf plates, a pine needle fork and a twig knife. There were three daisy heads on a laurel leaf for poached eggs, some slices of fuchsia petal cold beef, some lovely little rissoles made of earth and water and dandelion seeds, and the chocolate custard which she had decided to serve in the pawa shell she had cooked it in.

'You needn't trouble about my children,' said Mrs Smith graciously. 'If you'll just take this bottle and fill it at the tap—I mean at the dairy.'

'Oh, all right,' said Gwen, and she whispered to Mrs Jones: 'Shall I go and ask Alice for a little bit of real milk?'

But someone called from the front of the house and the luncheon party melted away, leaving the charming table, leaving the rissoles and the poached eggs to the ants and to an old snail who pushed his quivering horns over the edge of the garden seat and began to nibble a geranium plate.

'Come round to the front, children. Pip and Rags have come.'

The Trout boys were the cousins Kezia had mentioned to the storeman. They lived about a mile away in a house called Monkey Tree Cottage. Pip was tall for his age, with lank black hair and a white face, but Rags was very small and so thin that when he was undressed his shoulder blades stuck out like two little wings. They had a mongrel dog with pale blue eyes and a long tail turned up at the end who followed them everywhere; he was called Snooker. They spent half their time combing and brushing Snooker and dosing him with various awful mixtures concocted by Pip, and kept secretly by him in a broken jug covered with an old kettle lid. Even faithful little Rags was not allowed to know the full secret of these mixtures.... Take some carbolic tooth powder and a pinch of sulphur powdered up fine, and perhaps a bit of starch to stiffen up Snooker's coat.... But that was not all; Rags privately thought that the rest was gun-powder.... And he never was allowed to help with the mixing because of the danger.... 'Why, if a spot of this flew in your eye, you would be blinded for life,' Pip would say, stirring the mixture with an iron spoon. 'And there's always the chance—just the chance, mind you—of it exploding if you whack it hard enough.... Two spoons of this in a kerosene tin will be enough to kill thousands of fleas.' But Snooker spent all his spare time biting and snuffling, and he stank abominably.

'It's because he is such a grand fighting dog,' Pip would say. 'All fighting dogs smell.'

The Trout boys had often spent the day with the Burnells in town, but now that they lived in this fine house and boncer garden they were inclined to be very friendly. Besides, both of them liked playing with girls—Pip, because he could fox them so, and because Lottie was so easily frightened, and Rags for a shameful reason. He adored dolls. How he would look at a doll as it lay asleep, speaking in a whisper and smiling timidly, and what a treat it was to him to be allowed to hold one....

'Curve your arms round her. Don't keep them stiff like that. You'll drop her,' Isabel would say sternly.

Now they were standing on the veranda and holding back Snooker, who wanted to go into the house but wasn't allowed to because Aunt Linda hated decent dogs.

'We came over in the bus with mum,' they said, 'and we're going to spend the afternoon with you. We brought over a batch of our gingerbread for Aunt Linda. Our Minnie made it. It's all over nuts.'

'I skinned the almonds,' said Pip. 'I just stuck my hand into a saucepan of boiling water and grabbed them out and gave them a kind of pinch and the nuts flew out of the skins, some of them as high as the ceiling. Didn't they, Rags?'

Rags nodded. 'When they make cakes at our place,' said Pip, 'we always stay in the kitchen, Rags and me, and I get the bowl and he gets the spoon and the egg-beater. Sponge cake's the best. It's all frothy stuff, then.'

He ran down the veranda steps to the lawn, planted his hands on the grass, bent forward, and just did not stand on his head.

'That lawn's all bumpy,' he said. 'You have to have a flat place for standing on your head. I can walk round the monkey tree on my head at our place. Can't I, Rags?'

'Nearly,' said Rags faintly.

'Stand on your head on the veranda. That's quite flat,' said Kezia.

'No, smarty,' said Pip. 'You have to do it on something soft. Because if you give a jerk and fall over, something in your neck goes click, and it breaks off. Dad told me.'

'Oh, do let's play something,' said Kezia.

'Very well,' said Isabel quickly, 'we'll play hospitals. I will be the nurse and Pip can be the doctor and you and Lottie and Rags can be the sick people.'

Lottie didn't want to play that, because last time Pip had squeezed something down her throat and it hurt awfully.

'Pooh,' scoffed Pip. 'It was only the juice out of a bit of mandarin peel.'

'Well, let's play ladies,' said Isabel. 'Pip can be the father and you can be all our dear little children.'

'I hate playing ladies,' said Kezia. 'You always make us go to church hand in hand and come home and go to bed.'

Suddenly Pip took a filthy handkerchief out of his pocket. 'Snooker! Here, sir,' he called. But Snooker, as usual, tried to sneak away, his tail between his legs. Pip leapt on top of him, and pressed him between his knees.

'Keep his head firm, Rags,' he said, and he tied the handkerchief round Snooker's head with a funny knot sticking up at the top.

'Whatever is that for?' asked Lottie.

'It's to train his ears to grow more close to his head—see?' said Pip. 'All fighting dogs have ears that lie back. But Snooker's ears are a bit too soft.'

'I know,' said Kezia. 'They are always turning inside out. I hate that.'

Snooker lay down, made one feeble effort with his paw to get the handkerchief off, but finding he could not, trailed after the children, shivering with misery.

IX

Pat came swinging along; in his hand he held a little tomahawk that winked in the sun.

'Come with me,' he said to the children, 'and I'll show you how the kings of Ireland chop the head off a duck.'

They drew back—they didn't believe him, and besides, the Trout boys had never seen Pat before.

'Come on now,' he coaxed, smiling and holding out his hand to Kezia

'Is it a real duck's head? One from the paddock?'

'It is,' said Pat. She put her hand in his hard dry one, and he stuck the tomahawk in his belt and held out the other to Rags. He loved little children.

'I'd better keep hold of Snooker's head if there's going to be any blood about,' said Pip, 'because the sight of blood makes him awfully wild.' He ran ahead dragging Snooker by the handkerchief.

'Do you think we ought to go?' whispered Isabel. 'We haven't asked or anything. Have we?'

At the bottom of the orchard a gate was set in the paling fence. On the other side a steep bank led down to a bridge that spanned the creek, and once up the bank on the other side you were on the fringe of the paddocks. A little old stable in the first paddock had been turned into a fowl-house. The fowls had strayed far away across the paddock down to a dumping ground in a hollow, but the ducks kept close to that part of the creek that flowed under the bridge.

Tall bushes overhung the stream with red leaves and yellow flowers and clusters of blackberries. At some places the stream was wide and shallow, but at others it tumbled into deep little pools with foam at the edges and quivering bubbles. It was in these pools that the big white ducks had made themselves at home, swimming and guzzling along the weedy banks.

Up and down they swam, preening their dazzling breasts, and other ducks with the same dazzling breasts and yellow bills swam upside down with them.

'There is the little Irish navy,' said Pat, 'and look at the old admiral there with the green neck and the grand little flag-staff on his tail.'

He pulled a handful of grain from his pocket and began to walk towards the fowl-house, lazy, his straw hat with the broken crown pulled over his eyes.

'Lid. Lid—lid—lid—lid—' he called.

'Qua. Qua—qua—qua—qua—' answered the ducks, making for land, and flapping and scrambling up the bank they streamed after him in a long waddling line. He coaxed them, pretending to throw the grain, shaking it in his hands and calling to them until they swept round him in a white ring.

From far away the fowls heard the clamour and they too came running across the paddock, their heads thrust forward, their wings spread, turning in their feet in the silly way fowls run and scolding as they came.

Then Pat scattered the grain and the greedy ducks began to gobble. Quickly he stooped, seized two, one under each arm, and strode across to the children. Their darting heads and round eyes frightened the children—all except Pip.

'Come on, sillies,' he cried, 'they can't bite. They haven't any teeth. They've only got those two little holes in their beaks for breathing through.'

'Will you hold one while I finish with the other?' asked Pat. Pip let go of Snooker. 'Won't I? Won't I? Give us one. I don't mind how much he kicks.'

He nearly sobbed with delight when Pat gave the white lump into his arms.

There was an old stump beside the door of the fowl-house. Pat grabbed the duck by the legs, laid it flat across the stump, and almost at the same moment down came the little tomahawk and the duck's head flew off the stump. Up the blood spurted over the white feathers and over his hand.

When the children saw the blood they were frightened no longer. They crowded round him and began to scream. Even Isabel leaped about crying: 'The blood! The blood!' Pip forgot all about his duck. He simply threw it away from him and shouted, 'I saw it. I saw it,' and jumped round the wood block.

Rags, with cheeks as white as paper, ran up to the little head, put out a finger as if he wanted to touch it, shrank back again and then again put out a finger. He was shivering all over.

Even Lottie, frightened little Lottie, began to laugh and pointed at the duck and shrieked: 'Look, Kezia, look.'

'Watch it!' shouted Pat. He put down the body and it began to waddle—with only a long spurt of blood where the head had been; it began to pad away without a sound towards the steep bank that led to the stream. . . . That was the crowning wonder.

'Do you see that? Do you see that?' yelled Pip. He ran among the little girls tugging at their pinafores.

'It's like a little engine. It's like a funny little railway engine,' squealed Isabel.

But Kezia suddenly rushed at Pat and flung her arms round his legs and butted her head as hard as she could against his knees.

'Put head back! Put head back!' she screamed.

When he stooped to move her she would not let go or take her head away. She held on as hard as she could and sobbed: 'Head back! Head back!' until it sounded like a loud strange hiccup.

'It's stopped. It's tumbled over. It's dead,' said Pip.

Pat dragged Kezia up into his arms. Her sun-bonnet had fallen back, but she would not let him look at her face. No, she pressed her face into a bone in his shoulder and clasped her arms round his neck.

The children stopped screaming as suddenly as they had begun. They stood round the dead duck. Rags was not frightened of the head any more. He knelt down and stroked it now.

'I don't think the head is quite dead yet,' he said. 'Do you think it would keep alive if I gave it something to drink?'

But Pip got very cross: 'Bah! You baby.' He whistled to Snooker and went off.

When Isabel went up to Lottie, Lottie snatched away.

'What are you always touching me for, Isabel?'

'There now,' said Pat to Kezia. 'There's the grand little girl.'

She put up her hands and touched his ears. She felt something. Slowly she raised her quivering face and looked. Pat wore little round gold ear-rings. She never knew that men wore ear-rings. She was very much surprised.

'Do they come on and off?' she asked huskily.

X

Up in the house, in the warm tidy kitchen, Alice, the servant girl, was getting the afternoon tea. She was 'dressed'. She had on a black stuff dress that smelt under the arms, a white apron like a large sheet of paper, and a lace bow pinned on to her hair with two jetty pins. Also her comfortable carpet slippers were changed for a pair of black leather ones that pinched her corn on her little toe something dreadful. . . .

It was warm in the kitchen. A blowfly buzzed, a fan of whity steam came out of the kettle, and the lid kept up a rattling jig as the water bubbled. The clock ticked in the warm air, slow and deliberate, like the click of an old woman's knitting needle, and sometimes—for no reason at all, for there wasn't any breeze—the blind swung out and back, tapping the window.

Alice was making watercress sandwiches. She had a lump of butter on the table, a barracouta loaf, and the cresses tumbled in a white cloth.

But propped against the butter dish there was a dirty, greasy little book, half unstitched, with curled edges, and while she mashed the butter she read:

'To dream of black-beetles drawing a hearse is bad. Signifies death of one you hold near or dear, either father, husband, brother, son, or intended. If beetles crawl backwards as you watch them it means death from fire or from great height such as flight of stairs, scaffolding, etc.

Spiders. To dream of spiders creeping over you is good. Signifies large sum of money in near future. Should party be in family way an easy confinement may be expected. But care should be taken in sixth

month to avoid eating of probable present of
shellfish.... '

How many thousand birds I see.

Oh, life. There was Miss Beryl. Alice dropped the knife and
slipped the *Dream Book* under the butter dish. But she hadn't
time to hide it quite, for Beryl ran into the kitchen and up to the
table, and the first thing her eye lighted on were those greasy
edges. Alice saw Miss Beryl's meaning little smile and the way she
raised her eyebrows and screwed up her eyes as though she were
not quite sure what that could be. She decided to answer if Miss
Beryl should ask her: 'Nothing as belongs to you, Miss.' But she
knew Miss Beryl would not ask her.

Alice was a mild creature in reality, but she had the most
marvellous retorts ready for questions that she knew would never
be put to her. The composing of them and the turning of them
over and over in her mind comforted her just as much as if they'd
been expressed. Really, they kept her alive in places where she'd
been that chivvied she'd been afraid to go to bed at night with a
box of matches on the chair in case she bit the tops off in her sleep,
as you might say.

'Oh, Alice,' said Miss Beryl. 'There's one extra to tea, so heat a
plate of yesterday's scones, please. And put on the Victoria
sandwich as well as the coffee cake. And don't forget to put little
doyleys under the plates—will you? You did yesterday, you
know, and the tea looked so ugly and common. And, Alice, don't
put on that dreadful old pink and green cosy on the afternoon
teapot again. That is only for the mornings. Really, I think it
ought to be kept for the kitchen—it's so shabby, and quite smelly.
Put on the Japanese one. You quite understand, don't you?'

Miss Beryl had finished.

'That sing aloud from every tree ... '

she sang as she left the kitchen, very pleased with her firm
handling of Alice.

Oh, Alice was wild. She wasn't one to mind being told, but

there was something in the way Miss Beryl had of speaking to her that she couldn't stand. Oh, that she couldn't. It made her curl up inside, as you might say, and she fair trembled. But what Alice really hated Miss Beryl for was that she made her feel low. She talked to Alice in a special voice as though she wasn't quite all there; and she never lost her temper with her—never. Even when Alice dropped anything or forgot anything important Miss Beryl seemed to have expected it to happen.

'If you please, Mrs. Burnell,' said an imaginary Alice, as she buttered the scones, 'I'd rather not take my orders from Miss Beryl. I may be only a common servant girl as doesn't know how to play the guitar, but ... '

This last thrust pleased her so much that she quite recovered her temper.

'The only thing to do,' she heard, as she opened the dining-room door, 'is to cut the sleeves out entirely and just have a broad band of black velvet over the shoulders instead .... '

XI

The white duck did not look as if it had ever had a head when Alice placed it in front of Stanley Burnell that night. It lay, in beautifully basted resignation, on a blue dish—its legs tied together with a piece of string and a wreath of little balls of stuffing round it.

It was hard to say which of the two, Alice or the duck, looked the better basted; they were both such a rich colour and they both had the same air of gloss and strain. But Alice was fiery red and the duck a Spanish mahogany.

Burnell ran his eye along the edge of the carving knife. He prided himself very much upon his carving, upon making a first-class job of it. He hated seeing a woman carve; they were always too slow and they never seemed to care what the meat looked like afterwards. Now he did; he took a real pride in cutting delicate shaves of cold beef, little wads of mutton, just the right thickness, and in dividing a chicken or a duck with nice precision ....

'Is this the first of the home products?' he asked, knowing perfectly well that it was.

'Yes, the butcher did not come. We have found out that he only calls twice a week.'

But there was no need to apologise. It was a superb bird. It wasn't meat at all, but a kind of very superior jelly. 'My father would say,' said Burnell, 'this must have been one of those birds whose mother played to it in infancy upon the German flute. And the sweet strains of the dulcet instrument acted with such effect upon the infant mind . . . Have some more, Beryl? You and I are the only ones in this house with a real feeling for food. I'm perfectly willing to state, in a court of law, if necessary, that I love good food.'

Tea was served in the drawing-room, and Beryl, who for some reason had been very charming to Stanley ever since he came home, suggested a game of crib. They sat at a little table near one of the open windows. Mrs Fairfield disappeared, and Linda lay in a rocking-chair, her arms above her head, rocking to and fro.

'You don't want the light—do you, Linda?' said Beryl. She moved the tall lamp so that she sat under its soft light.

How remote they looked, those two, from where Linda sat and rocked. The green table, the polished cards, Stanley's big hands and Beryl's tiny ones, all seemed to be part of one mysterious movement. Stanley himself, big and solid, in his dark suit, took his ease, and Beryl tossed her bright head and pouted. Round her throat she wore an unfamiliar velvet ribbon. It changed her, somehow—altered the shape of her face—but it was charming, Linda decided. The room smelled of lilies; there were two big jars of arums in the fireplace.

'Fifteen two—fifteen four—and a pair is six and a run of three is nine,' said Stanley, so deliberately, he might have been counting sheep.

'I've nothing but two pairs,' said Beryl, exaggerating her woe because she knew how he loved winning.

The cribbage pegs were like two little people going up the road together, turning round the sharp corner, and coming down the road again. They were pursuing each other. They did not so much want to get ahead as to keep near enough to talk—to keep near, perhaps that was all.

But no, there was always one who was impatient and hopped

away as the other came up, and would not listen. Perhaps the white peg was frightened of the red one, or perhaps he was cruel and would not give the red one a chance to speak....

In the front of her dress Beryl wore a bunch of pansies, and once when the little pegs were side by side, she bent over and the pansies dropped out and covered them.

'What a shame,' said she, picking up the pansies. 'Just as they had a chance to fly into each other's arms.'

'Farewell, my girl,' laughed Stanley, and away the red peg hopped.

The drawing-room was long and narrow with glass doors that gave on to the veranda. It had a cream paper with a pattern of gilt roses, and the furniture, which had belonged to old Mrs Fairfield, was dark and plain. A little piano stood against the wall with yellow pleated silk let into the carved front. Above it hung an oil painting by Beryl of a large cluster of surprised-looking clematis. Each flower was the size of a small saucer, with a centre like an astonished eye fringed in black. But the room was not finished yet. Stanley had set his heart on a Chesterfield and two decent chairs. Linda liked it best as it was....

Two big moths flew in through the window and round and round the circle of lamplight.

'Fly away before it is too late. Fly out again.'

Round and round flew; they seemed to bring the silence and the moonlight in with them on their silent wings....

'I've two kings,' said Stanley. 'Any good?'

'Quite good,' said Beryl.

Linda stopped rocking and got up. Stanley looked across. 'Anything the matter, darling?'

'No, nothing. I'm going to find mother.'

She went out of the room and standing at the foot of the stairs she called, but her mother's voice answered her from the veranda.

The moon that Lottie and Kezia had seen from the storeman's wagon was full, and the house, the garden, the old woman and Linda—all were bathed in dazzling light.

'I have been looking at the aloe,' said Mrs Fairfield. 'I believe it is going to flower this year. Look at the top there. Are those buds, or is it only an effect of light?'

As they stood on the steps, the high grassy bank on which the aloe rested rose up like a wave, and the aloe seemed to ride upon it like a ship with the oars lifted. Bright moonlight hung upon the lifted oars like water, and on the green wave glittered the dew.

'Do you feel it, too,' said Linda, and she spoke to her mother with the special voice that women use at night to each other as though they spoke in their sleep or from some hollow cave—'Don't you feel that it is coming towards us?'

She dreamed that she was caught up out of the cold water into the ship with the lifted oars and the budding mast. Now the oars fell striking quickly, quickly. They rowed far away over the top of the garden trees, the paddocks and the dark bush beyond. Ah, she heard herself cry: 'Faster! Faster!' to those who were rowing.

How much more real this dream was than that they should go back to the house where the sleeping children lay and where Stanley and Beryl played cribbage.

'I believe those are buds,' said she. 'Let us go down into the garden, mother. I like that aloe. I like it more than anything here. And I am sure I shall remember it long after I've forgotten all the other things.'

She put her hand on her mother's arm and they walked down the steps, round the island and on to the main drive that led to the front gates.

Looking at it from below she could see the long sharp thorns that edged the aloe leaves, and at the sight of them her heart grew hard. . . . She particularly liked the long sharp thorns. . . . Nobody would dare to come near the ship or to follow after.

'Not even my Newfoundland dog,' thought she, 'that I'm so fond of in the daytime.'

For she really was fond of him; she loved and admired and respected him tremendously. Oh, better than anyone else in the world. She knew him through and through. He was the soul of truth and decency, and for all his practical experience he was awfully simple, easily pleased and easily hurt. . . .

If only he wouldn't jump at her so, and bark so loudly, and watch her with such eager, loving eyes. He was too strong for her; she had always hated things that rush at her, from a child. There were times when he was frightening—really frightening. When she just had not screamed at the top of her voice: 'You are killing me.' And at those times she had longed to say the most coarse, hateful things....

'You know I'm very delicate. You know as well as I do that my heart is affected, and the doctor has told you I may die any moment. I have had three great lumps of children already....'

Yes, yes, it was true. Linda snatched her hand from mother's arm. For all her love and respect and admiration she hated him. And how tender he always was after times like those, how submissive, how thoughtful. He would do anything for her; he longed to serve her.... Linda heard herself saying in a weak voice:

'Stanley, would you light a candle?'

And she heard his joyful voice answer: 'Of course I will, my darling.' And he leapt out of bed as though he were going to leap at the moon for her.

It had never been so plain to her as it was as this moment. There were all her feelings for him, sharp and defined, one as true as the other. And there was this other, this hatred, just as real as the rest. She could have done her feelings up in little packets and given them to Stanley. She longed to hand him that last one, for a surprise. She could see his eyes as he opened that....

She hugged her folded arms and began to laugh silently. How absurd life was—it was laughable, simply laughable. And why this mania of hers to keep alive at all? For it really was a mania, she thought, mocking and laughing.

'What am I guarding myself for so preciously? I shall go on having children and Stanley will go on making money and the children and the gardens will grow bigger and bigger, with whole fleets of aloes in them for me to choose from.'

She had been walking with her head bent, looking at nothing. Now she looked up and about her. They were standing by the red and white camellia trees. Beautiful were the rich dark leaves spangled with light and the round flowers that perch among them like red and white birds. Linda pulled a piece of verbena and crumpled it, and held her hands to her mother.

'Delicious,' said the old woman. 'Are you cold, child? Are you trembling? Yes, your hands are cold. We had better go back to the house.'

'What have you been thinking about?' said Linda. 'Tell me.'

'I haven't really been thinking of anything. I wondered as we passed the orchard what the fruit trees were like and whether we should be able to make much jam this autumn. There are splendid healthy currant bushes in the vegetable garden. I noticed them today. I should like to see those pantry shelves thoroughly well stocked with our own jam....'

XII

'MY DARLING NAN,

Don't think me a piggy wig because I haven't written before. I haven't had a moment, dear, and even now I feel so exhausted that I can hardly hold a pen.

Well, the dreadful deed is done. We have actually left the giddy whirl of town, and I can't see how we shall ever go back again, for my brother-in-law has bought this house "lock, stock and barrel," to use his own words.

In a way, or course, it is an awful relief, for he has been threatening to take a place in the country ever since I've lived with them—and I must say the house and garden are awfully nice—a million times better than that awful cubby-hole in town.

But buried, my dear. Buried isn't the word.

We have got neighbours, but they are only farmers—big louts of boys who seem to be milking all day, and two dreadful females with rabbit teeth who brought us some scones when we were moving and said they would be pleased to help. But my sister who lives a mile away doesn't know a soul here, so I am sure we never shall. It's pretty certain nobody will ever come out from town to see us, because though there is a bus it's an awful old rattling thing with black leather sides that any decent person would rather die than ride in for six miles.

Such a life. It's a sad ending for poor little B. I'll get to be a most awful frump in a year or two and come and see you in a mackintosh and a sailor hat tied on with a white china silk motor veil. So pretty.

Stanley says that now we are settled—for after the most awful week of my life we really are settled—he is going to bring out a couple of men from the club on Saturday afternoons for tennis. In fact, two are promised as a great treat today. But, my dear, if you could see Stanley's men from the club ... rather fattish, the type who look frightfully indecent without waistcoats—always with toes that turn in rather—so conspicuous when you are walking about a court in white shoes. And they are pulling up their trousers every minute—don't you know—and whacking at imaginary things with their rackets.

I used to play with them at the club last summer, and I am sure you will know the type when I tell you that after I'd been there about three times they all called me Miss Beryl. It's a dreary world. Of course mother simply loves the place, but then I suppose when I am mother's age I shall be content to sit in the sun and shell peas into a basin. But I'm not—not—not.

What Linda thinks about the whole affair, per usual, I haven't the slightest idea. Mysterious as ever....

My dear, you know that white satin dress of mine. I have taken the sleeves out entirely, put bands of black velvet across the shoulders and two big red poppies off my dear sister's *chapeau*. It is a great success, though when I shall wear it I do not know.'

Beryl sat writing this letter at a little table in her room. In a way, of course, it was all perfectly true, but in another way it was all the greatest rubbish and she didn't believe a word of it. No, that wasn't true. She felt all those things, but she didn't really feel them like that.

It was her other self who had written that letter. It not only bored, it rather disgusted her real self.

'Flippant and silly,' said her real self. Yet she knew that she'd send it and she'd always write that kind of twaddle to Nan Pym. In fact, it was a very mild example of the kind of letter she generally wrote.

Beryl leaned her elbows on the table and read it through again. The voice of the letter seemed to come up to her from the page. It was faint already, like a voice heard over the telephone, high, gushing, with something bitter in the sound. Oh, she detested it today.

'You've always got so much animation,' said Nan Pym. 'That's why men are so keen on you.' And she had added, rather mournfully, for men were not at all keen on Nan, who was a solid kind of girl, with fat hips and a high colour—'I can't understand how you can keep it up. But it is your nature, I suppose.'

What rot. What nonsense. It wasn't her nature at all. Good heavens, if she had ever been her real self with Nan Pym, Nannie would have jumped out of the window with surprise.... My dear, you know that white satin of mine.... Beryl slammed the letter-case to.

She jumped up and half unconsciously, half consciously she drifted over to the looking-glass.

There stood a slim girl in white—a white serge skirt, a white silk blouse, and a leather belt drawn in very tightly at her tiny waist.

Her face was heart-shaped, wide at the brows and with a pointed chin—but not too pointed. Her eyes, her eyes were perhaps her best feature; they were such a strange uncommon colour—greeny blue with little gold points in them.

She had fine black eyebrows and long lashes—so long, that when they lay on her cheeks you positively caught the light in them, someone or other had told her.

Her mouth was rather large. Too large? No, not really. Her underlip protruded a little; she had a way of sucking it in that somebody else had told her was awfully fascinating.

Her nose was her least satisfactory feature. Not that it was really ugly. But it was not half as fine as Linda's. Linda really had a perfect little nose. Hers spread rather—not badly. And in all probability she exaggerated the spreadiness of it just because it was her nose, and she was so awfully critical of herself. She pinched it with a thumb and first finger and made a little face....

Lovely, lovely hair. And such a mass of it. It had the colour of fresh fallen leaves, brown and red with a glint of yellow. When she did it in a long plait she felt it on her backbone like a long snake. She loved to feel the weight of it dragging her head back, and she loved to feel it loose, covering her bare arms. 'Yes, my dear, there is no doubt about it; you really are a lovely little thing.'

At the words her bosom lifted; she took a long breath of delight, half closing her eyes.

But even as she looked the smile faded from her lips and eyes. Oh, God, there she was, back again, playing the same old game.

False—false as ever. False as when she'd written to Nan Pym. False even when she was alone with herself, now.

What had that creature in the glass to do with her, and why was she staring? She dropped down to one side of her bed and buried her face in her arms.

'Oh,' she cried, 'I am so miserable—so frightfully miserable. I know that I'm silly and spiteful and vain; I'm always acting a part. I'm never my real self for a moment.' And plainly, plainly, she saw her false self running up and down the stairs, laughing a special trilling laugh if they had visitors, standing under the lamp if a man came to dinner, so that he should see the light on her hair, pouting and pretending to be a little girl when she was asked to play the guitar. Why? She even kept it up for Stanley's benefit. Only last night when he was reading the paper her false self had stood beside him and leaned against his shoulder on purpose. Hadn't she put her hand over his, pointing out something so that he should see how white her hand was beside his brown one.

How despicable! Despicable! Her heart was cold with rage. 'It's marvellous how you keep it up,' said she to the false self. But then it was only because she was so miserable—so miserable. If she had been happy and leading her own life, her false life would cease to be. She saw the real Beryl—a shadow . . . a shadow. Faint and unsubstantial she shone. What was there of her except the radiance? And for what tiny moments she was really she. Beryl could almost remember every one of them. At those times she had felt: 'Life is rich and mysterious and good, and I am rich and mysterious and good, too.' Shall I ever be that Beryl for ever? Shall I? How can I? And was there ever a time when I did not have a false self? . . . But just as she had got that far she heard the sound of little steps running along the passage; the door handle rattled. Kezia came in.

'Aunt Beryl, mother says will you please come down? Father is home with a man and lunch is ready.'

Botheration! How she had crumpled her skirt, kneeling in that idiotic way.

'Very well, Kezia.' She went over to the dressing-table and powdered her nose.

Kezia crossed too, and unscrewed a little pot of cream and sniffed it. Under her arm she carried a very dirty calico cat.

When Aunt Beryl ran out of the room she sat the cat up on the dressing-table and stuck the top of the cream jar over its ear.

'Now look at yourself,' she said sternly.

The calico cat was so overcome by the sight that it toppled over backwards and bumped and bumped on to the floor. And the top of the cream jar flew through the air and rolled like a penny in a round on the linoleum—and did not break.

But for Kezia it had broken the moment it flew through the air, and she picked it up, hot all over, and put it back on the dressing-table.

Then she tiptoed away, far too quickly and airily. . . .

Bliss

Although Bertha Young was thirty she still had moments like this when she wanted to run instead of walk, to take dancing steps on and off the pavement, to bowl a hoop, to throw something up in the air and catch it again, or to stand still and laugh at—nothing—at nothing, simply.

What can you do if you are thirty and, turning the corner of your own street, you are overcome, suddenly by a feeling of bliss—absolute bliss!—as though you'd suddenly swallowed a bright piece of that late afternoon sun and it burned in your bosom, sending out a little shower of sparks into every particle, into every finger and toe? . . .

Oh, is there no way you can express it without being 'drunk and disorderly'? How idiotic civilisation is! Why be given a body if you have to keep it shut up in a case like a rare, rare fiddle?

'No, that about the fiddle is not quite what I mean,' she thought, running up the steps and feeling in her bag for the key—she'd forgotten it, as usual—and rattling the letter-box. 'It's not what I mean, because— Thank you, Mary'—she went into the hall. 'Is nurse back?'

'Yes, M'm.'

'And has the fruit come?'

'Yes, M'm. Everything's come.'

'Bring the fruit up to the dining-room, will you? I'll arrange it before I go upstairs.'

It was dusky in the dining-room and quite chilly. But all the same Bertha threw off her coat; she could not bear the tight clasp of it another moment, and the cold air fell on her arms.

But in her bosom there was still that bright glowing place—that shower of little sparks coming from it. It was almost unbearable. She hardly dared to breathe for fear of fanning it higher, and yet she breathed deeply, deeply. She hardly dared to look into the cold mirror—but she did look, and it gave her back a woman, radiant, with smiling, trembling lips, with big, dark eyes and an air of listening, waiting for something . . . divine to happen . . . that she knew must happen . . . infallibly.

Mary brought in the fruit on a tray and with it a glass bowl, and a blue dish, very lovely, with a strange sheen on it as though it had been dipped in milk.

'Shall I turn on the light, M'm?'

'No, thank you. I can see quite well.'

There were tangerines and apples stained with strawberry pink. Some yellow pears, smooth as silk, some white grapes covered with a silver bloom and a big cluster of purple ones. These last she had bought to tone in with the new dining-room carpet. Yes, that did sound rather far-fetched and absurd, but it was really why she had bought them. She had thought in the shop: 'I must have some purple ones to bring the carpet up to the table.' And it had seemed quite sense at the time.

When she had finished with them and had made two pyramids of these bright round shapes, she stood away from the table to get the effect—and it really was most curious. For the dark table seemed to melt into the dusky light and the glass dish and the blue bowl to float in the air. This, of course, in her present mood, was so incredibly beautiful.... She began to laugh.

'No, no. I'm getting hysterical.' And she seized her bag and coat and ran upstairs to the nursery.

Nurse sat at a low table giving Little B her supper after her bath. The baby had on a white flannel gown and a blue woollen jacket, and her dark, fine hair was brushed up into a funny little peak. She looked up when she saw her mother and began to jump.

'Now, my lovey, eat it up like a good girl,' said nurse, setting her lips in a way that Bertha knew, and that meant she had come into the nursery at another wrong moment.

'Has she been good, Nanny?'

'She's been a little sweet all the afternoon,' whispered Nanny. 'We went to the park and I sat down on a chair and took her out of the pram and a big dog came along and put its head on my knee and she clutched its ear, tugged it. Oh, you should have seen her.'

Bertha wanted to ask if it wasn't rather dangerous to let her clutch at a strange dog's ear. But she did not dare to. She stood watching them, her hands by her side, like the poor little girl in front of the rich girl with the doll.

The baby looked up at her again, stared, and then smiled so charmingly that Bertha couldn't help crying:

'Oh, Nanny, do let me finish giving her her supper while you put the bath things away.'

'Well, M'm, she oughtn't to be changed hands while she's eating,' said Nanny, still whispering. 'It unsettles her; it's very likely to upset her.'

How absurd it was. Why have a baby if it has to be kept—not in a case like a rare, rare fiddle—but in another woman's arms?

'Oh, I must!' said she.

Very offended, Nanny handed her over.

'Now, don't excite her after her supper. You know you do, M'm. And I have such a time with her after!'

Thank heaven! Nanny went out of the room with the bath towels.

'Now I've got you to myself, my little precious,' said Bertha, as the baby leaned against her.

She ate delightfully, holding up her lips for the spoon and then waving her hands. Sometimes she wouldn't let the spoon go; and sometimes, just as Bertha had filled it, she waved it away to the four winds.

When the soup was finished Bertha turned round to the fire.

'You're nice—you're very nice!' said she, kissing her warm baby. 'I'm fond of you. I like you.'

And indeed, she loved Little B so much—her neck as she bent forward, her exquisite toes as they shone transparent in the firelight—that all her feeling of bliss came back again, and again she didn't know how to express it—what to do with it.

'You're wanted on the telephone,' said Nanny, coming back in triumph and seizing *her* Little B.

Down she flew. It was Harry.

'Oh, is that you, Ber? Look here. I'll be late. I'll take a taxi and come along as quickly as I can, but get dinner put back ten minutes—will you? All right?'

'Yes, perfectly. Oh, Harry!'

'Yes?'

What had she to say? She'd nothing to say. She only wanted to get in touch with him for a moment. She couldn't absurdly cry: 'Hasn't it been a divine day?'

'What is it?' rapped out the little voice.

'Nothing. *Entendu*,' said Bertha, and hung up the receiver, thinking how much more than idiotic civilisation was.

They had people coming to dinner. The Norman Knights—a very sound couple—he was about to start a theatre, and she was awfully keen on interior decoration, a young man, Eddie Warren, who had just published a little book of poems and whom everybody was asking to dine, and a 'find' of Bertha's called Pearl Fulton. What Miss Fulton did, Bertha didn't know. They had met at the club and Bertha had fallen in love with her, as she always did fall in love with beautiful women who had something strange about them.

The provoking thing was that, though they had been about together and met a number of times and really talked, Bertha couldn't make her out. Up to a certain point Miss Fulton was rarely, wonderfully frank, but the certain point was there, and beyond that she would not go.

Was there anything beyond it? Harry said 'No.' Voted her dullish, and 'cold like all blonde women, with a touch, perhaps, of anaemia of the brain.' But Bertha wouldn't agree with him; not yet, at any rate.

'No, the way she has of sitting with her head a little on one side, and smiling, has something behind it, Harry, and I must find out what that something is.'

'Most likely it's a good stomach,' answered Harry.

He made a point of catching Bertha's heels with replies of that kind ... 'liver frozen, my dear girl,' or 'pure flatulence,' or 'kidney disease,' ... and so on. For some strange reason Bertha liked this, and almost admired it in him very much.

She went into the drawing-room and lighted the fire; then, picking up the cushions, one by one, that Mary had disposed so carefully, she threw them back on to the chairs and the couches. That made all the difference; the room came alive at once. As she was about to throw the last one she surprised herself by suddenly hugging it to her, passionately, passionately. But it did not put out the fire in her bosom. Oh, on the contrary!

The windows of the drawing-room opened on to a balcony overlooking the garden. At the far end, against the wall, there was a tall, slender pear tree in fullest, richest bloom; it stood perfect, as though becalmed against the jade-green sky. Bertha couldn't help feeling, even from this distance, that it had not a single bud or a faded petal. Down below, in the garden beds, the red and yellow tulips, heavy with flowers, seemed to lean upon the dusk. A grey cat, dragging its belly, crept across the lawn, and a black one, its shadow, trailed after. The sight of them, so intent and so quick, gave Bertha a curious shiver.

'What creepy things cats are!' she stammered, and she turned away from the window and began walking up and down....

How strong the jonquils smelled in the warm room. Too strong? Oh, no. And yet, as though overcome, she flung down on a couch and pressed her hands to her eyes.

'I'm too happy—too happy!' she murmured.

And she seemed to see on her eyelids the lovely pear tree with its wide open blossoms as a symbol of her own life.

Really—really—she had everything. She was young. Harry and she were as much in love as ever, and they got on together splendidly and were really good pals. She had an adorable baby. They didn't have to worry about money. They had this absolutely satisfactory house and garden. And friends—modern, thrilling friends, writers and painters and poets or people keen on social questions—just the kind of friends they wanted. And then there were books, and there was music, and she had found a wonderful little dressmaker, and they were going abroad in the summer, and their new cook made the most superb omelettes....

'I'm absurd. Absurd!' She sat up; but she felt quite dizzy, quite drunk. It must have been the spring.

Yes, it was the spring. Now she was so tired she could not drag herself upstairs to dress.

A white dress, a string of jade beads, green shoes and stockings. It wasn't intentional. She had thought of this scheme hours before she stood at the drawing-room window.

Her petals rustled softly into the hall, and she kissed Mrs Norman Knight, who was taking off the most amusing orange coat with a procession of black monkeys round the hem and up the fronts.

' ... Why! Why! Why is the middle-class so stodgy—so utterly without a sense of humour! My dear, it's only by a fluke that I am here at all—Norman being the protective fluke. For my darling monkeys so upset the train that it rose to a man and simply ate me with its eyes. Didn't laugh—wasn't amused—that I should have loved. No, just stared—and bored me through and through.'

'But the cream of it was,' said Norman, pressing a large tortoiseshell-rimmed monocle into his eye, 'you don't mind me telling this, Face, do you?' (In their home and among their friends they called each other Face and Mug.) 'The cream of it was when she, being full fed, turned to the woman beside her and said: "Haven't you ever seen a monkey before?"'

'Oh, yes!' Mrs Norman Knight joined in the laughter. 'Wasn't that too absolutely creamy?'

And a funnier thing still was that now her coat was off she did look like a very intelligent monkey—who had even made that yellow silk dress out of scraped banana skins. And her amber ear-rings: they were like little dangling nuts.

'This is a sad, sad fall!' said Mug, pausing in front of Little B's perambulator. 'When the perambulator comes into the hall—' and he waved the rest of the quotation away.

The bell rang. It was lean, pale Eddie Warren (as usual) in a state of acute distress.

'It *is* the right house, *isn't it?*' he pleaded.

'Oh, I think so—I hope so,' said Bertha brightly.

'I have had such a *dreadful* experience with a taxi-man; he was *most* sinister. I couldn't get him to *stop*. The *more* I knocked and called the *faster* he went. And *in* the moonlight this *bizarre* figure with the *flattened* head *crouching* over the *lit-tle* wheel ... '

He shuddered, taking off an immense white silk scarf. Bertha noticed that his socks were white, too—most charming.

'But how dreadful!' she cried.

'Yes, it really was,' said Eddie, following her into the

drawing-room. 'I saw myself *driving* through Eternity in a *timeless* taxi.'

He knew the Norman Knights. In fact, he was going to write a play for N.K. when the theatre scheme came off.

'Well, Warren, how's the play?' said Norman Knight, dropping his monocle and giving his eye a moment in which to rise to the surface before it was screwed down again.

And Mrs Norman Knight: 'Oh, Mr Warren, what happy socks?'

'I *am* so glad you like them,' said he, staring at his feet. 'They seem to have got so *much* whiter since the moon rose.' And he turned his lean sorrowful young face to Bertha. 'There *is* a moon, you know.'

She wanted to cry: 'I am sure there is—often—often!'

He really was a most attractive person. But so was Face, crouched before the fire in her banana skins, and so was Mug, smoking a cigarette and saying as he flicked the ash: 'Why doth the bridegroom tarry?'

'There he is, now.'

Bang went the front door open and shut. Harry shouted: 'Hullo, you people. Down in five minutes.' And they heard him swarm up the stairs. Bertha couldn't help smiling; she knew how he loved doing things at high pressure. What, after all, did an extra five minutes matter? But he would pretend to himself that they mattered beyond measure. And then he would make a great point of coming into the drawing-room, extravagantly cool and collected.

Harry had such a zest for life. Oh, how she appreciated it in him. And his passion for fighting—for seeking in everything that came up against him another test of his power and of his courage—that, too, she understood. Even when it made him just occasionally, to other people, who didn't know him well, a little ridiculous perhaps .... For there were moments when he rushed into battle where no battle was.... She talked and laughed and positively forgot until he had come in (just as she had imagined) that Pearl Fulton had not turned up.

'I wonder if Miss Fulton has forgotten?'

'I expect so,' said Harry. 'Is she on the 'phone?'

'Ah! There's a taxi now.' And Bertha smiled with that little air of proprietorship that she always assumed while her women finds were new and mysterious. 'She lives in taxis.'

'She'll run to fat if she does,' said Harry coolly, ringing the bell for dinner. 'Frightful danger for blonde women.'

'Harry—don't!' warned Bertha, laughing up at him.

Came another tiny moment, while they waited, laughing and talking, just a trifle too much at their ease, a trifle too unaware. And then Miss Fulton, all in silver, with a silver fillet binding her pale blonde hair, came in smiling, her head a little on one side.

'Am I late?'

'No, not at all,' said Bertha. 'Come along.' And she took her arm and they moved into the dining-room.

What was there in the touch of that cool arm that could fan—fan—start blazing—blazing—the fire of bliss that Bertha did not know what to do with?

Miss Fulton did not look at her; but then she seldom did look at people directly. Her heavy eyelids lay upon her eyes and the strange half-smile came and went upon her lips as though she lived by listening rather than seeing. But Bertha knew, suddenly, as if the longest, most intimate look had passed between them—as if they had said to each other: 'You too?'—that Pearl Fulton, stirring the beautiful red soup in the grey plate, was feeling just what she was feeling.

And the others? Face and Mug, Eddie and Harry, their spoons rising and falling—dabbing their lips with their napkins, crumbling bread, fiddling with the forks and glasses and talking.

'I met her at the Alpha show—the weirdest little person. She'd not only cut off her hair, but she seemed to have taken a dreadfully good snip off her legs and arms and her neck and her poor little nose as well.'

'Isn't she very *liée* with Michael Oat?'

'The man who wrote *Love in False Teeth*?'

'He wants to write a play for me. One act. One man. Decides to commit suicide. Gives all the reasons why he should and why he shouldn't. And just as he has made up his mind either to do it or not to do it—curtain. Not half a bad idea.'

'What's he going to call it—"Stomach Trouble"?'

'I *think* I've come across the *same* idea in a lit-tle French review, *quite* unknown in England.'

No, they didn't share it. They were dears—dears—and she loved having them there, at her table, and giving them delicious food and wine. In fact, she longed to tell them how delightful they were, and what a decorative group they made, how they seemed to set one another off and how they reminded her of a play by Tchekof!

Harry was enjoying his dinner. It was part of his—well, not his nature, exactly, and certainly not his pose—his—something or other—to talk about food and to glory in his 'shameless passion for the white flash of the lobster' and 'the green of pistachio ices—green and cold like the eyelids of Egyptian dancers'.

When he looked up at her and said: 'Bertha, this is a very admirable *soufflé*!' she almost could have wept with child-like pleasure.

Oh, why did she feel so tender towards the whole world tonight? Everything was good—was right. All that happened seemed to fill again her brimming cup of bliss.

And still, in the back of her mind, there was the pear tree. It would be silver now, in the light of poor dear Eddie's moon, silver as Miss Fulton, who sat there turning a tangerine in her slender fingers that were so pale a light seemed to come from them.

What she simply couldn't make out—what was miraculous—was how she should have guessed Miss Fulton's mood so exactly and so instantly. For she never doubted for a moment that she was right, and yet what had she to go on? Less than nothing.

'I believe this does happen very, very rarely between women. Never between men,' thought Bertha. 'But while I am making the coffee in the drawing-room perhaps she will "give a sign".'

What she meant by that she did not know, and what would happen after that she could not imagine.

While she thought like this she saw herself talking and laughing. She had to talk because of her desire to laugh.

'I must laugh or die.'

But when she noticed Face's funny little habit of tucking something down the front of her bodice—as if she kept a tiny, secret hoard of nuts there, too—Bertha had to dig her nails into her hands—so as not to laugh too much.

It was over at last. And: 'Come and see my new coffee machine,' said Bertha.

'We only have a new coffee machine once a fortnight,' said Harry. Face took her arm this time; Miss Fulton bent her head and followed after.

The fire had died down in the drawing-room to a red, flickering 'nest of baby phoenixes', said Face.

'Don't turn up the light for a moment. It is so lovely.' And down she crouched by the fire again. She was always cold . . . 'without her little red flannel jacket, of course,' thought Bertha.

At that moment Miss Fulton 'gave the sign'.

'Have you a garden?' said the cool, sleepy voice.

This was so exquisite on her part that all Bertha could do was to obey. She crossed the room, pulled the curtains apart, and opened those long windows.

'There!' she breathed.

And the two women stood side by side looking at the slender, flowering tree. Although it was so still it seemed, like the flame of a candle, to stretch up, to point, to quiver in the bright air, to grow taller and taller as they gazed—almost to touch the rim of the round, silver moon.

How long did they stand there? Both, as it were, caught in that circle of unearthly light, understanding each other perfectly, creatures of another world, and wondering what they were to do in this one with all this blissful treasure that burned in their bosoms and dropped, in silver flowers, from their hair and hands?

For ever—for a moment? And did Miss Fulton murmur: 'Yes. Just *that*.' Or did Bertha dream it?

Then the light was snapped on and Face made the coffee and Harry said: 'My dear Mrs Knight, don't ask me about my baby. I never see her. I shan't feel the slightest interest in her until she has a lover,' and Mug took his eye out of the conservatory for a moment and then put it under glass again and Eddie Warren drank his coffee and set down the cup with a face of anguish as though he had drunk and seen the spider.

'What I want to do is to give the young men a show. I believe London is simply teeming with first-chop, unwritten plays. What I want to say to 'em is: "Here's the theatre. Fire ahead."'

'You know, my dear, I am going to decorate a room for the Jacob Nathans. Oh, I am so tempted to do a fried-fish scheme, with the backs of the chairs shaped like frying-pans and lovely chip potatoes embroidered all over the curtains.'

'The trouble with our young writing men is that they are still too romantic. You can't put out to sea without being seasick and wanting a basin. Well, why won't they have the courage of those basins?'

'A *dreadful* poem about a girl who was *violated* by a beggar *without* a nose in a lit-tle wood....'

Miss Fulton sank into the lowest, deepest chair and Harry handed round the cigarettes.

From the way he stood in front of her shaking the silver box and saying abruptly: 'Egyptian? Turkish? Virginian? They're all mixed up,' Bertha realised that she not only bored him; he really disliked her. And she decided from the way Miss Fulton said: 'No, thank you, I won't smoke,' that she felt it, too, and was hurt.

'Oh, Harry, don't dislike her. You are quite wrong about her. She's wonderful, wonderful. And, besides, how can you feel so differently about someone who means so much to me. I shall try to tell you when we are in bed tonight what has been happening. What she and I have shared.'

At those last words something strange and almost terrifying darted into Bertha's mind. And this something blind and smiling whispered to her: 'Soon these people will go. The house will be quiet—quiet. The lights will be out. And you and he will be alone together in the dark room—the warm bed....

She jumped up from her chair and ran over to the piano.

'What a pity someone does not play!' she cried. 'What a pity somebody does not play.'

For the first time in her life Bertha Young desired her husband.

Oh, she'd loved him—she'd been in love with him, of course, in every other way, but just not in that way. And equally, of course, she'd understood that he was different. They'd discussed it so often. It had worried her dreadfully at first to find that she was so cold, but after a time it had not seemed to matter. They were so frank with each other—such good pals. That was the best of being modern.

But now—ardently! ardently! The word ached in her ardent body! Was this what that feeling of bliss had been leading up to? But then, then—

'My dear,' said Mrs Norman Knight, 'you know our shame. We are the victims of time and train. We live in Hampstead. It's been so nice.'

'I'll come with you into the hall,' said Bertha. 'I loved having you. But you must not miss the last train. That's so awful, isn't it?'

'Have a whisky, Knight, before you go?' called Harry.

'No, thanks, old chap.'

Bertha squeezed his hand for that as she shook it.

'Good night, goodbye,' she cried from the top step, feeling that this self of hers was taking leave of them for ever.

When she got back into the drawing-room the others were on the move.

' . . . Then you can come part of the way in my taxi.'

'I shall be *so* thankful *not* to have to face *another* drive *alone* after my *dreadful* experience.'

'You can get a taxi at the rank just at the end of the street. You won't have to walk more than a few yards.'

'That's a comfort. I'll go and put on my coat.'

Miss Fulton moved towards the hall and Bertha was following when Harry almost pushed past.

'Let me help you.'

Bertha knew that he was repenting his rudeness—she let him go. What a boy he was in some ways—so impulsive—so—simple.

And Eddie and she were left by the fire.

'I *wonder* if you have seen Bilks' *new* poem called *Table d'Hôte,*' said Eddie softly. 'It's *so* wonderful. In the last Anthology. Have you got a copy? I'd *so* like to *show* it to you. It begins with an *incredibly* beautiful line: "Why Must it Always be Tomato Soup?"'

'Yes,' said Bertha. And she moved noiselessly to a table opposite the drawing-room door and Eddie glided noiselessly after her. She picked up the little book and gave it to him; they had not made a sound.

While he looked it up she turned her head towards the hall. And she saw ... Harry with Miss Fulton's coat in his arms and Miss Fulton with her back turned to him and her head bent. He tossed the coat away, put his hands on her shoulders and turned her violently to him. His lips said: 'I adore you,' and Miss Fulton laid her moonbeam fingers on his cheeks and smiled her sleepy smile. Harry's nostrils quivered; his lips curled back in a hideous grin while he whispered: 'Tomorrow,' and with her eyelids Miss Fulton said: 'Yes.'

'Here it is,' said Eddie. '"Why Must it Always be Tomato Soup?" It's so *deeply* true, don't you feel? Tomato soup is so *dreadfully* eternal.'

'If you prefer,' said Harry's voice, very loud, from the hall, 'I can 'phone you a cab to come to the door.'

'Oh, no. It's not necessary,' said Miss Fulton, and she came up to Bertha and gave her the slender fingers to hold.

'Goodbye. Thank you so much.'

'Goodbye,' said Bertha.

Miss Fulton held her hand a moment longer.

'Your lovely pear tree!' she murmured.

And then she was gone, with Eddie following, like the black cat following the grey cat.

'I'll shut up shop,' said Harry, extravagantly cool and collected.

'Your lovely pear tree—pear tree—pear tree!'

Bertha simply ran over to the long windows.

'Oh, what is going to happen now?' she cried.

But the pear tree was as lovely as ever and as full of flower and as still.

A Married Man's Story

It is evening. Supper is over. We have left the small, cold dining-room, we have come back to the sitting room where there is a fire. All is as usual. I am sitting at my writing-table which is placed across a corner so that I am behind it, as it were, and facing the room. The lamp with the green shade is alight; I have before me two large books of reference, both open, a pile of papers .... All the paraphernalia, in fact, of an extremely occupied man. My wife, with her little boy on her lap, is in a low chair before the fire. She is about to put him to bed before she clears away the dishes and piles them up in the kitchen for the servant girl tomorrow morning. But the warmth, the quiet, and the sleepy baby, have made her dreamy. One of his red woollen boots is off, one is on. She sits, bent forward, clasping the little bare foot, staring into the glow, and as the fire quickens, falls, flares again, her shadow—an immense Mother and Child—is here and gone again upon the wall ....

Outside it is raining. I like to think of that cold drenched window behind the blind, and beyond, the dark bushes in the garden, their broad leaves bright with rain, and beyond the fence, the gleaming road with the two hoarse little gutters singing against each other, and the wavering reflections of the lamps, like fishes' tails. While I am here, I am there, lifting my face to the dim sky, and it seems to me it must be raining all over the world—that the whole earth is drenched, is sounding with a soft, quick patter or hard, steady drumming, or gurgling and something that is like sobbing and laughing mingled together, and that light, playful splashing that is of water falling into still lakes and flowing rivers. And all at one and the same moment I am arriving in a strange city, slipping under the hood of the cab while the driver whips the cover off the breathing horse, running from shelter to shelter, dodging someone, swerving by someone else. I am conscious of tall houses, their doors and shutters sealed against the night, of dripping balconies and sodden flower-pots. I am brushing through deserted gardens and falling into moist smelling summer-houses (you know how soft and almost crumbling the wood of a summer-house is in the rain); I am standing on the dark quayside giving my ticket into the wet, red hand of the old sailor in an oilskin. How strong the sea smells! How loudly the tied-up boats knock against one another! I am crossing the wet stackyard, hooded in an old sack, carrying a lantern, while the house-dog, like a soaking doormat, springs, shakes himself over me. And now I am walking along a deserted road—it is impossible to miss the puddles, and the trees are stirring—stirring.

But one could go on with such a catalogue for ever—on and on—until one lifted the single arum lily leaf and discovered the tiny snails clinging, until one counted ... and what then? Aren't those just the signs, the traces of my feeling? The bright green streaks made by someone who walks over the dewy grass? Not the feeling itself. And as I think that a mournful, glorious voice begins to sing in my bosom. Yes, perhaps that is nearer what I mean. What a voice! What power! What velvety softness! Marvellous!

Suddenly my wife turns round quickly. She knows—how long has she known?—that I am not 'working'. It is strange that with her full, open gaze she should smile so timidly—and that she should say in such a hesitating voice, 'What are you thinking?'

I smile and draw two fingers across my forehead in the way I have. 'Nothing,' I answer softly.

At that she stirs and, still trying not to make it sound important, she says, 'Oh, but you must have been thinking of something!'

Then I really meet her gaze, meet it fully, and I fancy her face quivers. Will she never grow accustomed to these simple—one might say—everyday lies? Will she never learn not to expose herself—or to build up defences?

'Truly, I was thinking of nothing.'

There! I seem to see it dart at her. She turns away, pulls the other red sock off the baby, sits him up, and begins to unbutton him behind. I wonder if that little soft rolling bundle sees anything, feels anything? Now she turns him over on her knee, and in this light, his soft arms and legs waving, he is extraordinarily like a young crab. A queer thing is I can't connect him with my wife and myself—I've never accepted him as ours. Each time when I come into the hall and see the perambulator I catch myself thinking: 'H'm, someone has brought a baby!' Or, when his crying wakes me at night, I feel inclined to blame my wife for having brought the baby in from outside. The truth is, that though one might suspect her of strong maternal feelings, my wife doesn't seem to me the type of woman who bears children in her own body. There's an immense difference! Where is that ... animal ease and playfulness, that quick kissing and cuddling one has been taught to expect of young mothers? She hasn't a sign of it. I believe that when she ties its bonnet she feels like an aunt and not a mother. But of course I may be wrong; she may be passionately devoted .... I don't think so. At any rate, isn't it a trifle indecent to feel like this about one's own wife? Indecent or not, one has these feelings. And one other thing. How can I reasonably expect my wife, *a broken-hearted woman*, to spend her time tossing the baby? But that is beside the mark. She never even began to toss when her heart was whole.

And now she has carried the baby to bed. I hear her soft, deliberate steps moving between the dining-room and the kitchen, there and back again, to the tune of the clattering dishes. And now all is quiet. What is happening now? Oh, I know just as surely as if I'd gone to see—she is standing in the middle of the kitchen facing the rainy window. Her head is bent, with one finger she is tracing something—nothing—on the table. It is cold in the kitchen; the gas jumps; the tap drips; it's a forlorn picture. And nobody is going to come behind her, to take her in his arms, to kiss her soft hair, to lead her to the fire and to rub her hands warm again. Nobody is going to call her or to wonder what she is doing out there. And she knows it. And yet, being a woman, deep down, deep down, she really does expect the miracle to happen; she really could embrace that dark, dark deceit, rather than live—like this.

II

To live like this .... I write those words very carefully, very beautifully. For some reason I feel inclined to sign them, or to write underneath—Trying a New Pen. But, seriously, isn't it staggering to think what may be contained in one innocent-looking little phrase? It tempts me—it tempts me terribly. Scene: The supper-table. My wife has just handed me my tea. I stir it, lift the spoon, idly chase and then carefully capture a speck of tea-leaf, and having brought it ashore, I murmur, quite gently, 'How long shall we continue to live—like—this?' And immediately there is that famous 'blinding flash and deafening roar. Huge pieces of débris (I must say I like débris) are flung in to the air . . . and when the dark clouds of smoke have drifted away . . . ' But this will never happen; I shall never know it. It will be found upon me 'intact', as they say. 'Open my heart and you will see . . . '

Why? Ah, there you have me! There is the most difficult question of all to answer. Why do people stay together? Putting aside 'for the sake of the children', and 'the habit of years' and 'economic reasons' as lawyers' nonsense—it's not much more—if one really does try to find out why it is that people don't leave each other, one discovers a mystery. It is because they can't; they are bound. And nobody on earth knows what are the bonds that bind them except those two. Am I being obscure? Well, the thing itself isn't so frightfully crystal clear, is it? Let me put it like this. Supposing you are taken, absolutely, first into his confidence and then into hers. Supposing you know all there is to know about the situation. And having given it not only your deepest sympathy but your most honest impartial criticism, you declare, very calmly (but not without the slightest suggestion of relish—for there is—I swear there is—in the very best of us—something that leaps up and cries 'A-aah!' for joy at the thought of destroying), 'Well, my opinion is that you two people ought to part. You'll do no earthly good together. Indeed, it seems to me, it's the duty of either to set the other free.' What happens then? He—and she—agree. It is their conviction too. You are only saying what they have been thinking all last night. And away they go to act on your advice, immediately . . . . And the next time you hear of them they are still together. You see—you've reckoned without the unknown quantity—which is their secret relation to each other—and that they can't disclose even if they want to. Thus far you may tell and no further. Oh, don't misunderstand me! It need not necessarily have anything to do with their sleeping together . . . . But this brings me to a thought I've often half entertained. Which is that human beings, as we know them, don't choose each other at all. It is the owner, the second self inhabiting them, who makes the choice for his own particular purposes, and—this may sound absurdly far-fetched—it's the second self in the other which responds. Dimly—dimly—or so it has seemed to me—we realise this, at any rate to the extent that we realise the hopelessness of trying to escape. So that, what it all amounts to is—if the impermanent selves of my wife and me are happy—*tant mieux pour nous*—if miserable—*tant pis* .... But I don't know, I don't know. And it may be that it's something entirely individual in me—this sensation (yes, it is even a sensation) of how extraordinarily *shell-like* we are as we are—little creatures, peering out of the sentry-box at the gate, ogling through our glass case at the entry, wan little servants, who never can say for certain, even, if the master is out or in ....

The door opens ... My wife. She says, 'I am going to bed.'

And I look up vaguely, and vaguely say, 'You are going to bed.'

'Yes.' A tiny pause. 'Don't forget—will you?—to turn out the gas in the hall.'

And again I repeat, 'The gas in the hall.'

There was a time—the time before—when this habit of mine—it really has become a habit now—it wasn't one then—was one of our sweetest jokes together. It began, of course, when on several occasions I really was deeply engaged and I didn't hear. I emerged only to see her shaking her head and laughing at me, 'You haven't heard a word!'

'No. What did you say?'

Why should she think that so funny and charming? She did—it delighted her. 'Oh, my darling, it's so like you! It's so—so—' And I knew she loved me for it. I knew she positively looked forward to coming in and disturbing me, and so—as one does—I played up. I was guaranteed to be wrapped away every evening at 10.30 p.m. But now? For some reason I feel it would be crude to stop my performance. It's simplest to play on. But what is she waiting for tonight? Why doesn't she go? Why prolong this? She is going. No, her hand on the door-knob, she turns round again, and she says in the most curious, small, breathless voice, 'You're not cold?'

Oh, it's not fair to be as pathetic as that! That was simply damnable. I shuddered all over before I managed to bring out a slow 'No-o!' while my left hand ruffles the reference pages.

She is gone; she will not come back again tonight. It is not only I who recognise that—the room changes too. It relaxes, like an old actor. Slowly the mask is rubbed off; the look of strained attention changes to an air of heavy, sullen brooding. Every line, every fold breathes fatigue. The mirror is quenched; the ash whitens; only my sly lamp burns on ... But what a cynical indifference to me it all shows! Or should I perhaps be flattered? No, we understand each other. You know those stories of little children who are suckled by wolves and accepted by the tribe, and how for ever after they move freely among their fleet, grey brothers? Something like that has happened to me. But wait! That about the wolves won't do. Curious! Before I wrote it down, while it was still in my head, I was delighted with it. It seemed to express, and more, to suggest, just what I wanted to say. But written, I can smell the falseness immediately and the ... source of the smell is in that word fleet. Don't you agree? Fleet, grey brothers! 'Fleet.' A word I never use. When I wrote 'wolves' it skimmed across my mind like a shadow and I couldn't resist it. Tell me! Tell me! Why is it so difficult to write simply—and not simply only but *sotto voce*, if you know what I mean? That is how I long to write. No fine effects—no bravura. But just the plain truth, as only a liar can tell it.

III

I light a cigarette, lean back, inhale deeply—and find myself wondering if my wife is asleep. Or is she lying in her cold bed, staring into the dark, with those trustful, bewildered eyes? Her eyes are like the eyes of a cow that is being driven along a road. 'Why am I being driven—what harm have I done?' But I really am not responsible for that look; it's her natural expression. One day, when she was turning out a cupboard, she found a little old photograph of herself, taken when she was a girl at school. In her confirmation dress, she explained. And there were the eyes, even then. I remember saying to her, 'Did you always look so sad?' Leaning over my shoulder, she laughed lightly, 'Do I look sad? I think it's just ... me.' And she waited for me to say something about it. But I was marvelling at her courage at having shown it to me at all. It was a hideous photograph! And I wondered again if she realised how plain she was, and comforted herself with the idea that people who loved each other didn't criticise but accepted everything, or if she really rather liked her appearance and expected me to say something complimentary.

Oh, that was base of me! How could I have forgotten all the numberless times when I have known her turn away to avoid the light, press her face into my shoulders. And, above all, how could I have forgotten the afternoon of our wedding-day when we sat on the green bench in the Botanical Gardens and listened to the band; how, in an interval between two pieces, she suddenly turned to me and said in the voice in which one says, 'Do you think the grass is damp?' or 'Do you think it's time for tea?' ... 'Tell me, do you think physical beauty is so very important?' I don't like to think how often she had rehearsed that question. And do you know what I answered? At that moment, as if at my command, there came a great gush of hard, bright sound from the band, and I managed to shout above it cheerfully, 'I didn't hear what you said.' Devilish! Wasn't it? Perhaps not wholly. She looked like the poor patient who hears the surgeon say, 'It will certainly be necessary to perform the operation—but not now!'

IV

But all this conveys the impression that my wife and I were never really happy together. Not true! Not true! We were marvellously, radiantly happy. We were a model couple. If you had seen us together, any time, any place, if you had followed us, tracked us down, spied, taken us off our guard, you still would have been forced to confess, 'I have never seen a more ideally suited pair.' Until last autumn.

But really to explain what happened then I should have to go back and back—I should have to dwindle until my two hands clutched the banisters, the stair-rail was higher than my head, and I peered through to watch my father padding softly up and down. There were coloured windows on the landings. As he came up, first his bald head was scarlet, then it was yellow. How frightened

I was! And when they put me to bed, it was to dream that we were living inside one of my father's big coloured bottles. For he was a chemist. I was born nine years after my parents were married. I was an only child, and the effect to produce even me—small, withered bud I must have been—sapped all my mother's strength. She never left her room again. Bed, sofa, window, she moved between the three. Well I can see her, on the window days, sitting, her cheek in her hand, staring out. Her room looked over the street. Opposite there was a wall plastered with advertisements for travelling shows and circuses and so on. I stand beside her, and we gaze at the slim lady in a red dress hitting a dark gentleman over the head with her parasol, or at the tiger peering through the jungle while the clown, close by, balances a bottle on his nose, or at a little golden-haired girl sitting on the knee of an old black man in a broad cotton hat . . . . She says nothing. On sofa days there is a flannel dressing-gown that I loathe and a cushion that keeps on slipping off the hard sofa. I pick it up. It has flowers and writing sewn on. I ask what the writing says, and she whispers, 'Sweet Repose!' In bed her fingers plait, in tight little plaits, the fringe of the quilt and her lips are thin. And that is all there is of my mother, except the last queer 'episode' that comes later.

My father . . . Curled up in the corner on the lid of a round box that held sponges, I stared at my father so long, it's as though his image, cut off at the waist by the counter, has remained solid in my memory. Perfectly bald, polished head, shaped like a thin egg, creased, creamy cheeks, little bags under the eyes, large pale ears like handles. His manner was discreet, sly, faintly amused and tinged with impudence. Long before I could appreciate it I knew the mixture . . . I even used to copy him in my corner, bending forward, with a small reproduction of his faint sneer. In the evening his customers were, chiefly, young women; some of them came in every day for his famous fivepenny pick-me-up. Their gaudy looks, their voices, their free ways fascinated me. I longed to be my father, handing them across the counter the little glass of bluish stuff they tossed off so greedily. God knows what it was made of. Years after I drank some, just to see what it tasted like, and I felt as though someone had given me a terrific blow on the head; I felt stunned.

One of those evenings I remember vividly. It was cold; it must have been autumn, for the flaring gas was lighted after my tea. I sat in my corner and my father was mixing something; the shop was empty. Suddenly the bell jangled and a young woman rushed in, crying so loud, sobbing so hard, that it didn't sound real. She wore a green cape trimmed with fur and a hat with cherries dangling. My father came from behind the screen. But she couldn't stop herself at first. She stood in the middle of the shop and wrung her hands and moaned; I've never heard such crying since. Presently she managed to gasp out, 'Give me a pick-me-up!' Then she drew a long breath, trembled away from him and quavered, 'I've had *bad news*!' And in the flaring gaslight I saw the whole side of her face was puffed up and purple; her lip was cut and her eyelid looked as though it was gummed fast over the wet eye. My father pushed the glass across the counter, and she took the purse out of her stocking and paid him. But she couldn't drink; clutching the glass, she stared in front of her as if she could not believe what she saw. Each time she put her head back the tears spurted out again. Finally she put the glass down. It was no use. Holding the cape with one hand, she ran in the same way out of the shop again. My father gave no sign. But long after she had gone I crouched in my corner, and when I think back it's as though I felt my whole body vibrating—'So that's what it is outside,' I thought. 'That's what it's like out there.'

V

Do you remember your childhood? I am always coming across these marvellous accounts by writers who declare that they remember 'everything'. I certainly don't. The dark stretches, the blanks, are much bigger than the bright glimpses. I seem to have spent most of my time like a plant in a cupboard. Now and again, when the sun shone, a careless hand thrust me out on to the window-sill, and a careless hand whipped me in again—and that was all. But what happened in the darkness—I wonder? Did one grow? Pale stem ... timid leaves ... white reluctant bud. No wonder I was hated at school. Even the masters shrank from me. I somehow knew that my soft, hesitating voice disgusted them. I knew, too, how they turned away from my shocked, staring eyes. I

was small and thin and I smelled of the shop; my nickname was
Gregory Powder. School was a tin building, stuck on the raw
hillside. There were dark red streaks like blood in the oozing clay
banks of the playground. I hide in the dark passage, where the
coats hang, and am discovered there by one of the masters. 'What
are you doing there in the dark?' His terrible voice kills me; I die
before his eyes. I am standing in a ring of thrust-out heads; some
are grinning, some look greedy, some are spitting. And it is always
cold. Big crushed-up clouds press across the sky; the rusty water
in the school tank is frozen; the bell sounds numb. One day they
put a dead bird in my overcoat pocket. I found it just when I
reached home. Oh, what a strange flutter there was at my heart
when I drew out that terrible soft, cold little body, with the legs
thin as pins and the claws wrung. I sat on the back door step in the
yard and put the bird in my cap. The feathers round the neck
looked wet and there was a tiny tuft just above the closed eyes that
stood up too. How tightly the beak was shut! I could not see the
mark where it was divided. I stretched out one wing and touched
the soft, secret down underneath; I tried to make the claws curl
round my little finger. But I didn't feel sorry for it—no! I
wondered. The smoke from our kitchen chimney poured
downwards, and flakes of soot floated—soft, light in the air.
Through a big crack in the cement yard a poor-looking plant with
dull, reddish flowers had pushed its way. I looked at the dead bird
again . . . . And that is the first time that I remember singing—
rather . . . listening to a silent voice inside a little cage that was me.

VI

But what has all this to do with my married happiness? How
can all this affect my wife and me? Why—to tell what happened
last autumn—do I run all this way back into the Past? The
Past—what is the Past? I might say the star-shaped flake of soot on
a leaf of the poor-looking plant, and the bird lying on the quilted
lining of my cap, and my father's pestle and my mother's cushion
belong to it. But that is not to say they are any less mine than they
were when I looked upon them with my very eyes and touched
them with these fingers. No, they are more—they are a living part
of me. Who am I, in fact, as I sit here at this table, but my own

past? If I deny that, I am nothing. And if I were to try to divide my life into childhood, youth, early manhood and so on, it would be a kind of affectation; I should know I was doing it just because of the pleasantly important sensation it gives one to rule lines and to use green ink for childhood, red for the next stage, and purple for the period of adolescence. For, one thing I have learnt, one thing I do believe is, Nothing Happens Suddenly. Yes, that is my religion, I suppose.

My mother's death, for instance. Is it more distant from me today than it was then? It is just as close, as strange, as puzzling, and, in spite of all the countless times I have recalled the circumstances, I know no more now than I did then, whether I dreamed them, or whether they really occurred. It happened when I was thirteen and I slept in a little strip of a room on what was called the half-landing. One night I woke up with a start to see my mother, in her nightgown, without even the hated flannel dressing-gown, sitting on my bed. But the strange thing which frightened me was, she wasn't looking at me. Her head was bent; the short, thin trail of hair lay between her shoulders; her hands were pressed between her knees and my bed shook; she was shivering. It was the first time I had ever seen her out of her own room. I said, or I think I said, 'Is that you, Mother?' And as she turned round, I saw in the moonlight how queer she looked. Her face looked small—quite different. She looked like one of the boys at the school baths, who sits on a step, shivering just like that, and wants to go in and yet is frightened.

'Are you awake?' she said. Her eyes opened; I think she smiled. She leaned towards me. 'I've been poisoned,' she whispered. 'Your father's poisoned me.' And she nodded. Then, before I could say a word, she was gone; I thought I heard the door shut. I sat quite still, I couldn't move, I think I expected something else to happen. For a long time I listened for something; there wasn't a sound. The candle was by my bed, but I was too frightened to stretch out my hand for the matches. But even while I wondered what I ought to do, even while my heart thumped—everything became confused. I lay down and pulled the blankets round me. I fell asleep, and the next morning my mother was found dead of failure of the heart.

Did that visit happen? Was it a dream? Why did she come to tell me? Or why, if she came, did she go away so quickly? And her expression—so joyous under the frightened look—was that real? I believed it fully the afternoon of the funeral, when I saw my father dressed up for his part, hat and all. That tall hat so gleaming black and round was like a cork covered with black sealing-wax, and the rest of my father was awfully like a bottle, with his face for the label—*Deadly Poison*. It flashed into my mind as I stood opposite him in the hall. And Deadly Poison, or old D.P., was my private name for him from that day.

VII

Late, it grows late. I love the night. I love to feel the tide of darkness rising slowly and slowly washing, turning over and over, lifting, floating, all that lies strewn upon the dark beach, all that lies hid in rocky hollows. I love, I love this strange feeling of drifting—whither? After my mother's death I hated to go to bed. I used to sit on the window-sill, folded up, and watch the sky. It seemed to me the moon moved much faster than the sun. And one big, bright green star I chose for my own. My star! But I never thought of it beckoning to me or twinkling merrily for my sake. Cruel, indifferent, splendid—it burned in the airy night. No matter—it was mine! But, growing close up against the window, there was a creeper with small, bunched-up pink and purple flowers. These did know me. These, when I touched them at night, welcomed my fingers; the little tendrils, so weak, so delicate, knew I would not hurt them. When the wind moved the leaves I felt I understood their shaking. When I came to the window, it seemed to me the flowers said among themselves, 'The boy is here.'

As the months passed there was often a light in my father's room below. And I heard voices and laughter. 'He's got some woman with him,' I thought. But it meant nothing to me. Then the gay voice, the sound of the laughter, gave me the idea it was one of the girls who used to come to the shop in the evenings—and gradually I began to imagine which girl it was. It was the dark one in the red coat and skirt who once had given me a penny. A merry face stooped over me—warm breath tickled my neck—there were little beads of black on her long lashes, and when she opened her arms to kiss me there came a marvellous wave of scent! Yes, that was the one.

Time passed, and I forgot the moon and my green star and my shy creeper—I came to the window to wait for the light in my father's window, to listen for the laughing voice, until one night I dozed and I dreamed she came again—again she drew me to her, something soft, scented, warm and merry hung over me like a cloud. But when I tried to see, her eyes only mocked me, her red lips opened and she hissed, 'Little sneak! Little sneak!' but not as if she were angry,—as if she understood, and her smile somehow was like a rat—hateful!

The night after, I lighted the candle and sat down at the table instead. By and by, as the flame steadied, there was a small lake of liquid wax, surrounded by a white, smooth wall. I took a pin and made little holes in this wall and then sealed them up faster than the wax could escape. After a time I fancied the candle flame joined in the game; it leapt up, quivered, wagged; it even seemed to laugh. But while I played with the candle and smiled and broke off the tiny white peaks of wax that rose above the wall and floated them on my lake, a feeling of awful dreariness fastened on me—yes, that's the word. It crept up from my knees to my thighs, into my arms; I ached all over with misery. And I felt so strangely that I couldn't move. Something bound me there by the table—I couldn't even let the pin drop that I held between my finger and thumb. For a moment I came to a stop, as it were.

Then the shrivelled case of the bud split and fell, the plant in the cupboard came into flower. 'Who am I?' I thought. 'What is all this?' And I looked at my room, at the broken bust of the man called Hahnemann on top of the cupboard, at my little bed with the pillow like an envelope. I saw it all, but not as I had seen before . . . . Everything lived, everything. But that was not all. I was equally alive and—it's the only way I can express it—the barriers were down between us—I had come into my own world!

VIII

The barriers were down. I had been all my life a little outcast; but until that moment no one had 'accepted' me; I had lain in the cupboard—or the cave forlorn. But now I was taken, I was accepted, claimed. I did not consciously turn away from the world of human beings; I had never known it; but I from that night did beyond words consciously turn towards my silent brothers . . . .

Carnation

On those hot days Eve—curious Eve—always carried a flower. She snuffed it and snuffed it, twirled it in her fingers, laid it against her cheek, held it to her lips, tickled Katie's neck with it, and ended, finally, by pulling it to pieces and eating it, petal by petal.

'Roses are delicious, my dear Katie,' she would say, standing in the dim cloak-room, with a strange decoration of flowery hats on the hat pegs behind her—'but carnations are simply divine! They taste like—like—ah well!' And away her little thin laugh flew, fluttering among those huge, strange flower heads on the wall behind her. (But how cruel her little thin laugh was! It had a long sharp beak and claws and two bead eyes, thought fanciful Katie.)

Today it was a carnation. She brought a carnation to the French class, a deep, deep red one, that looked at though it had been dipped in wine and left in the dark to dry. She held it on the desk before her, half shut her eyes and smiled.

'Isn't it a darling?' said she. But—

'*Un peu de silence, s'il vous plaît,*' came from M. Hugo. Oh, bother! It was too hot! Frightfully hot! Grilling simply!

The two square windows of the French Room were open at the bottom and the dark blinds drawn half-way down. Although no air came in, the blind cord swung out and back and the blind lifted. But really there was not a breath from the dazzle outside.

Even the girls, in the dusky room, in their pale blouses, with stiff butterfly-bow hair ribbons perched on their hair, seemed to give off a warm, weak light, and M. Hugo's white waistcoat gleamed like the belly of a shark.

Some of the girls were very red in the face and some were white. Vera Holland had pinned up her black curls *à la japonaise* with a penholder and a pink pencil; she looked charming. Francie Owen pushed her sleeves nearly up to the shoulders, and then she inked the little blue vein in her elbow, shut her arm together, and then looked to see the mark it made; she had a passion for inking herself; she always had a face drawn on her thumb nail, with black, forked hair. Sylvia Mann took off her collar and tie, took them off simply, and laid them on the desk beside her, as calm as if she were going to wash her hair in her bedroom at home. She *had* a nerve! Jennie Edwards tore a leaf out of her notebook and wrote 'Shall we ask old Hugo-Wugo to give us a thrippenny vanilla on the way home!!!' and passed it across to Connie Baker, who turned absolutely purple and nearly burst out crying. All of them lolled and gaped, staring at the round clock, which seemed to have grown paler, too; the hands scarcely crawled.

'*Un peu de silence, s'il vous plaît,*' came from M. Hugo. He held up a puffy hand. 'Ladies, as it is so 'ot we will take no more notes today, but I will read you'—and he paused and smiled a broad, gentle smile—'a little French poetry.'

'Go—od God!' moaned Francie Owen.

M. Hugo's smile deepened. 'Well, Mees Owen, you need not attend. You can paint yourself. You can 'ave my red ink as well as your black one.'

How well they knew the little blue book with red edges that he tugged out of his coat-tail pocket! It had a green silk marker embroidered in forget-me-nots. They often giggled at it when he handed the book round. Poor old Hugo-Wugo! He adored reading poetry. He would begin, softly and calmly, and then gradually his voice would swell and vibrate and gather itself together, then it would be pleading and imploring and entreating, and then rising, rising triumphant, until it burst into light, as it were, and then—gradually again, it ebbed, it grew soft and warm and calm and died down into nothingness.

The great difficulty was, of course, if you felt at all feeble, not to get the most awful fit of the giggles. Not because it was funny, really, but because it made you feel uncomfortable, queer, silly, and somehow ashamed for old Hugo-Wugo. But—oh dear—if he was going to inflict it on them in this heat...!

'Courage, my pet,' said Eve, kissing the languid carnation.

He began, and most of the girls fell forward, over the desks, their heads on their arms, dead at the first shot. Only Eve and Katie sat upright and still. Katie did not know enough French to understand, but Eve sat listening, her eyebrows raised, her eyes half veiled, and a smile that was like the shadow of her cruel little laugh, like the wing shadows of that cruel little laugh fluttering over her lips. She made a warm, white cup of her fingers—the carnation inside. Oh, the scent! It floated across to Katie. It was too much. Katie turned away to the dazzling light outside the window.

Down below, she knew, there was a cobbled courtyard with stable buildings round it. That was why the French Room always smelled faintly of ammonia. It wasn't unpleasant; it was even part of the French language for Katie—something sharp and vivid and—and—biting!

Now she could hear a man clatter over the cobbles and the jing-jang of the pails he carried. And now *Hoo-hor-her! Hoo-hor-her!* as he worked the pump and a great gush of water followed. Now he was flinging the water over something, over the wheels of a carriage perhaps. And she saw the wheel, propped up, clear of the ground, spinning round, flashing scarlet and black, with great drops glancing off it. And all the while he worked the man kept up a high, bold whistling that skimmed over the noise of the water as a bird skims over the sea. He went away—he came back again leading a cluttering horse.

Hoo-hor-her! Hoo-hor-her! came from the pump. Now he dashed the water over the horse's legs and then swooped down and began brushing.

She *saw* him simply—in a faded shirt, his sleeves rolled up, his chest bare, all splashed with water—and as he whistled, loud and free, and as he moved, swooping and bending, Hugo-Wugo's voice began to warm, to deepen, to gather together, to swing, to rise—somehow or other to keep time with the man outside (Oh, the scent of Eve's carnation!) until they became one great rushing, rising, triumphant thing, bursting into light, and then—

The whole room broke into pieces.

'Thank you, ladies,' cried M. Hugo, bobbing at his high desk, over the wreckage.

And 'Keep it, dearest,' said Eve. '*Souvenir tendre*,' and she popped the carnation down the front of Katie's blouse.

This Flower

'But I tell you, my lord fool, out of this nettle, danger,
we pluck this flower, safety.'

As she lay there, looking up at the ceiling, she had her moment—yes, she had her moment! And it was not connected with anything she had thought or felt before, not even with those words the doctor had scarcely ceased speaking. It was single, glowing, perfect; it was like—a pearl, too flawless to match with another.... Could she describe what happened? Impossible. It was as though, even if she had not been conscious (and she certainly had not been conscious all the time) that she was fighting against the stream of life—the stream of life indeed!—she had suddenly ceased to struggle. Oh, more than that! She had yielded absolutely, down to every minutest pulse and nerve, and she had fallen into the bright bosom of the stream and it had borne her ... She was part of her room—part of the great bouquet of southern anemones, of the white net curtains that blew in stiff against the light breeze, of the mirrors, the white silky rugs; she was part of the high, shaking, quivering clamour, broken with little bells and crying voices that went streaming by outside—part of the leaves and the light.

Over. She sat up. The doctor had reappeared. This strange little figure with his stethoscope still strung round his neck—for she had asked him to examine her heart—squeezing and kneading his freshly washed hands, had told her ...

It was the first time she had ever seen him. Roy, unable, of course, to miss the smallest dramatic opportunity, had obtained his rather shady Bloomsbury address from the man in whom he always confided everything, who, although he'd never met her, knew 'all about them'.

'My darling,' Roy had said, 'we'd better have an absolutely unknown man just in case it's—well, what we don't either of us want it to be. One can't be too careful in affairs of this sort.

Doctors do talk. It's all damned rot to say they don't.' Then, 'Not that I care a straw who on earth knows. Not that I wouldn't—if you'd have me—blazon it on the skies, or take the front page of the Daily Mirror and have our two names on it, in a heart, you know—pierced by an arrow.'

Nevertheless, of course, his love of mystery and intrigue, his passion for 'keeping our secret beautifully' (his phrase!) had won the day, and off he'd gone in a taxi to fetch this rather sodden-looking little man.

She heard her untroubled voice saying, 'Do you mind not mentioning anything of this to Mr King? If you'd tell him that I'm a little run down and that my heart wants a rest. For I've been complaining about my heart.'

Roy had been really too right about the kind of man the doctor was. He gave her a strange, quick, leering look, and taking off the stethoscope with shaking fingers he folded it into his bag that looked somehow like a broken old canvas shoe.

'Don't you worry, my dear,' he said huskily. 'I'll see you through.'

Odious little toad to have asked a favour of! She sprang to her feet, and picking up her purple cloth jacket, went over to the mirror. There was a soft knock at the door, and Roy—he really did look pale, smiling his half-smile—came in and asked the doctor what he had to say.

'Well,' said the doctor, taking up his hat, holding it against his chest and beating a tattoo on it, 'all I've got to say is that Mrs—h'm—Madam wants a bit of a rest. She's a bit run down. Her heart's a bit strained. Nothing else wrong.'

In the street a barrel-organ struck up something gay, laughing, mocking, gushing, with little trills, shakes, jumbles of notes.

> That's *all* I got to say, to say,
> That's all I got to say,

it mocked. It sounded so near she wouldn't have been surprised if the doctor were turning the handle.

She saw Roy's smile deepen; his eyes took fire. He gave a little 'Ah!' of relief and happiness. And just for one moment he allowed himself to gaze at her without caring a jot whether the doctor saw or not, drinking her up with that gaze she knew so well, as she stood tying the pale ribbons of her camisole and drawing on the little purple cloth jacket. He jerked back to the doctor, 'She shall go away. She shall go away to the sea at once,' said he, and then, terribly anxious, 'What about her food?' At that, buttoning her jacket in the long mirror, she couldn't help laughing at him.

'That's all very well,' he protested, laughing back delightfully at her and at the doctor. 'But if I didn't manage her food, doctor, she'd never eat anything but caviare sandwiches and—and white grapes. About wine—oughtn't she to have wine?'

Wine would do her no harm.

'Champagne,' pleaded Roy. How he was enjoying himself!

'Oh, as much champagne as she likes,' said the doctor, 'and brandy and soda with her lunch if she fancies it.'

Roy loved that; it tickled him immensely.

'Do you hear that?' he asked solemnly, blinking and sucking in his cheeks to keep from laughing. 'Do you fancy a brandy and soda?'

And, in the distance, faint and exhausted, the barrel-organ:

> A brandy and so-da,
> A brandy and soda, please!
> A brandy and soda, please!

The doctor seemed to hear that, too. He shook hands with her, and Roy went with him into the passage to settle his fee.

She heard the front door close and then—rapid, rapid steps along the passage. This time he simply burst into her room, and she was in his arms, crushed up small while he kissed her with warm quick kisses, murmuring between them, 'My darling, my beauty, my delight. You're mine, you're safe.' Still keeping his arms round her he leant his head against her shoulder as though exhausted. 'If you knew how frightened I've been,' he murmured. 'I thought we were in for it this time. I really did. And it would have been so—fatal—so fatal!'

The Man Without a Temperament

He stood at the hall door turning the ring, turning the heavy signet ring upon his little finger while his glance travelled coolly, deliberately, over the round tables and basket chairs scattered about the glassed-in veranda. He pursed his lips—he might have been going to whistle—but he did not whistle—only turned the ring—turned the ring on his pink, freshly washed hands.

Over in the corner sat The Two Topknots, drinking a decoction they always drank at this hour—something whitish, greyish, in glasses, with little husks floating on the top—and rooting in a tin full of paper shavings for pieces of speckled biscuit, which they broke, dropped into the glasses and fished for with spoons. Their two coils of knitting, like two snakes, slumbered beside the tray.

The American Woman sat where she always sat against the glass wall, in the shadow of a great creeping thing with wide open purple eyes that pressed—that flattened itself against the glass, hungrily watching her. And she knoo it was there—she knoo it was looking at her just that way. She played up to it; she gave herself little airs. Sometimes she even pointed at it, crying: 'Isn't that the most terrible thing you've ever seen! Isn't that ghoulish!' It was on the other side of the veranda, after all ... and besides it couldn't touch her, could it, Klaymongso? She was an American Woman, wasn't she, Klaymongso, and she'd just go right away to her Consul. Klaymongso, curled in her lap, with her torn antique brocade bag, a grubby handkerchief, and a pile of letters from home on top of him, sneezed for reply.

The other tables were empty. A glance passed between the American and the Topknots. She gave a foreign little shrug; they waved an understanding biscuit. But he saw nothing. Now he was still, now from his eyes you saw he listened. 'Hoo-e-zip-zoo-oo!' sounded the lift. The iron cage clanged open. Light dragging steps sounded across the hall, coming towards him. A hand, like a leaf, fell on his shoulder. A soft voice said: 'Let's go and sit over there—where we can see the drive. The trees are so lovely.' And he moved forward with the hand still on his shoulder, and the light, dragging steps beside his. He pulled out a chair and she sank into it, slowly, leaning her head against the back, her arms falling along the sides.

'Won't you bring the other up closer? It's such miles away.' But he did not move.

'Where's your shawl?' he asked.

'Oh!' She gave a little groan of dismay. 'How silly I am, I've left it upstairs on the bed. Never mind. Please don't go for it. I shan't want it, I know I shan't.'

'You'd better have it.' And he turned and swiftly crossed the veranda into the dim hall with its scarlet plush and gilt furniture—conjuror's furniture—its Notice of Services at the English Church, its green baize board with the unclaimed letters climbing the black lattice, huge 'Presentation' clock that struck the hours at the half-hours, bundles of sticks and umbrellas and sunshades in the clasp of a brown wooden bear, past the two crippled palms, two ancient beggars at the foot of the staircase, up the marble stairs three at a time, past the life-size group on the landing of two stout peasant children with their marble pinnies full of marble grapes, and along the corridor, with its piled-up wreckage of old tin boxes, leather trunks, canvas holdalls, to their room.

The servant girl was in their room, singing loudly while she emptied soapy water into a pail. The windows were open wide, the shutters put back, and the light glared in. She had thrown the carpets and the big white pillows over the balcony rails; the nets were looped up from the beds; on the writing-table there stood a pan of fluff and match-ends. When she saw him her small, impudent eyes snapped and her singing changed to humming. But he gave no sign. His eyes searched the glaring room. Where the devil was the shawl!

'*Vous desirez, monsieur?*' mocked the servant girl.

No answer. He had seen it. He strode across the room, grabbed the grey cobweb and went out, banging the door. The servant girl's voice at its loudest and shrillest followed him along the corridor.

'Oh, there you are. What happened? What kept you? The tea's here, you see. I've just sent Antonio off for the hot water. Isn't it extraordinary? I must have told him about it sixty times at least, and still he doesn't bring it. Thank you. That's very nice. One does just feel the air when one bends forward.'

'Thanks.' He took his tea and sat down in the other chair. 'No, nothing to eat.'

'Oh do! Just one, you had so little at lunch and it's hours before dinner.'

Her shawl dropped off as she bent forward to hand him the biscuits. He took one and put it in his saucer.

'Oh, those trees along the drive,' she cried. 'I could look at them for ever. They are like the most exquisite huge ferns. And you see that one with the grey-silver bark and the clusters of cream-coloured flowers, I pulled down a head of them yesterday to smell, and the scent'—she shut her eyes at the memory and her voice thinned away, faint, airy—'was like freshly ground nutmegs.' A little pause. She turned to him and smiled. 'You do know what nutmegs smell like—do you Robert?'

And he smiled back at her. 'Now how am I going to prove to you that I do?'

Back came Antonio with not only the hot water—with letters on a salver and three rolls of paper.

'Oh, the post! Oh, how lovely! Oh, Robert, they mustn't be all for you! Have they just come, Antonio?' Her thin hands flew up and hovered over the letters that Antonio offered her, bending forward.

'Just this moment, Signora,' grinned Antonio. 'I took-a them from the postman myself. I made-a the postman give them for me.'

'Noble Antonio!' laughed she. 'There—those are mine, Robert; the rest are yours.'

Antonio wheeled sharply, stiffened, the grin went out of his face. His striped linen jacket and his flat gleaming fringe made him look like a wooden doll.

Mr Salesby put the letters into his pocket; the papers lay on the table. He turned the ring, turned the signet ring on his little finger and stared in front of him, blinking, vacant.

But she—with her teacup in one hand, the sheets of thin paper in the other, her head tilted back, her lips open, a brush of bright colour on her cheek-bones, sipped, sipped, drank ... drank ....

'From Lottie,' came her soft murmur. 'Poor dear ... such trouble ... left foot. She thought ... neuritis ... Doctor Blyth ... flat foot ... massage. So many robins this year ... maid most satisfactory ... Indian Colonel ... every grain of rice separate ... very heavy fall of snow.' And her wide lighted eyes looked up from the letter. 'Snow, Robert! Think of it!' And she touched the little dark violets pinned on her thin bosom and went back to the letter.

... Snow. Snow in London. Millie with the early morning cup of tea. 'There's been a terrible fall of snow in the night, sir.' 'Oh, has there, Millie?' The curtains ring apart, letting in the pale, reluctant light. He raises himself in the bed; he catches a glimpse of the solid houses opposite framed in white, of their window boxes full of great sprays of white coral .... In the bathroom—overlooking the back garden. Snow—heavy snow over everything. The lawn is covered with a wavy pattern of cat's-paws; there is a thick, thick icing on the garden table; the withered pods of the laburnum tree are white tassels; only here and there in the ivy is a dark leaf showing .... Warming his back at the dining-room fire, the paper drying over a chair. Millie with the bacon. 'Oh, if you please, sir, there's two little boys come as will do the steps and front for a shilling, shall I let them?' ... And then flying lightly, lightly down the stairs—Jinnie. 'Oh, Robert, isn't it wonderful! Oh, what a pity it has to melt. Where's the pussy-wee?' 'I'll get him from Millie.' ... 'Millie, you might just hand me up the kitten if you've got him down there.' 'Very good, sir.' He feels the little beating heart under his hand. 'Come on, old chap, your missus wants you.' 'Oh, Robert, do show him the snow—his first snow. Shall I open the window and give him a little piece on his paw to hold? ... '

'Well, that's very satisfactory on the whole—very. Poor Lottie! Darling Anne! How I only wish I could send them something of this,' she cried, waving her letters at the brilliant, dazzling garden. 'More tea, Robert? Robert dear, more tea?'

'No, thanks, no. It was very good,' he drawled.

'Well, mine wasn't. Mine was just like chopped hay. Oh, here comes the Honeymoon Couple.'

Half striding, half running, carrying a basket between them and rods and lines, they came up the drive, up the shallow steps.

'My! have you been out fishing?' cried the American Woman.

They were out of breath, they panted: 'Yes, yes, we have been out in a little boat all day. We have caught seven. Four are good to eat. But three we shall give away. To the children.'

Mrs Salesby turned her chair to look; the Topknots laid the snakes down. They were a very dark young couple—black hair, olive skin, brilliant eyes and teeth. He was dressed 'English fashion' in a flannel jacket, white trousers and shoes. Round his neck he wore a silk scarf; his head, with his hair brushed back, was bare. And he kept mopping his forehead, rubbing his hands with a brilliant handkerchief. Her white skirt had a patch of wet; her neck and throat were stained a deep pink. When she lifted her arms big half-hoops of perspiration showed under her arm-pits; her hair clung in wet curls to her cheeks. She looked as though her young husband had been dipping her in the sea and fishing her out again to dry in the sun and then—in with her again—all day.

'Would Klaymongso like a fish?' they cried. Their laughing voices charged with excitement beat against the glassed-in veranda like birds and a strange, saltish smell came from the basket.

'You will sleep well tonight,' said a Topknot, picking her ear with a knitting needle while the other Topknot smiled and nodded.

The Honeymoon Couple looked at each other. A great wave seemed to go over them. They gasped, gulped, staggered a little and then came up laughing—laughing..

'We cannot go upstairs, we are too tired. We must have tea just as we are. Here—coffee. No—tea. No—coffee. Tea—coffee, Antonio!' Mrs Salesby turned.

'Robert! Robert!' Where was he? He wasn't there. Oh, there he was at the other end of the veranda, with his back turned, smoking a cigarette. 'Robert, shall we go for our little turn?'

'Right.' He stumped the cigarette into an ash-tray and

sauntered over, his eyes on the ground. 'Will you be warm enough?'

'Oh, quite.'

'Sure?'

'Well,' she put her hand on his arm, 'perhaps'—and gave his arm the faintest pressure—'it's not upstairs, it's only in the hall—perhaps you'd get me my cape. Hanging up.'

He came back with it and she bent her small head while he dropped it on her shoulders. Then, very stiff, he offered her his arm. She bowed sweetly to the people of the veranda while he just covered a yawn, and they went down the steps together.

'*Vous avez voo ça!*' said the American Woman.

'He is not a man,' said the Two Topknots, 'he is an ox. I say to my sister in the morning and at night when we are in bed, I tell her—No man is he, but an ox!'

Wheeling, tumbling, swooping, the laughter of the Honeymoon Couple dashed against the glass of the veranda.

The sun was still high. Every leaf, every flower in the garden lay open, motionless, as if exhausted, and a sweet, rich, rank smell filled the quivering air. Out of the thick, fleshy leaves of a cactus there rose an aloe stem loaded with pale flowers that looked as though they had been cut out of butter; light flashed upon the lifted spears of the palms; over a bed of scarlet waxen flowers some black insects 'zoom-zoomed'; a great, gaudy creeper, orange splashed with jet, sprawled against the wall.

'I don't need my cape after all,' said she. 'It's really too warm.' So he took it off and carried it over his arm. 'Let us go down this path here. I feel so well today—marvellously better. Good heavens—look at those children! And to think it's November!'

In a corner of the garden there were two brimming tubs of water. Three little girls, having thoughtfully taken off their drawers and hung them on a bush, their skirts clasped to their waists, were standing in the tubs and tramping up and down. They screamed, their hair fell over their faces, they splashed one another. But suddenly, the smallest, who had a tub to herself, glanced up and saw who was looking. For a moment she seemed overcome with terror, then clumsily she struggled and strained out of her tub, and still holding her clothes above her waist, 'The

Englishman! The Englishman!' she shrieked and fled away to hide. Shrieking and screaming the other two followed her. In a moment they were gone; in a moment there was nothing but the two brimming tubs and their little drawers on the bush.

'How—very—extraordinary!' said she. 'What made them so frightened? Surely they were much too young to . . . ' She looked up at him. She thought he looked pale—but wonderfully handsome with that great tropical tree behind him with its long, spiked thorns.

For a moment he did not answer. Then he met her glance, and smiling his slow smile, '*Très* rum!' said he.

Très rum! Oh, she felt quite faint. Oh, why should she love him so much just because he said a thing like that. *Très* rum! That was Robert all over. Nobody else but Robert could ever say such a thing. To be so wonderful, so brilliant, so learned, and then to say in that queer, boyish voice . . . She could have wept.

'You know you're very absurd, sometimes,' said she.

'I am,' he answered. And they walked on.

But she was tired. She had had enough. She did not want to walk any more.

'Leave me here and go for a little constitutional, won't you? I'll be in one of these long chairs. What a good thing you've got my cape; you won't have to go upstairs for a rug. Thank you, Robert, I shall look at that delicious heliotrope . . . . You won't be gone long?'

'No—no. You don't mind being left?'

'Silly! I want you to go. I can't expect you to drag after your invalid wife every minute . . . . How long will you be?'

He took out his watch. 'It's just after half-past four. I'll be back at a quarter-past five.'

'Back at a quarter-past five,' she repeated, and she lay still in the long chair and folded her hands.

He turned away. Suddenly he was back again. 'Look here, would you like my watch?' And he dangled it before her.

'Oh!' She caught her breath. 'Very, very much.' And she clasped the watch, the warm watch, the darling watch in her fingers. 'Now go quickly.'

The gates of the Pension Villa Excelsior were open wide,

jammed open against some bold geraniums. Stooping a little, staring straight ahead, walking swiftly, he passed through them and began climbing the hill that wound behind the town like a great rope looping the villas together. The dust lay thick. A carriage came bowling along driving towards the Excelsior. In it sat the General and Countess; they had been for his daily airing. Mr Salesby stepped to one side but the dust beat up, thick, white, stifling like wool. The Countess just had time to nudge the General.

'There he goes,' she said spitefully.

But the General gave a loud caw and refused to look.

'It is the Englishman,' said the driver, turning round and smiling. And the Countess threw up her hands and nodded so amiably that he spat with satisfaction and gave the stumbling horse a cut.

On—on—past the finest villas in the town, magnificent palaces, palaces worth coming any distance to see, past the public gardens with the carved grottoes and statues and stone animals drinking at the fountain, into a poorer quarter. Here the road ran narrow and foul between high lean houses, the ground floors of which were scooped and hollowed into stables and carpenters' shops. At a fountain ahead of him two old hags were beating linen. As he passed them they squatted back on their haunches, stared, and then their 'A-hak-kak-kak!' with the slap, slap, of the stone on the linen sounded after him.

He reached the top of the hill; he turned a corner and the town was hidden. Down he looked into a deep valley with a dried-up river bed at the bottom. This side and that was covered with small dilapidated houses that had broken stone verandas where the fruit lay drying, tomato lanes in the garden and from the gates to the doors a trellis of vines. The late sunlight, deep, golden, lay in the cup of the valley; there was a smell of charcoal in the air. In the gardens the men were cutting grapes. He watched a man standing in the greenish shade, raising up, holding a black cluster in one hand, taking the knife from his belt, cutting, laying the bunch in a flat boat-shaped basket. The man worked leisurely, silently, taking hundreds of years over the job. On the hedges on the other side of the road there were grapes small as berries, growing among the stones. He leaned against a wall, filled his pipe, put a match to it . . . .

Leaned across a gate, turned up the collar of his mackintosh. It was going to rain. It didn't matter, he was prepared for it. You didn't expect anything else in November. He looked over the bare field. From the corner by the gate there came the smell of swedes, a great stack of them, wet, rank coloured. Two men passed walking towards the straggling village. 'Good day!' 'Good day!' By Jove! he had to hurry if he was going to catch that train home. Over the gate, across a field, over the stile, into the lane, swinging along in the drifting rain and dusk . . . . Just home in time for a bath and a change before supper . . . . In the drawing-room; Jinnie is sitting pretty nearly in the fire. 'Oh, Robert, I didn't hear you come in. Did you have a good time? How nice you smell! A present?' 'Some bits of blackberry I picked for you. Pretty colour.' 'Oh, lovely, Robert! Dennis and Beaty are coming to supper.' Supper—cold beef, potatoes in their jackets, claret, household bread. They are gay—everybody's laughing. 'Oh, we all know Robert,' says Dennis, breathing on his eyeglasses and polishing them. 'By the way, Dennis, I picked up a very jolly little edition of . . . '

A clock struck. He wheeled sharply. What time was it. Five? A quarter past? Back, back the way he came. As he passed through the gates he saw her on the look-out. She got up, waved and slowly she came to meet him, dragging the heavy cape. In her hand she carried a spray of heliotrope.

'You're late,' she cried gaily. 'You're three minutes late. Here's your watch, it's been very good while you were away. Did you have a nice time? Was it lovely? Tell me. Where did you go?'

'I say—put this *on*,' he said, taking the cape from her.

'Yes, I will. Yes, it's getting chilly. Shall we go up to our room?' When they reached the lift she was coughing. He frowned.

'It's nothing. I haven't been out too late. Don't be cross.' She sat down on one of the red plush chairs while he rang and rang, and then, getting no answer, kept his finger on the bell.

'Oh, Robert, do you think you ought to?'

'Ought to what?'

The door of the *salon* opened. 'What is that? Who is making that noise?' sounded from within. Klaymongso began to yelp. 'Caw! Caw! Caw!' came from the General. A Topknot darted out with one hand to her ear, opened the staff door, 'Mr Queet! Mr Queet!' she bawled. That brought the manager up at a run.

'Is that you ringing the bell, Mr Salesby? Do you want the lift? Very good, sir. I'll take you up myself. Antonio woudn't have been a minute, he was just taking off his apron—' And having ushered them in, the oily manager went to the door of the *salon*. 'Very sorry you should have been troubled, ladies and gentlemen.' Salesby stood in the cage, sucking in his cheeks, staring at the ceiling and turning the ring, turning the signet ring on his little finger . . . .

Arrived in their room he went swiftly over to the washstand, shook the bottle, poured her out a dose and brought it across.

'Sit down. Drink it. And don't talk.' And he stood over her while she obeyed. Then he took the glass, rinsed it and put it back in its case. 'Would you like a cushion?'

'No, I'm quite all right. come over here. Sit down by me just a minute, will you, Robert? Ah, that's very nice.' She turned and thrust the piece of heliotrope in the lapel of his coat. 'That,' she said, 'is most becoming.' And then she leaned her head against his shoulder and he put his arm round her.

'Robert—' her voice like a sigh—like a breath.

'Yes—'

They sat there for a long while. The sky flamed, paled; the two white beds were like two ships . . . . At last he heard the servant girl running along the corridor with the hot-water cans, and gently he released her and turned on the light.

'Oh, what time is it? Oh, what a heavenly evening. Oh, Robert, I was thinking while you were away this afternoon . . . '

They were the last couple to enter the dining-room. The Countess was there with her lorgnette and her fan, the General was there with his special chair and the air cushion and the small rug over his knees. The American Woman was there showing Klaymongso a copy of the *Saturday Evening Post* . . . 'We're having a feast of reason and a flow of soul.' The Two Topknots were there feeling over the peaches and the pears in their dish of fruit and putting aside all they considered unripe or overripe to show to the manager, and the Honeymoon Couple leaned across the table, whispering, trying not to burst out laughing.

Mr Queet, in everyday clothes and white canvas shoes, served the soup, and Antonio, in full evening dress, handed it round.

'No,' said the American Woman, 'take it away, Antonio. We can't eat soup. We can't eat anything mushy, can we, Klaymongso?'

'Take them back and fill them to the rim!' said the Topknots, and they turned and watched while Antonio delivered the message.

'What is it? Rice? Is it cooked?' The Countess peered through her lorgnette. 'Mr Queet, the General can have some of this soup if it is cooked.'

'Very good, Countess.'

The Honeymoon Couple had their fish instead.

'Give me that one. That's the one I caught. No, it's not. Yes, it is. No, it's not. Well, it's looking at me with its eye, so it must be. Tee! Hee! Hee!' Their feet were locked together under the table.

'Robert, you're not eating again. Is anything the matter?'

'No. Off food, that's all.'

'Oh, what a bother. There are eggs and spinach coming. You don't like spinach, do you. I must tell them in future . . . '

An egg and mashed potatoes for the General.

'Mr Queet! Mr Queet!'

'Yes, Countess.'

'The General's egg's too hard again.'

'Caw! Caw! Caw!'

'Very sorry, Countess. Shall I have you another cooked, General?'

. . . They are the first to leave the dining-room. She rises, gathering her shawl and he stands aside, waiting for her to pass, turning the ring, turning the signet ring on his little finger. In the hall Mr Queet hovers. 'I thought you might not want to wait for the lift. Antonio's just serving the finger bowls. And I'm sorry the bell won't ring, it's out of order. I can't think what's happened.'

'Oh, I do hope . . . ' from her.

'Get in,' says he.

Mr Queet steps after them and slams the door ....

... 'Robert, do you mind if I go to bed very soon? Won't you go down to the *salon* or out into the garden? Or perhaps you might smoke a cigar on the balcony. It's lovely out there. And I like cigar smoke. I always did. But if you'd rather ... '

'No, I'll sit here.'

He takes a chair and sits on the balcony. He hears her moving about in the room, lightly, lightly, moving and rustling. Then she comes over to him. 'Good night, Robert.'

'Good night.' He takes her hand and kisses the palm. 'Don't catch cold.'

The sky is the colour of jade. There are a great many stars; an enormous white moon hangs over the garden. Far away lightning flutters—flutters like a wing—flutters like a broken bird that tries to fly and sinks again and again struggles.

The lights from the *salon* shine across the garden path and there is the sound of a piano. And once the American Woman, opening the French window to let Klaymongso into the garden, cries: 'Have you seen this moon?' But nobody answers.

He gets very cold sitting there, staring at the balcony rail. Finally he comes inside. The moon—the room is painted white with moonlight. The light trembles in the mirrors; the two beds seem to float. She is asleep. He sees her through the nets, half sitting, banked up with pillows, her white hands crossed on the sheet. her white cheeks, her fair hair pressed against the pillow, are silvered over. He undresses quickly, stealthily and gets into bed. Lying there, his hands clasped behind his head ...

... In his study. Late summer. The virginia creeper just on the turn ....

'Well, my dear chap, that's the whole story. That's the long and the short of it. If she can't cut away for the next two years and give a decent climate a chance she don't stand a dog's—h'm—show. Better be frank about these things.' 'Oh, certainly .... ' 'And hang it all, old man, what's to prevent you going with her? It isn't as though you've got a regular job like us wage earners. You can do what you do wherever you are—' 'Two years.' 'Yes, I should give it two years. You'll have no trouble about letting this house, you know. As a matter of fact ... '

... He is with her. 'Robert, the awful thing is—I suppose it's my illness—I simply feel I could not go alone. You see—you're everything. You're bread and wine, Robert, bread and wine. Oh, my darling—what am I saying? Of course I could, of course I won't take you away ....'

He hears her stirring. Does she want something?

'Boogles?'

Good Lord! She is talking in her sleep. They haven't used that name for years.

'Boogles. Are you awake?'

'Yes, do you want anything?'

'Oh, I'm going to be a bother. I'm so sorry. Do you mind? There's a wretched mosquito inside my net—I can hear him singing. Would you catch him? I don't want to move because of my heart.'

'No, don't move. Stay where you are.' He switches on the light, lifts the net. 'Where is the little beggar? Have you spotted him?'

'Yes, there, over by the corner. Oh, I do feel such a fiend to have dragged you out of bed. Do you mind dreadfully?'

'No, of course not.' For a moment he hovers in his blue and white pyjamas. Then, 'got him,' he said.

'Oh, good. Was he a juicy one?'

'Beastly.' He went over to the washstand and dipped his fingers in water. 'Are you all right now? Shall I switch off the light?'

'Yes, please. No. Boogles! Come back here a moment. Sit down by me. Give me your hand.' She turns his signet ring. 'Why weren't you asleep? Boogles, listen. Come closer. I sometimes wonder—do you mind awfully being out here with me?'

He bends down. He kisses her. He tucks her in, he smooths the pillow.

'Rot!' he whispers.

The Daughters of the Late Colonel

I

The week after was one of the busiest weeks of their lives. Even when they went to bed it was only their bodies that lay down and rested; their minds went on, thinking things out, talking things over, wondering, deciding, trying to remember where . . .

Constantia lay like a statue, her hands by her sides, her feet just overlapping each other, the sheet up to her chin. She stared at the ceiling.

'Do you think father would mind if we gave his top-hat to the porter?'

'The porter?' snapped Josephine. 'Why ever the porter? What a very extraordinary idea!'

'Because,' said Constantia slowly, 'he must often have to go to funerals. And I noticed at—at the cemetery that he only had a bowler.' She paused. 'I thought then how very much he'd appreciate a top-hat. We ought to give him a present, too. He was always very nice to father.'

'But,' cried Josephine, flouncing on her pillow and staring across the dark at Constantia, 'father's head!' And suddenly, for one awful moment, she nearly giggled. Not, of course, that she felt in the least like giggling. It must have been habit. Years ago, when they had stayed awake at night talking, their beds had simply heaved. And now the porter's head, disappearing, popped out, like a candle, under father's hat . . . . The giggle mounted, mounted; she clenched her hands; she fought it down; she frowned fiercely at the dark and said 'Remember' terribly sternly.

'We can decide tomorrow,' she said.

Constantia had noticed nothing; she sighed.

'Do you think we ought to have our dressing-gowns dyed as well?'

'Black?' almost shrieked Josephine.

'Well, what else?' said Constantia. 'I was thinking—it doesn't seem quite sincere, in a way, to wear black out of doors and when we're fully dressed, and then when we're at home—'

'But nobody sees us,' said Josephine. She gave the bedclothes such a twitch that both her feet became uncovered and she had to creep up the pillows to get them well under again.

'Kate does,' said Constantia. 'And the postman very well might.'

Josephine though of her dark-red slippers, which matched her dressing-gown, and of Constantia's favourite indefinite green ones which went with hers. Black! Two black dressing-gowns and two pairs of black woolly slippers, creeping off to the bathroom like black cats.

'I don't think it's absolutely necessary,' said she.

Silence. Then Constantia said, 'We shall have to post the papers with the notice in them tomorrow to catch the Ceylon mail . . . . How many letters have we had up till now?'

'Twenty-three.'

Josephine had replied to them all, and twenty-three times when she came to 'We miss our dear father so much' she had broken down and had to use her handkerchief, and on some of them even to soak up a very light-blue tear with an edge of blotting-paper. Strange! She couldn't have put it on—but twenty-three times. Even now, though, when she said over to herself sadly 'We miss our dear father so much,' she could have cried if she'd wanted to.

'Have you got enough stamps?' came from Constantia.

'Oh, how can I tell?' said Josephine crossly. 'What's the good of asking me that now?'

'I was just wondering,' said Constantia mildly.

Silence again. There came a little rustle, a scurry, a hop.

'A mouse,' said Constantia.

'It can't be a mouse because there aren't any crumbs,' said Josephine.

'But it doesn't know there aren't,' said Constantia.

A spasm of pity squeezed her heart. Poor little thing! She wished she'd left a tiny piece of biscuit on the dressing-table. It was awful to think of it not finding anything. What would it do?

'I can't think how they manage to live at all,' she said slowly.

'Who?' demanded Josephine.

. And Constantia said more loudly than she meant to, 'Mice.'

Josephine was furious. 'Oh, what nonsense, Con!' she said. 'What have mice got to do with it? You're asleep.'

'I don't think I am,' said Constantia. She shut her eyes to make sure. She was.

Josephine arched her spine, pulled up her knees, folded her arms so that her fists came under her ears, and pressed her cheek hard against the pillow.

II

Another thing which complicated matters was they had Nurse Andrews staying on with them that week. It was their own fault; they had asked her. It was Josephine's idea. On the morning—well, on the last morning, when the doctor had gone, Josephine had said to Constantia, 'Don't you think it would be rather nice if we asked Nurse Andrews to stay on for a week as our guest?'

'Very nice,' said Constantia.

'I thought,' went on Josephine quickly, 'I should just say this afternoon, after I've paid her, "My sister and I would be very pleased, after all you've done for us, Nurse Andrews, if you would stay on for a week as our guest." I'd have to put that in about being our guest in case—'

'Oh, but she could hardly expect to be paid!' cried Constantia.

'One never knows,' said Josephine sagely.

Nurse Andrews had, of course, jumped at the idea. But it was a bother. It meant they had to have regular sit-down meals at the proper times, whereas if they'd been alone they could just have asked Kate if she wouldn't have minded bringing them a tray wherever they were. And meal-times now that the strain was over were rather a trial.

Nurse Andrews was simply fearful about butter. Really they couldn't help feeling that about butter, at least, she took advantage of their kindness. And she had that maddening habit of asking for just an inch more of bread to finish what she had on her plate, and then, at the last mouthful, absent-mindedly—of course it wasn't absent-mindedly—taking another helping. Josephine got very red when this happened, and she fastened her small, bead-like eyes on the table cloth as if she saw a minute strange insect creeping through the web of it. But Constantia's long, pale face lengthened and set, and she gazed away—away—far over the desert, to where that line of camels unwound like a thread of wool . . . .

'When I was with Lady Tukes,' said Nurse Andrews, 'she had such a dainty little contrayvance for the buttah. It was a silvah cupid balanced on the—on the bordah of a glass dish, holding a tayny fork. And when you wanted some buttah you simply pressed his foot and he bent down and speared you a piece. It was quite a gayme.'

Josephine could hardly bear that. But 'I think those things are very extravagant' was all she said.

'But whey?' asked Nurse Andrews, beaming through her eyeglasses. 'No one, surely, would take more buttah than one wanted—would one?'

'Ring, Con,' cried Josephine. She couldn't trust herself to reply.

And proud young Kate, the enchanted princess, came in to see what the old tabbies wanted now. She snatched away their plates of mock something or other and slapped down a white, terrified blancmange.

'Jam, please, Kate,' said Josephine kindly.

Kate knelt and burst open the sideboard, lifted the lid of the jam-pot, saw it was empty, put it on the table, and stalked off.

'I'm afraid,' said Nurse Andrews a moment later, 'there isn't any.'

'Oh, what a bother!' said Josephine. She bit her lip. 'What had we better do?'

Constantia looked dubious. 'We can't disturb Kate again,' she said softly.

Nurse Andrews waited, smiling at them both. Her eyes wandered, spying at everything behind her eyeglasses. Constantia in despair went back to her camels. Josephine frowned heavily—concentrated. If it hadn't been for this idiotic woman she and Con would, of course, have eaten their blancmange without. Suddenly the idea came.

'I know,' she said. 'Marmalade. There's some marmalade in the sideboard. Get it, Con.'

'I hope,' laughed Nurse Andrews—and her laugh was like a spoon tinkling against a medicine-glass—'I hope it's not very bittah marmalayde.'

III

But, after all, it was not long now, and then she'd be gone for good. And there was no getting over the fact that she had been very kind to father. She had nursed him day and night at the end. Indeed, both Constantia and Josephine felt privately she had rather overdone the not leaving him at the very last. For when they had gone in to say goodbye Nurse Andrews had sat beside his bed the whole time, holding his wrist and pretending to look at her watch. It couldn't have been necessary. It was so tactless, too. Supposing father had wanted to say something—something private to them. Not that he had. Oh, far from it! He lay there, purple, a dark, angry purple in the face, and never even looked at them when they came in. Then, as they were standing there, wondering what to do, he had suddenly opened one eye. Oh, what a difference it would have made, what a difference to their memory of him, how much easier to tell people about it, if he had only opened both! But no—one eye only. It glared at them a moment and then ... went out.

IV

It had made it very awkward for them when Mr Farolles, of St John's, called the same afternoon.

'The end was quite peaceful, I trust?' were the first words he said as he glided towards them through the dark drawing-room.

'Quite,' said Josephine faintly. They both hung their heads. Both of them felt certain that eye wasn't at all a peaceful eye.

'Won't you sit down?' said Josephine.

'Thank you, Miss Pinner,' said Mr Farolles gratefully. He folded his coat-tails and began to lower himself into father's armchair, but just as he touched it he almost sprang up and slid into the next chair instead.

He coughed. Josephine clasped her hands; Constantia looked vague.

'I want you to feel, Miss Pinner,' said Mr Farolles, 'and you, Miss Constantia, that I'm trying to be helpful. I want to be helpful to you both, if you will let me. These are the times,' said Mr Farolles, very simply and earnestly, 'when God means us to be helpful to one another.'

'Thank you very much, Mr Farolles,' said Josephine and Constantia.

'Not at all,' said Mr Farolles gently. He drew his kid gloves through his fingers and leaned forward. 'And if either of you would like a little Communion, either or both of you, here and now, you have only to tell me. A little Communion is often very help—a great comfort,' he added tenderly.

But the idea of a little Communion terrified them. What! In the drawing-room by themselves—with no—no altar or anything! The piano would be much too high, thought Constantia, and Mr Farolles could not possibly lean over it with the chalice. And Kate would be sure to come bursting in and interrupt them, thought Josephine. And supposing the bell rang in the middle? It might be somebody important—about their mourning. Would they get up reverently and go out, or would they have to wait . . . in torture?

'Perhaps you will send round a note by your good Kate if you would care for it later,' said Mr Farolles.

'Oh yes, thank you very much!' they both said.

Mr Farolles got up and took his black straw hat from the round table.

'And about the funeral,' he said softly. 'I may arrange that—as your dear father's old friend and yours, Miss Pinner—and Miss Constantia?'

Josephine and Constantia got up too.

'I should like it to be quite simple,' said Josephine firmly, 'and not too expensive. At the same time, I should like—'

'A good one that will last,' thought dreamy Constantia, as if Josephine were buying a nightgown. But, of course, Josephine didn't say that. 'One suitable to our father's position.' She was very nervous.

'I'll run round to our good friend Mr Knight,' said Mr Farolles soothingly. 'I will ask him to come and see you. I am sure you will find him very helpful indeed.'

V

Well, at any rate, all that part of it was over, though neither of them could possibly believe that father was never coming back. Josephine had had a moment of absolute terror at the cemetery, while the coffin was lowered, to think that she and Constantia had done this thing without asking his permission. What would father say when he found out? For he was bound to find out sooner or later. He always did. 'Buried. You two girls had me buried!' She heard his stick thumping. Oh, what would they say? What possible excuse could they make? It sounded such an appallingly heartless thing to do. Such a wicked advantage to take of a person because he happened to be helpless at the moment. The other people seemed to treat it all as a matter of course. They were strangers; they couldn't be expected to understand that father was the very last person for such a thing to happen to. No, the entire blame for it all would fall on her and Constantia. And the expense, she thought, stepping into the tight-buttoned cab. When she had to show him the bills. What would he say then?

She heard him absolutely roaring. 'And do you expect me to pay for this gimcrack excursion of yours?'

'Oh,' groaned poor Josephine aloud, 'we shouldn't have done it, Con!'

And Constantia, pale as a lemon in all that blackness, said in a frightened whisper, 'Done what, Jug?'

'Let them bu-bury father like that,' said Josephine, breaking down and crying into her new, queer-smelling mourning handkerchief.

'But what else could we have done?' asked Constantia wonderingly. 'We couldn't have kept him unburied. At any rate, not in a flat that size.'

Josephine blew her nose; the cab was dreadfully stuffy.

'I don't know,' she said forlornly. 'It is all so dreadful. I feel we ought to have tried to, just for a time at least. To make perfectly sure. One thing's certain'—and her tears sprang out again—'father will never forgive us for this—never!'

VI

Father would never forgive them. That was what they felt more than ever when, two mornings later, they went into his room to go through his things. They had discussed it quite calmly. It was even down on Josephine's list of things to be done. Go through father's things and settle about them. But that was a very different matter from saying after breakfast:

'Well, are you ready, Con?'

'Yes, Jug—when you are.'

'Then I think we'd better get it over.'

It was dark in the hall. It had been a rule for years never to disturb father in the morning, whatever happened. And now they were going to open the door without knocking even .... Constantia's eyes were enormous at the idea; Josephine felt weak in the knees.

'You—you go first,' she gasped, pushing Constantia.

But Constantia said, as she always had said on those occasions, 'No, Jug, that's not fair. You're the eldest.'

Josephine was just going to say—what at other times she wouldn't have owned to for the world—what she kept for her very last weapon, 'But you're the tallest,' when they noticed that the kitchen door was open, and there stood Kate ....

'Very stiff,' said Josephine, grasping the door-handle and doing her best to turn it. As if anything ever deceived Kate!

It couldn't be helped. That girl was ... Then the door was shut behind them, but—but they weren't in father's room at all. They might have suddenly walked through the wall by mistake into a different flat altogether. Was the door just behind them? They were too frightened to look. Josephine knew that if it was it was holding itself tight shut; Constantia felt that, like the doors in dreams, it hadn't any handle at all. It was the coldness which made it so awful. Or the whiteness—which? Everything was covered. The blinds were down, a cloth hung over the mirror, a sheet hid the bed; a huge fan of white paper filled the fireplace. Constantia timidly put out her hand; she almost expected a snowflake to fall. Josephine felt a queer tingling in her nose, as if her nose was freezing. Then a cab klop-klopped over the cobbles below, and the quiet seemed to shake into little pieces.

'I had better pull up a blind,' said Josephine bravely.

'Yes, it might be a good idea,' whispered Constantia.

They only gave the blind a touch, but it flew up and the cord flew after, rolling round the blind-stick, and the little tassel tapped as if trying to get free. That was too much for Constantia.

'Don't you think—don't you think we might put it off for another day?' she whispered.

'Why?' snapped Josephine, feeling, as usual, much better now that she knew for certain that Constantia was terrified. 'It's got to be done. But I do wish you wouldn't whisper, Con.'

'I didn't know I was whispering,' whispered Constantia.

'And why do you keep staring at the bed?' said Josephine, raising her voice almost defiantly. 'There's nothing on the bed.'

'Oh, Jug—don't say so!' said poor Connie. 'At any rate, not so loudly.'

Josephine felt herself that she had gone too far. She took a wide swerve over to the chest of drawers, put out her hand, but quickly drew it back again.

'Connie!' she gasped, and she wheeled round and leaned with her back against the chest of drawers.

'Oh, Jug—what?'

Josephine could only glare. She had the most extraordinary feeling that she had just escaped something simply awful. But how could she explain to Constantia that father was in the chest of drawers? He was in the top drawer with his handkerchiefs and neckties, or in the next with his shirts and pyjamas, or in the lowest of them all with his suits. He was watching there, hidden away—just behind the door-handle—ready to spring.

She pulled a funny old-fashioned face at Constantia, just as she used to in the old days when she was going to cry.

'I can't open,' she nearly wailed.

'No, don't, Jug,' whispered Constantia earnestly. 'It's much better not to. Don't let's open anything. At any rate, not for a long time.'

'But—but it seems so weak,' said Josephine, breaking down.

'But why not be weak for once, Jug?' argued Constantia, whispering quite fiercely. 'If it is weak.' And her pale stare flew from the locked writing-table—so safe—to the huge glittering wardrobe, and she began to breathe in a queer, panting away. 'Why shouldn't we be weak for once in our lives, Jug? It's quite excusable. Let's be weak—be weak, Jug. It's much nicer to be weak than to be strong.'

And then she did one of those amazingly bold things that she'd done about twice before in their lives: she marched over to the wardrobe, turned the key, and took it out of the lock. Took it out of the lock and held it up to Josephine, showing Josephine by her extraordinary smile that she knew what she'd done—she'd risked deliberately father being in there among his overcoats.

If the huge wardrobe had lurched forward, had crashed down on Constantia, Josephine wouldn't have been surprised. On the contrary, she would have thought it the only suitable thing to happen. But nothing happened. Only the room seemed quieter than ever, and the bigger flakes of cold air fell on Josephine's shoulders and knees. She began to shiver.

'Come, Jug,' said Constantia, still with that awful callous smile; and Josephine followed just as she had that last time, when Constantia had pushed Benny into the round pond.

VII

But the strain told on them when they were back in the dining-room. They sat down, very shaky, and looked at each other.

'I don't feel I can settle to anything,' said Josephine, 'until I've had something. Do you think we could ask Kate for two cups of hot water?'

'I really don't see why we shouldn't' said Constantia carefully. She was quite normal again. 'I won't ring. I'll go to the kitchen door and ask her.'

'Yes, do,' said Josephine, sinking down into a chair. 'Tell her, just two cups, Con, nothing else—on a tray.'

'She needn't even put the jug on, need she?' said Constantia, as though Kate might very well complain if the jug had been there.

'Oh no, certainly not! The jug's not at all necessary. She can pour it direct out of the kettle,' cried Josephine, feeling that would be a labour-saving indeed.

Their cold lips quivered at the greenish brims. Josephine curved her small red hands round the cup; Constantia sat up and blew on the wavy steam, making it flutter from one side to the other.

'Speaking of Benny,' said Josephine.

And though Benny hadn't been mentioned Constantia immediately looked as though he had.

'He'll expect us to send him something of father's, of course. But it's so difficult to know what to send to Ceylon.'

'You mean things get unstuck so on the voyage,' murmured Constantia.

'No, lost,' said Josephine sharply. 'You know there's no post. Only runners.'

Both paused to watch a black man in white linen drawers running through the pale fields for dear life, with a large brown-paper parcel in his hands. Josephine's black man was tiny; he scurried along glistening like an ant. But there was something blind and tireless about Constantia's tall, thin fellow, which made him, she decided, a very unpleasant person indeed .... On the veranda, dressed all in white and wearing a cork helmet, stood Benny. His right hand shook up and down, as father's did when he was impatient. And behind him, not in the least interested, sat Hilda, the unknown sister-in-law. She swung in a cane rocker and flicked over the leaves of the Tatler.

'I think his watch would be the most suitable present,' said Josephine.

Constantia looked up; she seemed surprised.

'Oh, would you trust a gold watch to a native?'

'But of course, I'd disguise it,' said Josephine. 'No one would know it was a watch.' She liked the idea of having to make a parcel such a curious shape that no one could possibly guess what it was. She even thought for a moment of hiding the watch in a narrow cardboard corset-box that she'd kept by her for a long time, waiting for it to come in for something. It was such beautiful, firm cardboard. But, no, it wouldn't be appropriate for this occasion. It had lettering on it: *Medium Women's 28. Extra Firm Busks*. It would be almost too much of a surprise for Benny to open that and find father's watch inside.

'And, of course, it isn't as though it would be going—ticking, I mean,' said Constantia, who was still thinking of the native love of jewellery. 'At least,' she added, 'it would be very strange if after all that time it was.'

VIII

Josephine made no reply. She had flown off on one of her tangents. She had suddenly thought of Cyril. Wasn't it more usual for the only grandson to have the watch? And then dear Cyril was so appreciative and a gold watch meant so much to a young man. Benny, in all probability, had quite got out of the habit of watches; men so seldom wore waistcoats in those hot climates. Whereas Cyril in London wore them from year's end to year's end. And it would be so nice for her and Constantia, when he came to tea, to know it was there. 'I see you've got on grandfather's watch, Cyril.' It would be somehow so satisfactory.

Dear boy! What a blow his sweet, sympathetic little note had been! Of course they quite understood; but it was most unfortunate.

'It would have been such a point, having him,' said Josephine.

'And he would have enjoyed it so,' said Constantia, not thinking what she was saying.

However, as soon as he got back he was coming to tea with his aunties. Cyril to tea was one of their rare treats.

'Now, Cyril, you mustn't be frightened of our cakes. Your Auntie Con and I bought them at Buszard's this morning. We know what a man's appetite is. So don't be ashamed of making a good tea.'

Josephine cut recklessly into the rich dark cake that stood for her winter gloves or the soling and heeling of Constantia's only respectable shoes. But Cyril was most unmanlike in appetite.

'I say, Aunt Josephine, I simply can't. I've only just had lunch, you know.'

'Oh, Cyril, that can't be true! It's after four,' cried Josephine. Constantia sat with her knife poised over the chocolate-roll.

'It is, all the same,' said Cyril. 'I had to meet a man at Victoria, and he kept me hanging about till ... there was only time to get lunch and to come on here. And he gave me—phew'—Cyril put his hand to his forehead—'a terrific blow-out,' he said.

It was disappointing—today of all days. But still he couldn't be expected to know.

'But you'll have a meringue, won't you, Cyril?' said Aunt

Josephine. 'These meringues were bought specially for you. Your dear father was so fond of them. We were sure you are, too.'

'I *am*, Aunt Josephine,' cried Cyril ardently. 'Do you mind if I take half to begin with?'

'Not at all, dear boy; but we mustn't let you off with that.'

'Is your dear father still so fond of meringues?' asked Auntie Con gently. She winced faintly as she broke through the shell of hers.

'Well, I don't quite know, Auntie Con,' said Cyril breezily.

At that they both looked up.

'Don't know?' almost snapped Josephine. 'Don't know a thing like that about your own father, Cyril?'

'Surely,' said Auntie Con softly.

Cyril tried to laugh it off. 'Oh, well,' he said, 'it's such a long time since—' He faltered. He stopped. Their faces were too much for him.

'Even *so*,' said Josephine.

And Auntie Con looked.

Cyril put down his teacup. 'Wait a bit,' he cried. 'Wait a bit, Aunt Josephine. What am I thinking of?'

He looked up. They were beginning to brighten. Cyril slapped his knee.

'Of course,' he said, 'it was meringues. How could I have forgotten? Yes, Aunt Josephine, you're perfectly right. Father's most frightfully keen on meringues.'

They didn't only beam. Aunt Josephine went scarlet with pleasure; Auntie Con gave a deep, deep sigh.

'And now, Cyril, you must come and see father,' said Josephine. 'He knows you were coming today.'

'Right,' said Cyril, very firmly and heartily. He got up from hs chair; suddenly he glanced at the clock.

'I say, Auntie Con, isn't your clock a bit slow? I've got to meet a man at—at Paddington just after five. I'm afraid I shan't be able to stay very long with grandfather.'

'Oh, he won't expect you to stay *very* long!' said Aunt Josephine.

Constantia was still gazing at the clock. She couldn't make up her mind if it was fast or slow. It was one or the other, she felt almost certain of that. At any rate, it had been.

Cyril still lingered. 'Aren't you coming along, Auntie Con?'

'Of course,' said Josephine, 'we shall all go. Come on, Con.'

IX

They knocked at the door, and Cyril followed his aunts into grandfather's hot, sweetish room.

'Come on,' said Grandfather Pinner. 'Don't hang about. What is it? What've you been up to?'

He was sitting in front of a roaring fire, clasping his stick. He had a thick rug over his knees. On his lap there lay a beautiful pale yellow silk handkerchief.

'It's Cyril, father,' said Josephine shyly. And she took Cyril's hand and led him forward.

'Good afternoon, grandfather,' said Cyril, trying to take his hand out of Aunt Josephine's. Grandfather Pinner shot his eyes at Cyril in the way he was famous for. Where was Auntie Con? She stood on the other side of Aunt Josephine; her long arms hung down in front of her; her hands were clasped. She never took her eyes off grandfather.

'Well,' said Grandfather Pinner, beginning to thump, 'what have you got to tell me?'

What had he, what had he got to tell him? Cyril felt himself smiling like a perfect imbecile. The room was stifling, too.

But Aunt Josephine came to his rescue. She cried brightly, 'Cyril says his father is still very fond of meringues, father dear.'

'Eh?' said Grandfather Pinner, curving his hand like a purple meringue-shell over one ear.

Josephine repeated, 'Cyril says his father is still very fond of meringues.'

'Can't hear,' said old Colonel Pinner. And he waved Josephine away with his stick, then pointed with his stick to Cyril. 'Tell me what she's trying to say,' he said.

(My God!) 'Must I?' said Cyril, blushing and staring at Aunt Josephine.

'Do, dear,' she smiled. 'It will please him so much.'

'Come on, out with it!' cried Colonel Pinner testily, beginning to thump again.

And Cyril leaned forward and yelled, 'Father's still very fond of meringues.'

At that Grandfather Pinner jumped as though he had been shot. 'Don't shout!' he cried. 'What's the matter with the boy? Meringues! What about 'em?'

'Oh, Aunt Josephine, must we go on?' groaned Cyril desperately.

'It's quite all right, dear boy,' said Aunt Josephine, as though he and she were at the dentist's together. 'He'll understand in a minute.' And she whispered to Cyril, 'He's getting a bit deaf, you know.' Then she leaned forward and really bawled at Grandfather Pinner, 'Cyril only wanted to tell you, father dear, that his father is still very fond of meringues.'

Colonel Pinner heard that time, heard and brooded, looking Cyril up and down.

'What an esstrordinary thing!' said old Grandfather Pinner. 'What an esstrordinary thing to come all this way here to tell me!'

And Cyril felt it *was*.

'Yes, I shall send Cyril the watch,' said Josephine.

'That would be very nice,' said Constantia. 'I seem to remember last time he came there was some little trouble about the time.'

X

They were interrupted by Kate bursting through the door in her usual fashion, as though she had discovered some secret panel in the wall.

'Fried or boiled?' asked the bold voice.

Fried or boiled? Josephine and Constantia were quite bewildered for the moment. They could hardly take it in.

'Fried or boiled what, Kate?' asked Josephine, trying to begin to concentrate.

Kate gave a loud sniff. 'Fish.'

'Well, why didn't you say so immediately?' Josephine reproached her gently. 'How could you expect us to understand, Kate? There are a great many things in this world you know, which are fried or boiled.' And after such a display of courage she said quite brightly to Constantia, 'Which do you prefer, Con?'

'I think it might be nice to have it fried,' said Constantia. 'On the other hand, of course, boiled fish is very nice. I think I prefer both equally well ... Unless you ... In that case—'

'I shall fry it,' said Kate, and she bounced back, leaving their door open and slamming the door of her kitchen.

Josephine gazed at Constantia; she raised her pale eyebrows until they rippled away into her pale hair. She got up. She said in a very lofty, imposing way, 'Do you mind following me into the drawing-room, Constantia? I've got something of great importance to discuss with you.'

For it was always to the drawing-room they retired when they wanted to talk over Kate.

Josephine closed the door meaningly. 'Sit down, Constantia,' she said, still very grand. She might have been receiving Constantia for the first time. And Con looked round vaguely for a chair, as though she felt indeed quite a stranger.

'Now the question is,' said Josephine, bending forward, 'whether we shall keep her or not.'

'That is the question,' agreed Constantia.

'And this time,' said Josephine firmly, 'we must come to a definite decision.'

Constantia looked for a moment as though she might begin going over all the other times, but she pulled herself together and said, 'Yes, Jug.'

'You see, Con,' explained Josephine, 'everything is so changed now.' Constantia looked up quickly. 'I mean,' went on Josephine, 'we're not dependent on Kate as we were.' And she blushed faintly. 'There's not father to cook for.'

'That is perfectly true,' agreed Constantia. 'Father certainly doesn't want any cooking now whatever else—'

Josephine broke in sharply, 'You're not sleepy, are you, Con?'

'Sleepy, Jug?' Constantia was wide-eyed.

'Well, concentrate more,' said Josephine sharply, and she returned to the subject. 'What it comes to is, if we did'—and this she barely breathed, glancing at the door—'give Kate notice'—she raised her voice again—'we could manage our own food.'

'Why not?' cried Constantia. She couldn't help smiling. The idea was so exciting. She clasped her hands. 'What should we live on, Jug?'

'Oh, eggs in various forms!' said Jug, lofty again. 'And, besides, there are all the cooked foods.'

'But I've always heard,' said Constantia, 'they are considered so very expensive.'

'Not if one buys them in moderation,' said Josephine. But she tore herself away from this fascinating bypath and dragged Constantia after her.

'What we've got to decide now, however, is whether we really do trust Kate or not.'

Constantia leaned back. Her flat little laugh flew from her lips.

'Isn't it curious, Jug,' said she, 'that just on this one subject I've never been able to quite make up my mind?'

XI

She never had. The whole difficulty was to prove anything. How did one prove things, how could one? Suppose Kate had stood in front of her and deliberately made a face. Mightn't she very well have been in pain? Wasn't it impossible, at any rate, to ask Kate if she was making a face at her? If Kate answered 'No'—and, of course, she would say 'No'—what a position! How undignified! Then, again, Constantia suspected, she was almost certain that Kate went to her chest of drawers when she and Josephine were out, not to take things but to spy. Many times she had come back to find her amethyst cross in the most unlikely places, under her lace ties or on top of her evening Bertha. More than once she had laid a trap for Kate. She had arranged things in a special order and then called Josephine to witness.

'You see, Jug?'

'Quite, Con.'

'Now we shall be able to tell.'

But, oh dear, when she did go to look, she was as far off from a proof as ever! If anything was displaced, it might so very well have happened as she closed the drawer; a jolt might have done it so easily.

'You come, Jug, and decide. I really can't. It's too difficult.'

But after a pause and a long glare Josephine would sigh, 'Now you've put the doubt into my mind, Con, I'm sure I can't tell myself.'

'Well, we can't postpone it again,' said Josephine. 'If we postpone it this time—'

XII

But at that moment in the street below a barrel-organ struck up. Josephine and Constantia sprang to their feet together.

'Run, Con,' said Josephine. 'Run quickly. There's sixpence on the—'

Then they remembered. It didn't matter. They would never have to stop the organ-grinder again. Never again would she and Constantia be told to make that monkey take his noise somewhere else. Never would sound that loud, strange bellow when father thought they were not hurrying enough. The organ-grinder might play there all day and the stick would not thump.

It never will thump again,
It never will thump again,

played the barrel-organ.

What was Constantia thinking? She had such a strange smile; she looked different. She couldn't be going to cry.

'Jug, Jug,' said Constantia softly, pressing her hands together. 'Do you know what day it is? It's Saturday. It's a week today, a whole week.'

A week since father died,
A week since father died,

cried the barrel-organ. And Josephine, too, forgot to be practical and sensible; she smiled faintly, strangely. On the Indian carpet there fell a square of sunlight, pale red; it came and went and came—and stayed, deepened—until it shone almost golden.

'The sun's out,' said Josephine, as though it really mattered.

A perfect fountain of bubbling notes shook from the barrel-organ, round, bright notes, carelessly scattered.

Constantia lifted her big, cold hands as if to catch them, and then her hands fell again. She walked over to the mantelpiece to her favourite Buddha. And the stone and gilt image, whose smile always gave her such a queer feeling, almost a pain and yet a pleasant pain, seemed today to be more than smiling. He knew something; he had a secret. 'I know something that you don't know,' said her Buddha. Oh, what was it, what could it be? And yet she had always felt there was . . . something.

The sunlight pressed through the windows, thieved its way in, flashed its light over the furniture and the photographs. Josephine watched it. When it came to mother's photograph, the enlargement over the piano, it lingered as though puzzled to find so little remained of mother, except the ear-rings shaped like tiny pagodas and a black feather boa. Why did the photographs of dead people always fade so? wondered Josephine. As soon as a person was dead their photograph died too. But, of course, this one of mother was very old. It was thirty-five years old. Josephine remembered standing on a chair and pointing out that feather boa to Constantia and telling her that it was a snake that had killed their mother in Ceylon . . . . Would everything have been different if mother hadn't died? She didn't see why. Aunt Florence had lived with them until they had left school, and they had moved three times and had their yearly holiday and . . . and there'd been changes of servants, of course.

Some little sparrows, young sparrows they sounded, chirped on the window-ledge. *Yeep—eyeep—yeep.* But Josephine felt they were not sparrows, not on the window-ledge. It was inside her, that queer little crying noise. *Yeep—eyeep—yeep.* Ah, what was it crying, so weak and forlorn?

If mother had lived, might they have married? But there had been nobody for them to marry. There had been father's Anglo-Indian friends before he quarrelled with them. But after that she and Constantia never met a single man except clergymen. How did one meet men? Or even if they'd met them, how could they have got to know men well enough to be more than strangers? One read of people having adventures, being followed, and so on. But nobody had ever followed Constantia and her. Oh yes, there had been one year at Eastbourne a mysterious man at their boarding-house who had put a note on the jug of hot water outside their bedroom door! But by the time Connie had found it the steam had made the writing too faint to read; they couldn't even make out to which of them it was addressed. And he had left next day. And that was all. The rest had been looking after father and at the same time keeping out of father's way. But now? But now? The thieving sun touched Josephine gently. She lifted her face. She was drawn over to the window by gentle beams . . . .

Until the barrel-organ stopped playing Constantia stayed before the Buddha, wondering, but not as usual, not vaguely. This time her wonder was like longing. She remembered the times she had come in here, crept out of bed in her nightgown when the moon was full, and lain on the floor with her arms outstretched, as though she was crucified. Why? The big, pale moon had made her do it. The horrible dancing figures on the carved screen had leered at her and she hadn't minded. She remembered too how, whenever they were at the seaside, she had gone off by herself and got as close to the sea as she could, and sung something, something she had made up, while she gazed all over that restless water. There had been this other life, running out, bringing things home in bags, getting this on approval, discussing them with Jug, and taking them back to get more things on approval, and arranging father's trays and trying not to annoy father. But it all seemed to have happened in a kind of tunnel. It wasn't real. It was only when she came out of the tunnel into the moonlight or by the sea or into a thunderstorm that she really felt herself. What did it mean? What was it she was always wanting? What did it all lead to? Now? Now?

She turned away from the Buddha with one of her vague gestures. She went over to where Josephine was standing. She wanted to say something to Josephine, something frightfully important, about—about the future and what . . .

'Don't you think perhaps—' she began.

But Josephine interrupted her. 'I was wondering if now—' she murmured. They stopped; they waited for each other.

'Go on, Con,' said Josephine.

'No, no, Jug; after you,' said Constantia.

'No, say what you were going to say. You began,' said Josephine.

'I . . . I'd rather hear what you were going to say first,' said Constantia.

'Don't be absurd, Con.'

'Really, Jug.'

'Connie!'

'Oh, *Jug*!'

A pause. Then Constantia said faintly, 'I can't say what I was going to say, Jug, because I've forgotten what it was ... that I was going to say.'

Josephine was silent for a moment. She stared at a big cloud where the sun had been. Then she replied shortly, 'I've forgotten too.'

Her First Ball

Exactly when the ball began Leila would have found it hard to say. Perhaps her first real partner was the cab. It did not matter that she shared the cab with the Sheridan girls and their brother. She sat back in her own little corner of it, and the bolster on which her hand rested felt like the sleeve of an unknown young man's dress suit; and away they bowled, past waltzing lamp-posts and houses and fences and trees.

'Have you really never been to a ball before, Leila? But, my child, how too weird—' cried the Sheridan girls.

'Our nearest neighbour was fifteen miles,' said Leila softly, gently opening and shutting her fan.

Oh dear, how hard it was to be indifferent like the others! She tried not to smile too much; she tried not to care. But every single thing was so new and exciting . . . Meg's tuberoses, Jose's long loop of amber, Laura's little dark head, pushing above her white fur like a flower through snow. She would remember for ever. It even gave her a pang to see her cousin Laurie throw away the wisps of tissue paper he pulled from the fastenings of his new gloves. She would like to have kept those wisps as a keepsake, as a remembrance. Laurie leaned forward and put his hand on Laura's knee.

'Look here, darling,' he said. 'The third and the ninth as usual. Twig?'

Oh, how marvellous to have a brother! In her excitement Leila felt that if there had been time, if it hadn't been impossible, she couldn't have helped crying because she was an only child and no brother had ever said 'Twig?' to her; no sister would ever say, as Meg said to Jose that moment, 'I've never known your hair go up more successfully than it has tonight!'

But, of course, there was not time. They were at the drill hall already; there were cabs in front of them and cabs behind. The road was bright on either side with moving fan-like lights, and on the pavement gay couples seemed to float through the air; little satin shoes chased each other like birds.

'Hold on to me, Leila; you'll get lost,' said Laura.

'Come on, girls, let's make a dash for it,' said Laurie.

Leila put two fingers on Laura's pink velvet cloak, and they were somehow lifted past the big golden lantern, carried along the passage, and pushed into the little room marked 'Ladies'. Here the crowd was so great there was hardly space to take off their things; the noise was deafening. Two benches on either side were stacked high with wraps. Two old women in white aprons ran up and down tossing fresh armfuls. And everybody was pressing forward trying to get at the little dressing-table and mirror at the far end.

A great quivering jet of gas lighted the ladies' room. It couldn't wait; it was dancing already. When the door opened again and there came a burst of tuning from the drill hall, it leaped almost to the ceiling.

Dark girls, fair girls were patting their hair, tying ribbons again, tucking handkerchiefs down the fronts of their bodices, smoothing marble-white gloves. And because they were all laughing it seemed to Leila that they were all lovely.

'Aren't there any invisible hairpins?' cried a voice. 'How most extraordinary! I can't see a single invisible hairpin.'

'Powder my back, there's a darling,' cried someone else.

'But I must have a needle and cotton. I've torn simply miles and miles of the frill,' wailed a third.

Then, 'Pass them along, pass them along!' The straw basket of programmes was tossed from arm to arm. Darling little pink-and-silver programmes, with pink pencils and fluffy tassels. Leila's fingers shook as she took one out of the basket. She wanted to ask someone, 'Am I meant to have one too?' but she had just time to read: 'Waltz 3. *Two, Two in a Canoe*. Polka 4. *Making the Feathers Fly*', when Meg cried, 'Ready, Leila?' and they pressed their way through the crush in the passage towards the big double doors of the drill hall.

Dancing had not begun yet, but the band had stopped tuning, and the noise was so great it seemed that when it did begin to play it would never be heard. Leila, pressing close to Meg, looking over Meg's shoulder, felt that even the little quivering coloured flags strung across the ceiling were talking. She quite forgot to be shy; she forgot how in the middle of dressing she had sat down on the bed with one shoe off and one shoe on and begged her mother to ring up her cousins and say she couldn't go after all. And the rush of longing she had had to be sitting on the veranda of their forsaken up-country home, listening to the baby owls crying 'More pork' in the moonlight, was changed to a rush of joy so sweet that it was hard to bear alone. She clutched her fan, and, gazing at the gleaming, golden floor, the azaleas, the lanterns, the stage at one end with its red carpet and gilt chairs and the band in a corner, she thought breathlessly, 'How heavenly; how simply heavenly!'

All the girls stood grouped together at one side of the doors, the men at the other, and the chaperones in dark dresses, smiling rather foolishly, walked with little careful steps over the polished floor towards the stage.

'This is my little country cousin Leila. Be nice to her. Find her partners; she's under my wing,' said Meg, going up to one girl after another.

Strange faces smiled at Leila—sweetly, vaguely. Strange voices answered, 'Of course, my dear.' But Leila felt the girls didn't really see her. They were looking towards the men. Why didn't the men begin? What were they waiting for? There they stood, smoothing their gloves, patting their glossy hair and smiling among themselves. Then, quite suddenly, as if they had only just made up their minds that that was what they had to do, the men came gliding over the parquet. There was a joyful flutter among the girls. A tall, fair man flew up to Meg, seized her programme, scribbled something; Meg passed him on to Leila. 'May I have the pleasure?' He ducked and smiled. There came a dark man wearing an eyeglass, then cousin Laurie with a friend, and Laura with a little freckled fellow whose tie was crooked. Then quite an old man—fat, with a big bald patch on his head—took her programme and murmured, 'Let me see, let me see!' And he was a long time comparing his programme, which looked black with names, with hers. It seemed to give him so much trouble that Leila was ashamed. 'Oh, please don't bother,' she said eagerly. But instead of replying the fat man wrote something, glanced at her again. 'Do I remember this bright little face?' he said softly. 'Is it known to me of yore?' At that moment the band began playing; the fat man disappeared. He was tossed away on a great wave of music that came flying over the gleaming floor, breaking the groups up into couples, scattering them, sending them spinning . . . .

Leila had learned to dance at boarding school. Every Saturday afternoon the boarders were hurried off to a little corrugated iron mission hall where Miss Eccles (of London) held her 'select' classes. But the difference between that dusty-smelling hall—with calico texts on the walls, the poor, terrified little woman in a brown velvet toque with rabbit's ears thumping the cold piano, Miss Eccles poking the girls' feet with her long white wand—and this, was so tremendous that Leila was sure if her partner didn't come and she had to listen to that marvellous music and to watch the others sliding, gliding over the golden floor, she would die at least, or faint, or lift her arms and fly out of one of those dark windows that showed the stars.

'Ours, I think—' Someone bowed, smiled, and offered her his arm; she hadn't to die after all. Someone's hand pressed her waist, and she floated away like a flower that is tossed into a pool.

'Quite a good floor, isn't it?' drawled a faint voice close to her ear.

'I think it's most beautifully slippery,' said Leila.

'Pardon!' The faint voice sounded surprised. Leila said it again. And there was a tiny pause before the voice echoed, 'Oh, quite!' and she was swung round again.

He steered so beautifully. That was the great difference between dancing with girls and men, Leila decided. Girls banged into each other and stamped on each other's feet; the girl who was gentleman always clutched you so.

The azaleas were separate flowers no longer; they were pink and white flags streaming by.

'Were you at the Bells' last week?' the voice came again. It sounded tired. Leila wondered whether she ought to ask him if he would like to stop.

'No, this is my first dance,' said she.

Her partner gave a little gasping laugh. 'Oh, I say,' he protested.

'Yes, it is really the first dance I've ever been to.' Leila was most fervent. It was such a relief to be able to tell somebody. 'You see, I've lived in the country all my life up till now . . . .'

At that moment the music stopped and they went to sit on two chairs against the wall. Leila tucked her pink satin feet under and fanned herself, while she blissfully watched the other couples passing and disappearing through the swing doors.

'Enjoying yourself, Leila?' asked Jose, nodding her golden head.

Laura passed and gave her the faintest little wink; it made Leila wonder for a moment whether she was quite grown up after all. Certainly her partner did not say very much. He coughed, tucked his handkerchief away, pulled down his waistcoat, took a minute thread off his sleeve. But it didn't matter. Almost immediately the band started and her second partner seemed to spring from the ceiling.

'Floor's not bad,' said the new voice. Did one always begin with the floor? And then, 'Were you at the Neaves' on Tuesday?' And again Leila explained. Perhaps it was a little strange that her partners were not more interested. For it was thrilling. Her first ball! She was only at the beginning of everything. It seemed to her that she had never known what the night was like before. Up till now it had been dark, silent, beautiful very often—oh yes—but mournful somehow. Solemn. And now it would never be like that again—it had opened dazzling bright.

'Care for an ice?' said her partner. And they went through the swing doors, down the passage, to the supper-room. Her cheeks burned, she was fearfully thirsty. How sweet the ices looked on little glass plates and how cold the frosted spoon was, iced too! And when they came back to the hall there was the fat man waiting for her by the door. It gave her quite a shock again to see how old he was; he ought to have been on the stage with the fathers and mothers. And when Leila compared him with her other partners he looked shabby. His waistcoat was creased, there was a button off his glove, his coat looked as if it was dusty with French chalk.

'Come along, little lady,' said the fat man. He scarcely troubled to clasp her, and they moved away so gently, it was more like walking than dancing. But he said not a word about the floor. 'Your first dance, isn't it?' he murmured.

'How *did* you know?'

'Ah,' said the fat man, 'that's what it is to be old!' He wheezed faintly as he steered her past an awkward couple. 'You see, I've been doing this kind of thing for the last thirty years.'

'Thirty years?' cried Leila. Twelve years before she was born!

'It hardly bears thinking about, does it?' said the fat man gloomily. Leila looked at his bald head, and she felt quite sorry for him.

'I think it's marvellous to be still going on,' she said kindly.

'Kind little lady,' said the fat man, and he pressed her a little closer and hummed a bar of the waltz. 'Of course,' he said, 'you can't hope to last anything like as long as that. No-o,' said the fat man, 'long before that you'll be sitting up there on the stage, looking on, in your nice black velvet. And these pretty arms will have turned into little short fat ones, and you'll beat time with such a different kind of fan—a black ebony one.' The fat man seemed to shudder. 'And you'll smile away like the poor old dears up there, and point to your daughter, and tell the elderly lady next to you how some dreadful man tried to kiss her at the club ball. And your heart will ache, ache'—the fat man squeezed her closer still, as if he really was sorry for that poor heart—'because no one wants to kiss you now. And you'll say how unpleasant these polished floors are to walk on, how dangerous they are. Eh, Mademoiselle Twinkletoes?' said the fat man softly.

Leila gave a light little laugh, but she did not feel like laughing. Was it—could it all be true? It sounded terribly true. Was this first ball only the beginning of her last ball, after all? At that the music seemed to change; it sounded sad, sad; it rose upon a great sigh. Oh, how quickly things changed! Why didn't happiness last for ever? For ever wasn't a bit too long.

'I want to stop,' she said in a breathless voice. The fat man led her to the door.

'No,' she said, 'I won't go outside. I won't sit down. I'll just stand here, thank you.' She leaned against the wall, tapping with her foot, pulling up her gloves and trying to smile. But deep inside her a little girl threw her pinafore over her head and sobbed. Why had he spoiled it all?

'I say, you know,' said the fat man, 'you mustn't take me seriously, little lady.'

'As if I should!' said Leila, tossing her small dark head and sucking her underlip . . . .

Again the couples paraded. The swing doors opened and shut. Now new music was given out by the bandmaster. But Leila didn't want to dance any more. She wanted to be home, or sitting on the veranda listening to those baby owls. When she looked through the dark windows at the stars they had long beams like wings . . . .

But presently a soft, melting, ravishing tune began, and a young man with curly hair bowed before her. She would have to dance, out of politeness, until she could find Meg. Very stiffly she walked into the middle; very haughtily she put her hand on his sleeve. But in one minute, in one turn, her feet glided, glided. The lights, the azaleas, the dresses, the pink faces, the velvet chairs, all became one beautiful flying wheel. And when her next partner bumped her into the fat man and he said, 'Par*don*,' she smiled at him more radiantly than ever. She didn't even recognise him again.

The Voyage

The Picton boat was due to leave at half-past eleven. It was a beautiful night, mild, starry, only when they got out of the cab and started to walk down the Old Wharf that jutted out into the harbour, a faint wind blowing off the water ruffled under Fenella's hat, and she put up her hand to keep it on. It was dark on the Old Wharf, very dark; the wool sheds, the cattle trucks, the cranes standing up so high, the little squat railway engine, all seemed carved out of solid darkness. Here and there on a rounded wood-pile, that was like the stalk of a huge black mushroom, there hung a lantern, but it seemed afraid to unfurl its timid, quivering light in all that blackness; it burned softly, as if for itself.

Fenella's father pushed on with quick, nervous strides. Beside him her grandma bustled along in her crackling black ulster; they went so fast that she had now and again to give an undignified little skip to keep up with them. As well as her luggage strapped into a neat sausage, Fenella carried clasped to her her grandma's umbrella, and the handle, which was a swan's head, kept giving her shoulder a sharp little peck as if it too wanted her to hurry .... Men, their caps pulled down, their collars turned up, swung by; a few women all muffled scurried along; and one tiny boy, only his little black arms and legs showing out of a white woolly shawl, was jerked along angrily between his father and mother; he looked like a baby fly that had fallen into the cream.

Then suddenly, so suddenly that Fenella and her grandma both leapt, there sounded from behind the largest wool shed, that had a trail of smoke hanging over it, *Mia-oo-oo-O-O!*

'First whistle,' said her father briefly, and at that moment they came in sight of the Picton boat. Lying beside the dark wharf, all strung, all beaded with round golden lights, the Picton boat looked as if she was more ready to sail among stars than out into the cold sea. People pressed along the gangway. First went her grandma, then her father, then Fenella. There was a high step down on to the deck, and an old sailor in a jersey standing by gave her his dry, hard hand. They were there; they stepped out of the

way of the hurrying people, and standing under a little iron
stairway that led to the upper deck they began to say goodbye.

'There, mother, there's your luggage!' said Fenella's father,
giving grandma another strapped-up sausage.

'Thank you, Frank.'

'And you've got your cabin tickets safe?'

'Yes, dear.'

'And your other tickets?'

Grandma felt for them inside her glove and showed him the
tips.

'That's right.'

He sounded stern, but Fenella, eagerly watching him, saw that
he looked tired and sad. *Mia-oo-oo-O-O!* The second whistle
blared just above their heads, and a voice like a cry shouted, 'Any
more for the gangway?'

'You'll give my love to father,' Fenella saw her father's lips say.
And her grandma, very agitated, answered, 'Of course I will, dear.
Go now. You'll be left. Go now, Frank. Go now.'

'It's all right, mother. I've got another three minutes.' To her
surprise Fenella saw her father take off his hat. He clasped
grandma in his arms and pressed her to him. 'God bless you,
mother!' she heard him say.

And grandma put her hand, with the black thread glove that
was worn through on her ring finger, against his cheek, and she
sobbed, 'God bless you, my own brave son!'

This was so awful that Fenella quickly turned her back on them,
swallowed once, twice, and frowned terribly at a little green star
on a mast head. But she had to turn round again; her father was
going.

'Goodbye, Fenella. Be a good girl.' His cold, wet moustache
brushed her cheek. But Fenella caught hold of the lapels of his
coat.

'How long am I going to stay?' she whispered anxiously. He
wouldn't look at her. He shook her off gently, and gently said,
'We'll see about that. Here! Where's your hand?' He pressed
something into her palm. 'Here's a shilling in case you should need
it.'

A shilling! She must be going away for ever! 'Father!' cried

Fenella. But he was gone. He was the last off the ship. The sailors put their shoulders to the gangway. A huge coil of dark rope went flying through the air and fell 'thump' on the wharf. A bell rang; a whistle shrilled. Silently the dark wharf began to slip, to slide, to edge away from them. Now there was a rush of water between. Fenella strained to see with all her might. 'Was that father turning round?'—or waving?—or standing alone?—or walking off by himself? The strip of water grew broader, darker. Now the Picton boat began to swing round steady, pointing out to sea. It was no good looking any longer. There was nothing to be seen but a few lights, the face of the town clock hanging in the air, and more lights, little patches of them, on the dark hills.

The freshening wind tugged at Fenella's skirts; she went back to her grandma. To her relief grandma seemed no longer sad. She had put the two sausages of luggage one on top of the other, and she was sitting on them, her hands folded, her head a little on one side. There was an intent, bright look on her face. Then Fenella saw that her lips were moving and guessed that she was praying. But the old woman gave her a bright nod as if to say the prayer was nearly over. She unclasped her hands, sighed, clasped them again, bent forward, and at last gave herself a soft shake.

'And now, child,' she said, fingering the bow of her bonnet-strings, 'I think we ought to see about our cabins. Keep close to me, and mind you don't slip.'

'Yes, grandma.'

Dark figures of men lounged against the rails. In the glow of their pipes a nose shone out, or the peak of a cap, or a pair of surprised-looking eyebrows. Fenella glanced up. High in the air a little figure, his hands thrust in his short jacket pockets, stood staring out to sea. The ship rocked ever so little and she thought the stars rocked too. And now a pale steward in a linen coat, holding a tray high in the palm of his hand, stepped out of a lighted doorway and skimmed past them. They went through that doorway. Carefully over the high brass-bound step on to the rubber mat and then down such a terribly steep flight of stairs that grandma had to put both feet on each step, and Fenella clutched the clammy brass rail and forgot all about the swan-necked umbrella.

At the bottom grandma stopped; Fenella was rather afraid she was going to pray again. But no, it was only to get out the cabin tickets. They were in the saloon. It was glaring bright and stifling; the air smelled of paint and burnt chop-bones and india-rubber. Fenella wished her grandma would go on, but the old woman was not to be hurried. An immense basket of ham sandwiches caught her eye. She went up to them and touched the top one delicately with her finger.

'How much are the sandwiches?' she asked.

'Tuppence!' bawled a rude steward, slamming down a knife and fork.

Grandma could hardly believe it.

'Twopence each?' she asked.

'That's right,' said the steward, and he winked at his companion.

Grandma made a small, astonished face. Then she whispered primly to Fenella, 'What wickedness!' And they sailed out at the further door and along a passage that had cabins on either side. Such a very nice stewardess came to meet them. She was dressed all in blue and her collar and cuffs were fastened with large brass buttons. She seemed to know grandma well.

'Well, Mrs Crane,' said she, unlocking their washstand. 'We've got you back again. It's not often you give yourself a cabin.'

'No,' said grandma. 'But this time my dear son's thoughtfulness—'

'I hope—' began the stewardess. Then she turned round and took a long, mournful look at grandma's blackness and at Fenella's black coat and skirt, black blouse, and hat with a crape rose.

Grandma nodded. 'It was God's will,' said she.

The stewardess shut her lips and, taking a deep breath, she seemd to expand.

'What I always say is,' she said, as though it was her own discovery, 'sooner or later each of us has to go, and that's a certingty.' She paused. 'Now, can I bring you anything, Mrs Crane? A cup of tea? I know it's no good offering you a little something to keep the cold out.'

Grandma shook her head. 'Nothing, thank you. We've got a few wine biscuits and Fenella has a very nice banana.'

'Then I'll give you a look later on,' said the stewardess; and she went out, shutting the door.

What a very small cabin it was! It was like being shut up in a box with grandma. The dark round eye above the washstand gleamed at them dully. Fenella felt shy. She stood against the door, still clasping her luggage and the umbrella. Were they going to get undressed in here? Already her grandma had taken off her bonnet, and, rolling up the strings, she fixed each with a pin to the lining before she hung the bonnet up. Her white hair shone like silk; the little bun at the back was covered with a black net. Fenella hardly ever saw her grandma with her head uncovered; she looked strange.

'I shall put on the woollen fascinator your dear mother crocheted for me,' said grandma, and, unstrapping the sausage, she took it out and wound it round her head; the fringe of grey bobbles danced at her eyebrows as she smiled tenderly and mournfully at Fenella. Then she undid her bodice, and something under that, and something else underneath that. Then there seemed a short, sharp tussle, and grandma flushed faintly. Snip! Snap! She had undone her stays. She breathed a sigh of relief and, sitting on the plush couch, she slowly and carefully pulled off her elastic-sided boots and stood them side by side.

By the time Fenella had taken off her coat and skirt and put on her flannel dressing-gown grandma was quite ready.

'Must I take off my boots, grandma? They're lace.'

Grandma gave them a moment's deep consideration. 'You'd feel a great deal more comfortable if you did, child,' said she. She kissed Fenella. 'Don't forget to say your prayers. Our dear Lord is with us when we are at sea even more than when we are on dry land. And because I am an experienced traveller,' said grandma briskly, 'I shall take the upper berth.'

'But, grandma, how ever will you get up there?'

Three little spider-like steps were all Fenella saw. The old woman gave a small silent laugh before she mounted them nimbly, and she peered over the high bunk at the astonished Fenella.

'You didn't think your grandma could do that, did you?' said she. And as she sank back Fenella heard her light laugh again.

The hard square of brown soap would not lather and the water in the bottle was like a kind of blue jelly. How hard it was, too, to turn down those stiff sheets; you simply had to tear your way in. If everything had been different, Fenella might have got the giggles .... At last she was inside, and while she lay there panting, there sounded from above a long, soft whispering, as though someone was gently, gently rustling among tissue paper to find something. It was grandma saying her prayers ....

A long time passed. Then the stewardess came in; she trod softly and leaned her hand on grandma's bunk.

'We're just entering the Straits,' she said.

'Oh!'

'It's a fine night, but we're rather empty. We may pitch a little.'

And indeed at that moment the Picton boat rose and rose and hung in the air just long enough to give a shiver before she swung down again, and there was the sound of heavy water slapping against her sides. Fenella remembered she had left the swan-necked umbrella standing up on the little couch. If it fell over, would it break? But grandma remembered too, at the same time.

'I wonder if you'd mind, stewardess, laying down my umbrella,' she whispered.

'Not at all, Mrs Crane.' And the stewardess, coming back to grandma, breathed, 'Your little granddaughter's in such a beautiful sleep.'

'God be praised for that!' said grandma.

'Poor little motherless mite!' said the stewardess. And grandma was still telling the stewardess all about what happened when Fenella fell asleep.

But she hadn't been asleep long enough to dream before she woke up again to see something waving in the air above her head. What was it? What could it be? It was a small grey foot. Now another joined it. They seemed to be feeling about for something; there came a sigh.

'I'm awake, grandma,' said Fenella.

'Oh, dear, am I near the ladder?' asked grandma. 'I thought it was this end.'

'No, grandma, it's the other. I'll put your foot on it. Are we there?' asked Fenella.

'In the harbour,' said grandma. 'We must get up, child. You'd better have a biscuit to steady yourself before you move.'

But Fenella had hopped out of her bunk. The lamp was still burning, but night was over, and it was cold. Peering through that round eye she could see far off some rocks. Now they were scattered over with foam; now a gull flipped by; and now there came a long piece of real land.

'It's land, grandma,' said Fenella, wonderingly, as though they had been at sea for weeks together. She hugged herself; she stood on one leg and rubbed it with the toes of the other foot; she was trembling. Oh, it had all been so sad lately. Was it going to change? But all her grandma said was, 'Make haste, child. I should leave your nice banana for the stewardess as you haven't eaten it.' And Fenella put on her black clothes again and a button sprang off one of her gloves and rolled to where she couldn't reach it. They went up on deck.

But if it had been cold in the cabin, on deck it was like ice. The sun was not up yet, but the stars were dim, and the cold pale sky was the same colour as the cold pale sea. On the land a white mist rose and fell. Now they could see quite plainly dark bush. Even the shapes of the umbrella ferns showed, and those strange silvery withered trees that are like skeletons .... Now they could see the landing-stage and some little houses, pale too, clustered together, like shells on the lid of a box. The other passengers tramped up and down, but more slowly than they had the night before, and they looked gloomy.

And now the landing-stage came out to meet them. Slowly it swam towards the Picton boat and a man holding a coil of rope, and a cart with a small drooping horse and another man sitting on the step, came too.

'It's Mr Penreddy, Fenella, come for us,' said grandma. She sounded pleased. Her white waxen cheeks were blue with cold, her chin trembled, and she had to keep wiping her eyes and her little pink nose.

'You've got my—'

'Yes, grandma.' Fenella showed it to her.

The rope came flying through the air and 'smack' it fell on to the deck. The gangway was lowered. Again Fenella followed her

grandma on to the wharf over to the little cart, and a moment later
they were bowling away. The hooves of the little horse drummed
over the wooden piles, then sank softly into the sandy road. Not a
soul was to be seen; there was not even a feather of smoke. The
mist rose and fell and the sea still sounded asleep as slowly it
turned on the beach.

'I seen Mr Crane yestiddy,' said Mr Penreddy. 'He looked
himself then. Missus knocked him up a batch of scones last week.'

And now the little horse pulled up before one of the shell-like
houses. They got down. Fenella put her hand on the gate, and the
big, trembling dew-drops soaked through her glove-tips. Up a
little path of round white pebbles they went, with drenched
sleeping flowers on either side. Grandma's delicate white picotees
were so heavy with dew that they were fallen, but their sweet smell
was part of the cold morning. The blinds were down in the little
house; they mounted the steps on to the veranda. A pair of old
bluchers was on one side of the door and a large red watering-can
on the other.

'Tut! tut! Your grandpa,' said grandma. She turned the handle.
Not a sound. She called, 'Walter!' And immediately a deep voice
that sounded half stifled called back, 'Is that you, Mary?'

'Wait, dear,' said grandma. 'Go in there.' She pushed Fenella
gently into a small dusky sitting-room.

On the table a white cat, that had been folded up like a camel,
rose, stretched itself, yawned, and then sprang on to the tips of its
toes. Fenella buried one cold little hand in the white, warm fur,
and smiled timidly while she stroked and listened to grandma's
gentle voice and the rolling tones of grandpa.

A door creaked. 'Come in, dear.' The old woman beckoned,
Fenella followed. There, lying to one side on an immense bed, lay
grandpa. Just his head with a white tuft and his rosy face and long
silver beard showed over the quilt. He was like a very old,
wide-awake bird.

'Well, my girl!' said grandpa. 'Give us a kiss!' Fenella kissed
him. 'Ugh!' said grandpa. 'Her little nose is as cold as a button.
What's that she's holding? Her grandma's umbrella?'

Fenella smiled again and crooked the swan neck over the

bedrail. Above the bed there was a big text in a deep black frame:

> Lost! One Golden Hour
> Set with Sixty Diamond Minutes.
> *No* Reward Is Offered
> For It Is GONE FOR EVER!

'Yer grandma painted that,' said grandpa. And he ruffled his white tuft and looked at Fenella so merrily she almost thought he winked at her.

At the Bay

I

Very early morning. The sun was not yet risen, and the whole of Crescent Bay was hidden under a white sea-mist. The big bush-covered hills at the back were smothered. You could not see where they ended and the paddocks and bungalows began. The sandy road was gone and the paddocks and bungalows the other side of it; there was no white dunes covered with reddish grass beyond them; there was nothing to mark which was beach and where was the sea. A heavy dew had fallen. The grass was blue. Big drops hung on the bushes and just did not fall; the silvery, fluffy toi-toi was limp on its long stalks, and all the marigolds and the pinks in the bungalow gardens were bowed to the earth with wetness. Drenched were the cold fuchsias, round pearls of dew lay on the flat nasturtium leaves. It looked as though the sea had beaten up softly in the darkness, as though one immense wave had come rippling, rippling—how far? Perhaps if you had waked up in the middle of the night you might have seen a big fish flicking in at the window and gone again . . .

Ah-Aah! sounded the sleepy sea. And from the bush there came the sound of little streams flowing, quickly, lightly, slipping between the smooth stones, gushing into ferny basins and out again; and there was the splashing of big drops on large leaves, and something else—what was it?—a faint stirring and shaking, the snapping of a twig and then such silence that it seemed someone was listening.

Round the corner of Crescent Bay, between the piled-up masses of broken rock, a flock of sheep came pattering. They were huddled together, a small, tossing, woolly mass, and their thin, stick-like legs trotted along quickly as if the cold and the quiet had frightened them. Behind them an old sheep-dog, his soaking paws covered with sand, ran along with his nose to the ground, but carelessly, as if thinking of something else. And then in the rocky gateway the shepherd himself appeared. He was a lean, upright old man, in a frieze coat that was covered with a web of tiny drops, velvet trousers tied under the knee, and a wideawake with a folded blue handkerchief round the brim. One hand was crammed into his belt, the other grasped a beautifully smooth yellow stick. And as he walked, taking his time, he kept up a very soft light whistling, an airy, far-away fluting that sounded mournful and tender. The old dog cut an ancient caper or two and then drew up sharp, ashamed of his levity, and walked a few dignified paces by his master's side. The sheep ran forward in little pattering rushes; they began to bleat, and ghostly flocks and herds answered them from under the sea. 'Baa! Baaa!' For a time they seemed to be always on the same piece of ground. There ahead was stretched the sandy road with shallow puddles; the same soaking bushes showed on either side and the same shadowy palings. Then something immense came into view; an enormous shock-haired giant with his arms stretched out. It was the big gum-tree outside Mrs Stubbs' shop, and as they passed by there was a strong whiff of eucalyptus. And now big spots of light gleamed in the mist. The shepherd stopped whistling; he rubbed his red nose and wet beard on his wet sleeve and, screwing up his eyes, glanced in the direction of the sea. The sun was rising. It was marvellous how quickly the mist thinned, sped away, dissolved from the shallow plain, rolled up from the bush and was gone as if in a hurry to escape; big twists and curls jostled and shouldered each other as the silvery beams broadened. The far-away sky—a bright, pure blue—was reflected in the puddles, and the drops, swimming along the telegraph poles, flashed into points of light. Now the leaping. glittering sea was so bright it made one's eyes ache to look at it. The shepherd drew a pipe, the bowl as small as an acorn, out of his breast pocket, fumbled for a chunk of speckled tobacco, pared off a few shavings and stuffed the bowl. He was a grave, fine-looking old man. As he lit up and the blue smoke wreathed his head, the dog, watching, looked proud of him.

'Baa! Baaa!' The sheep spread out into a fan. They were just clear of the summer colony before the first sleeper turned over and lifted a drowsy head; their cry sounded in the dreams of little children ... who lifted their arms to drag down, to cuddle the darling little woolly lambs of sleep. Then the first inhabitant appeared; it was the Burnells' cat Florrie, sitting on the gatepost, far too early as usual, looking for their milk-girl. When she saw the old sheep-dog she sprang up quickly, arched her back, drew in her tabby head, and seemed to give a little fastidious shiver. 'Ugh! What a coarse, revolting creature!' said Florrie. But the old sheep-dog, not looking up, waggled past, flinging out his legs from side to side. Only one of his ears twitched to prove that he saw, and thought her a silly young female.

The breeze of morning lifted in the bush and the smell of leaves and wet black earth mingled with the sharp smell of the sea. Myriads of birds were singing. A goldfinch flew over the shepherd's head and, perching on the tiptop of a spray, it turned to the sun, ruffling its small breast feathers. And now they had passed the fisherman's hut, passed the charred-looking little *whare* where Leila the milk-girl lived with her old Gran. The sheep strayed over a yellow swamp and Wag, the sheep-dog, padded after, rounded them up and headed them for the steeper, narrower rocky pass that led out of Crescent Bay and towards Daylight Cove. 'Baa! Baaa!' Faint the cry came as they rocked along the fast-drying road. The shepherd put away his pipe, dropping it into his breast-pocket so that the little bowl hung over. And straightway the soft airy whistling began again. Wag ran out along a ledge of rock after something that smelled, and ran back again disgusted. Then pushing, nudging, hurrying, the sheep rounded the bend and the shepherd followed after out of sight.

II

A few moments later the back door of one of the bungalows opened, and a figure in a broad-striped bathing suit flung down the paddock, cleared the stile, rushed through the tussock grass into the hollow, staggered up the sandy hillock, and raced for dear life over the big porous stones, over the cold, wet pebbles, on to the hard sand that gleamed like oil. Splish-Splosh! Splish-Splosh! The water bubbled round his legs as Stanley Burnell waded out exulting. First man in as usual! He'd beaten them all again. And he swooped down to souse his head and neck.

'Hail, brother! All hail, Thou Mighty One!' A velvety bass voice came booming over the water.

Great Scott! Damnation take it! Stanley lifted up to see a dark head bobbing far out and an arm lifted. It was Jonathan Trout—there before him! 'Glorious morning!' sang the voice.

'Yes, very fine!' said Stanley briefly. Why the dickens didn't the fellow stick to his part of the sea? Why should he come barging over to this exact spot? Stanley gave a kick, a lunge and struck out, swimming overarm. But Jonathan was a match for him. Up he came, his black hair sleek on his forehead, his short beard sleek.

'I had an extraordinary dream last night!' he shouted.

What was the matter with the man? This mania for conversation irritated Stanley beyond words. And it was always the same—always some piffle about a dream he'd had, or some cranky idea he'd got hold of, or some rot he'd been reading. Stanley turned over on his back and kicked with his legs till he was a living waterspout. But even then ... 'I dreamed I was hanging over a terrifically high cliff, shouting to someone below.' You would be! thought Stanley. He could stick no more of it. He stopped splashing. 'Look here, Trout,' he said, 'I'm in rather a hurry this morning.'

'You're WHAT?' Jonathan was so surprised—or pretended to be—that he sank under the water, then reappeared again blowing.

'All I mean is,' said Stanley, 'I've no time to—to—fool about. I want to get this over. I'm in a hurry. I've work to do this morning—see?'

Jonathan was gone before Stanley had finished. 'Pass, friend!' said the bass voice gently, and he slid away through the water with scarcely a ripple ... But curse the fellow! He'd ruined Stanley's bathe. What an unpractical idiot the man was! Stanley struck out to sea again, and then as quickly swam in again, and away he rushed up the beach. He felt cheated.

Jonathan stayed a little longer in the water. He floated, gently moving his hands like fins, and letting the sea rock his long, skinny body. It was curious, but in spite of everything he was fond of Stanley Burnell. True, he had a fiendish desire to tease him sometimes, to poke fun at him, but at bottom he was sorry for the fellow. There was something pathetic in his determination to make a job of everything. You couldn't help feeling he'd be caught out one day, and then what an almighty cropper he'd come! At that moment an immense wave lifted Jonathan, rode past him, and broke along the beach with a joyful sound. What a beauty! And now there came another. That was the way to live—carelessly, recklessly, spending oneself. He got on to his feet and began to wade towards the shore, pressing his toes into the firm, wrinkled sand. To take things easy, not to fight against the ebb and flow of life, but to give way to it—that was what was needed. It was this tension that was all wrong. To live—to live! And the perfect morning, so fresh and fair, basking in the light, as though laughing at its own beauty, seemed to whisper, 'Why not?'

But now he was out of the water Jonathan turned blue with cold. He ached all over; it was as though someone was wringing the blood out of him. And stalking up the beach, shivering, all his muscles tight, he too felt his bathe was spoilt. He'd stayed in too long.

III

Beryl was alone in the living-room when Stanley appeared, wearing a blue serge suit, a stiff collar and a spotted tie. He looked almost uncannily clean and brushed; he was going to town for the day. Dropping into his chair, he pulled out his watch and put it beside his plate.

'I've just got twenty-five minutes,' he said. 'You might go and see if the porridge is ready, Beryl?'

'Mother's just gone for it,' said Beryl. She sat down at the table and poured out his tea.

'Thanks!' Stanley took a sip. 'Hullo!' he said in an astonished voice, 'you've forgotten the sugar.'

'Oh, sorry!' But even then Beryl didn't help him; she pushed the basin across. What did this mean? As Stanley helped himself his blue eyes widened; they seemed to quiver. He shot a quick glance at his sister-in-law and leaned back.

'Nothing wrong, is there?' he asked carelessly, fingering his collar.

Beryl's head was bent; she turned her plate in her fingers.

'Nothing,' said her light voice. Then she too looked up, and smiled at Stanley. 'Why should there be?'

'O-oh! No reason at all as far as I know. I thought you seemed rather—'

At that moment the door opened and the three little girls appeared, each carrying a porridge plate. They were dressed alike in blue jerseys and knickers; their brown legs were bare, and each had her hair plaited and pinned up in what was called a horse's tail. Behind them came Mrs Fairfield with the tray.

'Carefully, children,' she warned. But they were taking the very greatest care. They loved being allowed to carry things. 'Have you said good morning to your father?'

'Yes, grandma.' They settled themselves on the bench opposite Stanley and Beryl.

'Good morning, Stanley!' Old Mrs Fairfield gave him his plate.

'Morning, mother! How's the boy?'

'Splendid! He only woke up once last night. What a perfect morning!' The old woman paused, her hand on the loaf of bread, to gaze out of the open door into the garden. The sea sounded. Through the wide-open window streamed the sun on to the yellow varnished walls and bare floor. Everything on the table flashed and glittered. In the middle there was an old salad bowl filled with yellow and red nasturtiums. She smiled, and a look of deep content shone in her eyes.

'You might *cut* me a slice of that bread, mother,' said Stanley. 'I've only twelve and a half minutes before the coach passes. Has anyone given my shoes to the servant girl?'

'Yes, they're ready for you.' Mrs Fairfield was quite unruffled.

'Oh, Kezia! Why are you such a messy child!' cried Beryl despairingly.

'Me, Aunt Beryl?' Kezia stared at her. What had she done now? She had only dug a river down the middle of her porridge, filled it, and was eating the banks away. But she did that every single morning, and no one had said a word up till now.

'Why can't you eat your food properly like Isabel and Lottie?' How unfair grown-ups are!

'But Lottie always makes a floating island, don't you, Lottie?'

'I don't,' said Isabel smartly. 'I just sprinkle mine with sugar and put on the milk and finish it. Only babies play with their food.'

Stanley pushed back his chair and got up.

'Would you get me those shoes, mother? And, Beryl, if you've finished, I wish you'd cut down to the gate and stop the coach. Run in to your mother, Isabel, and ask her where my bowler hat's been put. Wait a minute—have you children been playing with my stick?'

'No, father!'

'But I put it here,' Stanley began to bluster. 'I remember distinctly putting it in this corner. Now, who's had it? There's no time to lose. Look sharp! The stick's got to be found.'

Even Alice, the servant-girl, was drawn into the chase. 'You haven't been using it to poke the kitchen fire with by any chance?'

Stanley dashed into the bedroom where Linda was lying. 'Most extraordinary thing. I can't keep a single possession to myself. They've made away with my stick, now!'

'Stick, dear? What stick?' Linda's vagueness on these occasions could not be real, Stanley decided. Would nobody sympathize with him?

'Coach! Coach, Stanley!' Beryl's voice cried from the gate.

Stanley waved his arm to Linda. 'No time to say goodbye!' he cried. And he meant that as a punishment to her.

He snatched his bowler hat, dashed out of the house, and swung down the garden path. Yes, the coach was there waiting, and Beryl, leaning over the open gate, was laughing up at somebody or other just as if nothing had happened. The heartlessness of women! The way they took it for granted it was your job to slave away for them while they didn't even take the trouble to see that your walking-stick wasn't lost. Kelly trailed his whip across the horses.

'Goodbye, Stanley,' called Beryl, sweetly and gaily. It was easy enough to say goodbye! And there she stood, idle, shading her eyes with her hand. The worst of it was Stanley had to shout goodbye too, for the sake of appearances. Then he saw her turn, give a little skip and run back to the house. She was glad to be rid of him!

Yes, she was thankful. Into the living-room she ran and called 'He's gone!' Linda cried from her room: 'Beryl! Has Stanley gone.' Old Mrs Fairfield appeared, carrying the boy in his little flannel coatee.

'Gone?'

'Gone!'

Oh, the relief, the difference it made to have the man out of the house. Their very voices were changed as they called to one another; they sounded warm and loving and as if they shared a secret. Beryl went over to the table. 'Have another cup of tea, mother. It's still hot.' She wanted, somehow, to celebrate the fact that they could do what they liked now. There was no man to disturb them; the whole perfect day was theirs.

'No, thank you, child,' said old Mrs Fairfield, but the way at that moment she tossed the boy up and said 'a-goos-a-goos-a-ga!' to him meant that she felt the same. The little girls ran into the paddock like chickens let out of a coop.

Even Alice, the servant-girl, washing up the dishes in the kitchen, caught the infection and used the precious tank water in a perfectly reckless fashion.

'Oh, these men!' said she, and she plunged the teapot into the bowl and held it under the water even after it had stopped bubbling, as if it too was a man and drowning was too good for them.

IV

'Wait for me, Isa-bel! Kezia, wait for me!'

There was poor little Lottie, left behind again, because she found it so fearfully hard to get over the stile by herself. When she stood on the first step her knees began to wobble; she grasped the post. Then you had to put one leg over. But which leg? She never could decide. And when she did finally put one leg over with a sort of stamp of despair—then the feeling was awful. She was half in the paddock still and half in the tussock grass. She clutched the post desperately and lifted up her voice. 'Wait for me!'

'No, don't you wait for her, Kezia!' said Isabel. 'She's such a little silly. She's always making a fuss. Come on!' And she tugged Kezia's jersey. 'You can use my bucket if you come with me,' she said kindly. 'It's bigger than yours.' But Kezia couldn't leave Lottie all by herself. She ran back to her. By this time Lottie was very red in the face and breathing heavily.

'Here, put your other foot over,' said Kezia.

'Where?'

Lottie looked down at Kezia as if from a mountain height.

'Here where my hand is.' Kezia patted the place.

'Oh, *there* do you mean?' Lottie gave a deep sigh and put the second foot over.

'Now—sort of turn round and sit down and slide,' said Kezia.

'But there's nothing to sit down *on*, Kezia,' said Lottie.

She managed it at last, and once it was over she shook herself and began to beam.

'I'm getting better at climbing over stiles, aren't I, Kezia?'

Lottie's was a very hopeful nature.

The pink and the blue sunbonnet followed Isabel's bright red sunbonnet up that sliding, slipping hill. At the top they paused to decide where to go and to have a good stare at who was there already. Seen from behind, standing against the skyline, gesticulating largely with their spades, they looked like minute puzzled explorers.

The whole family of Samuel Josephs was there already with their lady-help, who sat on a camp-stool and kept order with a whistle that she wore tied round her neck, and a small cane with which she directed operations. The Samuel Josephs never played by themselves or managed their own game. If they did, it ended in the boys pouring water down the girls' necks or the girls trying to put little black crabs into the boys' pockets. So Mrs S. J. and the poor lady-help drew up what she called a 'brogramme' every morning to keep them 'abused and out of bischief'. It was all competitions or races or round games. Everything began with a piercing blast of the lady-help's whistle and ended with another. There were even prizes—large, rather dirty paper parcels which the lady-help with a sour little smile drew out of a bulging string kit. The Samuel Josephs fought fearfully for the prizes and cheated and pinched one another's arms—they were all expert pinchers. The only time the Burnell children ever played with them Kezia had got a prize, and when she undid three bits of paper she found a very small rusty button-hook. She couldn't understand why they made such a fuss ...

But they never played with the Samuel Josephs now or even went to their parties. The Samuel Josephs were always giving children's parties at the Bay and there was always the same food. A big washhand basin of very brown fruit-salad, buns cut into four and a washhand jug full of something the lady-help called 'Limmonadear'. And you went away in the evening with half the frill torn off your frock or something spilled all down the front of your open-work pinafore, leaving the Samuel Josephs leaping like savages on their lawn. No! They were too awful.

On the other side of the beach, close down to the water, two little boys, their knickers rolled up, twinkled like spiders. One was digging, the other pattered in and out of the water, filling a small bucket. They were the Trout boys, Pip and Rags. But Pip was so busy digging and Rags was so busy helping that they didn't see their little cousins until they were quite close.

'Look!' said Pip. 'Look what I've discovered.' And he showed them an old wet, squashed-looking boot. The three little girls stared.

'Whatever are you going to do with it?' asked Kezia.

'Keep it, of course!' Pip was very scornful. 'It's a find—see?'

Yes, Kezia saw that. All the same . . .

'There's lots of things buried in the sand,' explained Pip. 'They get chucked up from wrecks. Treasure. Why—you might find—'

'But why does Rags have to keep on pouring water in?' asked Lottie.

'Oh, that's to moisten it,' said Pip, 'to make the work a bit easier. Keep it up, Rags.'

And good little Rags ran up and down, pouring in the water that turned brown like cocoa.

'Here, shall I show you what I found yesterday?' said Pip mysteriously, and he stuck his spade into the sand. 'Promise not to tell.'

They promised.

'Say, cross my heart straight dinkum.'

The little girls said it.

Pip took something out of his pocket, rubbed it a long time on the front of his jersey, then breathed on it and rubbed it again.

'Now turn round!' he ordered.

They turned round.

'All look the same way! Keep still! Now!'

And his hand opened; he held up to the light something that flashed, that winked, that was a most lovely green.

'It's a nemeral,' said Pip solemnly.

'Is it really, Pip?' Even Isabel was impressed.

The lovely green thing seemed to dance in Pip's fingers. Aunt Beryl had a nemeral in a ring, but it was a very small one. This one was as big as a star and far more beautiful.

V

As the morning lengthened whole parties appeared over the sand-hills and came down on the beach to bathe. It was understood that at eleven o'clock the women and children of the summer colony had the sea to themselves. First the women undressed, pulled on their bathing dresses and covered their heads in hideous caps like sponge bags; then the children were unbuttoned. The beach was strewn with little heaps of clothes and shoes; the big summer hats, with stones on them to keep them from blowing away, looked like immense shells. It was strange that even the sea seemed to sound differently when all those leaping, laughing figures ran into the waves. Old Mrs Fairfield, in a lilac cotton dress and a black hat tied under the chin, gathered her little brood and got them ready. The little Trout boys whipped their shirts over their heads, and away the five sped, while their grandma sat with one hand in her knitting-bag ready to draw out the ball of wool when she was satisfied they were safely in.

The firm compact little girls were not half so brave as the tender, delicate-looking boys. Pip and Rags, shivering, crouching down, slapping the water, never hesitated. But Isabel, who could swim twelve strokes, and Kezia, who could nearly swim eight, only followed on the strict understanding they were not to be splashed. As for Lottie, she didn't follow at all. She liked to be left to go in her own way, please. And that way was to sit down at the edge of the water, her legs straight, her knees pressed together, and to make vague motions with her arms as if she expected to be wafted out to sea. But when a bigger wave than usual, an old whiskery one, came lolloping along in her direction, she scrambled to her feet with a face of horror and flew up the beach again.

'Here, mother, keep those for me, will you?'

Two rings and a thin gold chain were dropped into Mrs Fairfield's lap.

'Yes, dear. But aren't you going to bathe here?'

'No-o,' Beryl drawled. She sounded vague. 'I'm undressing farther along. I'm going to bathe with Mrs Harry Kember.'

'Very well.' But Mrs Fairfield's lips set. She disapproved of Mrs Harry Kember. Beryl knew it.

Poor old mother, she smiled, as she skimmed over the stones. Poor old mother! Old! Oh, what joy, what bliss it was to be young...

'You look very pleased,' said Mrs Harry Kember. She sat hunched up on the stones, her arms round her knees, smoking.

'It's such a lovely day,' said Beryl, smiling down at her.

'Oh my *dear*!' Mrs Harry Kember's voice sounded as though she knew better than that. But then her voice always sounded as though she knew something more about you than you did yourself. She was a long, strange-looking woman with narrow hands and feet. Her face, too, was long and narrow and exhausted-looking; even her fair curled fringe looked burnt out and withered. She was the only woman at the Bay who smoked, and she smoked incessantly, keeping the cigarette between her lips while she talked, and only taking it out when the ash was so long you could not understand why it did not fall. When she was not playing bridge—she played bridge every day of her life—she spent her time lying in the full glare of the sun. She could stand any amount of it; she never had enough. All the same, it did not seem to warm her. Parched, withered, cold, she stretched on the stones like a piece of tossed-up driftwood. The women at the Bay thought she was very, very fast. Her lack of vanity, her slang, the way she treated men as though she was one of them, and the fact that she didn't care twopence about her house and called the servant Gladys 'Glad-eyes', was disgraceful. Standing on the veranda steps Mrs Kember would call in her indifferent, tired voice, 'I say, Glad-eyes, you might heave me a handkerchief if I've got one, will you?' And Glad-eyes, a red bow in her hair instead of a cap, and white shoes, came running with an impudent smile. It was an absolute scandal! True, she had no children, and her husband ... Here the voices were always raised; they became fervent. How can he have married her? How can he, how can he? It must have been money, of course, but even then!

Mrs Kember's husband was at least ten years younger than she was, and so incredibly handsome that he looked like a mask or a most perfect illustration in an American novel rather than a man. Black hair, dark blue eyes, red lips, a slow sleepy smile, a fine tennis player, a perfect dancer, and with it all a mystery. Harry Kember was like a man walking in his sleep. Men couldn't stand him, they couldn't get a word out of the chap; he ignored his wife just as she ignored him. How did he live? Of course there were stories, but such stories! They simply couldn't be told. The women he's been seen with, the places he'd been seen in ... but nothing was ever certain, nothing definite. Some of the women at the Bay privately thought he'd commit a murder one day. Yes, even while they talked to Mrs Kember and took in the awful concoction she was wearing, they saw her, stretched as she lay on the beach; but cold, bloody, and still with a cigarette stuck in the corner of her mouth.

Mrs Kember rose, yawned, unsnapped her belt buckle, and tugged at the tape of her blouse. And Beryl stepped out of her skirt and shed her jersey, and stood up in her short white petticoat, and her camisole with ribbon bows on the shoulders.

'Mercy on us,' said Mrs Harry Kember, 'what a little beauty you are!'

'Don't!' said Beryl softly; but, drawing off one stocking and then the other, she felt a little beauty.

'My dear—why not?' said Mrs Harry Kember, stamping on her own petticoat. Really—her underclothes! A pair of blue cotton knickers and a linen bodice that reminded one somehow of a pillowcase ... 'And you don't wear stays, do you?' She touched Beryl's waist, and Beryl sprang away with a small affected cry. Then 'Never!' she said firmly.

'Lucky little creature,' sighed Mrs Kember, unfastening her own.

Beryl turned her back and began the complicated movements of someone who is trying to take off her clothes and to pull on her bathing-dress all at one and the same time.

'Oh, my dear—don't mind me,' said Mrs Harry Kember. 'Why be shy! I shan't eat you. I shan't be shocked like those other ninnies.' And she gave her strange neighing laugh and grimaced at the other women.

But Beryl was shy. She never undressed in front of anybody. Was that silly? Mrs Harry Kember made her feel it was silly, even something to be ashamed of. Why be shy indeed! She glanced quickly at her friend standing so boldly in her torn chemise and lighting a fresh cigarette; and a quick, bold, evil feeling started up in her breast. Laughing recklessly, she drew on the limp, sandy-feeling bathing-dress that was not quite dry and fastened the twisted buttons.

'That's better,' said Mrs Harry Kember. They began to go down the beach together. 'Really, it's a sin for you to wear clothes, my dear. Somebody's got to tell you some day.'

The water was quite warm. It was that marvellous transparent blue, flecked with silver, but the sand at the bottom looked gold; when you kicked with your toes there rose a little puff of gold-dust. Now the waves just reached her breast. Beryl stood, her arms outstretched, gazing out, and as each wave came she gave the slightest little jump, so that it seemed it was the wave which lifted her so gently.

'I believe in pretty girls having a good time,' said Mrs Harry Kember. 'Why not? Don't you make a mistake, my dear. Enjoy yourself.' And suddenly she turned turtle, disappeared, and swam away quickly, quickly, like a rat. Then she flicked round and began swimming back. She was going to say something else. Beryl felt that she was being poisoned by this cold woman, but she longed to hear. But oh, how strange, how horrible! As Mrs Harry Kember came up close she looked, in her black waterproof bathing-cap, with her sleepy face lifted above the water, just her chin touching, like a horrible caricature of her husband.

VI

In a steamer chair, under a manuka tree that grew in the middle of the front grass patch, Linda Burnell dreamed the morning away.

She did nothing. She looked up at the dark, close, dry leaves of the manuka, at the chinks of blue between, and now and again a tiny yellowish flower dropped on her. Pretty—yes, if you held one of those flowers on the palm of your hand and looked at it closely, it was an exquisite small thing. Each pale yellow petal shone as if each was the careful work of a loving hand. The tiny tongue in the centre gave it the shape of a bell. And when you turned it over the outside was a deep bronze colour. But as soon as they flowered, they fell and were scattered. You brushed them off your frock as you talked; the horrid little things got caught in one's hair. Why, then, flower at all? Who takes the trouble—or the joy—to make all these things that are wasted, wasted ... It was uncanny.

On the grass beside her, lying between two pillows, was the boy. Sound asleep he lay, his head turned away from his mother. His fine dark hair looked more like a shadow than like real hair, but his ear was a bright, deep coral. Linda clasped her hands above her head and crossed her feet. It was very pleasant to know that all these bungalows were empty, that everybody was down on the beach, out of sight, out of hearing. She had the garden to herself; she was alone.

Dazzling white the picotees shone; the golden-eyed marigold glittered; the nasturtiums wreathed the veranda poles in green and gold flame. If only one had time to look at these flowers long enough, time to get over the sense of novelty and strangeness, time to know them! But as soon as one paused to part the petals, to discover the under-side of the leaf, along came Life and one was swept away. And, lying in her cane chair, Linda felt so light; she felt like a leaf. Along came Life like a wind and she was seized and shaken; she had to go. Oh dear, would it always be so? Was there no escape?

... Now she sat on the veranda of their Tasmanian home, leaning against her father's knee. And he promised, 'As soon as you and I are old enough, Linny, we'll cut off somewhere, we'll escape. Two boys together. I have a fancy I'd like to sail up a river in China.' Linda saw that river, very wide, covered with little rafts and boats. She saw the yellow hats of the boatmen and she heard their high, thin voices as they called ...

'Yes, papa.'

But just then a very broad young man with bright ginger hair walked slowly past their house, and slowly, solemnly even, uncovered. Linda's father pulled her ear teasingly, in the way he had.

'Linny's beau,' he whispered.

'Oh, papa, fancy being married to Stanley Burnell!'

Well, she was married to him. And what was more she loved him. Not the Stanley whom everyone saw, not the everyday one; but a timid, sensitive, innocent Stanley who knelt down every night to say his prayers, and who longed to be good. Stanley was simple. If he believed in people—as he believed in her, for instance—it was with his whole heart. He could not be disloyal; he could not tell a lie. And how terribly he suffered if he thought anyone—she—was not being dead straight, dead sincere with him! 'This is too subtle for me!' He flung out the words, but his open quivering, distraught look was like the look of a trapped beast.

But the trouble was—here Linda felt almost inclined to laugh, though Heaven knows it was no laughing matter—she saw *her* Stanley so seldom. There were glimpses, moments, breathing spaces of calm, but all the rest of the time it was like living in a house that couldn't be cured of the habit of catching on fire, on a ship that got wrecked every day. And it was always Stanley who was in the thick of the danger. Her whole time was spent in rescuing him, and restoring him, and calming him down, and listening to his story. And what was left of her time was spent in the dread of having children.

Linda frowned; she sat up quickly in her steamer chair and clasped her ankles. Yes, that was her real grudge against life; that was what she could not understand. That was the question she asked and asked, and listened in vain for the answer. It was all very well to say it was the common lot of women to bear children. It wasn't true. She, for one, could prove that wrong. She was broken, made weak, her courage was gone, through child-bearing. And what made it doubly hard to bear was, she did not love her children. It was useless pretending. Even if she had had the strength she never would have nursed and played with the little girls. No, it was as though a cold breath had chilled her through and through on each of those awful journeys; she had no warmth left to give them. As to the boy—well, thank Heaven, mother had taken him; he was mother's, or Beryl's or anybody's who wanted him. She had hardly held him in her arms. She was so indifferent about him that as he lay there ... Linda glanced down.

The boy had turned over. He lay facing her, and he was no longer asleep. His dark-blue, baby eyes were open; he looked as though he was peeping at his mother. And suddenly his face dimpled; it broke into a wide, toothless smile, a perfect beam, no less.

'I'm here!' that happy smile seemed to say. 'Why don't you like me?'

There was something so quaint, so unexpected about that smile that Linda smiled herself. But she checked herself and said to the boy coldly, 'I don't like babies.'

'Don't like babies?' The boy couldn't believe her. 'Don't like *me*?' He waved his arms foolishly at his mother.

Linda dropped off her chair on to the grass.

'Why do you keep on smiling?' she said severely. 'If you knew what I was thinking about, you wouldn't.'

But he only squeezed up his eyes, slyly, and rolled his head on the pillow. He didn't believe a word she said.

'We know all about that!' smiled the boy.

Linda was so astonished at the confidence of this little creature ... Ah no, be sincere. That was not what she felt; it was something far different, it was something so new, so ... The tears danced in her eyes; she breathed in a small whisper to the boy, 'Hallo, my funny!'

But by now the boy had forgotten his mother. He was serious again. Something pink, something soft waved in front of him. He made a grab at it and it immediately disappeared. But when he lay back, another, like the first, appeared. This time he determined to catch it. He made a tremendous effort and rolled right over.

VII

The tide was out; the beach was deserted; lazily flopped the warm sea. The sun beat down, beat down hot and fiery on the fine sand, baking the grey and blue and black and white-veined pebbles. It sucked up the little drop of water that lay in the hollow of the curved shells; it bleached the pink convolvulus that threaded through and through the sand-hills. Nothing seemed to move but the small sand-hoppers. Pit-pit-pit! They were never still.

Over there on the weed-hung rocks that looked at low tide like shaggy beasts come down to the water to drink, the sunlight seemed to spin like a silver coin dropped into each of the small rock pools. They danced, they quivered, and minute ripples laved the porous shores. Looking down, bending over, each pool was like a lake with pink and blue houses clustered on the shores; and oh! the vast mountainous country behind those houses—the ravines, the passes, the dangerous creeks and fearful tracks that led to the water's edge. Underneath waved the sea-forest—pink thread-like trees, velvet anemones, and orange berry-spotted weeds. Now a stone on the bottom moved, rocked, and there was a glimpse of a black feeler; now a thread-like creature wavered by and was lost. Something was happening to the pink, waving trees; they were changing to a cold moonlight blue. And now there sounded the faintest 'plop'. Who made that sound? What was going on down there? And how strong, how damp the seaweed smelt in the hot sun . . .

The green blinds were drawn in the bungalows of the summer colony. Over the verandas, prone on the paddock, flung over the fences, there were exhausted-looking bathing-dresses and rough striped towels. Each back window seemed to have a pair of sand-shoes on the sill and some lumps of rock or a bucket or a collection of pawa shells. The bush quivered in a haze of heat; the sandy road was empty except for the Trouts' dog Snooker, who lay stretched in the very middle of it. His blue eye was turned up, his legs stuck out stiffly, and he gave an occasional desperate-sounding puff, as much as to say he had decided to make an end of it and was only waiting for some kind cart to come along.

'What are you looking at, my grandma? Why do you keep stopping and sort of staring at the wall?'

Kezia and her grandmother were taking their siesta together. The little girl, wearing only her short drawers and her under-bodice, her arms and legs bare, lay on one of the puffed-up pillows of her grandma's bed, and the old woman, in a white ruffled dressing-gown sat in a rocker at the window, with a long piece of pink knitting in her lap. This room that they shared, like the other rooms of her bungalow, was of light varnished wood and the floor was bare. The furniture was of the shabbiest, the simplest. The dressing-table, for instance, was a packing-case in a sprigged muslin petticoat, and the mirror above was very strange; it was as though a little piece of forked lightning was imprisoned in it. On the table there stood a jar of seapinks, pressed so tightly together they looked more like a velvet pincushion, and a special shell which Kezia had given her grandma for a pin-tray, and another even more special which she had thought would make a very nice place for a watch to curl up in.

'Tell me, grandma,' said Kezia.

The old woman sighed, whipped the wool twice round her thumb, and drew the bone needle through. She was casting on.

'I was thinking of your Uncle William, darling,' she said quietly.

'My Australian Uncle William?' said Kezia. She had another.

'Yes, of course.'

'The one I never saw?'

'That was the one.'

'Well, what happened to him?' Kezia knew perfectly well, but she wanted to be told again.

'He went to the mines, and he got a sunstroke there and died,' said old Mrs Fairfield.

Kezia blinked and considered the picture again ... A little man fallen over like a tin soldier by the side of the big black hole.

'Does it make you sad to think about him, grandma?' She hated her grandma to be sad.

It was the old woman's turn to consider. Did it make her sad? To look back, back. To stare down the years, as Kezia had seen her doing. To look after them as a woman does, long after they were out of sight. did it make her sad? No, life was like that.

'No, Kezia.'

'But why?' asked Kezia. She lifted one bare arm and began to draw things in the air. 'Why did Uncle William have to die? He wasn't old.'

Mrs Fairfield began counting the stitiches in threes. 'It just happened,' she said in an absorbed voice.

'Does everybody have to die?' asked Kezia.

'Everybody!'

'*Me?*' Kezia sounded fearfully incredulous.

'Some day, my darling.'

'But, grandma.' Kezia waved her left leg and waggled the toes. They felt sandy. 'What if I just won't?'

The old woman sighed again and drew a long thread from the ball.

'We're not asked, Kezia,' she said sadly. 'It happens to all of us sooner or later.'

Kezia lay still thinking this over. She didn't want to die. It meant she would have to leave here, leave everywhere, for ever, leave—leave her grandma. She rolled over quickly.

'Grandma,' she said in a startled voice.

'What, my pet!'

'*You're* not to die.' Kezia was very decided.

'Ah, Kezia'—her grandma looked up and smiled and shook her head—'don't let's talk about it.'

'But you're not to. You couldn't leave me. You couldn't not be there.' This was awful. 'Promise me you won't ever do it, grandma,' pleaded Kezia.

The old woman went on knitting.

'Promise me! Say never!'

But still her grandma was silent.

Kezia rolled off her bed; she couldn't bear it any longer, and lightly she leapt on to her grandma's knees, clasped her hand round the old woman's throat and began kissing her, under the chin, behind the ear, and blowing down her neck.

'Say never ... say never ... say never—' She gasped between kisses. And then she began, very softly and lightly to tickle her grandma.

'Kezia!' The old woman dropped her knitting. She swung back in the rocker. She began to tickle Kezia. 'Say never, say never, say never,' gurgled Kezia, while they lay there laughing in each other's arms. 'Come, that's enough, my squirrel! That's enough, my wild pony!' said old Mrs Fairfield, setting her cap straight. 'Pick up my knitting.'

Both of them had forgotten what the 'never' was about.

VIII

The sun was still full on the garden when the back door of the Burnells' shut with a bang, and a very gay figure walked down the path to the gate. It was Alice, the servant-girl, dressed for her afternoon out. She wore a white cotton dress with such large red spots on it, and so many that they made you shudder, white shoes and a leghorn turned up under the brim with poppies. Of course she wore gloves, white ones, stained at the fastenings with iron-mould, and in one hand she carried a very dashed-looking sunshade which she referred to as her *perishall*.

Beryl, sitting in the window, fanning her freshly-washed hair, thought she had never seen such a guy. If Alice had only blacked her face with a piece of cork before she started out, the picture would have been complete. And where did a girl like that go to in a place like this? The heart-shaped Fijian fan beat scornfully at that lovely bright mane. She supposed Alice had picked up some horrible common larrikin and they'd go off into the bush together. Pity to have made herself so conspicuous; they'd have hard work to hide with Alice in that rig-out.

But no, Beryl was unfair. Alice was going to tea with Mrs Stubbs, who'd sent her an 'invite' by the little boy who called for orders. She had taken ever such a liking to Mrs Stubbs ever since the first time she went to the shop to get something for her mosquitoes.

'Dear heart!' Mrs Stubbs had clapped her hand to her side. 'I never seen anyone so eaten. You might have been attacked by canningbals.'

Alice did wish there'd been a bit of life on the road though. Made her feel so queer, having nobody behind her. Made her feel all weak in the spine. She couldn't believe that someone wasn't watching her. And yet it was silly to turn round; it gave you away. She pulled up her gloves, hummed to herself and said to the distant gum-tree, 'Shan't be long now.' But that was hardly company.

Mrs Stubbs's shop was perched on a little hillock just off the road. It had two big windows for eyes, a broad veranda for a hat, and the sign on the roof, scrawled MRS STUBBS'S, was like a little card stuck rakishly in the hat crown.

On the veranda there hung a long string of bathing-dresses, clinging together as though they'd just been rescued from the sea rather than waiting to go in, and beside them there hung a cluster of sand-shoes so extraordinarily mixed that to get at one pair you had to tear apart and forcibly separate at least fifty. Even then it was the rarest thing to find the left that belonged to the right. So many people had lost patience and gone off with one shoe that fitted and one that was a little too big ... Mrs Stubbs prided herself on keeping something of everything. The two windows, arranged in the form of precarious pyramids, were crammed so tight, piled so high, that it seemed only a conjurer could prevent them from toppling over. In the left-hand corner of one window, glued to the pane by four gelatine lozenges, there was—and there had been from time immemorial—a notice.

LOST! HANSOME GOLE BROOCH
SOLID GOLD
ON OR NEAR BEACH
REWARD OFFERED

Alice pressed open the door. The bell jangled, the red serge curtains parted, and Mrs Stubbs appeared. With her broad smile and the long bacon knife in her hand, she looked like a friendly brigand. Alice was welcomed so warmly that she found it quite difficult to keep up her 'manners'. They consisted of persistent little coughs and hems, pulls at her gloves, tweaks at her skirt, and a curious difficulty in seeing what was set before her or understanding what was said.

Tea was laid on the parlour table—ham, sardines, a whole pound of butter, and such a large johnny cake that it looked like an advertisement for somebody's baking-powder. But the Primus stove roared so loudly that it was useless to try to talk above it. Alice sat down on the edge of a basket chair while Mrs Stubbs pumped the stove still higher. Suddenly Mrs Stubbs whipped the cushion off a chair and disclosed a large brown-paper parcel.

'I've just had some new photers taken, my dear,' she shouted cheerfully to Alice. 'Tell me what you think of them.'

In a very dainty, refined way Alice wet her finger and put the

tissue back from the first one. Life? How many there were! There
were three dozzing at least. And she held hers up to the light.

Mrs Stubbs sat in an armchair, leaning very much to one side.
There was a look of mild astonishment on her large face. and well
there might be. For though the armchair stood on a carpet, to the
left of it, miraculously skirting the carpet-border, there was a
dashing waterfall. On her right stood a Grecian pillar with a giant
fern-tree on either side of it, and in the background towered a
gaunt mountain, pale with snow.

'It is a nice style, isn't it?' shouted Mrs Stubbs; and Alice had
just screamed 'Sweetly' when the roaring of the Primus stove died
down, fizzled out, ceased, and she said 'Pretty' in a silence that
was frightening.

'Draw up your chair, my dear,' said Mrs Stubbs, beginning to
pour out. 'Yes,' she said thoughtfully, as she handed the tea, 'but I
don't care about the size. I'm having an enlargemint. All very well
for Christmas cards, but I never was the one for small photers
myself. You get no comfort out of them. To say the truth, I find
them dis'eartening.'

Alice quite saw what she meant.

'Size,' said Mrs Stubbs. 'Give me size. That was what my poor
dear husband was always saying. He couldn't stand anything
small. Gave him the creeps. And, strange as it may seem my
dear'—here Mrs Stubbs creaked and seemed to expand herself at
the memory—'it was dropsy that carried him off at the larst.
Many's the time they drawn one and a half pints from 'im at the
'ospital . . . It seemed like a judgemint.'

Alice burned to know exactly what it was that was drawn from
him. She ventured, 'I suppose it was water.'

But Mrs Stubbs fixed Alice with her eyes and replied meaningly,
'It was *liquid*, my dear.'

Liquid! Alice jumped away from the word like a cat and came
back to it, nosing and wary.

'That's 'im!' said Mrs Stubbs, and she pointed dramatically to
the life-size head and shoulders of a burly man with a dead white
rose in the button-hole of his coat that made you think of a curl of
cold mutting fat. Just below, in silver letters on a red cardboard
ground, were the words, 'Be not afraid, it is I.'

'It's ever such a fine face,' said Alice faintly.

The pale-blue bow on the top of Mrs Stubbs's fair frizzy hair quivered. She arched her plump neck. What a neck she had! It was bright pink where it began and then it changed to warm apricot, and that faded to the colour of a brown egg and then to a deep creamy.

'All the same, my dear,' she said surprisingly, 'freedom's best!' Her soft, fat chuckle sounded like a purr. 'Freedom's best,' said Mrs Stubbs again.

Freedom! Alice gave a loud, silly little titter. She felt awkward. Her mind flew back to her own kitching. Ever so queer! She wanted to be back in it again.

IX

A strange company assembled in the Burnells' washhouse after tea. Round the table there sat a bull, a rooster, a donkey that kept forgetting it was a donkey, a sheep and a bee. The washhouse was the perfect place for such a meeting because they could make as much noise as they liked, and nobody ever interrupted. It was a small tin shed standing apart from the bungalow. Against the wall there was a deep trough and in the corner a copper with a basket of clothes-pegs on top of it. The little window, spun over with cobwebs, had a piece of candle and a mouse-trap on the dusty sill. There were clothes-lines criss-crossed overhead and, hanging from a peg on the wall, a very big, a huge, rusty horseshoe. The table was in the middle with a form at either side.

'You can't be a bee, Kezia. A bee's not an animal. It's a ninseck.'

'Oh, but I do want to be a bee frightfully,' wailed Kezia ... A tiny bee, all yellow-furry, with striped legs. She drew her legs up under her and leaned over the table. She felt she was a bee.

'A ninseck must be an animal,' she said stoutly. 'It makes a noise. It's not like a fish.'

'I'm a bull, I'm a bull!' cried Pip. And he gave such a tremendous bellow—how did he make that noise?—Lottie looked quite alarmed.

'I'll be a sheep,' said little Rags. 'A whole lot of sheep went past this morning.'

'How do you know?'

'Dad heard them. Baa!' He sounded like the little lamb that trots behind and seems to wait to be carried.

'Cock-a-doodle-do!' shrilled Isabel. With her red cheeks and bright eyes she looked like a rooster.

'What'll I be?' Lottie asked everybody, and she sat there smiling, waiting for them to decide for her. It had to be an easy one.

'Be a donkey, Lottie.' It was Kezia's suggestion. 'Hee-haw! You can't forget that.'

'Hee-haw!' said Lottie solemnly. 'When do I have to say it?'

'I'll explain, I'll explain,' said the bull. It was he who had the cards. He waved them round his head. 'All be quiet! All listen!' And he waited for them. 'Look here, Lottie.' He turned up a card. 'It's got two spots on it—see? Now, if you put that card in the middle and somebody else has one with two spots as well, you say "Hee-haw", and the card's yours.'

'Mine?' Lottie was round-eyed. 'To keep?'

'No, silly. Just for the game, see? Just while we're playing.' The bull was very cross with her.

'Oh, Lottie, you *are* a little silly,' said the proud rooster.

Lottie looked at both of them. Then she hung her head; her lip quivered. 'I don't want to play,' she whispered. The others glanced at one another like conspirators. All of them knew what that meant. She would go away and be discovered somewhere standing with her pinny thrown over her head, in a corner, or against a wall, or even behind a chair.

'Yes, you do, Lottie. It's quite easy,' said Kezia.

And Isabel, repentant, said exactly like a grown-up, 'Watch me, Lottie, and you'll soon learn.'

'Cheer up, Lot,' said Pip. 'There, I know what I'll do. I'll give you the first one. It's mine, really, but I'll give it to you. Here you are.' And he slammed the card down in front of Lottie.

Lottie revived at that. But now she was in another difficulty. 'I haven't got a hanky,' she said; 'I want one badly, too.'

'Here, Lottie, you can use mine.' Rags dipped into his sailor blouse and brought up a very wet-looking one, knotted together. 'Be very careful,' he warned her. 'Only use that corner. Don't undo it. I've got a little starfish inside I'm going to try and tame.'

'Oh, come on, you girls,' said the bull. 'And mind—you're not to look at your cards. You've got to keep your hands under the table till I say "Go".'

Smack went the cards round the table. They tried with all their might to see, but Pip was too quick for them. It was very exciting, sitting there in the washhouse; it was all they could do not to burst into a little chorus of animals before Pip had finished dealing.

'Now, Lottie, you begin.'

Timidly Lottie stretched out a hand, took the top card off her pack, had a good look at it—it was plain she was counting the spots—and put it down.

'No, Lottie, you can't do that. You mustn't look first. You must turn it the other way over.'

'But then everybody will see it the same time as me,' said Lottie.

The game proceeded. Mooe-ooo-er! The bull was terrible. He charged over the table and seemed to eat the cards up.

Bss-ss! said the bee.

Cock-a-doodle-do! Isabel stood up in her excitement and moved her elbows like wings.

Baa! Little Rags put down the King of Diamonds and Lottie put down the one they called the King of Spain. She had hardly any cards left.

'Why don't you call out, Lottie?'

'I've forgotten what I am,' said the donkey woefully.

'Well, change! Be a dog instead! Bow-wow!'

'Oh yes. That's much easier.' Lottie smiled again. But when she and Kezia both had a one Kezia waited on purpose. The others made signs to Lottie and pointed. Lottie turned very red; she looked bewildered, and at last she said, 'Hee-haw! Ke-zia.'

'Ss! Wait a minute!' They were in the very thick of it when the bull stopped them, holding up his hand. 'What's that? What's that noise?'

'What noise? What do you mean?' asked the rooster.

'Ss! Shut up! Listen!' They were mouse-still. 'I thought I heard a—a sort of knocking,' said the bull.

'What was it like?' asked the sheep faintly.

No answer.

The bee gave a shudder. 'Whatever did we shut the door for?' she said softly. Oh, why, why had they shut the door?

While they were playing, the day had faded; the gorgeous sunset had blazed and died. And now the quick dark came racing over the sea, over the sandhills, up the paddock. You were frightened to look in the corners of the washhouse, and yet you had to look with all your might. And somewhere, far away, grandma was lighting a lamp. The blinds were being pulled down; the kitchen fire leapt in the tins on the mantelpiece.

'It would be awful now,' said the bull, 'if a spider was to fall from the ceiling on to the table, wouldn't it?'

'Spiders don't fall from ceilings.'

'Yes, they do. Our Min told us she'd seen a spider as big as a saucer, with long hairs on it like a gooseberry.'

Quickly all the little heads were jerked up; all the little bodies drew together, pressed together.

'Why doesn't somebody come and call us?' cried the rooster.

Oh, those grown-ups, laughing and snug, sitting in the lamplight, drinking out of cups! They'd forgotten about them. No, not really forgotten. That was what their smile meant. They had decided to leave them there all by themselves.

Suddenly Lottie gave such a piercing scream that all of them jumped off the forms, all of them screamed too. 'A face—a face looking!' shrieked Lottie.

It was true, it was real. Pressed against the window was a pale face, black eyes, a black beard.

'Grandma! Mother! Somebody!'

But they had not got to the door, tumbling over one another, before it opened for Uncle Jonathan. He had come to take the little boys home.

X

He had meant to be there before, but in the front garden he had come upon Linda walking up and down the grass, stopping to pick off a dead pink or give a top-heavy carnation something to lean against, or to take a deep breath of something, and then walking on again, with her little air of remoteness. Over her white frock she wore a yellow, pink-fringed shawl from the chinaman's shop.

'Hallo, Jonathan!' called Linda. And Jonathan whipped off his shabby panama, pressed it against his breast, dropped on one knee, and kissed Linda's hand.

'Greeting, my Fair One! Greeting, my Celestial Peach Blossom!' boomed the bass voice gently. 'Where are the other noble dames?'

'Beryl's out playing bridge and mother's giving the boy his bath . . . Have you come to borrow something?'

The Trouts were for ever running out of things and sending across to the Burnells' at the last moment.

But Jonathan only answered, 'A little love, a little kindness;' and he walked by his sister-in-law's side.

Linda dropped into Beryl's hammock under the manuka tree, and Jonathan stretched himself on the grass beside her, pulled a long stalk and began chewing it. They knew each other well. The voices of children cried from the other gardens. A fisherman's light cart shook along the sandy road, and from far away they heard a dog barking; it was muffled as though the dog had its head in a sack. If you listened you could just hear the soft swish of the sea at full tide sweeping the pebbles. The sun was sinking.

'And so you go back to the office on Monday, do you, Jonathan?' asked Linda.

'On Monday the cage door opens and clangs to upon the victim for another eleven months and a week,' answered Jonathan.

Linda swung a little. 'It must be awful,' she said slowly.

'Would ye have me laugh, my fair sister? Would ye have me weep?'

Linda was so accustomed to Jonathan's way of talking that she paid no attention to it.

'I suppose,' she said vaguely, 'one gets used to it. One gets used to anything.'

'Does one? Hum!' the 'Hum' was so deep it seemed to boom from underneath the ground. 'I wonder how it's done,' brooded Jonathan; 'I've never managed it.'

Looking at him as he lay there, Linda thought again how attractive he was. It was strange to think that he was only an ordinary clerk, that Stanley earned twice as much money as he. What was the matter with Jonathan? He had no ambition; she supposed that was it. And yet one felt he was gifted, exceptional. He was passionately fond of music; every spare penny he had went on books. He was always full of new ideas, schemes, plans.

But nothing came of it all. The new fire blazed in Jonathan; you almost heard it roaring softly as he explained, described and dilated on the new thing; but a moment later it had fallen in and there was nothing but ashes, and Jonathan went about with a look like hunger in his black eyes. At these times he exaggerated his absurd manner of speaking, and he sang in church—he was the leader of the choir—with such fearful dramatic intensity that the meanest hymn put on an unholy splendour.

'It seems to me just as imbecile, just as infernal, to have to go to the office on Monday,' said Jonathan, 'as it always has done and always will do. To spend all the best years of one's life sitting on a stool from nine to five, scratching in somebody's ledger! It's a queer use to make of one's ... one and only life, isn't it? Or do I fondly dream?' He rolled over on the grass and looked up at Linda. 'Tell me, what is the difference between my life and that of an ordinary prisoner? The only difference I can see is that I put myself in jail and nobody's ever going to let me out. That's a more intolerable situation than the other. For if I'd been—pushed in, against my will—kicking, even—once the door was locked, or at any rate in five years or so, I might have accepted the fact and begun to take an interest in the flight of flies or counting the warder's steps along the passage with particular attention to variations of tread and so on. But as it is, I'm like an insect that's flown into a room of its own accord. I dash against the walls, dash against the windows, flop against the ceiling, do everything on God's earth, in fact, except fly out again. And all the while I'm thinking, like that moth, or that butterfly, or whatever it is, "The shortness of life! The shortness of life!" I've only one night or one day, and there's this vast dangerous garden, waiting out there, undiscovered, unexplored.'

'But, if you feel like that, why—' began Linda quickly.

'*Ah*!' cried Jonathan. And that '*Ah*!' was somehow almost exultant. 'There you have me. Why? Why indeed? There's the maddening, mysterious question. Why don't I fly out again? There's the window or the door or whatever it was I came in by. It's not hopelessly shut—is it? Why don't I find it and be off? Answer me that, little sister.' But he gave her no time to answer.

'I'm exactly like that insect again. For some reason'—Jonathan paused between the words—'it's not allowed, it's forbidden, it's against the insect law, to stop banging and flopping and crawling up the pane even for an instant. Why don't I leave the office? Why don't I seriously consider, this moment, for instance, what it is that prevents me leaving? It's not as though I'm tremendously tied. I've two boys to provide for, but, after all, they're boys. I could cut off to sea, or get a job up-country, or—' Suddenly he smiled at Linda and said in a changed voice, as if he were confiding a secret, 'Weak ... weak. No stamina. No anchor. No guiding principle, let us call it.' But then the dark velvety voice rolled out:

> Would ye hear the story
> How it unfolds itself ...

and they were silent.

The sun had set. In the western sky there were great masses of crushed-up rose-coloured clouds. Broad beams of light shone through the clouds and beyond them as if they would cover the whole sky. Overhead the blue faded; it turned a pale gold, and the bush outlined against it gleamed dark and brilliant like metal. Sometimes when those beams of light show in the sky they are very awful. They remind you that up there sits Jehovah, the jealous God, the Almighty, Whose eye is upon you, ever watchful, never weary. You remember that at His coming the whole earth will shake into one ruined graveyard; the cold, bright angels will drive you this way and that, and there will be no time to explain what could be explained so simply ... But tonight it seemed to Linda there was something infinitely joyful and loving in those silver beams. And now no sound came from the sea. It breathed softly as if it would draw that tender, joyful beauty into its own bosom.

'It's all wrong, it's all wrong,' came the shadowy voice of Jonathan. 'It's not the scene, it's not the setting for ... three stools, three desks, three ink pots and a wire blind.'

Linda knew that he would never change, but she said, 'Is it too late, even now?'

'I'm old—I'm old,' intoned Jonathan. He bent towards her, he passed his hand over his head. 'Look!' His black hair was speckled all over with silver, like the breast plumage of a black fowl.

Linda was surprised. She had no idea that he was grey. And yet, as he stood up beside her and sighed and stretched, she saw him, for the first time, not resolute, not gallant, not careless, but touched already with age. He looked very tall on the darkening grass, and the thought crossed her mind, 'He is like a weed.'

Jonathan stooped again and kissed her fingers.

'Heaven reward thy sweet patience, lady mine,' he murmured. 'I must go seek those heirs to my fame and fortune . . . ' He was gone.

XI

Light shone in the windows of the bungalow. Two square patches of gold fell upon the pinks and the peaked marigolds. Florrie, the cat, came out on to the veranda, and sat on the top step, her white paws close together, her tail curled round. She looked content, as though she had been waiting for this moment all day.

'Thank goodness, it's getting late,' said Florrie. 'Thank goodness, the long day is over.' Her greengage eyes opened.

Presently there sounded the rumble of the coach, the crack of Kelly's whip. It came near enough for one to hear the voices of the men from town, talking loudly together. It stopped at the Burnell's gate.

Stanley was half-way up the path before he saw Linda. 'Is that you, darling?'

'Yes, Stanley.'

He leapt across the flower-bed and seized her in his arms. She was enfolded in that familiar, eager, strong embrace.

'Forgive me, darling, forgive me,' stammered Stanley, and he put his hand under her chin and lifted her face to him.

'Forgive you?' smiled Linda. 'But whatever for?'

'Good God! You can't have forgotten,' cried Stanley Burnell. 'I've thought of nothing else all day. I've had the hell of a day. I made up my mind to dash out and telegraph, and then I thought the wire mightn't reach you before I did. I've been in tortures, Linda.'

'But, Stanley,' said Linda, 'what must I forgive you for?'

'Linda!'—Stanley was very hurt—'didn't you realize—you must have realized—I went away without saying goodbye to you this morning? I can't imagine how I can have done such a thing.

My confounded temper, of course. But—well'—and he sighed and took her in his arms again—'I've suffered for it enough today.'

'What's that you've got in your hand?' asked Linda. 'New gloves? Let me see.'

'Oh, just a cheap pair of wash-leather ones,' said Stanley humbly. 'I noticed Bell was wearing some in the coach this morning, so, as I was passing the shop, I dashed in and got myself a pair. What are you smiling at? You don't think it was wrong of me, do you?'

'On the *con*-trary, darling,' said Linda, 'I think it was most sensible.'

She pulled one of the large, pale gloves on her own fingers and looked at her hand, turning it this way and that. She was still smiling.

Stanley wanted to say, 'I was thinking of you the whole time I bought them.' It was true, but for some reason he couldn't say it. 'Let's go in,' said he.

XII

Why does one feel so different at night? Why is it so exciting to be awake when everybody else is asleep? Late—it is very late! And yet every moment you feel more and more wakeful, as though you were slowly almost with every breath, waking up into a new, wonderful, far more thrilling and exciting world than the daylight one. And what is this queer sensation that you're a conspirator? Lightly, stealthily you move about your room. You take something off the dressing-table and put it down again without a sound. And everything, even the bedposts, knows you, responds, shares your secret...

You're not very fond of your room by day. You never think about it. You're in and out, the door opens and slams, the cupboard creaks. You sit down on the side of your bed, change your shoes and dash out again. A dive down to the glass, two pins in your hair, powder your nose and off again. But now—it's suddenly dear to you. It's a darling little funny room. It's yours. Oh, what a joy it is to own things! Mine—my own!

'My very own for ever?'

'Yes.' Their lips met.

No, of course, that had nothing to do with it. That was all nonsense and rubbish. But, in spite of herself, Beryl saw so plainly two people standing in the middle of her room. Her arms were round his neck; he held her. And now he whispered, 'My beauty, my little beauty!' She jumped off her bed, ran over to the window and kneeled on the windowseat, with her elbows on the sill. But the beautiful night, the garden, every bush, every leaf, even the white palings, even the stars, were conspirators too. So bright was the moon that the flowers were bright as by day; the shadow of the nasturtiums, exquisite lily-like leaves and wide-open flowers, lay across the silvery veranda. The manuka tree, bent by the southerly winds, was like a bird on one leg stretching out a wing.

But when Beryl looked at the bush, it seemed to her the bush was sad.

'We are dumb trees, reaching up in the night, imploring we know not what,' said the sorrowful bush.

It is true when you are by yourself and you think about life, it is always sad. All that excitement and so on has a way of suddenly leaving you, and it's as though, in the silence, somebody called your name, and you heard your name for the first time. 'Beryl!'

'Yes, I'm here. I'm Beryl. Who wants me?'

'Beryl!'

'Let me come.'

It is lonely living by oneself. Of course, there are relations, friends, heaps of them; but that's not what she means. She wants someone who will find the Beryl they none of them know, who will expect her to be that Beryl always. She wants a lover.

'Take me away from all these other people, my love. Let us go far away. Let us live our life, all new, all ours, from the very beginning. Let us make our fire. Let us sit down to eat together. Let us have long talks at night.'

And the thought was almost, 'Save me, my love. Save me!'

... 'Oh, go on! Don't be a prude, my dear. You enjoy yourself while you're young. That's my advice.' And a high rush of silly laughter joined Mrs Harry Kember's loud, indifferent neigh.

You see, it's so frightfully difficult when you've nobody. You're so at the mercy of things. You can't just be rude. And you've always this horror of seeming inexperienced and stuffy like the other ninnies at the Bay. And—and it's fascinating to know you've power over people. Yes, that is fascinating . . .

Oh why, oh why doesn't 'he' come soon?

If I go on living here, thought Beryl, anything may happen to me.

'But how do you know he is coming at all?' mocked a small voice within her.

But Beryl dismissed it. She couldn't be left. Other people, perhaps, but not she. It wasn't possible to think that Beryl Fairfield never married, that lovely fascinating girl.

'Do you remember Beryl Fairfield?'

'Remember her! As if I could forget her! It was one summer at the Bay that I saw her. She was standing on the beach in a blue'—no, pink—'muslin frock, holding on a big cream'—no, black—'straw hat. But it's years ago now.'

'She's as lovely as ever, more so if anything.'

Beryl smiled, bit her lip, and gazed over the garden. As she gazed, she saw somebody, a man, leave the road, step along the paddock beside their palings as if he was coming straight towards her. Her heart beat. Who was it? Who could it be? It couldn't be a burglar, certainly not a burglar, for he was smoking and he strolled lightly. Beryl's heart leapt; it seemed to turn right over, and then to stop. She recognized him.

'Good evening, Miss Beryl,' said the voice softly.

'Good evening.'

'Won't you come for a little walk?' it drawled.

Come for a walk—at that time of night! 'I couldn't. Everybody's in bed. Everybody's asleep.'

'Oh,' said the voice lightly, and a whiff of sweet smoke reached her. 'What does everybody matter? Do come! It's such a fine night. There's not a soul about.'

Beryl shook her head. But already something stirred in her, something reared its head.

The voice said, 'Frightened?' It mocked, 'Poor little girl!'

'Not in the least,' said she. As she spoke that weak thing within her seemed to uncoil, to grow suddenly tremendously strong; she longed to go!

And just as if this was quite understood by the other, the voice said, gently and softly, but finally, 'Come along!'

Beryl stepped over her low window, crossed the veranda, ran down the grass to the gate. He was there before her.

'That's right,' breathed the voice, and it teased, 'You're not frightened, are you? You're not frightened?'

She was; now she was here she was terrified, and it seemed to her everything was different. The moonlight stared and glittered; the shadows were like bars of iron. Her hand was taken.

'Not in the least,' she said lightly. 'Why should I be?'

Her hand was pulled gently, tugged. She held back.

'No, I'm not coming any farther,' said Beryl.

'Oh, rot!' Harry Kember didn't believe her. 'Come along! We'll just go as far as that fuchsia bush. Come along!'

The fuchsia bush was tall. It fell over the fence in a shower. There was a little pit of darkness beneath.

'No, really, I don't want to,' said Beryl.

For a moment Harry Kember didn't answer. Then he came close to her, turned to her, smiled and said quickly, 'Don't be silly! Don't be silly!'

His smile was something she'd never seen before. Was he drunk? That bright, blind, terrifying smile froze her with horror. What was she doing? How had she got here? The stern garden asked her as the gate pushed open, and quick as a cat Harry Kember came through and snatched her to him.

'Cold little devil! Cold little devil!' said the hateful voice.

But Beryl was strong. She slipped, ducked, wrenched free.

'You are vile, vile,' said she.

'Then why in God's name did you come?' stammered Harry Kember.

Nobody answered him.

A cloud, small, serene, floated across the moon. In that moment of darkness the sea sounded deep, troubled. Then the cloud sailed away, and the sound of the sea was a vague murmur, as though it waked out of a dark dream. All was still.

The Garden Party

And after all the weather was ideal. They could not have had a more perfect day for a garden party if they had ordered it. Windless, warm, the sky without a cloud. Only the blue was veiled with a haze of light gold, as it is sometimes in early summer. The gardener had been up since dawn, mowing the lawns and sweeping them, until the grass and the dark flat rosettes where the daisy plants had been seemed to shine. As for the roses, you could not help feeling they understood that roses are the only flowers that impress people at garden parties; the only flowers that everybody is certain of knowing. Hundreds, yes, literally hundreds, had come out in a single night; the green bushes bowed down as though they had been visited by archangels.

Breakfast was not yet over before the men came to put up the marquee.

'Where do you want the marquee put, mother?'

'My dear child, it's no use asking me. I'm determined to leave everything to you children this year. Forget I am your mother. Treat me as an honoured guest.'

But Meg could not possibly go and supervise the men. She had washed her hair before breakfast, and she sat drinking her coffee in a green turban, with a dark wet curl stamped on each cheek. Jose, the butterfly, always came down in a silk petticoat and a kimono jacket.

'You'll have to go, Laura; you're the artistic one.'

Away Laura flew, still holding her piece of bread-and-butter. It's so delicious to have an excuse for eating out of doors, and besides, she loved having to arrange things; she always felt she could do it so much better than anybody else.

Four men in their shirt-sleeves stood grouped together on the garden path. They carried staves covered with rolls of canvas, and they had big tool-bags slung on their backs. They looked impressive. Laura wished now that she was not holding that piece of bread-and-butter, but there was nowhere to put it, and she couldn't possibly throw it away. She blushed and tried to look severe and even a little bit short-sighted as she came up to them.

'Good morning,' she said, copying her mother's voice. But that sounded so fearfully affected that she was ashamed, and stammered like a little girl, 'Oh—er—have you come—is it about the marquee?'

'That's right, miss,' said the tallest of the men, a lanky, freckled fellow, and he shifted his tool-bag, knocked back his straw hat and smiled down at her. 'That's about it.'

His smile was so easy, so friendly, that Laura recovered. What nice eyes he had, small, but such a dark blue! And now she looked at the others, they were smiling too. 'Cheer up, we won't bite,' their smile seemed to say. How very nice workmen were! And what a beautiful morning! She mustn't mention the morning; she must be business-like. The marquee.

'Well, what about the lily-lawn? Would that do?'

And she pointed to the lily-lawn with the hand that didn't hold the bread-and-butter. They turned, they stared in the direction. A little fat chap thrust out his under-lip, and the tall fellow frowned.

'I don't fancy it,' said he. 'Not conspicuous enough. You see, with a thing like a marquee,' and he turned to Laura in his easy way, 'you want to put it somewhere where it'll give you a bang slap in the eye, if you follow me.'

Laura's upbringing made her wonder for a moment whether it was quite respectful of a workman to talk to her of bangs slap in the eye. But she did quite follow him.

'A corner of the tennis-court,' she suggested. 'But the band's going to be in one corner.'

'H'm, going to have a band, are you?' said another of the workmen. He was pale. He had a haggard look as his dark eyes scanned the tennis-court. What was he thinking?

'Only a very small band,' said Laura gently. Perhaps he wouldn't mind so much if the band was quite small. But the tall fellow interrupted.

'Look here, miss, that's the place. Against those trees. Over there. That'll do fine.'

Against the karakas. Then the karaka-trees would be hidden. And they were so lovely, with their broad, gleaming leaves, and their clusters of yellow fruit. They were like trees you imagined growing on a desert island, proud, solitary, lifting their leaves and fruits to the sun in a kind of silent splendour. Must they be hidden by a marquee?

They must. Already the men had shouldered their staves and were making for the place. Only the tall fellow was left. He bent down, pinched a sprig of lavender, put his thumb and forefinger to his nose and snuffed up the smell. When Laura saw that gesture she forgot all about the karakas in her wonder at him caring for things like that—caring for the smell of lavender. How many men that she knew would have done such a thing. Oh, how extraordinarily nice workmen were, she thought. Why couldn't she have workmen for her friends rather than the silly boys she danced with and who came to Sunday night supper? She would get on much better with men like these.

It's all the fault, she decided, as the tall fellow drew something on the back of an envelope, something that was to be looped up or left to hang, of these absurd class distinctions. Well, for her part, she didn't feel them. Not a bit, not an atom ... And now there came the chock-chock of wooden hammers. Someone whistled, someone sang out, 'Are you right there, matey?' 'Matey!' The friendliness of it, the—the— Just to prove how happy she was, just to show the tall fellow how at home she felt, and how she despised stupid conventions, Laura took a big bite of her bread-and-butter as she stared at the little drawing. She felt just like a work-girl.

'Laura, Laura, where are you? Telephone, Laura!' a voice cried from the house.

'Coming!' Away she skimmed, over the lawn, up the path, up the steps, across the veranda, and into the porch. In the hall her father and Laurie were brushing their hats ready to go to the office.

'I say, Laura,' said Laurie very fast, 'you might just give a squiz at my coat before this afternoon. See if it wants pressing.'

'I will,' said she. Suddenly she couldn't stop herself. She ran at Laurie and gave him a small, quick squeeze. 'Oh, I do love parties, don't you?' gasped Laura.

'Ra-ther,' said Laurie's warm, boyish voice, and he squeezed his sister too, and gave her a gentle push. 'Dash off to the telephone, old girl.'

The telephone. 'Yes, yes; oh yes. Kitty? Good morning, dear. Come to lunch? Do, dear. Delighted of course. It will only be a very scratch meal—just the sandwich crusts and broken meringue-shells and what's left over. Yes, isn't it a perfect morning? Your white? Oh, I certainly should. One moment— hold the line. Mother's calling.' And Laura sat back. 'What, mother? Can't hear.'

Mrs Sheridan's voice floated down the stairs. 'Tell her to wear that sweet hat she had on last Sunday.'

'Mother says you're to wear that sweet hat you had on last Sunday. Good. One o'clock. Bye-bye.'

Laura put back the receiver, flung her arms over her head, took a deep breath, stretched and let them fall. 'Huh,' she sighed, and the moment after the sigh she sat up quickly. She was still, listening. All the doors in the house seemed to be open. The house was alive with soft, quick steps and running voices. The green baize door that led to the kitchen regions swung open and shut with a muffled thud. And now there came a long, chuckling absurd sound. It was the heavy piano being moved on its stiff castors. But the air! If you stopped to notice, was the air always like this? Little faint winds were playing chase in at the tops of the windows, out at the doors. And there were two tiny spots of sun, one on the inkpot, one on a silver photograph frame, playing too. Darling little spots. Especially the one on the inkpot lid. It was quite warm. A warm little silver star. She could have kissed it.

The front door bell pealed, and there sounded the rustle of Sadie's print skirt on the stairs. A man's voice murmured; Sadie answered, careless, 'I'm sure I don't know. Wait. I'll ask Mrs Sheridan.'

'What is it, Sadie?' Laura came into the hall.

'It's the florist, Miss Laura.'

It was, indeed. There, just inside the door, stood a wide, shallow tray full of pots of pink lilies. No other kind. Nothing but lilies—canna lilies, big pink flowers, wide open, radiant, almost frighteningly alive on bright crimson stems.

'O-oh, Sadie!' said Laura, and the sound was like a little moan. She crouched down as if to warm herself at that blaze of lilies; she felt they were in her fingers, on her lips, growing in her breast.

'It's some mistake,' she said faintly. 'Nobody ever ordered so many. Sadie, go and find mother.'

But at that moment Mrs Sheridan joined them.

'It's quite right,' she said calmly. 'Yes, I ordered them. Aren't they lovely?' She pressed Laura's arm. 'I was passing the shop yesterday, and I saw them in the window. And I suddenly thought for once in my life I shall have enough canna lilies. The garden party will be a good excuse.'

'But I thought you said you didn't mean to interfere,' said Laura. Sadie had gone. The florist's man was still outside at his van. She put her arm round her mother's neck and gently, very gently, she bit her mother's ear.

'My darling child, you wouldn't like a logical mother, would you? Don't do that. Here's the man.'

He carried more lilies still, another whole tray.

'Bank them up, just inside the door, on both sides of the porch, please,' said Mrs Sheridan. 'Don't you agree, Laura?'

'Oh, I *do*, mother.'

In the drawing-room Meg, Jose and good little Hans had at last succeeded in moving the piano.

'Now, if we put this chesterfield against the wall and move everything out of the room except the chairs, don't you think?'

'Quite.'

'Hans, move these tables into the smoking-room, and bring a sweeper to take these marks off the carpet and—one moment, Hans—' Jose loved giving orders to the servants, and they loved obeying her. She always made them feel they were taking part in some drama. 'Tell mother and Miss Laura to come here at once.'

'Very good, Miss Jose.'

She turned to Meg. 'I want to hear what the piano sounds like, just in case I'm asked to sing this afternoon. Let's try over "This life is Weary".'

Pom! Ta ta ta *Tee* ta! The piano burst out so passionately that Jose's face changed. She clasped her hands. She looked mournfully and enigmatically at her mother and Laura as they came in.

> This Life is *Wee*-ary,
> A Tear—a Sigh.

> A Love that *Chan*-ges,
>   This Life is *Wee*-ary,
> A Tear—a Sigh.
> A Love that *Chan*-ges,
> And then ... Goodbye!

But at the word 'Goodbye', and although the piano sounded more desperate than ever, her face broke into a brilliant, dreadfully unsympathetic smile.

'Aren't I in good voice, mummy?' she beamed.

> This Life is *Wee*-ary,
> Hope comes to Die.
> A Dream—a *Wa*-kening.

But now Sadie interrupted them. 'What is it, Sadie?'

'If you please, m'm, cook says have you got the flags for the sandwiches?'

'The flags for the sandwiches, Sadie?' echoed Mrs Sheridan dreamily. And the children knew by her face that she hadn't got them. 'Let me see.' And she said to Sadie firmly, 'Tell cook I'll let her have them in ten minutes.'

Sadie went.

'Now, Laura,' said her mother quickly, 'come with me into the smoking-room. I've got the names somewhere on the back of an envelope. You'll have to write them out for me. Meg, go upstairs this minute and take that wet thing off your head. Jose, run and finish dressing this instant. Do you hear me, children, or shall I have to tell your father when he comes home tonight? And—and, Jose, pacify cook if you do go into the kitchen, will you? I'm terrified of her this morning.'

The envelope was found at last behind the dining-room clock, though how it had got there Mrs Sheridan could not imagine.

'One of you children must have stolen it out of my bag, because I remember vividly—cream-cheese and lemon-curd. Have you done that?'

'Yes.'

'Egg and—' Mrs Sheridan held the envelope away from her. 'It looks like mice. It can't be mice, can it?'

'Olive, pet,' said Laura, looking over her shoulder.

'Yes, of course, olive. What a horrible combination it sounds. Egg and olive.'

They were finished at last, and Laura took them off to the kitchen. She found Jose there pacifying the cook, who did not look at all terrifying.

'I have never seen such exquisite sandwiches,' said Jose's rapturous voice. 'How many kinds did you say there were, cook? Fifteen?'

'Fifteen, Miss Jose.'

'Well, cook, I congratulate you.'

Cook swept up crusts with the long sandwich knife and smiled broadly.

'Godber's has come,' announced Sadie, issuing out of the pantry. She had seen the man pass the window.

That meant the cream puffs had come. Godber's were famous for their cream puffs. Nobody ever thought of making them at home.

'Bring them in and put them on the table, my girl,' ordered cook.

Sadie brought them in and went back to the door. Of course Laura and Jose were far too grown-up to really care about such things. All the same, they couldn't help agreeing that the puffs looked very attractive. Very. Cook began arranging them, shaking off the extra icing sugar.

'Don't they carry one back to all one's parties?' said Laura.

'I suppose they do,' said practical Jose, who never liked to be carried back. 'They look beautifully light and feathery, I must say.'

'Have one each, my dears,' said cook in her comfortable voice. 'Yer ma won't know.'

Oh, impossible. Fancy cream puffs so soon after breakfast. The very idea made one shudder. All the same, two minutes later Jose and Laura were licking their fingers with that absorbed inward look that only comes from whipped cream.

'Let's go into the garden, out by the back way,' suggested Laura. 'I want to see how the men are getting on with the marquee. They're such awfully nice men.'

But the back door was blocked by cook, Sadie, Godber's man and Hans.

Something had happened.

'Tuk-tuk-tuk,' clucked cook like an agitated hen. Sadie had her hand clapped to her cheek as though she had toothache. Hans's face was screwed up in the effort to understand. Only Godber's man seemed to be enjoying himself; it was his story.

'What's the matter? What's happened?'

'There's been a horrible accident,' said cook. 'A man's been killed.'

'A man killed! Where? How? When?'

But Godber's man wasn't going to have his story snatched from under his nose.

'Know those little cottages just below here, miss?' Know them? Of course, she knew them. 'Well, there's a young chap living there, name of Scott, a carter. His horse shied at a traction-engine, corner of Hawke Street this morning, and he was thrown out on the back of his head. Killed.'

'Dead!' Laura stared at Godber's man.

'Dead when they picked him up,' said Godber's man with relish. 'They were taking the body home as I come up here.' And he said to the cook, 'He's left a wife and five little ones.'

'Jose, come here.' Laura caught hold of her sister's sleeve and dragged her through the kitchen to the other side of the green baize door. There she paused and leaned against it. 'Jose!' she said, horrified, 'however are we going to stop everything?'

'Stop everything, Laura!' cried Jose in astonishment. 'What do you mean?'

'Stop the garden party, of course.' Why did Jose pretend?

But Jose was still more amazed. 'Stop the garden party? My dear Laura, don't be so absurd. Of course we can't do anything of the kind. Nobody expects us to. Don't be so extravagant.'

'But we can't possibly have a garden party with a man dead just outside the front gate.'

That really was extravagant, for the little cottages were in a lane to themselves at the very bottom of a steep rise that led up to the house. A broad road ran between. True, they were far too near. They were the greatest possible eyesore, and they had no right to be in that neighbourhood at all. They were little mean dwellings painted a chocolate brown. In the garden patches there was nothing but cabbage stalks, sick hens and tomato cans. The very smoke coming out of their chimneys was poverty-stricken. Little rags and shreds of smoke, so unlike the great silvery plumes that uncurled from the Sheridans' chimneys. Washerwomen lived in the lane and sweeps and a cobbler, and a man whose house-front was studded all over with minute bird-cages. Children swarmed. When the Sheridans were little they were forbidden to set foot there because of the revolting language and of what they might catch. But since they were grown up, Laura and Laurie on their prowls sometimes walked through. It was disgusting and sordid. They came out with a shudder. But still one must go everywhere; one must see everything. So through they went.

'And just think of what the band would sound like to that poor woman,' said Laura.

'Oh, Laura!' Jose began to be seriously annoyed. 'If you're going to stop a band playing every time someone has an accident, you'll lead a very strenuous life. I'm every bit as sorry about it as you. I feel just as sympathetic.' Her eyes hardened. She looked at her sister just as she used to when they were little and fighting together. 'You won't bring a drunken workman back to life by being sentimental,' she said softly.

'Drunk! Who said he was drunk?' Laura turned furiously on Jose. She said just as they had used to say on those occasions, 'I'm going straight up to tell mother.'

'Do, dear,' cooed Jose.

'Mother, can I come into your room?' Laura turned the big glass door-knob.

'Of course, child. Why, what's the matter? What's given you such a colour?' And Mrs Sheridan turned round from her dressing-table. She was trying on a new hat.

'Mother, a man's been killed,' began Laura.

'Not in the garden?' interrupted her mother.

'No, no!'

'Oh, what a fright you gave me!' Mrs Sheridan sighed with relief, and took off the big hat and held it on her knees.

'But listen, mother,' said Laura. Breathless, half-choking, she told the dreadful story. 'Of course, we can't have our party, can we?' she pleaded. 'The band and everybody arriving. They'd hear us, mother; they're our neighbours!'

To Laura's astonishment her mother behaved just like Jose; it was harder to bear because she seemed amused. she refused to take Laura seriously.

'But, dear child, use your common sense. It's only by accident we've heard of it. If someone had died there normally—and I can't understand how they keep alive in those poky little holes—we should still be having our party, shouldn't we?'

Laura had to say 'yes' to that, but she felt it was all wrong. She sat down on her mother's sofa and pinched the cushion frill.

'Mother, isn't it terribly heartless of us?' she asked.

'Darling!' Mrs Sheridan got up and came over to her, carrying the hat. Before Laura could stop her she had popped it on. 'My child!' said her mother, 'the hat is yours. It's made for you. It's much too young for me. I have never seen you look such a picture. Look at yourself!' And she held up her hand-mirror.

'But, mother,' Laura began again. She couldn't look at herself; she turned aside.

This time Mrs Sheridan lost patience just as Jose had done.

'You are being very absurd, Laura,' she said coldly. 'People like that don't expect sacrifices from us. And it's not very sympathetic to spoil everybody's enjoyment as you're doing now.'

'I don't understand,' said Laura, and she walked quickly out of the room into her own bedroom. There, quite by chance, the first thing she saw was this charming girl in the mirror, in her black hat trimmed with gold daisies, and a long black velvet ribbon. Never had she imagined she could look like that. Is mother right? she thought. And now she hoped her mother was right. Am I being extravagant? Perhaps it was extravagant. Just for a moment she had another glimpse of that poor woman and those little children, and the body being carried into the house. But it all seemed blurred, unreal, like a picture in the newspaper. I'll remember it again after the party's over, she decided. And somehow that seemed quite the best plan . . .

Lunch was over by half past one. By half past two they were all ready for the fray. The green-coated band had arrived and was established in a corner of the tennis-court.

'My dear!' trilled Kitty Maitland, 'aren't they too like frogs for words? You ought to have arranged them round the pond with the conductor in the middle on a leaf.'

Laurie arrived and hailed them on his way to dress. At the sight of him Laura remembered the accident again. She wanted to tell him. If Laurie agreed with the others, then it was bound to be all right. And she followed him into the hall.

'Laurie!'

'Hallo!' he was half-way upstairs, but when he turned round and saw Laura he suddenly puffed out his cheeks and goggled his eyes at her. 'My word, Laura! You do look stunning,' said Laurie. 'What an absolutely topping hat!'

Laura said faintly 'Is it?' and smiled up at Laurie, and didn't tell him after all.

Soon after that people began coming in streams. The band struck up; the hired waiters ran from the house to the marquee. Wherever you looked there were couples strolling, bending to the flowers, greeting, moving on over the lawn. They were like bright birds that had alighted in the Sheridans' garden for this one afternoon, on their way to—where? Ah, what happiness it is to be with people who all are happy, to press hands, press cheeks, smile into eyes.

'Darling Laura, how well you look!'

'What a becoming hat, child!'

'Laura, you look quite Spanish. I've never seen you look so striking.'

And Laura, glowing, answered softly, 'Have you had tea? Won't you have an ice? The passion-fruit ices really are rather special.' She ran to her father and begged him. 'Daddy darling, can't the band have something to drink?'

And the perfect afternoon slowly ripened, slowly faded, slowly its petals closed.

'Never a more delightful garden-party...' 'The greatest success...' 'Quite the most...'

Laura helped her mother with the goodbyes. They stood side by side in the porch till it was all over.

'All over, all over, thank heaven,' said Mrs Sheridan. 'Round up the others, Laura. Let's go and have some fresh coffee. I'm exhausted. Yes, it's been very successful. But oh, these parties, these parties! Why will you children insist on giving parties!' And they all of them sat down in the deserted marquee.

'Have a sandwich, daddy dear. I wrote the flag.'

'Thanks.' Mr Sheridan took a bite and the sandwich was gone. He took another. 'I suppose you didn't hear of a beastly accident that happened today?' he said.

'My dear,' said Mrs Sheridan, holding up her hand, 'we did. It nearly ruined the party. Laura insisted we should put it off.'

'Oh, mother!' Laura didn't want to be teased about it.

'It was a horrible affair all the same,' said Mr Sheridan. 'The chap was married too. Lived just below in the lane, and leaves a wife and half a dozen kiddies, so they say.'

An awkward little silence fell. Mrs Sheridan fidgeted with her cup. Really, it was very tactless of father . . .

Suddenly she looked up. There on the table were all those sandwiches, cakes, puffs, all un-eaten, all going to be wasted. She had one of her brilliant ideas.

'I know,' she said. 'Let's make up a basket. Let's send that poor creature some of this perfectly good food. At any rate, it will be the greatest treat for the children. Don't you agree? And she's sure to have neighbours calling in and so on. What a point to have it all ready prepared. Laura!' She jumped up. 'Get me the big basket out of the stairs cupboard.'

'But, mother, do you really think it's a good idea?' said Laura.

Again, how curious, she seemed to be different from them all. To take scraps from their party. Would the poor woman really like that?

'Of course! What's the matter with you today? An hour or two ago you were insisting on us being sympathetic, and now—'

Oh well! Laura ran for the basket. It was filled, it was heaped by her mother.

'Take it yourself, darling,' said she. 'Run down just as you are. No, wait, take the arum lilies too. People of that class are so impressed by arum lilies.'

'The stems will ruin her lace frock,' said practical Jose.

So they would. Just in time. 'Only the basket, then. And,

Laura!'—her mother followed her out of the marquee—'don't on any account—'

'What mother?'

No, better not put such ideas into the child's head! 'Nothing! Run along.'

It was just growing dusky as Laura shut their garden gates. A big dog ran by like a shadow. The road gleamed white, and down below in the hollow the little cottages were in deep shade. How quiet it seemed after the afternoon. Here she was going down the hill to somewhere where a man lay dead, and she couldn't realize it. Why couldn't she? She stopped a minute. And it seemed to her that kisses, voices, tinkling spoons, laughter, the smell of crushed grass were somehow inside her. She had no room for anything else. How strange! She looked up at the pale sky, and all she thought was, 'Yes, it was the most successful.'

Now the broad road was crossed. The lane began, smoky and dark. Women in shawls and men's tweed caps hurried by. Men hung over the palings; the children played in the doorways. A low hum came from the mean little cottages. In some of them there was a flicker of light, and a shadow, crab-like, moved across the window. Laura bent her head and hurried on. She wished now she had put on a coat. How her frock shone! And the big hat with the velvet streamer—if only it was another hat! Were the people looking at her? They must be. It was a mistake to have come; she knew all along it was a mistake. Should she go back even now?

No, too late. This was the house. It must be. A dark knot of people stood outside. Beside the gate an old, old woman with a crutch sat in a chair, watching. She had her feet on a newspaper. The voices stopped as Laura drew near. The group parted. It was as though she was expected, as though they had known she was coming here.

Laura was terribly nervous. Tossing the velvet ribbon over her shoulder, she said to a woman standing by, 'Is this Mrs Scott's house?' and the woman, smiling queerly, said, 'It is, my lass.'

Oh, to be from this! She actually said, 'Help me, God,' as she walked up the tiny path and knocked. To be away from those staring eyes, or be covered up in anything, one of those women's shawls even. I'll just leave the basket and go, she decided. I shan't even wait for it to be emptied.

Then the door opened. A little woman in black showed in the gloom.

Laura said, 'Are you Mrs Scott?' But to her horror the woman answered, 'Walk in, please, miss,' and she was shut in the passage.

'No,' said Laura, 'I don't want to come in. I only want to leave this basket. Mother sent—'

The little woman in the gloomy passage seemed not to have heard her. 'Step this way, please, miss,' she said in an oily voice, and Laura followed her.

She found herself in a wretched little low kitchen, lighted by a smoky lamp. There was a woman sitting before the fire.

'Em,' said the little creature who had let her in. 'Em! It's a young lady.' She turned to Laura. She said meaningly, 'I'm her sister, miss. You'll excuse 'er, won't you?'

'Oh, but of course!' said Laura. 'Please, please don't disturb her. I—I only want to leave—'

But at that moment the woman at the fire turned round. Her face, puffed up, red, with swollen eyes and swollen lips, looked terrible. She seemed as though she couldn't understand why Laura was there. What did it mean? Why was this stranger standing in the kitchen with a basket? What was it all about? And the poor face puckered up again.

'All right, my dear,' said the other. 'I'll thenk the young lady.'

And again she began, 'You'll excuse her, miss, I'm sure,' and her face, swollen too, tried an oily smile.

Laura only wanted to get out, to get away. She was back in the passage. The door opened. She walked straight through into the bedroom where the dead man was lying.

'You'd like a look at 'im, wouldn't you?' said Em's sister, and she brushed past Laura over to the bed. 'Don't be afraid, my lass,'—and now her voice sounded fond and sly, and fondly she drew down the sheet—''e looks a picture. There's nothing to show. Come along, my dear.'

Laura came.

There lay a young man, fast asleep—sleeping so soundly, so deeply, that he was far, far away from them both. Oh, so remote, so peaceful. He was dreaming. Never wake him up again. His head was sunk in the pillow, his eyes were closed; they were blind under the closed eyelids. He was given up to his dream. What did garden parties and baskets and lace frocks matter to him? He was far from all those things. He was wonderful, beautiful. While they were laughing and while the band was playing, this marvel had come to the lane. Happy ... happy ... All is well, said that sleeping face. This is just as it should be. I am content.

But all the same you had to cry, and she couldn't go out of the room without saying something to him. Laura gave a loud childish sob.

'Forgive my hat,' she said.

And this time she didn't wait for Em's sister. She found her way out of the door, down the path, past all those dark people. At the corner of the lane she met Laurie.

He stepped out of the shadow. 'Is that you, Laura?'

'Yes.'

'Mother was getting anxious. Was it all right?'

'Yes, quite. Oh, Laurie!' She took his arm, she pressed up against him.

'I say, you're not crying, are you?' asked her brother.

Laura shook her head. She was.

Laurie put his arm round her shoulder. 'Don't cry,' he said in his warm, loving voice. 'Was it awful?'

'No,' sobbed Laura. 'It was simply marvellous. But Laurie—' She stopped, she looked at her brother. 'Isn't life,' she stammered, 'isn't life—' But what life was she couldn't explain. No matter. He quite understood.

'*Isn't* it, darling?' said Laurie.

And when they came out of the lace shop there was their own driver and the cab they called their own cab waiting for them under a plane tree. What luck! Wasn't it luck? Fanny pressed her husband's arm. These things seemed always to be happening to them ever since they—came abroad. Didn't he think so too? But George stood on the pavement edge, lifted his stick, and gave a loud 'Hi!' Fanny sometimes felt a little uncomfortable about the way George summoned cabs, but the drivers didn't seem to mind, so it must have been all right. Fat, good-natured, and smiling, they stuffed away the little newspaper they were reading, whipped the cotton cover off the horse, and were ready to obey.

'I say,' George said as he helped Fanny in, 'suppose we go and have tea at the place where the lobsters grow. Would you like to?'

'Most awfully,' said Fanny fervently, as she leaned back wondering why the way George put things made them sound so very nice.

'R-right, *bien.*' He was beside her. '*Allay,*' he cried gaily, and off they went.

Off they went, spanking along lightly, under the green and gold shade of the plane trees, through the small streets that smelled of lemons and fresh coffee, past the fountain square where women, with water-pots lifted, stopped talking to gaze after them, round the corner past the café, with its pink and white umbrellas, green tables, and blue siphons, and so to the sea front. There a wind, light, warm, came flowing over the boundless sea. It touched George, and Fanny it seemed to linger over while they gazed at the dazzling water. And George said, 'Jolly, isn't it?' And Fanny, looking dreamy, said, as she said at least twenty times a day since they—came abroad: 'Isn't it extraordinary to think that here we are quite alone, away from everybody, with nobody to tell us to go home, or to—to order us about except ourselves?'

George had long since given up answering 'Extraordinary!' As a rule he merely kissed her. But now he caught hold of her hand, stuffed it into his pocket, pressed her fingers, and said, 'I used to keep a white mouse in my pocket when I was a kid.'

'Did you?' said Fanny, who was intensely interested in everything George had ever done. 'Were you very fond of white mice?'

'Fairly,' said George, without conviction. He was looking at something, bobbing out there beyond the bathing steps. Suddenly he almost jumped in his seat. 'Fanny!' he cried. 'There's a chap out there bathing. Do you see? I'd no idea people had begun. I've been missing it all these days.' George glared at the reddened face, the reddened arm, as though he could not look away. 'At any rate,' he muttered, 'wild horses won't keep me from going in tomorrow morning.'

Fanny's heart sank. She had heard for years of the frightful dangers of the Mediterranean. It was an absolute death-trap. Beautiful, treacherous Mediterranean. There it lay curled before them, its white, silky paws touching the stones and gone again....But she'd made up her mind long before she was married that never would she be the kind of woman who interfered with her husband's pleasures, so all she said was, airily, 'I suppose one has to be very up in the currents, doesn't one?'

'Oh, I don't know,' said George. 'People talk an awful lot of rot about the danger.'

But now they were passing a high wall on the land side, covered with flowering heliotrope, and Fanny's little nose lifted. 'Oh, George,' she breathed. 'The smell! The most divine ... '

'Topping villa,' said George. 'Look, you can see it through the palms.'

'Isn't it rather large?' said Fanny, who somehow could not look at any villa except as a possible habitation for herself and George.

'Well, you'd need a crowd of people if you stayed there long,' replied George. 'Deadly, otherwise. I say, it is ripping. I wonder who it belongs to.' And he prodded the driver in the back.

The lazy, smiling driver, who had no idea, replied, as he always did on these occasions, that it was the property of a wealthy Spanish family.

'Masses of Spaniards on this coast,' commented George, leaning back again, and they were silent until, as they rounded a bend, the big, bone-white hotel-restaurant came into view. Before it there was a small terrace built up against the sea, planted with umbrella palms, set out with tables, and at their approach, from the terrace, from the hotel, waiters came running to receive, to welcome Fanny and George, to cut them off from any possible kind of escape.

'Outside?'

Oh, but of course they would sit outside. The sleek manager, who was marvellously like a fish in a frock-coat, skimmed forward.

'Dis way, sir. Dis way, sir. I have a very nice little table,' he gasped. 'Just the little table for you, sir, over in de corner. Dis way.'

So George, looking most dreadfully bored, and Fanny, trying to look as though she'd spent years of life threading her way through strangers, followed after.

'Here you are, sir. Here you be very nice,' coaxed the manager, taking the vase off the table, and putting it down again as if it were a fresh little bouquet out of the air. But George refused to sit down immediately. He saw through these fellows; he wasn't going to be done. These chaps were always out to rush you. So he put his hands in his pockets, and said to Fanny, very calmly, 'This all right for you? Anywhere else you'd prefer? How about over there?' And he nodded to a table right over the other side.

What it was to be a man of the world! Fanny admired him deeply, but all she wanted to do was to sit down and look like everybody else.

'I—I like this,' said she.

'Right,' said George hastily, and he sat down almost before Fanny, and said quickly, 'Tea for two and chocolate éclairs.'

'Very good, sir,' said the manager, and his mouth opened and shut as though he was ready for another dive under the water. 'You will not 'ave toasts to start with? We 'ave very nice toasts, sir.'

'No,' said George shortly. 'You don't want toast, do you, Fanny?'

'Oh no, thank you, George,' said Fanny, praying the manager would go.

'Or perhaps de lady might like to look at de live lobsters in de tank while de tea is coming?' And he grimaced and smirked and flicked his serviette like a fin.

George's face grew stony. He said 'No' again, and Fanny bent over the table, unbuttoning her gloves. When she looked up the man was gone. George took off his hat, tossed it on to a chair, and pressed back his hair.

'Thank God,' said he, 'that chap's gone. These foreign fellows bore me stiff. The only way to get rid of them is simply to shut them up as you saw I did. Thank heaven!' sighed George again, with so much emotion that if it hadn't been ridiculous Fanny might have imagined that he had been as frightened of the manager as she. As it was she felt a rush of love for George. His hands were on the table, brown large hands that she knew so well. She longed to take one of them and squeeze it hard. But, to her astonishment, George did just that thing. Leaning across the table, he put his hand over hers, and said, without looking at her, 'Fanny, darling Fanny!'

'Oh, George!' It was in that heavenly moment that Fanny heard a *twing-twing-tootle-tootle*, and a light strumming. There's going to be music, she thought, but the music didn't matter just then. Nothing mattered except love. Faintly smiling she gazed into that faintly smiling face, and the feeling was so blissful that she felt inclined to say to George, 'Let us stay here—where we are—at this table. It's perfect, and the sea is perfect. Let us stay.' But instead her eyes grew serious.

'Darling,' said Fanny. 'I want to ask you something fearfully important. Promise me you'll answer. Promise.'

'I promise,' said George, too solemn to be quite as serious as she.

'It's this.' Fanny paused a moment, looked down, looked up again. 'Do you feel,' she said softly, 'that you really know me now? But really, really know *me*?'

It was too much for George. Know his Fanny? He gave a broad, childish grin. 'I should jolly well think I do,' he said emphatically. 'Why, what's up?'

Fanny felt he hadn't quite understood. She went on quickly: 'What I mean is this. So often people, even when they love each

other, don't seem to—to—it's so hard to say—know each other
perfectly. They don't seem to want to. And I think that's awful.
They misunderstand each other about the most important things
of all.' Fanny looked horrified. 'George, we couldn't do that,
could we? We never could.'

'Couldn't be done,' laughed George, and he was just going to
tell her how much he liked her little nose, when the waiter arrived
with the tea and the band struck up. It was a flute, a guitar, and a
violin, and it played so gaily that Fanny felt if she wasn't careful
even the cups and saucers might grow little wings and fly away.
George absorbed three chocolate éclairs, Fanny two. The
funny-tasting tea—'Lobster in the kettle,' shouted George above
the music—was nice all the same, and when the tray was pushed
aside and George was smoking, Fanny felt bold enough to look at
the other people. But it was the band grouped under one of the
dark trees that fascinated her most. The fat man stroking the
guitar was like a picture. The dark man playing the flute kept
raising his eyebrows as though he was astonished at the sounds
that came from it. The fiddler was in shadow.

The music stopped as suddenly as it had begun. It was then she
noticed a tall old man with white hair standing beside the
musicians. Strange she hadn't noticed him before. He wore a very
high, glazed collar, a coat green at the seams, and shamefully
shabby button boots. Was he another manager? He did not look
like a manager, and yet he stood there gazing over the tables as
though thinking of something different and far away from all this.
Who could he be?

Presently, as Fanny watched him, he touched the points of his
collar with his fingers, coughed slightly, and half turned to the
band. It began to play again. Something boisterous, reckless, full
of fire, full of passion, was tossed into the air, was tossed to that
quiet figure, which clasped its hands, and still with that far-away
look, began to sing.

'Good Lord!' said George. It seemed that everybody was
equally astonished. Even the little children eating ices stared, with
their spoons in the air . . . .Nothing was heard except a thin, faint
voice, the memory of a voice singing something in Spanish. It
wavered, beat on, touched the high notes, fell again, seemed to

implore, to entreat, to beg for something, and then the tune changed, and it was resigned, it bowed down, it knew it was denied.

Almost before the end a little child gave a squeak of laughter, but everybody was smiling—except Fanny and George. Is life like this too? thought Fanny. There are people like this. There is suffering. And she looked at that gorgeous sea, lapping the land as though it loved it, and the sky, bright with the brightness before evening. Had she and George the right to be so happy? Wasn't it cruel? There must be something else in life which made all these things possible. What was it? She turned to George.

But George had been feeling differently from Fanny. The poor old boy's voice was funny in a way, but, God, how it made you realise what a terrific thing it was to be at the beginning of everything, as they were, he and Fanny! George, too, gazed at the bright, breathing water, and his lips opened as if he could drink it. How fine it was! There was nothing like the sea for making a chap feel fit. And there sat Fanny, his Fanny, leaning forward, breathing so gently.

'Fanny!' George called to her.

As she turned to him something in her soft, wondering look made George feel that for two pins he would jump over the table and carry her off.

'I say,' said George rapidly, 'let's go, shall we? Let's go back to the hotel. Come. Do, Fanny darling. Let's go now.'

The band began to play. 'Oh, God!' almost groaned George. 'Let's go before the old codger begins squawking again.'

And a moment later they were gone.